HOME STATION

*Also by Jeanne Williams
in Large Print:*

The Unplowed Sky
Daughter of the Storm
The Island Harp
Home Mountain

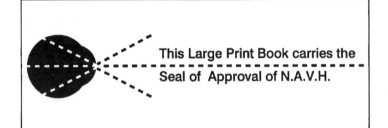

This Large Print Book carries the
Seal of Approval of N.A.V.H.

HOME STATION

Jeanne Williams

Thorndike Press • Thorndike, Maine

Published in 1997 by arrangement with St. Martin's Press, Inc.

Thorndike Large Print ® Romance Series.

The tree indicium is a trademark of Thorndike Press.

The text of this Large Print edition is unabridged.
Other aspects of the book may vary from the original edition.

Set in 16 pt. Bookman Old Style by Minnie B. Raven.

Printed in the United States on permanent paper.

Library of Congress Cataloging in Publication Data

Williams, Jeanne, 1930–
    Home station / Jeanne Williams.
        p.   cm.
    ISBN 0-7862-0928-3 (lg. print : hc)
    1. Young women — Oklahoma — History — 20th century —
Fiction.   2. Large type books.   I. Title.
    [PS3573.I44933H64   1997]
    813'.54—dc20   96-44124

TO DAVE WEBB

Who loves history and shows that love through his work, teaching, and writing. Without his encouragement and help, this book would never have been written.

Author's Note

Dave Webb of the Kansas Heritage Center told me several years ago that I should write a book about railroads, but I didn't get excited about it till, through him, I caught a glimpse of how the depot used to be the center of a small town, how crops were shipped and supplies arrived by train, and how the news and messages from outside came through by telegraph.

Charmed by this vision of community in a different age, I began to try to make it real. Dave very kindly sent me material on early railroads and telegraphers. His own book, *Protection Paragraphs*, Comanche Press, Protection, Kansas, 1984, brilliantly gives the flavor and life of a town from 1880 to 1930, the town where Dave lives in the old depot with his cats, Atchison and Fe, whose names I begged to borrow for this story. I must also thank Dave for reading the manuscript with his expert's knowledge. Any mistakes

I made in spite of him are my own.

I also found much fascinating information in Webb's *399 Kansas Characters*, Kansas Heritage Center, Dodge City, Kansas, 1992. Other sources were *All Aboard, The Golden Age of American Train Travel*, edited by Bill Yenne, Brompton Books Corp., Greenwich, Connecticut, 1989; *Rails Across America*, consultant editor William L. Withuhn, Smithmark Publishers, New York, 1993; *Rails West*, by George B. Abdill, Bonanza Books, New York, 1960; *The Railroaders*, by Keith Wheeler and the editors of Time-Life Books, Time, Inc., New York, 1973; *Yonder Comes the Train*, by Lance Phillips, Galahad Books, New York, 1993; *The Trains We Rode*, by Lucius Beebe and Charles Clegg, Promontory Press, New York, 1993; *Metropolitan Corridor*, by John Stilgoe, Yale University Press, New Haven and London, 1983; *Railroads Triumphant*, by Albro Martin, Oxford University Press, New York and Oxford, 1992; and *Highways to Heaven*, by Christopher Finch, HarperCollins, New York, 1992.

For details of small-town life at the century's turn, I drew on many sources, but of these the most readable are *The Townsmen*, by Keith Wheeler and the editors of Time-Life Books, Time, Inc., New York, 1975; and *This Fabulous Century 1900–1910*, by the editors of Time-Life Books, Time, Inc., 1969. George Scofield's unpublished manuscript about small-town living and building a railroad across the Oklahoma Panhandle is full of fascinating details, and I want to thank George, of Ponca City, Oklahoma, for sharing these memories that he wrote down for his children and grandchildren.

The experiences of station agents' families come alive in *Living in the Depot*, by H. Roger Grant, University of Iowa Press, Iowa City, Iowa, 1993. The human and political struggles over the use of alcohol are thoroughly, often humorously, told in *Prohibition in Kansas*, by Robert Smith Bader, University Press of Kansas, Lawrence, Kansas, 1986.

The story of the first woman telegrapher in the United States, Sarah Bagley, is told in Madeleine Stern's *We the Women*, University of Nebraska Press, Lincoln, Nebraska, 1994. *Wires West*, by Philip Ault, Dodd, Mead & Co.,

New York, 1974, gives a lively view of frontier telegraphy and tells the fascinating story of the attempt to string wires from Alaska through Siberia to Saint Petersburg.

Two sets of audiocassettes, *Listen to the Land — Prairie Pioneers and Town Builders*, recorded by Robert Manley, and lent to me by the Kansas Heritage Center, gave the flavor of small towns and made me realize how horse-centered they were — watering troughs, hitching posts, blacksmiths, liveries, saddleries, harness shops, and so on.

For a background of the times, I relied on *A People's History of the United States*, by Howard Zinn, HarperCollins, New York, 1990; *Chronicle of the 20th Century*, editor in chief Clifton Daniel, Chronicle Publications, Mount Kisco, New York, 1987; and *Annals of Kansas*, Volume 1, 1886–1911, edited by Kirke Mecham, Kansas State Historical Society, Topeka, Kansas, 1954.

It's been said that in a degree, the transcontinental railroad healed the wounds of the Civil War and bound the country together. For half a century at least, until automobiles and trucks became common, the train was vitally important, its comings and goings high-lights of the day. My neighbor Dr. Walter Spofford gleefully recalls how he and other boys begged rides in the cab of the train that stopped in his town, and how they watched the fireman shovel coal from the tender into the firebox.

This book is for those who remember trains and depots from their own lives, and the greater number like me, who love to "remember" times that ended before they were born.

1

OKLAHOMA TERRITORY
July 1900

Through the bay window of the depot, Lesley Morland watched the throng crowd around the vestibule of the train — businessmen in suits and ties; farmers in overalls; town and country women in their best, hats decked with plumes, bows, flowers, fruits, or birds; spurred, big-hatted cowboys; and Osages in both buckskin and ordinary garb.

"Theodore Roosevelt, likely nominee for vice president, is on the way to the July Fourth celebration in Oklahoma City, but he is stopping here in Sunflower to address a gathering of thousands." She tapped the message in Morse code on the telegraph key. Pausing, she bit her lip. "A half dozen Rough Riders are here in uniform. So are veterans of the Civil War, some in blue, some in gray. Roosevelt is shaking hands with them. The crowd is cheering —"

Then suddenly it wasn't. It was howling.

Lesley couldn't see why, but her insides twisted and she went sick with apprehension. Daddy, even when sober, called Roosevelt a warmonger, and he had been drinking more steadily than usual since they learned the potential vice president would stop here. Her father had been asleep in their quarters at one end of the depot when she came out to take charge of the duties of a stationmaster, but he could have slipped out the back door without her seeing him.

She signed off with her father's initials — his name was Lesley, too, Lesley Edwin, and she was Lesley Edwina — and hurried to the door as her father broke free of the mayor, fire chief, and town marshal to vault to the red-white-and-blue-ribboned rear platform of the train.

"Cuban freedom!" Ed Morland shouted, flapping his empty sleeve in the potential vice president's astonished face. "Cuban independence! That's why

13

I volunteered — why I lost this arm!"

"My good old fellow —" began Roosevelt. He tried to set his hand on Morland's shoulder, but the station agent jerked away.

"Devil a bit of freedom the Cubans have for all their hopes and fighting and starving! The old officials appointed by the Queen of Spain left to run things! The U.S. declaring it has the right to interfere anytime it wants! Cuban patriots who fought for their country are kept out of the government because they want freedom! And the Philippines! Shooting unarmed civilians —"

Marshal Tawney and several firemen dragged Ed Morland off the train and hauled him toward the courthouse and jail. He fought every inch of the way. "Murderer!" he yelled. "You're wading in blood! We fought over the price of sugar — for new markets — for everything but freedom! You —"

Tawney and the others hustled Lesley's father into the jail. Commanding her trembling fingers, she tapped, "A one-armed Spanish-American War veteran interrupted Roosevelt's speech to protest this country's domination of Cuba and the war in the Philippines.

14

He has been arrested. Now Roosevelt is saying the United States must expand in order to be strong."

The sounder that clicked out incoming messages started chattering, amplified by a strategically wedged Prince Albert tobacco can. From the rapidity and skill of the sender, she knew it was Harry Eckman at Guthrie. "Do you know the veteran's name? Was he hired by labor agitators to raise a ruckus?"

"The veteran is Lesley Edwin Morland." She hesitated. Then her fingers moved swiftly, firmly, on the key. "No one had to hire him to tell the truth."

That would set the wire humming. One message she could count on was from the railroad's division superintendent. It, like others before, would tersely inform Lesley Edwin Morland that he was forthwith no longer an employee of the railroad and his temporary replacement would arrive on the next train.

What would the charges be? She hoped for just "drunk and disorderly," though she feared it could be a lot worse. At least he hadn't hit or threatened the much-admired politician.

The sounder started again. Lesley left

it clattering to hurry to the back door. Shy young Marshal Tawney hung around the depot a lot more than necessary. She was sure he liked her. Maybe he wouldn't lock her father up if she promised to get him out of town quickly.

Only, where would they go? After this, who would hire Ed Morland as a station agent? In spite of her most dire economies, doctor bills and whiskey devoured her father's salary and the savings she had scrimped from working as a waitress in Kansas City while her father was off at war. His old company, the Chicago, Rock Island and Pacific, had given him a station on his return, but traveling officials found him drunk. This was his fourth job in less than two years.

It was going to be up to her to earn their living, but right now she had to get him released. Slipping out the door, she almost collided head-on with a leather vest. She was tall, but the owner of the vest was taller. The hands that steadied her were large and strong and confident. They lingered on her upper arms till she drew back, looking from the vest and plaid shirt up a column of brown throat to a lean, hard jaw, long mouth, and eyes the color of a blue norther, a kind of smoky gray.

"I just want to say, ma'am, that your father's sentiments are mine entirely." The stern mouth softened in a grin. He proffered an arm. "I know you're Miss Lesley Morland. I'm Jim Kelly. Let's sashay over to the courthouse. I'll be honored to pay your father's fine."

She ignored his arm and set off for the courthouse two blocks away. "How did you know —" She broke off, choked with humiliation. She loved her father. When he was sober, he was the kindest and most entertaining of companions. She thought he was right about the war. But how long had it been since she'd felt proud of him, been glad he was her father?

The stranger matched his stride to hers. "Some lady was saying what a pity it was that your pa had disgraced you again and that you're really the one that runs the station."

"I won't anymore," she said bitterly. "I just hope one of our conductor friends will let us ride the train to someplace where I can get work."

"You can't stay here?"

"After this? We've only been here three

months. Before that, we moved around over Kansas." She clamped her teeth down hard on her lip to keep it from trembling. "We don't have any real friends."

No need to add that all most Sunflower people knew about them was that Lesley Edwin Morland, usually called Ed, had lost his arm in the war, drank a lot, and refused to go to any of the town's churches, Baptist, Methodist, or Episcopalian.

"You can make friends. Starting with me." His smile made him look like a boy instead of the mature man bespoken by crinkly lines at the edges of his eyes and the strand of white hair above a scar on his right temple that made black hair seem even blacker. "Clearwater, the town I'm freighting out of right now, is going to have a railroad real soon. That'll just about put me out of business and I'll be hunting a new location, but I'll bet there'd be a way for you folks to make a living there. I'd sure put in some good words for you. It's the county seat and trading center for that part of the Region."

"Region?"

"That's what folks used to call all the

area south of Dodge City as far as Tascosa in Texas and Camp Supply in Indian Territory that got their supplies from wagon freighters. Slow travel, but folks along the wagon routes knew and cared about each other even if they lived a hundred miles apart."

"You can remember that?"

She had never lived anywhere long enough to feel she had neighbors. After her mother died when she, Lesley, was three years old, Ed Morland searched for something he couldn't find. When seeking an appointment to a different station, though, he made sure there was a school. He didn't understand that it was hard for a strange child to fit in with children who'd grown up together, especially when her dresses weren't nicely starched and ironed and her hair was tangled in back where she couldn't reach it. Once, she had made friends with Mary Dunnigan, daughter of the section crew boss. They made a bower of tumbleweeds lodged against tall sunflower stalks and played there every day after school. Then Daddy tired of the town. Lesley didn't want to make friends after that. For a long time her heart felt as if a big piece had been torn

19

out of it. She enjoyed her father's stories and company when he was sober. When he wasn't, she took refuge in reading, and in learning to cook from a recipe book of her mother's. She liked to imagine her mother, real and alive, was teaching her. And she learned to use the telegraph key.

"Remember the big days of wagon freighting?" Jim Kelly chuckled and then sighed. "My folks ran a way station. I knew all the freighters. Learned to take care of the horses and mules as soon as I was big enough to take off their harnesses. Started driving to Tascosa for P. J. Reynolds when I was sixteen."

"That's a long way!"

"Two hundred and forty miles from Dodge. Figured it was a good trip if we made it in eighteen days. It could take considerably longer, depending on the weather and what mood the Cimarron was in." His mouth quirked. "The last five or six years my little freighting outfit has mostly hauled freight twenty miles to and from the railroad to Clearwater. Right now I'm hauling supplies for the crew building the new line. I miss my folks, but I'm kind of glad they didn't have to learn a new way of living. Dad died of heart failure, and pneumonia took Mama a few months later. Guess she wanted to be with him. When the tracks get to Clearwater, I'll move along."

A shadow bulked against them. The massive stranger in the well-cut pale gray Prince Albert frock coat briefly acknowledged Lesley by taking off a hat the same color and softness as a dove's breast. From a widow's peak cleaving a tanned forehead, hair that was either silver or extremely fair swept thickly back and almost covered ears that were a trifle pointed. Fair eyebrows rose to a point at the outer edges above eyes that looked black till the sun struck emerald fire from their depths. Broad nose, wide nostrils, a surprisingly full mouth. A wizard's face, it seemed to Lesley, at once young and old.

"You're supposed to be hauling ties to my crew, Kelly, not wasting time in town."

"Am I behind, Benedict?"

"When you are, it'll be too late to worry. Load up and hit the road."

"I've got business to attend to first."

Only their eyes clashed, but Lesley got

the overpowering impression of two bulls locking horns. "You'll do what I've hired you for — now — or I'll find another freighter."

Kelly's head swung back, but when he spoke, his tone was careless. "Do that." He turned to Lesley. "Don't you reckon we better go along and get your dad out of jail?"

Benedict's voice rasped with disbelief. "You'll throw away more money for a summer's work than you generally make in a year?"

"We'd never last the summer, Benedict. You hired my teams and wagons, not my backbone. Come on, Miss Morland."

The other man loomed in front of them. He stared at Lesley, first with boldness, then with a quizzical softening. "Allow me to escort you, ma'am. My name is Adam Benedict. I want to offer your father a job."

She glanced at Kelly. His jaw clamped hard. After a moment, he shrugged. "Benedict can do that, Miss Morland. He owns his own railroad." He paused. "Guess you don't need me now. If you do, I'll be at Clearwater another month or two."

Why did she want to stop him, keep him from going away? It wasn't just because she was wary of Adam Benedict. "Thanks for your help, Mr. Kelly." That sounded stiff and prim against what she wanted to say. *Thanks for being my friend — thanks for caring when I thought no one did.*

How a smile transformed the hard angles of his face! "Miss Morland, ma'am, I sure do wish you all the luck in the world. I'd appreciate a note when you're settled. Just to let me know you're doing fine."

They had almost reached the courthouse. Jim Kelly veered around it. She watched him vanish with a curious sense of loss. How could that be when ten minutes ago she hadn't known he existed?

"There goes a fool." Benedict's tone was scornfully amused. "Hanging on to the past while the train — literally — leaves without him. He'd couldn't stay in business if he didn't haul stuff to and from the railroad."

"He must be a good freighter or you wouldn't have hired him."

"Being the best freighter around just makes him more the idiot for tossing my business back in my face."

"You both had your tempers up. Surely you don't mean to fire him over a few words."

"I have."

As she stared, he set his hand under her elbow to help her up the narrow steps. She balked, turning to face him.

"Why would you hire my father?"

"Because he's like my father." At her startled look, he amended, "My father was a drunkard. Oddly enough, he also had only one arm. Left the other at Gettysburg. I suppose that's why he drank. All I knew at the time was that he stank worse than a slaughterhouse. Still, he was good to me in his way . . ."

"I'm sorry." Lesley meant that. "But —"

Benedict moved his shoulders as if to throw off unwelcome memories. "Let it suffice that I have a soft spot for one-armed former soldiers who hug the bottle — along with sympathy for any child of theirs."

A job for her father? Lesley could scarcely credit such luck — but then, it had been hard to believe her father's outrageous behavior, though she had seen and heard it all too clearly.

"Where would Father's station be?"

"The middle of nowhere, I'm afraid. That is to say, southwestern Kansas about forty miles southwest of Dodge City. Not much in Bountiful except the station and a few falling-down buildings left from when it was an end-of-track town and boomed for a couple of weeks."

Benedict watched her for a reaction she did not have. A town without people might be the best place for them. Father couldn't get into arguments. There'd be no one to witness and mock his binges. And ghosts can't snub you.

"It sounds fine to me," she said. "Anyway, as you know, sir, we can't be choosy."

Again that swift, searching gaze, that speculative lift of eyebrows that made her add hastily, "Choosy about a station, I mean."

"Of course." He inclined his head solemnly, but his lip twitched. "Bountiful's due for a new start toward townhood. I'm going to build a railroad south of it — The Great Plains and Western — to Meridian in the Texas Panhandle, where it'll link up with a line an associate's building from El Paso. You and your father won't be isolated long."

More's the pity, she almost said. She didn't allow herself the often-crushed fantasy that a new place, a fresh start, would induce her father to stop drinking.

Benedict opened one side of the heavy courthouse double door for her. "Wait here, Miss Morland," he said.

Just then Ed Morland, none too steadily, empty coat sleeve flapping, came down the broad hall. Lesley ran to him. "Daddy! Did —"

Shamefacedly, he patted her hand. "I'm sorry, Les." He spoke in that slow, fumbling way that told her he was very drunk indeed.

"Are you all right?" She pinned up the sleeve and studied him for any signs of abuse.

"Tawney's a good man. He wouldn't let the others teach me respect for the Rough Rider soon-to-be vice prez."

"They just let you go?"

He shook a head that shone pink between side fringes of wispy gray hair. "Young feller paid my fine — said you were on your way with a man who'd offered me a job. Sheriff was tickled to have me off his hands." Morland peered through thick lenses at Benedict. "That right, mister? You got a station for me?"

"I do." Benedict shook hands and gave his name, but he couldn't conceal discomfiture at Jim Kelly's maneuver. "Let's go back to the depot, Mr. Morland, and you can consider my proposition."

"Not much to consider, Mr. Benedict." Father's grin was rueful. "I bet my discharge has already been wired in by the superintendent." As he had so often before, he took his daughter's hands. Tears glinted in his soft brown eyes.

Again he said, "I'm sorry, child."

Child? She had never been able to be one. Much as he loved her, he had stolen that. "I want you more than sorry." She hadn't known she was gong to say it until she did. "I want you sober!" Her breath came in a gasp as she fought tears, shocked and ashamed to say this, especially in front of a stranger, but unable to stop herself. "I mean this, Daddy. The next time you get drunk, I'm leaving."

"Honey, I —"

Sobs overcame her. She evaded Benedict's outstretched well-manicured hand and hurried toward the depot. He caught up with her. Cumbered by skirts, she couldn't walk fast enough to escape.

"I understand why you said what you did to your father, Miss Morland. But could you really do it? Leave him?"

"I certainly intend to try!" she said fiercely. Bolting into the depot, she shut the door to their quarters and began to pack.

Four days later, the last flush of color had faded from the endless sky when the westbound train clanged to a halt beside a deserted depot of the kind that was mass-produced to cut costs. Across the track and westward a bit, a huge windmill creaked as it pumped water into a big closed tank and a smaller open one for watering teams of mules and horses.

"Here you are, folks." Jared Crane, the jovial ruddy-faced conductor, placed the wooden steps for Lesley and helped her father and the brakeman deposit their trunks and crates of provisions in the handcart sitting on the platform. "You can keep each other company, so I'm sure you'll like Bountiful more than the last agent. He only lasted a month. Got on the eastbound last week. Said he was going to the dentist. He got off in Dodge City and no one's seen him since."

The conductor stepped back on the train and gave a friendly wave. With a long, lonely whistle, the locomotive snorted a fog of cinders, and the pistons began to clang. The train chugged off, gathering speed that soon made it look like a toy train disappearing over the rim of the plains.

Lesley's heart sank as she glanced at the ramshackle buildings scattered along the track across from the depot, and beyond them, abandoned fields. Densely rooted sod, undisturbed for thousands of years, once thoroughly broken to the plow, could not return to its virgin state but lay exposed and naked except for tumbleweeds, cockleburs, and jaunty sunflowers that could survive anything. This evidence of earlier dwellers made the place more lonesome than if only prairie surrounded the building.

"Bountiful!" Her father's tone was full of scorn for the mockery of a name, and for himself. "Les, honey, I'm so ashamed

— you shouldn't have to live like this."

She threw back her shoulders. "You've got a job and we've got a place to live."

"A dratted boxcar!"

"We can fix it up." She picked up their valises. "Let's get a lamp lit and see what the boxcar's like."

In spite of her cheering words, Lesley's heart sank again as the yellow light flickering through a sooty lamp chimney revealed a rickety table, two chairs, a kerosene stove, cupboards made of apple crates, and two steel cots with thin mattresses pushed together like a double bed. The floor was linoleum marred to the color of mud, and the walls were almost as smoke-stained as the lamp.

"Aw, Les —" began her father.

No wonder the previous agent had left after a month! Only exiles would live here, those who weren't wanted anywhere else. Swallowing the lump in her throat, Lesley set down the valises and took charge as she had so many times before.

"I guess we're lucky the last agent didn't take the furniture. We'll paint the walls and get new linoleum. I'll make some curtains. But for now, will you fill the water buckets while I locate some pans and figure out what to fix for supper?"

2

Soft radiance rimmed the prairie horizon on all sides while twilight darkened the vaulted sky above. Stars began to twinkle, a few more sparkling with each moment. On these high plains, sundown brought blessed respite from the searing early August heat as Lesley neared the prairie dog town that spread for many acres beginning a quarter mile south of the railroad tracks.

Most of the small, short-legged ground squirrels had retired into their underground sleeping chambers, but a few sat upright on their mounds, chirping at her approach. The closest one dropped flat on its belly, chirping faster and louder, then dived into its hole with a flick of its stubby black tail. Lesley perched on a split railroad tie.

"Funny little beasties! I won't hurt you. Don't you let rattlesnakes and burrowing owls live in holes you don't use anymore when both of them aren't above snagging your babies?" She considered. "Of course, I suppose there's not a lot you can do about it."

Snakes would be venturing out to hunt. She kept a cautious watch for them as she approached a family of long-legged burrowing owls that peered at her from yellow eyes set beneath tufted white broadened Vs that looked like joined eyebrows. One of the adults had a black collar across a white bib, which made it look like an irascible gentleman unwillingly dressed for a formal occasion. In contrast to the neatly kept prairie dog mounds, the pile of debris outside the owls' home would have delighted a pack rat — owl pellets and tiny bones, hair, teeth, and other remains of prey. They were used to her now. When she had first begun her evening visits, the young had startled her with their distress signal, which sounded very much like the whir of a rattler.

In the five weeks since the Morlands had come to Bountiful, she had found amusement and wonder in watching the village's small inhabitants, a welcome relief from her father's morose company. He *had* stayed sober, but his misery and self-reproaches made her sometimes almost wish he would drink. He hadn't even whistled "Casey Jones," the song immortalizing the engineer who had died that April in the wreck of the famed Cannonball out of Memphis. In contrast to the shacks of Bountiful, abandoned except for a family of valentine-faced barn owls, the prairie dog town teemed from dawn to dusk with adults and half-grown youngsters born that spring. Scores of them stood guard from the tops of their mounds while the others clipped grasses. The shadow of a hawk or eagle, the stealthy approach of a coyote, badger, or fox, would set off furious chirping and, if the threat increased, headlong disappearance into the nearest holes.

These numerous refuges and the posting of sentinels allowed the dogs to thrive. Alone, or in small numbers, they would fall easy prey to winged or four-footed predators.

In spite of the lingering heat, Lesley felt chilled as she looked back toward the dilapidated shacks across from the depot. These still gave her a forsaken feeling, as did the passing of trains coming from the outer world and speeding on to it after sometimes taking on water from the tank or adding coal to the tender, if it was needed, from a great pile of coal near the windmill. Usually only the morning eastbound and evening westbound locals needed these facilities. The two red ball, high-speed freights and the one main-line passenger train daily sped at forty to fifty miles an hour past the blink of the eye that was Bountiful.

Still, that blink was Lesley's home. Deprived of human company, she treasured the small neighbors of the prairie dog village and the birds that somehow made a living in this desolate region, meadowlarks, mockingbirds, gossipy crows, and perky little sparrows that came to drink gratefully at the water trough.

Some creature, probably a coyote, had dug out a small pool filled by overflow from the tank. Long-eared jackrabbits and their smaller white-tailed cousins drank here, as did coyotes and smaller creatures.

The animals were at home, but for humans, the station was very much betwixt and between. Passengers rarely got off at Bountiful, nor did they get on. Occasionally freight or mail was unloaded to be collected in a day or two by a farmer driving his wagon in from some hardscrabble homestead. Plagued by drought, grasshoppers, and the nationwide financial panic of 1893 that had caused hundreds of hopefully plowed and planted fields to be abandoned, not many settlers had managed to hang on, though the experiment with irrigation farther west around Garden City was encouraging farmers to hope for good crops oftener than one year out of three. Maybe someday deserted farms would yield grain again, but for now they only scarred the prairie.

Like the boxcar. It was as clean now as scrubbing and new paint, curtains, and linoleum could make it, but nothing could make it a home. If only . . . *Quit feeling sorry for yourself! There's the lovely twilight and the funny little prairie dogs and owls. Your father has work, and at least there's no place he can buy whiskey!*

She amended that. He might ask Jared Crane, the conductor who dropped off their supplies every week, to find him a bottle. Kansas, after years of determined campaigning by the Women's Christian Temperance Union, passed a law in 1880 against selling whiskey, beer, and wine except by druggists for medicinal purposes. At first, a doctor's prescription was required, and doctors were to account regularly for these, but physicians had rebelled at the paperwork and what they considered an insult to their integrity. All a person had to do now was write down the condition for which they needed the "medicine." Father's amputated arm did pain him. A drink to ease the ache was legal and acceptable, but he couldn't stop with a drink. In spite of their isolation, Lesley feared the temptations a real town would bring.

Benedict had said Bountiful would be the junction with the railroad he meant to build south, but railroad schemes were ephemeral. Not for the first time, Lesley thought of Jim Kelly, the way he'd succored her on that terrible day of despairing humiliation.

Warmth filled her at the memory of his hand beneath her arm. How wonderful to have someone care! But even in those overwrought moments, she had felt more than comforted. Those gray eyes reached untouched, unknown depths within her. She had felt a strange sense of loss when he walked away.

Where would he go when the rails reached Clearwater? He couldn't out-run rails forever. Several times she had tried to write him a letter expressing her thanks, but when she read the missives, they said too much or too little. Finally she had simply thanked him for settling her father's fine and enclosed money to repay him.

There'd been no answer. She had tried to stop remembering his eyes, the curve of his mouth, the strength of his long brown fingers. He'd probably forgotten all about her — yet he'd thrown up a lucrative contract in order to escort her to the jail, hadn't he? Though perhaps that had been more masculine pride than concern for her.

Distant thunder rumbled nearer. Number 82, the 7:30 P.M. eastbound local to Dodge City and points beyond, was only an hour late. She hurried inside the depot. Her father sat at his desk in the bay window, gazing dispir-itedly at the mute sounder and his telegraph key with the pad and pencil nearby for writing out messages. He hadn't opened the windows, and the room was sweltering.

Once he had enjoyed visiting with other telegraph operators, but after word of his verbal attack on Roosevelt spread, he had been frozen out of the wire conversations. One telegrapher had even called him a traitor.

Opening the windows, Lesley said, "Will you take care of the orders for the eastbound or shall I do it?"

"You can."

She wanted to shake him. Between pity and exasperation, she lit the lantern, picked up the two copies of engineer's and conductor's orders her father had written out from the telegraph signals, and placed them under the clamps of the bamboo train order hoops that had handles about a yard long.

The engineer would lean out of the cab, the conductor off the caboose, as the train clanged by, and she had to hold first the engineer's hoop, then the conductor's, at just the right level for them to slip their arms through the hoops. The train crew would toss off any messages they were carrying. Then they'd unclip the messages Lesley had handed up and toss the hoops out along the track. In the dark, they could be hard to find.

The orange eye of the train glared like that of some elongated Cyclopian monster as its whistle sounded over the roar. It was too dark to see the smoke billowing from the engine.

What did the prairie dogs think of it, and the owls and other creatures? At first they may have feared it was a prairie fire, panicked as it shook the earth, but since it came every day and was gone in minutes, they must have developed some kind of tolerance for it.

The prairie dog town had once reached across the track, to judge from a number of abandoned holes beyond the derelict scatter of shanties. Building the track had destroyed the burrows in its way, of course, and the fleeting end-of-track town wrecked that part of a happy, bustling community that had quite probably existed for centuries.

Who, much less the cardsharps, saloon keepers, and prostitutes who swarmed to end-of-track, would give a thought to ravaging the homes of rodents and owls, let alone rattlesnakes? It seemed almost instinct for people to kill snakes, though Lesley never had, opening the doors of several homes or depots to shoo the reptiles outside with a broom.

She raised the lantern, steeling herself to stand close enough to hold the engineer's hoop steady, but instead of merely slowing, the train groaned and wheezed to a stop.

The young engineer greeted her appreciatively as he unclamped his orders from the hoop. She wished him a good run east and took the conductor's orders to the caboose.

"Howdy, Miss Morland!" Jared Crane freed his orders from the clamp as the brakeman helped her father unload some crates, big ones, into the handcart kept on the platform. In the yellow wash of the lantern light, the conductor's teeth flashed beneath a bushy gray mustache.

"I think you're about to see a big change in Bountiful. Mr. Benedict's private car will be along tomorrow. He's ready to start that line south."

Why wasn't she glad? The force of Adam Benedict's personality was overpowering, but he'd be too busy overseeing his railroad to bother her.

41

Dismay must have shown on her face, because Mr. Crane squinted in puzzlement. "Aren't you tickled? This is going to be a town! You and your dad will have someone to talk to besides the prairie dogs." He laughed at his joke, little guessing that she did indeed talk to prairie dogs, and owls, too.

Dazed by the conductor's news, Lesley took the lantern inside and blew it out. Ed Morland summoned the waver of a smile.

"So there's going to be a town to go with the station. You'll have company again, honey."

Company? Didn't he understand that his way of life had cut them off from others as effectively as distance? Anywhere a rail-laying crew collected, there'd be whiskey.

"Daddy —" She hated herself for saying it, yet she had to, and for that, she almost hated him. "I meant what I said. No drinking."

He turned slowly, painfully red. "I hope I may die, Les, if I take another swallow. I know I've shamed you — got us sent out here to the edge of nowhere —"

She held out her arms as if he were

her child, her erring but beloved child, and hugged him close. How frail he was! Skin over bone. He never had much appetite in hot weather, but he was scarcely eating at all.

"Let's hope Bountiful makes a good town, one we'll want to stay in." She patted his cheek. "Now that it's cooler, why don't we sit out on the platform and have some rice pudding?"

He chuckled for the first time since his disgrace. "And listen to the coyote serenade?"

It was the most companionable evening they'd spent since he'd heard of Roosevelt's impending stop at Sunflower. That was over and done. Maybe this time they really could have neighbors, have a home.

Even though the station never had passengers, Ed Morland meticulously kept the schedule on the blackboard up to the minute with the latest telegraphed information.

TWENTY MINUTES LATE, he chalked carefully beside Number 82. "I wish I'd asked Mr. Crane which train will bring Mr. Benedict's private car," he mused nervously.

He scanned the room and crossed it to completely shut the door to the freight room where last night's crates still waited. Nothing strange in that. Rather than risk having to make another trip to the depot, those expecting freight usually waited till it was sure to be there. "Do you think Mr. Benedict will be satisfied?"

It hurt to hear the question from a telegrapher who could once send 120 words a minute, who had, in Lesley's first memories, been trusted with the busiest telegraph centers along the Rock Island line. Gradually he had slid to night operator, then to stations like Sunflower where he was both station agent and telegrapher. Bountiful was about as far as one could fall and still have a job.

Because her heart ached for her father, Lesley's tone was sharper than she'd intended. "Of course he'll be satisfied! What could he find fault with?"

Still, she almost scoured the floor with the broom as she gave the station its daily sweeping out. Even its minimal furnishings were more than were needed at present. The operator's desk was located in a gabled bay window. On either side ran a shelf-desk. The cubbyholes on one were empty except for two stacks of unused tickets. On the other, the telegraph key and sounder were connected by wires to the pole outside, one of the column that dwindled out of sight on east and west.

In this part of the country, telegraph wires were strung above the prairie at the same time railroad tracks were laid across it, invading air and earth and changing the region forever in a way the rutted tracks of the Santa Fe Trail had never done. When a wagon train passed out of sight, the prairie world closed in again, but wires and tracks sundered that ancient whole into man-made divisions and man-made uses.

Lesley swept the tin plate that in winter protected the wood floor from the heat of the potbellied black iron stove dominating the center of the room. Hard to believe now how welcome that warmth would be by November! A good thing they got their coal free from the supply kept for the trains.

She whisked the broom under unused benches, two straight-backed chairs, and propelled the results through the door to the platform, which she swept from end to end.

"Les," ventured her father from the window. "Do you think we should invite Mr. Benedict to supper?"

The very notion panicked her. Offer Benedict beans and cornbread and dried peach pie served at the table in the end of the boxcar that was the kitchen, crowded with a kerosene cookstove and cupboard? Father's bed and trunk and her bed and trunk were divided from each other and the living area with the same blue gingham she used for curtains. There was a table-cloth of the same material. A small shelf held their treasured books. On top was the silver-framed photograph of her mother and father on their wedding day.

Lesley both cherished the portrait and detested it because the proud, handsome man was so different from the one she knew. She had never known, not to remember, the radiant woman with the crown of curly hair that could not be tamed by the veiled tiara.

"You look just like your mother," Ed Morland often told his daughter. When she was little, that made her feel as if she herself were no one, only a fraudulent imitation of the lovely, kind-faced woman in the picture. Perhaps she still did?

Lesley shut out that painful question. "I'm sure Mr. Benedict has his own dining arrangements," she pointed out, not quite able to keep the acid out of her tone.

Her father winced. Repenting, Lesley said, "I'm making peach pie. If you like, we could invite him to sit out on the platform after sundown and have dessert and coffee."

Ed Morland brightened and brushed the flyaway gray hair back from his ears. "I'd like to show him courtesy. Your mother was such a gracious hostess . . . Thank you, Les."

After supper, when Lesley suggested they sit on the platform to have their pie, her father hesitated. "Should we save the pie for tomorrow?"

"I baked two along with the cornbread. In this weather, I'm certainly not heating up the place for one pie."

They were enjoying the coolness and coyote chorus as much as the dessert when the telegraph began to chatter. Ed Morland's practiced ear could decipher the messages of the swiftest operator, though he still wrote them down, of course. Lesley could mentally decode the signals of only a deliberate telegrapher. It was a good thing that operators were required to repeat train orders to the dispatcher.

"Mr. Benedict's coming tonight!" Ed Morland called as he hurried in to acknowledge the transmission. "He's dining in his private car with a kitchen — he doesn't like cooking odors in his quarters. I have to be sure the siding near the wye's in good repair. The engine will switch Benedict's cars onto it and go on to Dodge."

"It's his railroad." Lesley shrugged. "I guess he can run a special train if he wants to." Still, the extravagance irked her. She added under her breath, "He saves money by not overpaying his station agents!"

"I'm lucky to have a job at all," her father admonished. He added hopefully, "If Bountiful grows and there's more station business, I'll get a raise."

She lit the lantern. They both went out to make sure that indeed the sandy earth hadn't undermined the Y-shaped tracks and the side track leading off the main railroad. How long would Benedict stay? Lesley was suddenly anxious for there to be more people in Bountiful. She didn't want, from the brief experience she'd had, to be exposed too long, too often, to the railroad magnate without other people around to absorb some of the force of his dominating nature.

He would be here in an hour.

A major benefit of living at an isolated station was not having to wear a corset, the affliction of womanhood she most abhorred. After numerous excruciating ordeals, she had located a Sears, Roebuck sateen corset waist with flexible stays front and back and side steels that could be removed.

Remove them, she had. She was so slender and her breasts so firm and high that the corset waist met the demands of decency without torment or leaving red welts on her torso.

The combination was in her trunk. In this brutal weather, she wore only drawers and a long chemise beneath her skirts and waists. She was positive that even by lamp and lantern light, Adam Benedict could tell at a glance that she wasn't wearing a corset.

Resentfully, she opened the trunk,

sighed, and got out the ecru corset waist. She paused. After another sigh, with an imprecation, she thrust the side steels in place.

However, since she had to undress, she decided to put her brown polka dot waist and skirt in the laundry and wear her rose and white striped lawn with lace trim at collar and sleeves and around the skirt. She sighed again, regarding the yards of hem that would collect dust with every step.

Bustles were gone for good, thank heaven, after reaching the limits of deformity in the early 1890s. Father had grumbled that fashionable women resembled "rump-sprung centaurs." Compared to the voluminous skirts worn over those monstrosities, this skirt was simplicity and ease, but she wondered if the day would ever come when women weren't cumbered with yards of material that dragged the ground. Even raising hems to the ankle would help, as was accepted for bicyclists.

Wind had loosened her hair, but there wasn't time to brush and put it up. She pinned the straying red-brown hair as severely as she could, dusted her nose with talcum powder — why wasn't it straight and patrician instead of short and slightly uptilted? — and wished her eyes were blue or gray or even green instead of what her father called russet — a nice word for brownish orange. At least her eyebrows were shapely and deep brown like her eyelashes.

Her mirrored face showed sudden consternation. She needn't have gone to all this bother! She wasn't the station agent. She could just tell her father her head ached — it was starting to! — and she didn't feel like inviting his employer for dessert. Then she wouldn't have to see the man till next day.

But she had to see him sometime, and Daddy was so eager to be welcoming . . . Hypocrite! she told herself. You're a little afraid of Adam Benedict, but he's an interesting change from Mr. Crane's shouting a few words out the window as the train clanks by. Whatever else he may be, he *is* a kind of magician, building railroads, creating towns.

But would a town of his be like Jim Kelly's? A place of neighbors? A whistle sounded, long and piercing. She went out into the wind and the darkness lit by oblongs of lamplight from windows.

The glaring dragon eye drew closer as the rumbling vibrated through the earth beneath her feet. Though she had grown up with trains, as this one neared, she felt a sudden primitive fear, as if she had never seen an engine before, as if it were indeed a fire-breathing terror.

It was veering off the track! It was roaring down upon her! She choked back the scream in her throat, hurrying for the platform. Of course the train had veered. It was moving onto the wye, growling to a halt, snorting like a dying behemoth.

Her father came out of the depot with the lantern. In spite of the heat, he had put on his station agent's coat and cap. "You look very smart and official, Mr. Morland," she said in his ear, and gave his hand a squeeze.

How strange it was, encouraging your father as if he were younger than you! But maybe there was an apprehensive child buried deep in everyone. She hoped she looked cool and composed, but that was not in the least how she felt as Adam Benedict filled the entrance of the car from which the engine was being uncoupled. A uniformed man hurried to place a stepbox under the steps at the end of the car.

Without acknowledging the service, Benedict strode toward the Morlands. "Holding down the outpost, Mr. Morland?" He gave his employee's hand a hearty shake, then captured Lesley's, though she had not offered it.

He held rather than shook it, released it only when she withdrew fingers that tingled from the warm pressure of his. "The high plains seem to agree with you, Miss Morland." Lantern light made a silver nimbus of his hair, evoked green brilliance in the depths of dark, unreadable eyes. "My chef has prepared his specialties. I hope you'll both join me for dinner."

"Thank you, we've dined." None of his business that it had been on cornbread and beans. She groaned inwardly as her father added, "Lesley makes delicious peach pie, Mr. Benedict. We intended to invite you for dessert —"

White teeth flashed. "Don't, I beg you, rescind the invitation. Henri will be devastated if I don't do justice to his Chateaubriand with béarnaise sauce. Perhaps you'll sit with me and have a glass of wine?"

Lesley was appalled. She'd have to make it clear to Benedict that he must not offer her father alcohol. Ed Morland gulped. "No, thank you, sir. We'll just sit on the platform and enjoy the cool."

"Twenty minutes then." Benedict checked in midstride. "Perhaps you'd like to see my traveling quarters?"

Lesley didn't want to compare their boxcar to a luxurious private car, but her father fell in step with the entrepreneur and launched into one of his favorite grumbling subjects. "Did you know, Mr. Benedict, that George Pullman stole the idea of his sleeping car from a Canadian named Tom Burnley?"

"I didn't, but good for Pullman."

Ed Morland stopped in his tracks. "Surely, sir, you don't think it was fair to cut his factory workers' wages in 'ninety-four?"

"Times were hard and profits down."

"He wouldn't even try to negotiate."

"Why should he? If the workers didn't want their jobs, there were plenty who did. Besides, traffic was stopped into Chicago by trains manned by men who belonged to the American Railway Union. They were paralyzing commerce."

Ed Morland's empty sleeve jerked as

if the stub were moving in agitation. "Then you think President Cleveland was right to send in regular troops to help the Chicago police and state militia?"

"The government has the responsibility to keep the mail trains running."

"Yes. But it doesn't do anything about the way railroad companies fire union leaders and send their names around so they won't be hired anywhere. U.S. marshals are on hand when there's a strike, but they don't lift a finger when Pinkerton strikebreakers threaten workers or beat them up."

Morland stopped at the door of the private car. Regret deepened the lines in his face as he glanced at Lesley, but his voice was stronger than she had heard it since he assailed Roosevelt. "You won't want me working for you now, Mr. Benedict. I'll naturally stay till you find a replacement."

To the Morlands' amazement, Adam Benedict laughed, body shaking. "Do you know something, Mr. Morland? My father died the year of the Pullman strike. The last editorial he wrote for his paper said almost precisely what you just did." The magnate's hand fell on the older man's shoulder. "I can't replace you. I don't want to try."

For a moment, Lesley was afraid her father would resign on principle. She breathed again when he said a trifle stiffly, "Well, sir, as long as we understand each other —"

"We do indeed." Benedict's hand closed under Lesley's elbow as he helped her up the steps. "By the way, I do know that Pullman made notes about and sketches of the railroad car Tom Burnley was building in Ontario for the Prince of Wales to travel in during his visit to Canada in 1860. The prince — poor fellow, will he ever get to be king? Queen Victoria may outlive him! — liked the coach so much that he didn't stay in hotels at all and lived in it the whole two months of his tour."

"The prince's car can't have been more elegant than this!" Morland exclaimed.

"No gilded coats of arms," Benedict chuckled.

It couldn't lack much else. Three big overstuffed chairs and a sofa were upholstered in the same wine red velvet as the gold fringed and tasseled draperies. Gold-framed mirrors reflected the clear white flame of the ornate gas lamp fixed in the middle of the domed ceiling of inlaid wood. Trains had become much safer during this last decade as dangerous, flammable kerosene lamps were replaced with Pintsch lamps fueled by gas from a tank carried beneath the car.

A walnut desk with carved legs and drawers faced a long window, a snugly filled bookshelf beside it. A folded brocade screen revealed a table gleaming with silver, fine china, and crystal arranged on a damask tablecloth. Yellow roses gave out their fragrance from a cut-glass vase.

A middle-aged man, face made ruddier by a blue uniform, entered from the car beyond, the same one who had placed the steps. His clever blue eyes seemed not to observe the Morlands, but Lesley was sure he could have described them to the eyelash.

"I'm not quite ready, Matthew. Tell Henri ten minutes. And that I'll be having dessert with Mr. and Miss Morland."

"As you say, sir." Matthew nodded and withdrew, giving a glimpse, in the next compartment, of a marble basin and claw-footed tub.

"You might like to see the kitchen dining car, Miss Morland." Benedict smiled. "It has every convenience, but we'd better wait till Henri's not using it." It wouldn't be proper for him to exhibit his bathroom.

He escorted them back to the platform. "I'll be eating Henri's handiwork, but I'll be thinking of your pie," he vowed, inclining his head to Lesley. "Is coffee a nuisance?"

"Of course not," she lied, and hurried to light her kerosene stove and put on the coffeepot.

3

The lantern would attract a throng of moths and those especially annoying beetles called June bugs, so they had their pie in the soft light shed through the station window. Lesley had spread a tablecloth over the crate they used for a table, but there was no way to prettify the blue-rimmed buff stoneware, tinned steel forks, and enameled coffeepot she had wrapped in a towel to keep hot.

"Your pastry is better than Henri's," complimented Benedict. "Could I have another cup of your excellent coffee?"

As she filled his cup, Lesley could not avoid being silhouetted against the window. Though his face was impassive, she was uncomfortably convinced that he knew her corset waist had side steels but that she was wearing the lightest undergirding she could find. Their eyes met for an instant. Shock knifed through her as if at a touch. She was glad to turn her back on that calm appraisal, but as she poured her father's second cup, she was sure that Benedict could not only describe her undergarments but what they concealed.

Strangely, she suspected that was not what most interested him about her, or her face, either. He *was* interested. The Morlands had never lived anywhere long enough for a courtship to develop beyond being escorted to a few dances or parties, but long before she put her hair up at seventeen, she had fended off male overtures when her father was either occupied or befuddled by drink.

Benedict was interested. Was she? Certainly he was fascinating, a cresting surge of energy in this ghost town, but he was alarming, too. He'd been gentle with her father, but she had seen hard-driving ruthlessness flash when Jim Kelly defied him. He hadn't achieved his power and wealth by being kind to one-armed men who drank too much.

Unlike Ed Morland, Benedict didn't add a copious amount of the canned Pet cream Lesley had served in a small pitcher. "We'd best enjoy this peaceful evening," he said. "The grading contractor will be here tomorrow."

"Did you finish the railroad to Clearwater?" Lesley asked.

"Clearwater?" He seemed to mentally sort records for a moment before he laughed. "Yes, that little stretch is finished, though I had to hire another freighter to replace — what was his name, Kelly?"

"Jim Kelly." With a pang, Lesley realized that building the line that had destroyed Kelly's Clearwater business must have been, to Benedict, only one of a number of such ventures.

"The Great Plains and Western's route is already surveyed," Benedict said. "Because of grades — it looks flat here, but it's not — my engineer has the line start several miles west. Construction headquarters will be there. The grading crews will set up camps along the sections they're supposed to build the roadbed for. The engineer reckons they can do the hundred and thirty miles in six weeks since there it's mostly sandy alluvial soil. Supplies will have to be hauled from the jump-off point, so the contractor's hired half a dozen farmers with wagons to do that. We'll have to order food from Dodge City till it can be locally supplied, but the men will haul water from here for the closest crew."

"Locally supplied?" Lesley echoed.

"Of course. The existing railroad, to be reasonably profitable, needs a good-sized community in this area, one with stores and services that will make it a hub for farmers in all directions. Supplying the railroad builders will give enterprising merchants a very handsome start — especially since I'm offering free lots and, to men with good credit, substantial loans at low interest."

"And to women of good credit?" Lesley demanded.

"My dear Miss Morland" — his tone was lazily amused — "my bank will lend you capital for any venture you choose to embark upon, though I believe you and your father will keep fully occupied with the station."

"But there aren't many farmers," Ed Morland said ruefully.

"There will be." That confident smile flashed. "When nearly all the farms around here were foreclosed on in the late eighties and early nineties, I bought the land — if you'll pardon the expression — dirt cheap. I'm capitalizing the Citizens Bank of Bountiful to finance buyers and lend those who need it money for getting started. My railroad will provide free transportation for buyers and their possessions. It will supply each farmer enough Turkey Red seed wheat to plant eighty acres. They can plant this fall. By this time next year, their crop will be in the elevator I'm going to build."

"I can see why you're rich, sir." Morland's tone was dry. "You're a champion salesman."

"I've been lucky enough to be in the right places at the right times with a little money and lots of nerve." Benedict's eyes twinkled. "Now, Mr. Morland, if you were a farmer who'd lost everything in the bad times, could you resist such a prospect?"

"Farmers have to be optimists or they'd never choose that way of life, especially not in western Kansas, where they can count on drought, grasshoppers, and hail a lot more reliably than good crops." Ed Morland looked shrewdly at his guest — or since the guest owned the station, was it the other way around? "They say farmers out here raise three crops, wheat, credit, and freight charges. I'd guess your customers are going to have bumper yields of the last two anyhow."

"Not as much as you'd think. Thanks to the Railroad Commission Kansas set up in 1883, freight and passenger rates are fixed at what the commissioners consider a fair amount, and they stick their noses into working conditions, too."

"Sometimes I'm proud of Kansas," Morland said. "Like when we elected Jerry Simpson to the House of Representatives for a third term."

"Sockless Jerry?" The points of Benedict's eyebrows rose almost level with his silvery widow's peak. "That hayseed's done his best to hamstring railroads and bankers!"

"Can't blame him much. And he's about as simple as a fox. Worked his way from cabin boy to captain on the Great Lakes, came to Kansas with ten thousand dollars and started ranching. Did fine till the 1886 blizzard wiped him out. Then he got ten dollars a week as Medicine Lodge's marshal and also dug sewers to make enough to live."

"You've certainly made a study of his career." Benedict's tone was acid.

"Admired his grit. He got beat when he ran for the state legislature, but he won a seat in Congress in 1890 — and I'm glad I voted for him. The Populists have kind of lost out, but they had the right idea, giving ordinary folks more to say about government."

"That sounds just like the hogwash my dad used to write in the little newspaper I bought him. I remember in 'eighty-nine when there was a record corn crop and the price dropped to ten cents a bushel, he managed to blame it on banks and railroads."

"Most farmers burned their corn for fuel," Ed Morland said. "Not much wonder fifty thousand Kansans left the state that year to make the Land Rush to Oklahoma Territory."

Benedict leaned over to rest his hand on the older man's shoulder. "Well, my friend, get set for a land rush here. In a month, you won't know the place."

He rose. His dark suit concentrated the light on his silver hair and mustache, peaked eyebrows, and broad cheekbones and jaw. The unfathomable eyes were dark as the night as they fixed on Lesley. "Thank you for the marvelous dessert and coffee — and the pleasure of your company."

Why did she feel as if those big hands

had seized her when they hung loose at his sides? She said automatically, "The pleasure was ours, sir." He vanished into the night to reappear again at the door of his lighted car.

Intriguing, the evening had surely been. But a pleasure? A bedazzling glimpse of what power and money could accomplish, but more an encounter with a man of implacable will.

"He admires you, honey."

She turned to her father. "I think I'd just as soon be admired by a bolt of lightning — all very exciting so long as there's a safe distance in between."

"He'll keep a safe distance while I'm around," her father promised. "And you can bet I will be, long as you want me."

"I know, Dad." She kissed his cheek, but as she collected the dishes, she wondered if, where Adam Benedict was concerned, there was a safe distance.

The Morlands could see the smoke of a westbound train next morning as it stopped a few miles away. "Must be unloading the graders," Father surmised.

No one had come out of the private car, but half an hour later, as the train

66

announced its coming with a long wail, Benedict emerged and strolled to the platform with Matthew close behind.

A flatcar came in view at the end of the train as it huffed and groaned to a stop, spewing cinders and smoke. Secured to the flatbed with stout ropes was something carefully shrouded in tarpaulins. The brakeman set about untying the ropes. He drew away the canvas with great care, as if unveiling a work of art as well as trying not to shake dust all over the spectators. Ordinarily, such a car would be left on a siding to unload later, but Benedict could, of course, delay a train if he wished.

"Will you look at that?" breathed Father. "Oldsmobile, is it, sir?"

"Made to my specifications." Adam Benedict looked pleased as a boy with his first bicycle. "Ransom Olds is a friend of mine. When his factory at Detroit burned, about all that was rescued was a pioneer version of this carriage. He'll put it on the open market next year."

"It looks like a sleigh on high wheels," Lesley exclaimed. "I like the jaunty way the front curves back."

"It's lighter than I'd choose and I'd prefer to have backseats, but this is just Ransom's beginning, and I believe in buying American automobiles, though I'll confess I was tempted by a Daimler. The French have more experience than any nation in making internal-combustion-powered machines and turn out half of the world's production. I think America can outstrip the foreigners, but it won't if Americans buy their horseless carriages from abroad."

Not that many Americans could afford any kind of the contrivances. During the nineties, a number of inventors had assembled motor-run tricycles and carriages. In 1896 a young man named Henry Ford had driven his quadricycle through Detroit, and soon after, several makes of carriages were on the market, but they cost thousands of dollars and were expensive and difficult to maintain. It was hard to see how they would ever be more than a rich man's toy.

The conductor and eight male passengers swarmed out to stare at the astonishing black vehicle trimmed in red that resembled a topless carriage with a closed elongated front equipped with brass-encased lamps. A tiller on a long rod thrust toward the padded leather front seat.

"Ain't she a beauty?" crooned a ginger-haired man in a derby. "How fast will she go?"

"Depends on the road," said Benedict. "Here, where I'll jounce along on tracks made by horse teams, I don't hope for more than ten miles an hour."

Several men whistled, but one, whose wistful look at the vehicle contradicted his words, said in a scornful tone, "You'll spend most of that hour fixing flat tires and cranking the engine when it dies. Give me a Stanley Steamer anytime."

Benedict disdained to answer, but Matthew bristled. "A Stanley takes twenty minutes to build up a head of steam. You call that efficient?"

"You're sitting over an explosion when you use gasoline," put in a bushy-bearded older man. "I favor Pope's electric carriages. My wife and I saw one when we were visiting her folks in Boston a few months ago. It purred like a kitten and went as fast as any sane person would want to."

"Yes, but the batteries have to be recharged every forty or fifty miles," sniffed the man in the derby. "Give me a Steamer any day."

While Lesley's father unloaded a big metal box and what looked like steel milk cans with spigots, all the train crew except the engineer helped place a ramp from flatcar to platform and cautiously push the automobile down it. The engineer tootled, crew and passengers reboarded, and the train chugged off.

"Have you driven a horseless carriage before, Mr. Benedict?" Lesley ventured.

"I tried a Peugeot, a Benz, a Daimler, and a Fiat when I was in Europe last winter. Matthew also drives." Benedict nodded at the wood crate and big metal box in the baggage cart. "With that crate of extra tire casings, inner tubes, and spare parts and that repair kit Hammacher Schlemmer of New York put together for me, we'll keep it running." His glance included both Morlands. "Once I have it figured out and handling nicely, may I take you for a drive?"

"We can't both leave the station at the same time," Lesley demurred.

"We could take turns," her father said eagerly. What was it about men that

70

attracted them so to anything with an engine?

Benedict's eyes flickered. "So you could. Fine, then. In a day or two we'll take a spin. This morning, as soon as Matthew gets the buggy fueled and humming, I must make sure the grading crews are competent."

"Doesn't your contractor see to that?" asked Ed Morland.

"You might say," Benedict said, grinning, "that I see to it that he sees to it that his men know their jobs — and do them. Harve Steele's the best contractor I've ever had. I want to keep him that way." He paused, obviously running problems through his head. "We're going to need more freighters. Farmers leave you in the lurch when their crops need attention. If anyone with a wagon and reasonable intelligence shows up, I'd appreciate your hiring him — provisionally — on my behalf."

"Someone's got some freight to collect," Morland said. "If he has a good outfit, I'll ask if he's interested."

Matthew, without direct orders, had already opened the crate to produce a hose, which he fastened to the spigot of one of the large steel cans and began

71

to fill the tank beneath the front seat. "I'll have to buy an interest in an oil company," Benedict mused. "Up to now, the main use has been kerosene for lamps, but automobiles are going to change that faster than new wells can be drilled."

Immersed in the prospect, he nodded almost absently to the Morlands and sauntered toward his palatial, if temporary, abode. Did he really have a *home?* A place where his questing spirit rested? Somehow, Lesley doubted it.

Her father lingered to watch Matthew fuss over the Oldsmobile, so Lesley went inside to complete the paperwork on Bountiful's most exciting shipment to date. A tap came on the never-used passenger window. She looked up to meet keen blue eyes set in a face adorned with a furled waxed mustache and pointed gray Vandyke beard that belied skin so weathered that it would ordinarily have proclaimed him an outdoor man. From his starched, poufed white hat and apron, this could scarcely be anyone other than Henri, the prized and temperamental cook.

"*Bonjour,* lady," he said, and thrust a written message toward her. If his eyebrows, too, had not been waxed, they would surely have bristled in wild profusion. He lifted them and produced a worn leather wallet. "How much?"

A phrase any foreigner would have to learn, but his accent was not what she'd expected — not that she'd heard French spoken, but she had learned a smattering of German when they were at a station near a Mennonite community. Henri talked as if he had marbles in his mouth and was trying to keep them from falling out.

She counted the words in a hard-to-read scrawled hand with frequent misspellings, and as she usually had for the Mennonites, wrote down the charge. He gave her exact change and leaned on the window shelf as she sent his message, an order to a St. Louis merchant for foodstuffs she'd never heard of before.

Signing off, Lesley gave the cook an encouraging smile. He probably understood much more than he could say. After all, the order was written in English, though some of the items had foreign names. "The wire went through just fine. You should have the things in about a week, Mr. —"

73

"Champagne," he supplied, but his gaze was fixed on a team and wagon just now coming near enough for the clop of hooves to carry.

"That's a very French name," Lesley said, looking out the bay window.

"Mmm. *Oui. Merci,* lady." It sounded like Wee. Mercy.

"Oh, there was no mercy, Mr. Champagne. It's my job and you paid —"

He cut in with a jerk of his spiked beard toward the nearing wagon. "Who?"

Lesley shaded her eyes against the sun and got a shock. The driver wore a plaid shirt, bandanna, and trousers, but long, waving yellow hair like that hadn't appeared under a man's slouch hat since Custer lost his at the Little Big Horn. The driver handled the reins with skill, and the names and adjurations directed at long-eared mules were profane but loving and delivered in a throaty, carrying woman's voice.

"I don't know her, Mr. Champagne. She may be the owner of some stored freight." Lesley hurried out as the driver slowed the team to a sedate pace. They stopped without a "Whoa!" at the hitching rack and the driver swung down and tied them, practiced motions tightening Levi's and shirt over what were definitely feminine curves.

She turned. Green eyes widened as they settled on Henri. A delighted smile broadened a thin face that was as weathered as Henri's. "Well, I'll be spavined if you ain't the cutest critter I ever saw, mister! Where in the ever-lovin' world did you come from and who might you be?"

He blinked and opened his mouth, but it just hung agape. His eyes gleamed with admiration, but he seemed unable to summon words. Trying to help him, Lesley said, "He's Henri Champagne from Paris. He cooks for Mr. Benedict, who owns this railroad and is building another south."

"That's the bird I want to see soon as I haul the stuff I've got to pick up here to our lots."

"Lots?" repeated Lesley.

The woman jerked a thumb toward the rickety buildings. "My partner bought four big lots. We're settin' up in business."

"What kind of business?"

"Freightin'. Should be a good place to set up headquarters. From the sound of it, this neck of the woods is goin' to settle up again, this time for keeps 'cause there's no more decent cheap or free land to grab. Folks will be needin' freight hauled to their stores, farms, and ranches, and there's a few inland towns can be served from here."

Inland towns were communities not located on a railroad. Jim Kelly had talked of finding a new location. Could he possibly be this woman's partner? Lesley tried to work up the nerve to ask but was afraid of being disappointed.

The remarkable teamster looked around. Her gaze lit on the Oldsmobile with Matthew and Ed Morland bent over it. "Is that one of them infernal horseless carriages?"

"That's what it is. Father!" Lesley had to rouse her father to his duty. "This lady's here for some freight."

He straightened reluctantly from inspecting the undercarriage, oblivious, till summoned, to the arrival of a customer. To Lesley's surprise and discomfort, he, like Henri, almost gasped at the luxuriant yellow ringlets and undulations so accentuated by tight-fitting male garments.

"Good day to you, ma'am." He swept

off his cap with a flourish. "Some crates arrived several days ago. If you'll just give me your name —"

"I'm Bella Ballard, mister, and don't call me Mrs. My last hubby died a year ago, God rest his darling soul. Everybody calls *me* Bella. But the shipment's in my partner's name. James H. Kelly."

Even though Lesley had hoped this might be true, she was astonished at the sudden warm lilt of the blood in her veins. She scarcely knew Jim Kelly, she reasoned — had been with him less than ten minutes. But oh, in those moments when she was distraught, angry, and desperate, he had sustained her, offered his friendship. It was the first time in her life she had felt she could depend on another human. He had lost a profitable contract in order to go with her to the courthouse jail, and he had confirmed that Benedict could indeed give her father a station.

He had paid her father's fine and gone his way without waiting for gratitude. She hadn't been able to properly phrase her thanks in the letter she had sent him, but now she should be able to tell him how much his help had meant.

"When's Mr. Kelly coming?" she asked Bella.

"Soon's he winds up loose ends in Clearwater. Then he'll be along with our other teamster, Micajah Schatz." Bella grinned. That erased some of the lines in her face and made it look almost as youthful as her figure and bright hair.

How old was she? Certainly not young, but with her skin contradicting her figure and flowing curls, she could have been anywhere from thirty to fifty. "Kelly depends on me to line up most of our business. Before he turns up, I want to make a deal with Benedict. Jim won't like it — yes, I know the two fell out, though I never heard exactly why — but while the country builds up, it'll sure help if we haul for the construction gangs."

Ed trundled the crates to the edge of the platform next to the endgate of the wagon. When Bella let it down, he stretched a movable ramp from platform to wagon bed and pulled the cart into the wagon. Bella started to help unload the crates.

"No!" Henri shouted, dashing forward. *"Non!"* He piloted the startled teamster gallantly to the platform and hurried to assist Ed Morland.

"Henri!" Adam Benedict had come up without anyone hearing him. "I don't pay you to wrestle freight. I want a lunch packed and —"

Bella didn't have the same devastating effect on Benedict that she had on Henri and Morland, but he did stop talking as she crossed the platform to him — and he couldn't watch her rhythmically shifting posterior as did the other mesmerized men.

"Say, young fella, you Adam Benedict?"

The peaked brows arched high. "I am."

She didn't notice or didn't heed his note of hauteur but thrust out her hand and gave his a vigorous shake. "I'm Bella Ballard. Hear you need some good freighters."

"I do, but —"

She might well be the first person who had ever interrupted Benedict. "Our outfit's the best. Aim to set up headquarters here on some lots we bought for back taxes."

"So *that's* what happened to the lots that were already sold when I bought up the abandoned ones."

"Yep. My partners and me were lookin'

for a good place to roost. What with the new railroad you're buildin', this seemed a prime spot. We've got three experienced teamsters."

"*You're* a teamster?"

"Twenty years, son. Me'n my three husbands, Lord rest 'em, hauled out of Dodge to Tascosa and Camp Supply. In spite of blizzards, quicksand, and floods, we never lost a shipment."

Grudgingly amused, Benedict said, "By the sound of it, ma'am, you must have lost a few husbands."

"Poor Arch," she sighed. "Got caught with one too many aces up his sleeve in the Long Branch Saloon. George —" Her tone hardened. "He fell down the stairs of a — place he had no business to be. If he hadn't broke his neck, I'd have done it for him, no extra charge. Howard —" She considered. "Some say he doesn't count because he had an apoplexy fit on his way to the church for the weddin'. But he was willin', God love him, he was willin'. I say he counts."

"So would I, ma'am." Benedict chuckled. "All right. Your company's hired." He jerked his head in the direction of the construction camp. "Report to the contractor as soon as you can, see what he needs brought in. He'll be pleased to have some professionals. Where are your other wagons?"

"They'll be along in a couple of days." She glanced fondly toward her mules. "My honeys need to rest today, but they'll be rarin' to go in the morning." She pumped his hand again, thanked the men who had loaded her cargo with a flashing smile, untied the team, and maneuvered across the tracks.

"Henri!" Benedict sounded indulgent but determined. "Mrs. Ballard is indeed a fine figure of a woman, but I do want my lunch."

"*Oui,* m'sieur." Henri nodded, but as he moved toward the private car, he kept his eyes on Bella.

She halted her team a short distance beyond the huddle of dilapidated buildings. She at once set about unharnessing the mules, slipped on halters, and led them to drink at the trough by the railroad water tank, patting and praising them on the way. Father, unlike Henri, had no immediate chores. With a spring in his step that Lesley hadn't seen for years, he crossed the track to help her with the mules and unloading.

"Well, Miss Morland," said Benedict with a smile, "your father may have more dash left in him than you think. I wish him luck, the more so since I don't want to lose my cook."

Father marry again? He had never returned the interest of the several ladies who had genteelly pursued him; in fact, they had left one town because of a persistent widow who haunted the depot. Lesley tested the idea gingerly, as one might explore the tissue around an aching tooth, and discovered to her surprise that it didn't hurt as it once had. If Bella could keep a sparkle in his eye and make him prance like a colt, that was worlds better than melancholy, drunk or sober.

"I wish him luck, too," she found herself saying.

Benedict looked surprised. She was saved from whatever he might have said by the sound of the telegraph. As she hurried inside, Matthew straightened and flicked a speck off the fender with a chamois.

"Ready, sir. And here comes that Frenchie with your lunch."

"Good." Benedict's voice filled Lesley's ears, though she was trying to concentrate on the announcement of the departure of a special supply train from Pueblo. "Crank the buggy, Matthew, and let's have a look at that grading crew."

Acknowledging the Pueblo message, Lesley transcribed it and watched Matthew's face redden as he turned a kind of handle thing protruding from the engine space beneath the driver's seat. The labor evidently got harder, and he was careful not to take pressure off the handle as he paused on the downsweeps.

The engine growled. Benedict performed some magic and the growl became a thunderous purr. Matthew dragged the ramp to the end of the platform, leaped up beside his employer, and away they went, jouncing beside the railroad tracks.

What'll Benedict do when he finds out he's hired Jim Kelly? Lesley wondered. With a stab of anxiety, she added, For that matter, what will Jim do?

Worry couldn't long dampen the sweet, secret glow inside her caused by knowing that he'd be coming soon. Had he chosen Bountiful as his new headquarters not only for the business prospects but because she was there?

She dared to hope so. Out of bubbling high spirits, she tapped to the Dodge operator, "It's a beautiful, wonderful, glorious day!" and signed off the initials she shared with her father.

"Hotter than Hades," came back the answer. "You're drinking something stronger than lemonade over there, L.M.! Wish I had some."

Father came in, a bemused smile touching his lips. She tried to see him as Bella might. The natty blue uniform cap hid his baldness and he did have deep-set warm brown eyes. "Spiritual," the persistent widow woman had called them.

"I invited Bella — Mrs. Ballard — for dinner," he said with a hint of apology. "If that won't put you out."

"Why, I'd love to have Mrs. Ballard — that is, Bella — for dinner," Lesley teased. "Should we offer to let her sleep in the depot?"

"She's got a tent, and when Kelly and Micajah come, they'll repair the old livery stable and house that sit on their lots." Father peered out the ticket window. "If you can hold things down here, Les, I'd like to go help Bella pitch that tent."

"Go ahead." Lesley gave her father a quick hug and kiss. "Just get back in time for me to fix dinner."

He went off like a schoolboy let out early. How good to see him eager about something! And how more than good it would be to see Jim Kelly! Lesley whistled as she tidied and swept out the depot. The stream of life had stagnated for weeks. Now it was racing, with suddenly more currents and twists than she could think about.

All she was sure of in the tumult was that it was wonderful to watch Father move so jauntily, that she didn't trust Adam Benedict no matter how benevolent he might act, and most of all, that seeing Jim Kelly again would be like the dawning of the first day of the world.

4

Bella had supper with the Morlands as well as dinner, contributing to the evening meal a can of pears and a box of Cracker Jacks apiece. "I sure like these," she said, crunching a big handful of the sticky carameled popcorn and peanuts. "Buy 'em by the hundred-package case from good old Sears, Roebuck. We take gettin' most anything we want for granted now, but I remember when there wasn't any Sears or Monkey Ward and no trains west of Kansas City. When I first saw Dodge City back in the early 1870s, it was nothin' but a stinkin' camp for buffalo hunters, and Comanches — as I have durn good reason to know — were still on the prowl all over the South Plains, to say nothin' of Kiowa."

Lesley shook her head in wonder. "Less than thirty years ago!"

"That's right." Bella looked reflectively at Lesley. " 'Course, folks my age are kind of walkin' history books. I was eleven when the Civil War began, only where we lived on the Missouri border, the war'd been going on ever since I could remember between proslavery men from Missouri, and Kansans who were ready to die — and kill — to keep slavery out of the state."

"Bleeding Kansas," Lesley remembered from her history lessons. It seemed so long ago, yet here was Bella, who had seen it and was still far from old.

"My daddy was one of the New England folks who moved to Kansas to vote it into the Union as a free state. Got killed in Quantrill's raid on Lawrence — them Southern gentlemen who liked to brag on how polite they were to women dragged Mama out of the way and shot him in front of her."

Lesley looked a horrified question. Bella shook her head. "My little brothers and me didn't see it. Mama sent us into the cellar when the shooting and yelling woke us up. Quantrill had three hundred raiders. They galloped into town that bloody dawn, killed every man they could find, and set fire to most of the buildings. Daddy's store burned to the ground, but neighbors built it back and stocked it. Mama ran it till she died ten years ago."

"She was a brave lady," Father said.

"She had more to bear. My big brother, Ernie — he was almost fifteen — was workin' at a farm ten miles up the Kaw River. When he heard what happened, he went off and joined the army. He was killed in his first battle just a few days shy of his fifteenth birthday."

"Your poor mother!" Lesley cried.

"You lived through it or you didn't," Bella said. "She prayed every night that the war would end before Tom and Danny were old enough to fight."

"I wanted to fight like my two older brothers," Ed said, "but I was only fourteen when the war ended." He glanced at his empty sleeve. "Guess that's why I volunteered to fight for Cuba's freedom — at least that's what I thought I was doing."

"I didn't know you had brothers who fought in the Civil War, Daddy," said Lesley, a bit aggrieved.

He shrugged. "They died before you were born, honey, and neither of them married, so they didn't leave wives or kids. Jack lost a leg at Shiloh and died a few years after the war from the morphine he used to dull the pain — and the memories, too, I guess. Charlie went to Arizona and got killed when a Tombstone mine caved in."

"Never has been any lack of ways to die," observed Bella. "Especially not in the West. Used to be you hardly ever saw an old person out here." She sighed, then grinned her irrepressible grin. "Now I'm gettin' old myself."

"Not you, Bella," said Ed gallantly. "You move like a girl" — he didn't specify *what* she moved so youthfully — "and I never saw a finer head of yellow curls."

"I'd hope not. It cost me plenty." When the Morlands stared, she twiddled a curl between thumb and finger. "Twenty-four inches long sewed to a silk foundation. Eighteen dollars fifty cents."

She smiled in gratification at their gasps. "I could never figger," she mused, "why the old codgers who got scalped wore stocking caps or such instead of getting a nice wig."

Lesley blinked. Her father's jaw dropped. "Bella!" he started, then broke off.

"Well, sure, it's a wig," she said. "What I have left of my own hair is plumb gray."

"You —" Lesley began, but stopped at the unthinkable.

Bella had no such scruples. She even laughed. "My hair *was* yellow and curly then; I was only twenty-four. For all I know, it's still decoratin' some old warrior's shield down at the Fort Sill Reservation — may give him somethin' enjoyable to remember. It happened the summer of seventy-four, a week or so before Adobe Walls."

Lesley must have shown her puzzlement. After a stare of incredulity, Bella shrugged and laughed. "You weren't born yet and maybe the perfessers who write the history books didn't put it in, but that was the first and last time a bunch of different tribes got together to try to run the whites off their hunting grounds. There was Quanah Parker leadin' the Quahadi Comanche along with a medicine man who was supposed to vomit up loads of ammunition and stop bullets in the air. The Cheyenne and Arapaho joined in, and the Kiowas. Some say there was a couple hundred warriors, some say eight hundred. Anyhow, they came down on the buffalo hunters' stockade at Adobe Walls in the Texas Panhandle, but the hunters stood 'em off. As the warriors was a-gatherin', they killed any whites they came across. I was haulin' supplies to the stockade and didn't know about the trouble till a bunch of painted braves on horseback swarmed around my wagon."

"Bella!" Father was horrified. "What was your husband thinking of, letting you be out there alone?"

" 'Twasn't his fault 'ceptin' for puttin' away so much red-eye that he had to sleep it off. I was sore at him and figgered I'd show him. Guess I did! He found me."

"I thought scalping killed people." Lesley spoke gingerly although Bella seemed almost bragging.

"Bless you, folks were lots of times dead or mortal wounded before they got scalped. That itself wasn't enough to kill a grown-up unless the warrior was fumble-fingered or mighty rough. 'Twasn't my warrior's fault I didn't die. He ran a lance clean through me."

"Bella!" Father shuddered.

"They didn't necessarily take all the

hair, you know," Bella continued in a confidential tone. "Sometimes the skin part was small as a silver dollar, though it could be stretched a sight bigger if the owner — well, not the real owner, of course, but the one who took it off the other feller's head — could start workin' on it while it was still pretty fresh." She cocked her head solicitously. "Feelin' puny, Ed? You look sorta green around the gills."

"Mmphmf." He jolted down several swallows of black coffee and managed to sound cool and scientifically interested. "Is it true that Comanches thought scalping kept the victim from having a life after death?"

"Way I understand it is only if he or she got their hair raised after they was dead. Someone scalped while they were still alive didn't lose their shot at the Happy Hunting Ground. Warriors would risk death to rescue a pal's body so it wouldn't lose its scalp and chance to rise again. It was mighty bad luck to die in the dark or by strangling." She got to her feet, patting back a yawn. "Glad we've had a chance to get acquainted some before I start work. Let me help you redd up the dishes, Lesley?"

Lesley shook her head. "It won't take long and you must be tired."

"Not as limber as I used to be," Bella admitted. She paused at the door of their boxcar. "I may not be back for several days if the contractor has me haul supplies to crews workin' further south. If I'm gone when Kelly and Micajah turn up, tell 'em I've made a deal with Benedict. All they have to do is report to the contractor."

"From what happened last time Mr. Kelly met Adam Benedict," said Lesley, "I think they're both going to be surprised and not too happy."

"The more fools they," retorted Bella. "Benedict needs us, we need work." She swept her gaze over the uninhabited plains, the deserted buildings. "The bank we bought our properties from painted Jim a pretty picture from which he reckoned there'd be enough farmers and inland towns to keep us busy. When he sees this —" She gave Lesley a long look of appraisal. "I've known Jim since he was a skinny kid currying my team at his folks' way station on the Jones-Plummer Trail. He's never been a lad to leap before he looks." Her gaze probed till Lesley felt herself blushing.

Bella smiled suddenly. "Guess this time he was lookin' at somethin' beyond the leap. But he can just pull in his horns and get along with Benedict, at least till we get some new customers."

"Mr. Benedict's building a bank —"

"He would." Bella gave a toss of blond hair. "The bank I had my savin's in — six thousand hard-earned dollars — shut down in 'ninety-three. I never got a dime. No more banks for me! I'd rather get robbed with a gun than a bunch of figures." She covered Lesley's hand with her brown, steel-like fingers. "Thanks for bein' neighborly. That's what makes a town."

"We're glad you're our neighbor," Lesley said. "And I have a feeling that however many we get, you'll always be the nicest one."

Bella's green eyes opened wide. "Aw, honey, I'm not nice!"

"You certainly are," declared Ed. "And I'm going to walk you home — well, anyhow, to your tent."

Lesley watched them go. Her feelings were as tangled as a beginner's telegraph signals. It was good to see her father so lively and interested, but she had been used to his undivided attention all her life, at least when he was sober.

She was collecting the dishes when she heard Henri Champagne's voice. "M'sieu Morland! M'sieu!" She looked out. Henri was holding a paper under Father's nose — doubtless another list of delicacies.

He thrust it into Father's hand, bowed to him, and then, pivoting, proffered his arm to Bella. It was all done too quickly to allow Lesley to hurry up and offer to send the message. Ed stared after the abductor and not-too-unwilling abducted, growled something, and vanished inside the depot. Scalped or not, Bella had no trouble attracting men.

When was Benedict going to eat all this food his chef was ordering? It was twilight and the Oldsmobile hadn't returned. She heard the whistle of an eastbound train. Father was in the station, so he'd pass on any orders. She dumped the dishwater on bare ground and the rinse water on a small sandhill plum bush she was trying to nurture.

As night thickened, the train took on water and clanged on its way. Coyotes laughed somewhere to the south. A whippoorwill lamented. Overhead, a nighthawk called, "Peeent!" After enduring the broiling day, moving and breathing only enough to survive, the plains and its creatures seemed to breathe deep and come alive again. It was much cooler outside than in. Lesley hung up the dishpans and wandered toward the prairie dog town. They had retired for the night, but the burrowing owls would be hunting, snatching insects and whatever small prey they could seize from air or earth.

Cautious of the rattlesnakes who would be hunting, too, she sat down on the railroad tie, folding her skirts across her lap so they wouldn't attract and harbor anything like tarantulas, scorpions, or centipedes. If Bountiful became a human town again as Benedict intended, she hoped this other town would not be disturbed. But if someone bought it — well, people didn't buy land and leave it to owls and prairie dogs.

She would, though. The thought galvanized her. Of course! Buy the acres of mounds and tunnels and leave their dwellers in peace.

But she didn't have the money. Thanks to their isolation, the last paycheck hadn't been used. She thought

Father would agree to using the check however she wished. He said, by rights, it was half hers. But that wouldn't buy the stretch of burrows, which she guessed must cover twenty acres.

The sound of a motor reached her at the same time two wavering lights beamed into view. Here came the man who almost certainly owned the little village — and he was setting up a bank. Banks lent money. If father would share his salary with her, and she was sure he would, she could borrow enough to buy the land before someone else did, someone who would level the mounds and destroy the underground dwellings.

This might not be the most propitious time to approach Benedict. He must be weary from a long, hot, dusty day. She was afraid to leave it, though. His advertising might lead, any time, to someone's buying it sight unseen.

Lifting her skirts to avoid collecting burrs and spears of dry grass, she hurried toward the rails and followed them to the siding. The automobile churned up dust that made her cough as the lights glittered like an undulating monster's eyes. She reached the private car only seconds before the Oldsmobile ground up beside it. The lights washed her in failing brightness before they flickered off, but the lamp above the door showed the way Adam Benedict sprang out of the vehicle and hastened, gray silk duster trailing behind him, goggles pushed up on his forehead, to reach Lesley and take her hands between his.

"Miss Morland! You make me forget a weary day." Matthew eased him out of the duster, took the hat and goggles, and retreated to a safe distance to shake out the clouds of dirt. His employer's face was streaked with sweat and dust except for a pale mask the goggles had protected. Henri appeared in the entrance. Bella must not have encouraged him to linger. "I'm sure you've dined," Benedict went on, "but perhaps you'd have iced tea or lemonade while I apply myself to whatever Henri has ready."

Iced tea? It sounded deliciously refreshing, but respectable women didn't sit with a gentleman in what was actually his home even if his cook and — what would you call Matthew? — were present.

Lesley detested the word "servant." "Valet" was no better. It didn't belong in America, but "hired man" would scarcely do. Having tended to his employer's immediate needs, Matthew was examining the Oldsmobile as an anxious mother might a child who'd just done something strenuous.

Mechanic. That was better. She'd call him that. Benedict was waiting. The lamp lit the green depths of his eyes, reminding her of a large cat surveying its quarry. "I came on business," she said, regretting the iced tea with a physical pang. "Perhaps if you're not too tired after your supper, you'd have coffee with Father and me on the platform?"

"I've got a better idea." His tone was good-humoredly resigned. "Why don't you and your father join me for dessert in about forty-five minutes? Or, if that's too late for his convenience, perhaps Mrs. Ballard would be your chaperone." Teeth flashed white in his travel-stained face. "A lady who's had three husbands should make a watchdog — pardon me, a guardian — vigilant enough to satisfy the most exacting standards."

He thought her prudish, stuck in the

past century. Her cheeks burned and she started to make some protest, but then decided it was safest to let him hold that opinion.

"I'll ask Father." She took herself off with a whisk of skirts, pursued by soft, delighted laughter.

Let him laugh, she told herself. Let him think she got her code of conduct direct from Queen Victoria! He could think whatever he chose to, so long as she got the loan.

Ed Morland was not at the depot, nor was he in their home. That left one place. Lesley started for the soft glow of light across the tracks, for Bella's throaty laughter and Ed Morland's voice, deepened and masculine.

Lesley smiled in the darkness. He must have hotfooted it over the minute Henri left. Whether or not Bella was agreeable to having a fourth husband, she must be enjoying the attention. After all she had gone through — and Lesley was sure they'd heard only a fraction of her trials and tribulations — it was cheering to be around her. Lesley felt a sting of jealousy and guilt as her father's laughter joined Bella's.

I guess I haven't been very good com-

pany. But I might have been if he'd stayed sober, if we'd lived in one place where we'd have made friends, if he hadn't gone off to war . . .

"Daddy!" she called. A lantern stood on a crate by the tent. Either to avoid the insects fluttering around it, or for more privacy, Bella and Ed sat in the shadows on smaller boxes.

"Here I am, Les," he said. "Saw you talking with Mr. Benedict. Looks like he survived his first day with the Oldsmobile."

"He looked like he'd been in a coal bin! And that silk duster! When Matthew shook it, the dust boiled out till you couldn't believe there was any left on the road."

"Wonder how many flats he had," pondered Bella, with the undertone of glee felt by drivers of animals for the frequent travails of those depending on motorcars. "Nothin' tickles me more than haulin' a dadburned horseless carriage out of the mud or a ditch. Somehow my old mules can't quite do it unless the owner gets in there and pushes hard as he can."

"Matthew will do the pushing, you bet, and he'll fix the flats, too," said Lesley.

She hesitated, not much wanting, in front of Bella, to ask her father to co-operate in her plan. Still, if it worked, Bella would know. It would be a long time, if ever, that anyone bought land in Bountiful without everybody knowing all the details. Lesley squared her shoulders.

"Daddy," she said in a rush, "I want to buy the prairie dog town before someone does who'd wreck it. Will you help me get a loan from Mr. Benedict?"

"Prairie dogs!" sniffed Bella. "I lost a good mule once on account of them. Stepped in a burrow and snapped his leg."

"That wasn't the prairie dog's fault," defended Lesley.

"If farms go in around them and they start munchin' on crops instead of grass and weeds, they'll get poisoned," Bella warned.

"Maybe the surrounding land will be sold for grazing," Lesley countered.

"Then for sure a rancher won't want them stealin' his grass and cripplin' his cattle with their danged holes."

"If we get a neighbor who'd hurt them, I — I'll fence them in," Lesley vowed rashly. She was all too aware that Bella was likely to be right.

"Lesley girl," began Father. Then he stopped. Maybe he remembered his arrest in Sunflower and all the times before when he had brought shame on them. "All right, angel. If we can buy that funny little town, we will."

He started to rise, but Lesley pressed him back. "Mr. Benedict's freshening up and eating right now, but he's invited us to have dessert with him — and he has *iced* tea."

"I should hope. The train dropped off a three-hundred-pound block of ice this evening, all wrapped in tarps and packing. If it hadn't been sealed up so snug, I'd have chipped off a piece."

"Daddy!"

"Just my tip for trundlin' it over to Henri." Father's chuckle was unrepentant. "Bella, if I can figger out a way to keep it from melting, I'll bring you some ice to cool off that Parker's Ginger Tonic you say you take right before you go to bed."

"Champion stuff!" she praised. "Takes the ache out of my shoulders and arms. I just fall into sleep like sinkin' into a featherbed. It sure beats Lydia Pinkham's compound all hollow."

"No wonder." Lesley's father sounded wistful. "The tonic's got forty-two percent alcohol compared to Pinkham's eighteen percent, which is about the strength of wine. And the tonic eases your sore muscles because it's got lots of morphine."

Bella's tone cracked like a whip. "Are you callin' me a dope fiend, Ed Morland? I'll have you know I'm a dues-payin' member of the WCTU! And my tonic is recommended for mothers nursin' babies. Helps them both rest."

"Morphine'll do that," said Father. At Bella's outraged gasp, he added hastily, "Lord, Bella! After driving a team all day, you sure are entitled to something to help you relax."

"I'm glad you think so." Her tone started off frosty but then turned a bit embarrassed. "Don't worry about the ice, Ed. Henri brought me a pitcher of it."

"He would!" yelped Father. "Now, Bella, you got to be careful around Frenchies. They've got a terrible reputation as lady-killers!"

"Thanks for warning me," said Bella, too sweetly.

"I'll meet you at Benedict's car in half

an hour," Lesley promised, and left her father to smooth over the result of his chiding and his intimate familiarity with every extract or nostrum that boasted alcohol.

The Morlands had had an icebox in Sunflower, and a block was delivered every other day, so they had often had iced tea or lemonade. That seemed long ago, though, and the summer at Bountiful had been so unrelenting that the tea Matthew brought on a silver tray was the most refreshing drink Lesley could remember, crushed ice glittering in the crystal glasses with slices of lemon on the rims. Matthew replenished the glasses from a silver pitcher as soon as they were half-empty, and though Lesley disliked the idea of servants, she found it remarkably pleasant to be waited on rather than herself jumping up to see to others' needs.

One thing Benedict's wealth could not do was cool his luxurious abode. It was nearly as hot as the Morlands' boxcar, so a table, spread with a damask cloth, had been set on striped straw matting spread on obviously leveled earth by the siding. Improbable roses, yellow, blush pink, and deepest red, swayed in the slight breeze that radiated their fragrance.

Such gracious entertaining called for the kind of gown that Lesley had never owned, something exquisite and frothy, daringly off the shoulder like the evening dresses sometimes worn by the Gibson Girl in *Life.* Her rose and white lawn, in spite of the lace, didn't do justice to the occasion. *You're here on business,* she reminded herself sternly. *Anyway, once Adam Benedict goes off in his private car with his silver, crystal, roses, and ice, there'll be no place to wear such a gown.*

Henri's dessert was delicate lemon ice in footed crystal bowls served with crisp wafer spirals filled with bittersweet chocolate. The elegance of presentation and the sophisticated contrast of flavors and textures were so different from the dried peach pie and coffee Lesley had served their host the night before that she lost some of her appetite for the tempting food. Still, she could not resist enjoying the tea and letting ice melt in her mouth as Benedict spoke of his day's excursion.

"The men all seem to know their work.

Blake, the contractor, knows I won't stand for incompetence. I want this road finished before winter." He had quickly eaten three bowls of lemon ice and devoured the dainty wafers in a bite, not pausing to taste them. Eating was for him a nervous habit, Lesley decided, like chewing gum.

"I'm going to build a brick factory," he planned. "There won't be enough rocks blasted out along the way for bridges and culverts, and I intend to encourage merchants to erect brick buildings. That gives a town a permanent, prosperous look. The bank will be a frame structure at first, but I'll replace it with brick as soon as possible."

When the last wafer was gone, Matthew cleared the table and brought bowls of mixed nuts and chocolate bonbons and a silver box of cigars. "May we?" Benedict asked Lesley.

Father looked so longingly at the indulgence to which he rarely treated himself that Lesley nodded. Tobacco smoke made her a trifle nauseated, but they were outside and the breeze should carry the fumes the other direction. Father, thank goodness, didn't chew tobacco or use snuff, so she tolerated his occasional savoring of a Havana.

Matthew lit the cigars. Sharing a male ritual, the two relished drawing on the cigars and then blew puffs of smoke that vanished on the night wind. Lesley was glad her father was enjoying the evening, but she feared the disappointment and hurt he'd feel if Benedict dropped this cordiality as abruptly as he'd begun it. She'd seen how he had behaved with Jim Kelly. That same ruthlessness, directed at her father in his vulnerable position, might well destroy him.

"Mr. Benedict," she said at last, "do you own the land south of the tracks?"

"Clear to the Oklahoma border. Twenty sections running east and west of Bountiful, and about the same on the north except for a few farms that've hung on and a few town lots with adjacent lands that someone bought before I got around to it."

Jim Kelly's land was an island in the midst of Benedict's over twenty-five thousand acres. Chill fingered Lesley's spine. She hoped Bella could prevent clashes between the men till the time, probably short, that Benedict moved on to a new challenge.

Lesley tried to sound confident and businesslike. "My father and I would like to buy about twenty acres of land south of the depot. Can your bank lend us the money or arrange a mortgage or whatever is customary?"

"You could hold the payments out of my salary every month till the land's paid for," Ed put in.

Benedict studied them both, then fixed his gaze on Lesley. "My dear Miss Morland, unless I'm mistaken, you wish to buy a prairie dog town."

Good grief! Why did he have to know that? Before she could think of some useful equivocation, he said, "I do apologize for your present living quarters. I have an architect designing a model depot for Bountiful that will be built at all future stations on my lines. Because most of these stations don't warrant having a separate night operator, accommodations must adjoin the depot so the agent can hear incoming messages on the telegraph. The dwelling space, however, will be roomy and comfortable."

"That sounds wonderful, sir," Ed Morland said, beaming at Lesley. He had taken living in the boxcar much harder than she had, as if it were evidence of an abysmal failure on his part to provide for her.

"So," Benedict resumed, "if you were thinking it necessary to procure land and build a house, I assure you that before bitter weather comes, you'll have a most adequate home."

"It's good of you to consider the station agents and their families," Lesley told him. "But we still wish to buy the property."

The arched eyebrows rose. "You want to speculate in selling town lots? Let me advise you that ridding the land of those mounds and burrows will take considerable time and effort. Even if you have it plowed up —"

"That's what I don't want to happen!" Lesley burst out.

The swift uptilt of his lips beneath the silvery mustache confirmed the flicker of satisfaction in his eyes. She'd fallen into a trap. Would he consider the village a detriment to his schemes and refuse to sell?

"Are you that softhearted, Miss Morland? You'd incur a considerable debt to preserve the abodes of pesky barking rodents, owls, and rattlers?"

"They were here first."

He astonished her by voicing her thoughts. "And they're diverting, the way they greet each other when they meet in the morning, bustle around mowing their lawns, stand on their little volcano craters like sentries, and dive into their holes when the menace gets too close."

"You've watched them!" Lesley exclaimed. He hadn't observed all that in one hurried glance.

"Many times. As an engineer, I admire their building skills. They dike around their entrances to keep their burrows from flooding and repair them immediately after a rain. The burrow drops straight, sometimes more than ten feet, before it levels out, but there's a listening niche about three feet below the entrance. No educated prairie dog rushes out without making sure no coyote or hawk is waiting for it."

"I hope you didn't excavate a burrow to learn all this!"

"I dug out a number of abandoned ones. Scientific curiosity. After the tunnel turns, there's a sleeping chamber lined with grass and usually smaller side rooms. One or more of these may be used as privies, though the dogs aren't always too fastidious. The burrows I investigated all had an escape tunnel dug close to the surface. In case the burrow does flood, Mr. Dog and his family can stay there high and dry, but I expect the main use is as an easy place to claw through and give the slip to hungry ferrets or badgers who're digging him out."

Stunned at the tycoon's knowledge, Lesley absorbed the fascinating details. "Since you know all this about them," she said after a moment, "how could you think of destroying their town?"

"I find them interesting, Miss Morland, and admire their building competence, but I am not sentimental."

"Business is business?"

"Indeed."

She blinked back tears of frustration. If he'd meant to deny her, why had he made the prairie dogs all the more appealing? She rose to her feet. "Please tell Henri the ice and wafers were delectable. Thank you for your time, sir, if not for your decision."

"Decision?" He got lazily to his feet. "I've made no decision."

Hope rushed back. "You mean —"

"I'll ponder it. Meanwhile, Miss Morland, perhaps you'd like a ride in the Oldsmobile. Have you ever seen a railroad being built?"

"No. The railroad was always there before we were."

"Then you might find it illuminating to see how it's done. Mr. Morland, could you spare your daughter for a morning?"

"She needs an outing. I've laid rails myself, so that's nothing new to me."

"But a motorcar is. If Miss Morland will go in the morning, I'll return her at noon, and if you like, you could drive with me in the afternoon."

"That would be capital, sir!" Father's eyes shone. "You can handle the station, can't you, Les?"

As if she hadn't done that more often than not these past eight years . . . She stifled the thought. Father was sober now, thank goodness, and would scarcely have a chance to be morose with Bella for a neighbor.

"Of course I'll tend the depot," she promised. "You'll probably be home before the evening train, and not much else is likely to happen."

She forbore, because of her father's enthusiasm about the ride, to point out that she had never consented to go. By bringing her father into it, Benedict had neatly maneuvered her into a position that made her feel compelled to accept his offer. Still, it was flattering to have an intriguing and powerful man devise schemes to have her company. As for riding in the motorcar, she wanted to experience what it was like but was considerably nervous about it. Which, come to think of it, was how she felt about spending hours with Benedict even though his mechanic would be along.

"Is it convenient for you to leave at seven, Miss Morland? I'd like to spare you as much of the heat of the day as possible."

"Seven will be fine."

She didn't try to keep the acid note from her voice. He only smiled. "You need the widest-brimmed hat you have and a scarf to tie it on. I have extra goggles." He scowled suddenly. "I don't suppose you have a duster? You'll need something to protect your clothes."

"I certainly can't wear my winter coat, and Father's slicker would be just as miserable. Perhaps —"

"I have a linen duster."

"It'll be much too large."

"Matthew is excellent at alterations. He'll have it ready in the morning."

"But that would ruin it! And it's late! There won't be time —"

"You can do it, can't you, Matthew?"

The dapper man of all capabilities gave her a swift, detached appraisal. "I can, sir, but you'll look humorous if you ever try to get into it again. Without my sewing machine, about all I can undertake tonight is hemming up the sleeves and bottom. It'll fit the lady like a tent."

"So much the better. That'll give the air room to circulate." Pleased at finding a way out of the dilemma — did he ever fail? — Benedict shook Father's hand and bowed over Lesley's. "At seven, then, Miss Morland. Pleasant dreams."

As they made their way by Father's lantern, Lesley grumbled, "I doubt if I'll sleep at all, worrying about getting into that — that contraption!" An old-fashioned word, but that was how she felt when she contemplated jouncing across the plains in the scary invention.

"Aw, Les! It'll be fun." Her father

added wistfully, "I wish Bella could come along."

"I'll bet *she* doesn't. She likes her mules. The railroad started putting teamsters out of business, and now, providing they're not just a fad, motor-cars will finish the job — and probably cut into railroad profits, too."

"Ouch!" teased Father, gently tweaking her ear. "You're sure in a grouchy mood for a young woman who's just been served lemon ice, quarts of iced tea, and been offered a ride in a rich man's Oldsmobile."

"That's why I'm grouchy. Neither of you waited for me to say whether I wanted to go or not. You just jumped in and arranged everything so I couldn't back out without a big fuss."

He stopped and stared at her. "Why, Les girl, I never dreamed you wouldn't like a ride. If you don't fancy it, I'll go back right now and beg off — for both of us," he added with obvious regret.

"No, dear, I'll go." He still looked worried. She giggled and kissed his cheek. "It's just that no woman likes to be taken for granted."

"Seems to me he's not doin' that when he carves up his duster so you can go,"

Ed said dryly. "Must be he's really taken a shine to you, Les."

"I think it's more his scientific curiosity."

"He'd better not get too curious, even if he is the boss."

"Matthew will be right there. Anyway, Daddy, I've been fending off drummers and all sizes and shapes of lechers since I stopped wearing pigtails."

He shook his head. "Honey, it makes me sick to look back and see that I didn't take good care of you. If your mother knew —"

"Maybe she does." With an ache in her throat, Lesley remembered using her mother's cookbook and pretending the pretty woman in the wedding portrait was there, smiling and encouraging. "Maybe she took care of us both as much as she could. Anyway, things are all right now. We're going to have a good life here in Bountiful."

"We sure will. Especially if — Do you think Bella —"

Lesley wasn't ready for that yet. She gave her father a hug and kiss. "I like Bella more than any woman I ever met, but right now it's time we went to bed!"

5

Lesley's only scarf was a winter one of heavy wool, but she remembered some short net curtains in the bottom of a trunk. There was no time to heat an iron on the stove and press out the fold-lines, but she swathed it over her summer hat, a straw sailor with a wide blue ribbon, tied it under her chin in a rather fat bow, and thought it passable. Her navy polka dot percale skirt with white pique trim looked neat and fresh with her best white lawn shirtwaist under which she wore her corset waist. As long as Benedict was in the vicinity, she would wear the side steels.

She didn't expect Benedict to come to her door with the Oldsmobile. Her knowledge of gasoline engines was sketchy, but didn't they have to warm up something in the fashion that boilers in a steam engine had to build up a certain amount of pressure before they could power anything? Once the automobile was cranked into life, Benedict would surely want to keep going for a while before stopping.

Opening the door, she almost collided with Matthew. He stepped back quickly. "Mr. Benedict sent me to escort you, ma'am." His blue eyes danced. "May I say you're looking so nice that it's a shame to cover you up with this?" He held up the duster, a sage green lined with paler satin. "I hope you'll find it satisfactory. Perhaps a belt —"

It was already hot. On top of wearing the lined duster for hours, the prospect of adding one more constriction around her body was unbearable. "It will do very well, thank you, Mr. Reid. It was kind of you to do the alterations on such short notice."

"It's my job to carry out Mr. Benedict's wishes, ma'am. He pays me hand-somely, though I must say I have a lot more duties when we're traveling than when we're at home, where, of course, there's a complete staff."

Of course. He proffered his arm. Lesley took it because she was wearing her patent leather sandals and didn't want to slip on the uneven footing and scratch them. Benedict, emerging from his abode, came to meet her. The silk duster was lustrous gray, as was his matching cap.

"A shame to hide such an attractive ensemble." His admiring gaze changed to one of dismay. "Is that your broadest-brimmed hat, Miss Morland?"

It was her only hat except for a winter hood. "I'm afraid it is."

"I can't have you burned with sun and wind. Matthew, do you think my Panama —"

"Sir," said Matthew with a poker face but glint in his eyes, "your cousin traveled with you from Denver to Pueblo. Perhaps you've forgotten, but you took her shopping in Denver."

"Why, yes." Benedict explained to Lesley, "She's a favorite cousin and it was her birthday. She picked out several hats."

"Yes, sir. And when she left us at Pueblo, she hadn't room for her old one, so she very kindly told me I could give it to someone. It has, as I recall, quite a wide brim."

"I do believe you're right. You always have a solution, Matthew. Fetch the hat."

Lesley caught her breath at the sight of the exquisite creation, which was in

120

the fashionable Gainsborough style, one side tilted dashingly high with swaths of tucked pale green chiffon, and a cascade of crushed velvet yellow roses and buds surrounded by green foliage.

"Oh, I can't tie a scarf over that! It would press down the flowers and leaves."

"So much the better." Benedict gave the hat a disparaging look and handed her a pair of goggles. "Put these on first, Miss Morland. Then we'll fasten the hat down to shade your face."

He made no comment on the net curtain as she untied it. "Here, Matthew," he said, handing the mechanic the straw sailor. "Be so good as to return this to Miss Morland's house. Now, dear lady, if you will allow me to be your mirror —"

Head to one side as if studying the effect, he set the confection on her head, moved it several times before he nodded. "Now to anchor it." He arranged the material over the hat, then brought it down, deft fingers brushing her ears and the sides of her face, then her throat, as he tied a bow beneath her chin. Did his hands linger a second longer than necessary?

She glanced up, involuntarily took a step back from the flicker of green flame in his eyes. It was like confronting a handsome, powerful cougar. Wishing for Matthew's speedy return, she defended herself, from Benedict but more from the bewildering sensations he caused in her, at once frightening and pleasurable.

"I don't know how your cousin could bear to part with this hat."

"Easily. I assure you. It has no egret plumes, and those, she informed me, are all the rage."

"Doesn't she know egrets and ostriches are slaughtered for their feathers?" Lesley had read some horrifying accounts put out by the Audubon Society, a group founded to battle this atrocious fad.

He grimaced. "I told her that the plumes looked better on the egret than they did on her, but I had promised to buy whatever she wanted." His tone hardened. "I won't make that mistake again."

"Even if she's your favorite cousin?"

He studied Lesley a moment. "I dislike deception unless it's required. Yvonne

D'Aubignon is no more my cousin than she is French. My obligations to her, from hats to more mundane matters, are thoroughly discharged, and she is by now, with my blessing, in San Francisco, where she will doubtless befuddle some millionaire and wind up in a mansion on Nob Hill. Now then, let's drape you in my duster."

The sleeves and bottom were the proper length, but the shoulders came halfway to her elbows, and it was indeed like wearing a tent since the garment, flaring from the knee, was styled to fit loosely on Benedict's large frame. The collar that would button snugly under his chin exposed her stand-up collar and top of her shirtwaist.

Matthew arrived, assessed the problem, and suggested, "Turn up the collar, sir, and a few safety pins should make it protect the lady's clothes. Though the pins won't do the coat any good —"

"A duster that reaches little below my knees and elbows is no use to me anyway, Matthew. By all means, try the pins. You place them, with Miss Morland's permission. You're better at such things than I am."

After a moment, Matthew emerged

with several good-sized pins. It took three to expertly fasten the collar. "There you are, ma'am." The mischief in his eyes belied his decorous tone. "May I say the hat becomes you much more than it did Mr. Benedict's cousin?"

"We'll dispense with further mention of Miss D'Aubignon," his employer said. "Bear up, Miss Morland! The automobile will move fast enough to make all this bundling less oppressive."

Matthew lowered a metal step that fitted beneath the carriage. The fenders were metal half circles secured well above the tires. Benedict started to help Lesley up, but she stopped with one foot on the step. "There's no room for Mr. Reid!"

"Lord love you, ma'am," said Matthew heartily, "after I crank the engine, I'll just hop on behind the seat."

Lesley eyed the smooth boxlike rear anxiously. "Won't you bounce off?"

"If the ride gets jouncy, I can hold on to the bars that hold the back of the seat in place," Matthew assured her.

Benedict almost lifted her onto the tufted leather seat and went around to climb in on the other side. He moved with surprising grace for such a heavy-set man, settling himself behind the tiller, a long rod with a padded handle. Matthew cranked vigorously, sweat dripping from his florid brow. The instant the motor rumbled, Benedict pressed his foot on a pedal on the floor beneath the curved dashboard. Lesley tensed and gripped the edge of the seat, stomach churning at the racket throbbing beneath her.

Was it going to explode? Her terror subsided at Benedict's calm air. Matthew clambered up behind, grabbed hold of the seat bars, and gasped, "Ready, sir!"

They were off, bumping with each revolution of the wheels. Uncanny for a vehicle to move without horses or a steam engine! Because of train schedules and the need to constantly record times, Lesley was attuned to judging them. In less than ten minutes, as she was breathing easier and rather beginning to enjoy the rush of wind that cooled her face and made the duster less sweltering, they came in sight of a tent village situated a distance from the long, level-topped mound that began at the present tracks and formed the bed where rails would be laid.

Five wagons drawn by teams of horses traveled back and forth between the roadbed and a big machine pulled by a steam engine that belched spiraling clouds of vapor. From a train window, Lesley had seen a few such engines threshing wheat, and of course, trains were powered by steam, but she had never seen an invention like the one towed by the engine. A man on a platform behind a huge plowshare used levers to lower it to dig a furrow and toss the earth onto a big belt. Another lever raised the belt to dump the load into a wagon driven along the side opposite to where the plow operated.

"That's the grader." Benedict spoke in her ear so his voice would carry above the racket of machinery and teamsters exhorting their beasts. "The power for the conveyor belt is supplied by gears from the wheels. That's my contractor running the steam engine and his son-in-law on the grader. Right now the water wagon for the engine fills up at the Bountiful tank, and the next outfit gets water from an existing cattle tank and windmill, but we'll drill wells in between present ones so the water wagons can keep the boilers going. If engines have to shut down for lack of water, the whole crew is idled."

Lesley watched the man who drove the coal wagon breaking coal to egg size and feeding it into the firebox. "I suppose the coal comes in by train."

Benedict nodded. "So will the ties and rails and supplies, though freighters like our estimable Mrs. Ballard will have to haul them to the work crews until roadbed is made to start laying rails. As the rails go down, a train can travel right behind the crew with everything they need."

Lesley thought of the other grading crews working deep into the Texas Panhandle, of the rail layers who'd follow. "It's a tremendous undertaking."

"Oh, compared to building the first transcontinental railroad, this is trifling. Jay Gould said he could walk from Omaha to California on the bodies of the men who died building the line." At her horrified look, Benedict laughed. "Considering that about three hundred thousand workers built the road, Central Pacific building from the West Coast, Union Pacific from Nebraska, plenty of them survived."

Lesley thought back to her U.S. history books. "It was started during the Civil War, wasn't it, but precious little got done till afterwards?"

"That's right. They got moving in 1866, and the Golden Spike — and a silver one, too — were driven in May of 1869 at Promontory Point in Utah Territory. The telegraph sent the news in both directions."

"The whole country celebrated." Lesley tried to imagine how the feat of little over forty years ago must have excited people. "Coast to coast in eight or ten days. To anyone who'd traveled west by stagecoach, it must have seemed like magic."

"Yes, and there was a good deal of rhetoric about the railroad binding the nation together and healing the wounds of the Civil War." Benedict added sardonically, "My father took me to California when I was six years old. We still had to take a ferry across the Missouri River. The bridge was finally built the next year, 1872, between Council Bluffs, Iowa, and Omaha."

Lesley did a little arithmetic. He was thirty-five. Young to have acquired his power and wealth. "What kind of ties will your railroad have?" she asked. "Cottonwoods are about the only trees out here, and they only grow along creeks and rivers. I remember reading that the Union Pacific tried treating cottonwood ties with zinc chloride, but they still wouldn't stand up to heavy use."

"After the UP used up most of the big oaks and walnuts of the Missouri Valley, the builders brought in red cedar ties. I'll use oak from Missouri."

All the while he talked with Lesley, Benedict kept a watchful eye on the grader, steam engine, wagons, and the men and scrapers leveling the roadbed. With a nod of satisfaction, he said to his mechanic, "Crank her up again, Matthew. We've got time to see how the well drillers are doing before we start back. The place they're trying is only about twenty miles from here."

A day's journey by carriage or wagon unless you exhausted your horses. It was hard to believe that this sleighlike vehicle perched on high wheels could travel more than double that distance in a morning.

"Sir," protested Matthew, "I understand that a teamster got stuck in sand on the way there yesterday. He had to almost completely unload his wagon before the team could pull it out."

"Then he was doubtless trying to haul more than was advisable."

"Yes, sir." Matthew slipped off the back of the automobile and turned the crank.

Hooves and wagon wheels roughly marked a track through short buffalo grass, paralleling the survey stakes that faded into the distance till they were indistinguishable from the occasional yucca or soapweed spire. Unlike the land north of the railroad, this region had obviously remained grazing country. A group of pronghorn antelope skimmed along a slope and vanished like a dream.

"Did you see buffalo when you went west with your father?" she asked.

"Herds that spread out of sight. Passengers shot them from the train. They were left along the way to rot."

And the Indians saw, Comanche, Cheyenne, Arapaho, Kiowa, and others, all the peoples who lived from the buffalo, and a few years later they saw the hide hunters come and slaughter the beasts by the hundreds of thousands.

So there was that futile attack on Adobe Walls, and a good many scalps, like Bella's, decorated lances and shields.

Lesley sighed. She was glad that she wasn't going to get scalped today, but all the same —

"Penny for your thoughts," Benedict said in her ear.

"I was just thinking that when the buffalo went, so did the way the Indians lived. For those who remember roaming all over the plains, it must be awful to live on reservations."

"Some of them raise cattle," Benedict said.

"That can't be anything like the great buffalo hunts they used to have."

"Everything changes. They don't have to stay on reservations. They can get educations and succeed like anyone else."

"Indian men your age can remember the old times, the buffalo, the way it was. How could they not regret them?"

"They can regret and still get on with a new kind of life."

"But —"

"My dear Miss Morland, the glamorous phenomenon of the Plains Indian on horseback existed for only a few centuries. Before Spaniards brought horses to the Southwest, Indians used dogs to haul their few belongings and killed buffalo by running herds over cliffs. If you think that wasn't wasteful! Winter starvation was frequent. It was a rough, harsh life, and usually short —"

"Where were your ancestors two hundred years ago? How did they live?"

He cast her a glance of amused respect. "Family tradition doesn't go back that far, and all I know about my mother is that she was a Pennsylvania farmer's daughter. I do know my father's father was a weaver — most likely it was a family trade, passed on from father to son. He was a leader in the Luddite riots of 1812, wrecking the machinery that was putting hand weavers out of work. When he got out of jail, he signed on as a sailor, jumped ship in Boston Harbor, and eventually married a Kentucky widow who ran a tavern. I guess my father came naturally by his fondness for whiskey."

"So if you lost everything you have, would it comfort you to ask if you'd rather be a hand weaver thrown out of work because of a machine?"

"My grandfather started over. So would I. Wear sackcloth if you will for the Indians, Miss Morland, but they happily killed each other and forced weaker bands off desirable territory long before white men set that example."

"It still isn't right."

"It's how things are."

Maybe so, but she didn't have to like it. She intended to try, when she had a chance, to thwart progress of the kind that would destroy the prairie dog town and sacrifice everything to what was viewed as civilization.

Brooding, she was literally jerked back to reality by the abrupt halt of the Oldsmobile as the front wheels buried themselves almost to the axles. Benedict tried to steer the vehicle to the side, but it whined in protest and the engine died.

"I've got a shovel, sir." Matthew opened a compartment of the boxlike rear and brought out a small spade. "I'll have us out in a jiffy."

It took longer than that. They were in a shallow, wide, dry streambed. As soon as Matthew tossed out a shovelful of the pulverized sand, more sifted around

133

the tires, but at last he had dug it from around the tires and laboriously made tracks for the tires to follow out of the loose sand. His shirt was soaked, his florid complexion was alarmingly red, and he huffed for breath as he stowed the shovel.

"There we are, sir. Now we'll crank it up and be on our way —"

"Mr. Reid," interrupted Lesley, "is there any water?"

"Henri fixed a jug of iced tea, ma'am."

"Then please oblige me by drinking some — slowly." She got out her handkerchief and handed it to him. "As long as there's no sugar in the tea, it would cool you to wet this and wipe your face."

Matthew looked helplessly at his employer. "Do it," Benedict ordered. "Pour some tea for us as well, Matthew. While we're stopped and before the ice melts, we might as well enjoy it." He took Lesley's handkerchief from his mechanic's hand and replaced it with one of his own. "Use this for your ablutions."

The tea was refreshing, but Lesley was too uneasy to enjoy it to the fullest. Without the breeze forced by the automobile's speed, it was getting hotter every minute inside the lined duster that encased her from chin to toe. She was grateful for the shading brim of the hat.

Matthew stowed the glasses and canvas-wrapped tea jar in the rear compartment. His appearance was a little less alarming. Didn't it bother Adam Benedict to watch another man overexert himself because of his stubbornness? Most likely he believed that paying someone a good wage put him entirely at his disposal.

What was it Jim Kelly had said to him? *You hired my wagons, not my backbone.* Benedict expected to hire that, too. What was going to happen when he found out Bella's partner was Jim?

The engine sputtered fitfully as Matthew cranked, but it refused to start. "Give it up," Benedict growled when his man was panting heavily and repeated efforts had failed. "Maybe the engine overheated. We *do* have the repair kit?"

"You bet we do, sir." Matthew gratefully leaned his arms on the rear of the automobile. "Besides all the stuff for tires and lots of tools, we've got an extra fan belt, radiator hose and clips, spark plugs, gaskets." He attempted a small joke. "We've even got a towing line."

Benedict scowled. "If this thing has to be towed, I may ship it back to Ransom Olds and tell him to design a better machine! Besides, who's going to tow us? It must be ten miles back to the camp."

"I can walk it, sir." Matthew forbore to point out that Mr. Olds could scarcely have thought anyone would drive his invention off any sort of road and through deep sand. The natty little man tried to sound confident, but he looked thoroughly exhausted. "While a team comes for you, I'll send someone to tell Mr. Morland that you're all right, ma'am, just a trifle inconvenienced."

"Inconvenienced! Stranded here in the middle of nowhere! I should have bought that Daimler."

"I think we should all stay where we are," said Lesley. "Or better yet, get on the shady side of that sandhill plum thicket. If we're not back by early afternoon, Daddy will take a handcar to the camp and they'll send someone after us. We have plenty of tea and —"

"And there's two canvas bags of

water," said Matthew. "And tins of sardines and smoked oysters and fruit."

"It looks like there are still plums on the bushes," said Lesley, unbuttoning the duster. "We can have a picnic."

"Picnic!" roared Benedict, glaring at them both.

"Why not?" asked Lesley. "I promise you one thing. If Mr. Reid starts back, I'm going with him."

"You are *not* trudging ten miles through this wasteland."

"Then neither is he."

"I suppose you think I should tramp it myself?"

"Yes, I do, since you ignored Mr. Reid's warning." Lesley's rising temper edged her words. For a moment she glowered back at her host.

He amazed her then by exploding into laughter. "Very well. Let's gather plums, by all means, and if the wretched machine won't start after that, Matthew and I will have a look at the innards. If it's nothing we can fix, we'll do as you suggest, Miss Morland, settle in the best shade we can find and lunch al fresco. Here, let me help you off with that duster."

Divested of the voluminous coats, they started for the plum bushes, Matthew following with a pail unearthed from the trove of supplies.

6

The tallest clumps of the thicket were six feet high, level with Benedict's head. Birds and wild creatures had eaten most of the fruit, but here and there towards the top a small red-orange plum gleamed among the long yellowish green leaves.

Benedict plucked the highest, plumpest one and offered it to Lesley. The fruit was warm, but the juicy tanginess was refreshing. "Wild fruit always tastes better to me than tame," Benedict said, tasting one himself. "I used to wander through the woods with a certain pretty girl and find wild strawberries for her, red and sweet as her lips."

It was hard to imagine this man as young and vulnerable. "She married the banker's son." Benedict gave a short laugh of self-mockery. "I decided then and there that I'd have a bank one day."

"How did you —" Lesley began, and checked herself. "I'm sorry. That's none of my business."

"Ah, but I want you to know I worked my way through college, Miss Morland." His teeth flashed and the hint of a dimple showed in his broad chin. "I worked as a construction engineer for the Rock Island line, invested most of my wages, and eventually became a partner in a small railroad company that prospered. It's difficult to acquire beginning capital, but after that, with luck — I had that — perseverance — I have that — and drive, money almost seems to multiply itself."

They picked in silence for a few minutes. Turning suddenly, he popped a fruit into her surprised mouth. The jade depths of his dark eyes seemed to draw her into them. "It's been a long time, too long, since I gathered fruit for a pretty lady."

Wrenching her gaze from his, Lesley spoke against the pulse beating fast in her throat. "Isn't it time to see if the crank works?"

"I suppose we may as well if I can't beguile you with wild plums."

The crank evoked no response, though Matthew, dripping with sweat, kept trying. "Leave it, Matthew," Benedict said. "Let's have our picnic. Then we'll get se-

rious about repairing this fickle convey-
ance."

No one lingered over the impromptu
meal. While Lesley put away the food
and put utensils and empty cans into
a sack, the men tilted the seat back and
peered at the engine.

"The fan belt's fine." Matthew
scratched his ear. "Radiator has plenty
of water. Guess we could try a new
spark plug."

After their ministrations, the Oldsmobile still wouldn't crank. "I'd best walk
back to the work gang, sir," Matthew
said. His face was fiery red and he
sounded breathless.

"Mr. Reid, I refuse to let you exert
yourself like that in this heat." Lesley
turned to Benedict. "As I said, my father
will certainly send someone to look for
us when we're not back by early afternoon."

"So you prefer that we just sit here
and await rescue?"

"Yes, indeed."

"Please, ma'am," began Matthew, wiping his forehead. "It's no problem —"

"It is for me," Lesley said, and cast
Benedict a defiant look. "If you go, so
do I."

141

"We'll all wait then," conceded Benedict grudgingly. He raised a silencing hand. "Listen! Something's coming."

Matthew's face was wreathed in a grin. "Something with wheels, sir! We're in luck."

Lesley gazed south toward the rumble. Sunlight glinted off metal. She could make out moving animals in front of what must be a wagon.

"Won't be here for another ten minutes," Benedict said grumpily. "We'd better wait in such shade as there is." He spread the lap robe for Lesley where she did get some shelter from the thicket, but he and Matthew stood with their eyes fixed on the slowly approaching vehicle.

Inordinately galling, it must be to Benedict to have his automobile succored by mules or horses, especially with Lesley watching, but she thought it salutary for him to have a defeat now and then.

He sucked in his breath before he released it explosively. "It's that —" He swallowed the word. "It's Kelly!"

Jim Kelly? As if a bolt of lightning coursed through her, Lesley sprang up and shielded her eyes, only then realizing how much she had longed to see him again, how much she needed to know whether she was mistaking her feeling for him because of her over-wrought state at the time he came out of nowhere to befriend her. Benedict had not been far behind, of course, but she could never forget how, in the darkest and most humiliating time of her life, Jim Kelly had smiled breezily and taken her arm, walking her to the jail as if they were honored guests approaching a celebration.

Now here he was! At his command, six horses and a green and yellow Studebaker wagon stopped with a creaking of wood and harness. Dusty tarpaulins were lashed over the load. Kelly took off a hat that was bleached and weathered to the color of sand, inclining his dark head to Lesley before recognition brought straight black brows rushing together.

Her heart pounded. She stepped forward to greet him, but an impassive mask closed over the shock on his face. "Looks like you folks are having a little trouble."

"Kelly, do me the courtesy of not crowing." Benedict brought out his wallet.

"I'll pay you handsomely to tow my automobile back to the railroad."

"You won't," said Kelly.

Benedict's hands clenched. "You won't tow me?"

"Sure I will."

"Then I'll pay. I don't want favors from you, Kelly."

"I've never taken money for helping someone out of a fix and I'm not starting now." Kelly pulled his hat down against the rising wind. "Miss Morland, I'm headed for Bountiful. I reckon you'd better ride with me. Shall I send someone back for you, Benedict?"

"You stubborn —" Benedict gritted. "I won't be obligated to you!"

"That's up to you. Miss Morland?"

"Tow the automobile," Benedict growled. "I'm responsible for the lady. I'm not letting her out of my sight."

Matthew's relief was evident. "Splendid!" he said heartily. "I'll just stow away the tools and get the towing cable." He cast an admiring glance at the bay horses, sweaty but in excellent condition. "Can your horses pull their load and the Oldsmobile, sir?"

"They can pull six thousand pounds. My load's less than three thousand."

Kelly appraised the automobile. "That little cricket can't weigh a thousand pounds. My team won't even notice it."

"It can travel more miles in an hour than you can all day," said Benedict.

"Sure," Jim Kelly said, and grinned.

Benedict crimsoned and hurried to help Matthew attach the cable to the chassis of the auto and the running gear of the wagon.

"Miss Morland will ride up here with me." Kelly's tone allowed no argument. He leaned over to extend his hand to her. Matthew gave her a discreet assist by steadying her under the elbow as she clambered up, grateful that at least she wasn't smothered and encumbered by the duster. As if her flesh burned him, Kelly let go of her the moment she was securely seated, and tossed over his shoulder, "I'd suggest you men hunker down in the softest spots you can find on the wagon."

"I prefer to ride in my automobile," said Benedict.

"Suit yourself, but it's going to get awful dusty."

"Sir!" pleaded Matthew. Climbing into the wagon bed, he patted and shifted cargo till he defined a kind of seat.

"Here, sir, this will do nicely."

Benedict allowed himself to be coaxed into the wagon. Jim Kelly called to his team. Their muscles ridged with the effort of getting stationary weight into motion again. There was a sucking sound as the back wheels of the Oldsmobile plunged through loose sand. Then it was on solid ground again and moved more easily.

"It's fortunate you came along," Lesley said above the clop of hooves and assorted squeaks and groans of both vehicles. She liked the skilled assurance with which he handled the lines. "Bella Ballard's already got your business going." Lesley had no intention of being the one to tell either Kelly or Benedict that they once again had a contract with each other. Since she hadn't seen Bella that day, she assumed the freighter was hauling supplies to the next construction camp and that Kelly, coming from the east, had struck the tracks along the survey line above that location.

A smile softened the grim set of Kelly's angular face. "Bella's wonderful. Mighty good teamster, too."

Silence grew heavy between them,

seemed to put down roots. Why, Lesley wondered, did she feel guilty at his finding her with Benedict? She wanted to explain that her father's chance to delight in the Oldsmobile depended on her accepting a ride, but after all, why should she make excuses? Good grief, she'd only met this man once in her life, couldn't have spent much more than five minutes in his company! Still, the silence was unendurable, and she didn't think their voices could carry to Benedict over all the racket.

"Bella says you and she have bought some lots and property around Bountiful."

"Yeah." Gray-blue eyes touched her briefly before fixing on the way ahead. "We were looking for a place to move our outfit. When we heard that Bountiful was coming back to life, it sounded like a good location."

Was it partly because you knew I'd be there? If so, to judge from his coolness, he had changed his mind. "I hope you got my letter and repayment of my father's fine," she said.

He nodded. "I didn't want it back, so I gave it to a widow with a bunch of kids."

"What you did with it is none of my concern," she said stiffly. "I just wanted to be sure you did get the money."

"You don't owe me a thing," he assured her.

How often she had dreamed of seeing him again, and now it was turning out like this! Vexed almost to tears, she tilted her chin high and stared intently at the not-very-intriguing landscape.

Neither of them spoke for so long that his voice made her start. "That's a mighty stylish hat. Bet you didn't find it in Bountiful, or over in Oklahoma Territory, either."

"My hat didn't have a wide enough brim for riding in the automobile." She was furious at herself for blushing. "Mr. Benedict loaned me this one."

"Loaned, my dear Miss Morland?" inquired Benedict in an astonished tone. Blast his keen ears! "I thought I made it clear that the hat was yours to keep."

"You did nothing of the kind!" She unknotted the net curtain-scarf with trembling fingers, yanked off the hat, and thrust it towards Benedict. "We're not going fast now. I don't need it."

"Yes, you do," cut in Jim Kelly. "You'll sunburn bad at this time of day in less than half an hour."

"I don't care!"

"You will when the blisters puff up and break. However you came by the hat, ma'am, you need it now. Put it on."

"Sensible advice," approved Benedict.

Glaring at them both, but suspecting that Kelly would tie it on her if she didn't, Lesley put the hat on and was still simmering when they passed the construction camp.

"I can get a team here to take me into Bountiful," yelled Benedict to Kelly.

"No need. I'm headed that way."

"You are? Why?"

"Bountiful's my new headquarters."

"What?"

"I think your ears are pretty good."

"Bountiful's my town."

"Not all of it."

Benedict digested that. After a moment, he demanded, "Are you by any infernal chance Bella Ballard's partner?"

"Sure am. Whatever business it is of yours."

"It's considerably my business!" Benedict sounded as if he were swallowing to get control of his voice. "That — that woman hoodwinked me into signing on your outfit to haul for my new railroad!"

"She did?" roared Kelly.

"She did!" roared Benedict.

Kelly burst out laughing. "Doggone Bella! This is nerve, even for her. She knew I quit you —"

"I fired you, Kelly!"

"No, I quit. And I can sure quit again!"

"Not unless I fire you. I signed a contract with your partner —"

"Then you can't fire me!"

The men exchanged mutual glowers before Kelly turned back to his driving. They reached the railroad tracks and rattled along toward Bountiful. Coming in from this direction, Lesley got a different view than she ever had before and was staggered at the desolation of the place. The water tank and windmill across from the depot was the highest structure. Beyond the derelict buildings, Bella's tent looked a lot whiter than it was. Hard to believe it would ever really be a town . . .

"Listen, Kelly." Benedict had somehow schooled himself to sound reasonable. "I need freighters. You're a good one. You need work. Let's forget what's past and start over."

Kelly thought awhile. "All right," he agreed reluctantly. "But before we scrub the slate clean, you owe me money for that last load of ties I hauled to your crew."

"You did that after I fired you."

"No. I did it after I quit — but it didn't make sense not to haul a load I already had lashed onto my wagon. Let's see: That was forty-five hundred pounds hauled twenty miles —"

"Matthew!" snapped Benedict. "Be so good as to clamber up and put these bills in Mr. Kelly's pocket. No need to quibble like a huckster, Kelly! This is *not* pay for a delivery I didn't engage you to make — it's pay for towing my vehicle."

"I won't take pay for doing a neighborly thing."

"And I won't pay for freighting I didn't ask for!"

Lesley covered her ears. "For heaven's sake, stop it! You sound like babies!"

"Stop and leave the Oldsmobile at my private car," Benedict ordered.

"I might if you said please."

Lesley wailed. "Oh, for the love of mud! Let me off, Mr. Kelly, or I'll jump!"

"You'll stay put," he growled, but he

did stop by the private car. "Those shoes you're wearing aren't made for walking along railroad tracks."

It only took a few minutes for Matthew and Benedict to unhook the vehicle from Kelly's wagon. "Thank you, Mr. Kelly," called Matthew.

"You're welcome, I'm sure," returned Kelly with a sarcastic glance at Benedict.

Lesley untied the beautiful hat and gave it to Matthew. "You'd better save this for Mr. Benedict's cousin."

Unruffled, Benedict told her, "We'll have a better ride next time." His tone lowered intimately. "Shall I drop by this evening to discuss your — business proposal?"

"You mean selling me the land with the prairie dog town? I thought you had to analyze everything and decide whether it was a good commercial decision."

He smiled. "I can analyze considerable in an afternoon."

"Good. When you're through analyzing, let me know."

Kelly spoke to the horses. As the wagon rumbled along to the depot, he glanced toward the mounds of the prairie dogs. "Have I got this right, Miss Morland? You want to buy that prairie dog village?"

She nodded, unwilling to tell him why. He'd probably think she was crazy.

"How come?" he pursued. "It's pretty useless."

"It's useful to the things that live there."

"That'd be rattlesnakes and burrowing owls as well as the dogs."

"So?"

"Most folks don't like rattlesnakes."

"I don't exactly like them, but they get away from people if they have the chance and they usually warn you before they strike."

"So you wouldn't plan on killing out the critters and leveling the mounds?"

Forced to the truth, she said, "That's why I want to buy the land. So it won't be built on." They were at the depot. She got down quickly before he could help her. She hesitated. After all, she and her father did owe this man a debt of gratitude — and after this day's rescue, she owed him a double one. "Won't you join us for supper, Mr. Kelly? About sundown? Bring Bella, too, if she comes back."

Eyes the color of autumn haze studied her. "Thanks," he said abruptly. "I'll be here."

He turned the horses across the tracks and drove toward Bella's tent. Lesley watched him, brooding. Why did he have to find her with Benedict? And even so, why did he behave as if she'd done something criminal? Matthew had been with them all the time, and a breakdown in searing August heat was scarcely romantic.

"Honey?" Her father stood in the door. "You okay? I was about to send someone from camp looking for you."

"I'm fine, Daddy," she assured him. "The automobile got stuck in a dry streambed and wouldn't start even after poor Matthew dug sand away from the wheels. Jim Kelly, the man who — who — helped us out in Sunflower and who's Bella's partner — he came along and towed the Oldsmobile."

Ed Morland whistled. "Guess that didn't set real well with Mr. Benedict!"

"Especially not when Mr. Kelly wouldn't accept pay." Lesley laughed reluctantly. "However, he said Mr. Benedict still owed him for hauling ties. Mr. Benedict says he didn't, but he handed over some money. He calls it payment for the tow, Mr. Kelly calls it payment for hauling — and I call them both stubborn mules!"

Father's brown eyes twinkled. "Mules are 'its,' Les. I wouldn't call Mr. Benedict that, and from the sound of it, your Mr. Kelly is sure a man."

"He's not my Mr. Kelly," Lesley flung over her shoulder as she started to the boxcar to change clothes. "They both acted like bratty little boys. Bella's going to have her hands full keeping any kind of peace between them."

"Bella can do it," Ed said worshipfully.

"I hope so," Lesley groused. "*I* certainly never want to be in between them again!"

It was stifling inside the boxcar. The lawn shirtwaist stuck to her skin. It would have to be washed and ironed. She examined the skirt and decided a pressing would make it presentable. Her corset waist was soaked with sweat. Lesley hung it over a chair to dry and wished irritably that she didn't have to put on her other one. In a gesture of exasperation, she took out the side steels.

There! Jim Kelly wouldn't know they

155

were gone, and as for Benedict — well, it would probably be dark before he finished his gourmet meal and loitered over to give the peasants his decision.

Great howling cats! She'd invited Kelly for supper. She couldn't feed him fried mush and canned green beans, the meal she had planned. Next summer they were going to have a garden. Even a small plot would grow tomatoes, lettuce, green onions, chard, string beans, new potatoes so delicious with creamed tender peas . . .

Her mouth watered at the thought. With a jolt of shock, she realized that this was the first time in years she'd counted on being at a station the following spring, unconsciously assumed there'd be time to plant and harvest. But that was next summer. She sighed glumly as she surveyed her resources.

No time to soak and cook beans. Anyway, they weren't company fare. But she made good biscuits. Men always liked biscuits even when there wasn't any butter. She could mash potatoes with evaporated Pet and use the rest of the cream to make a sauce for canned peas. She could dip onion slices in cornmeal batter, fry them crisp, and make a salmon loaf.

Dessert? She shut out the memory of Henri's lemon ice and chocolate-filled wafers. Dried apples, soaked in sugar water and spiced with cinnamon, made quite acceptable dumplings. Her crusts usually turned out deliciously light and flaky.

Cheered that she wouldn't have to apologize for the meal, she set about her preparations. Somehow she found the heat of the boxcar less stifling because she was making food she thought Jim Kelly would enjoy — and even though she'd yearned to bang his and Benedict's heads together, she felt as if now that he was here, her life was opening like a long-clenched bud bursting suddenly into bloom. She even sang a little as she put the apples to soak and began to peel the potatoes.

7

To Father's disappointment, Bella must have overnighted at the camp she was hauling to or somewhere along the trail, for Jim Kelly crossed the tracks alone in the blessed relief sundown brought from the broiling heat.

"Good evening, Mr. Kelly," Lesley greeted him. "I don't believe you've met my father."

The two shook hands. Lesley was proud of her father when he cleared his throat and said, "I'm glad to have a chance to thank you in person, young man. It was mighty good of you to pay my fine when they were about to lock me up in the Sunflower hoosegow."

"You only told Roosevelt what I'd have liked to," Kelly said. His grin was savage. "Here we're still fighting the Filipinos, slaughtering men, women, and children by the thousands so whoever's left will have the benefits of being governed by a Christian nation."

Father nodded so emphatically that the stump of his arm jerked. "What was it Senator Algin Beveridge told the Senate early this year? That he didn't think that among five million Filipinos, a hundred understood the meaning of Anglo-Saxon self-government? Why the devil should they? They want their freedom from us as much or more than ever they wanted it from Spain."

"What can you expect from a senator who claims that 'the trade of the world must and should be ours'? The United States is on the grab." Kelly's tone held disgusted shame. "We annexed Hawaii a couple of years ago. During the war with Spain, we took over Guam, Wake Island, and Puerto Rico."

"We want raw materials and markets for our products," Ed said. "Look at the way United Fruit and the American Tobacco Company swarmed into Cuba. McKinley talks piously of educating, uplifting, civilizing, and Christianizing the Filipinos, but the truth is, we've taken over all these peoples to serve our business interests, pure and simple."

"Not so pure," said Jim. His hand brushed the scar that ridged his cheek.

"But the Anti-Imperialist League can't make much headway against all the flag-waving."

"If there is a judgment, God will mark it to Andrew Carnegie's credit that he's a member of the League," Ed said. "Did you know that when he was sixteen, he was one of the first telegraphers in the country who was able to take messages by sound alone?"

"Carnegie was a telegrapher?" Lesley asked. It was difficult to imagine that the man who controlled virtually all U.S. steel production had ever held such a job.

"He was only eighteen when he became private secretary and telegrapher to the president of the Pennsylvania Railroad." Her father loved producing bits of telegraphy lore. "During the Civil War, he served the Union brilliantly as superintendent of the eastern military and telegraph lines. But when his poverty-ridden parents brought him to the States when he was thirteen, he worked in a cloth factory for a dollar twenty-five a week."

"It can happen in America," Kelly said. "I guess the best thing we have is hope, the chance to change. I sure hope to heaven our government will."

"We'd better eat while the biscuits are hot," Lesley interposed. "Why don't we fill our plates inside and carry them to the depot platform? It'll be a lot cooler."

Kelly sniffed the mingled aromas. "Smells scrumptious. It was mighty kind of you to invite me, Miss Morland."

Was it a trick of light or did his eyes, the color of the deepening sky, glow as they rested on her? Trick or not, sweet flame swept through her. Trying not to sound as breathless as she felt, Lesley said, "It's nothing compared to what you've done for us. Please help yourself, Mr. Kelly."

"Can't we use first names, Les?" her father asked. "After all, we're going to be neighbors."

"It's fine with me if it is with Mr. —"

"Jim," he said quickly. And then, as if it slipped out without his permission, he added, "I've always called you Lesley in my mind."

So he had thought about her! A melting radiance spread from her heart through her whole body, bringing her alive in a way she had never been. If he had — thought about her — surely he'd get over his ill temper at finding her out for a drive with Benedict.

"These are the best biscuits I ever ate," Jim said, accepting his fourth. "And I reckon it's close to the best meal I ever had."

"Save room for the apple dumplings," Ed advised.

Lesley served these with sprinkles of brown sugar and Pet cream. As she brought coffee, a rumbling traveled through the air. "Bet that's Micajah," Jim said. "He left Clearwater when I did but veered east a little to visit some friends on their homestead." Jim chuckled. "He must have smelled your apple dumplings, Miss Lesley." Maybe he called her Lesley in his mind, but he apparently couldn't bring himself to drop some form of title. "He purely loves them."

"There's plenty of everything left for him to have supper," she said.

"Don't put yourself out. He'll have to water and curry his team before he can eat, and it's no use my offering to do it. He treats those mules like they were his kids and their mama was dead."

"Why do you drive horses when Bella and Mr. Micajah use mules?" Lesley wondered.

"It's kind of six of the one and half a dozen of the other, ma'am. The reason I don't drive mules is they almost drowned me in the Cimarron one time in water so shallow, they had to bury their noses in it to have a problem. Mules are that way about water."

Lesley glanced around the arid countryside. "I shouldn't think water would be much of a worry on these plains."

"It is when it rains and you get a flash flood because there's nothing to hold the water and it pours like crazy into dry washes like that one you got stuck in today, or creeks that generally trickle a few inches of water if any, or the Cimarron, which, like they say, can be a mile wide, an inch deep, and that inch too thick to drink and too wet to plow except when it floods. Then, what with quicksand, it's about the most treacherous river the devil could dream up in his nastiest spell."

Lesley shuddered. "It sounds awful! Did Bella drive across it?"

"She did more times than I can count, and with mules, too. Me, that time after I lost my load, two mules, and almost my hide, I switched to horses."

Heralded by increasing squeaks,

creaks, and clopping hooves, a team and wagon took form in the light from the depot. Rising, Jim said over his shoulder, "Better not call Micajah 'Mr.' or he'll pass out, Miss Lesley. He's practically forgotten his last name — it's Schatz."

"That you, Jimmy?" came a gravelly voice. "What kinda ghost town is this you've picked for our new headquarters?"

"It's going to change, and till then, we'll haul for the railroad that's being built south. Where've you been? I was getting scared you'd had trouble or that widow lady had roped and hog-tied you."

"You watch your tongue about Miz Lilyun O'Brien or you won't get none of these nice watermelons and other garden plunder she sent." A patch of yellow light revealed only eyes and a long broken nose between a slouched-down hat and bushy gray whiskers. "Where'm I supposed to park this wagon? That a water trough over by the tank?"

"That's what it is," said Jim. "I'll help you unharness, but first say howdy to Miss Lesley Morland and her father, Ed Morland, who's the station agent here."

"Howdy, ma'am." Micajah Schatz doffed his hat with a gallant sweep. "Howdy, Ed."

"When you've finished with your team, sir," said Lesley, "won't you have some supper?"

"I'd sure admire to, ma'am, if it ain't too much trouble. I been smellin' apple pie or apple dumplin's — couldn't tell which — ever time the wind came from this direction. Thought I was havin' haluc— hallucin— well, anyhow, whatever them things are that you see or smell or hear when they ain't there."

"It's apple dumplings and no trouble at all," she promised.

He cackled happily. "I'll be back soon's I unhitch and look after my babies here."

"And slosh a little water over your face," Jim added.

"First, Jimmy, unload four-five of them watermelons. Miz O'Brien sent a bunch more'n we can eat. More roastin' ears and tomatoes and squash and chili peppers, too. Lift out that crate of stuff, son —" Beneath the dust, the wagon was painted red, white, and black, the old German imperial colors often seen in Texas or other places where Germans had settled.

"Oh, don't give us all that!" Lesley protested. "Your friend gave it to you."

"Yeah, but she's not here to cook it, ma'am, and it looks like neither is Bella, so lots of it would go plumb to waste or get tossed to the coyotes."

"I'll be more than glad to cook it, but you'll have to come help eat it."

"You bet I will!" He dropped his tone confidentially. "Sure wouldn't let Miz O'Brien know, but I hate squash!"

Lesley thought of a recipe in her mother's book. "Maybe you'll like the way I fix it, but if you don't, you can fill up on something else."

"I'll put those watermelons in the trough to cool," Ed said.

"And I'll carry the other stuff to your place, Miss Lesley." Jim hoisted the crate to his shoulder. "It was sure a great supper. All right if I come back with Micajah?"

"Of course." Lesley collected plates and utensils. "Have more coffee and another apple dumpling if you want it."

"You can bet I'm in line for any crumbs Micajah leaves," Jim laughed. He set the heaped box of fresh things on a chair by the table. For a moment they were so close in the darkness that delicious little electric shocks prickled her skin before he quickly turned away. "I'll be back soon as we take care of the team," he promised.

Her heart sang as she lit the lamp. He seemed to be thawing. For pride's sake, she couldn't directly explain how she came to be out with Benedict, but some way might come up to slip it into the conversation.

She lit the burners to reheat the food. The biscuits, left in the oven, were still warm. Then, as if admiring treasures, she examined the vegetables in the crate. What a glory of colors and textures!

The bottom of the crate was filled with roasting ears, fine silk curling out of pale green husks that protected juicy kernels. Next were golden crookneck squash, shiny red and green chili peppers, and plump scarlet tomatoes mounded as high as they could be without rolling off.

What a feast they'd have tomorrow! But thoroughly as her appetite was appeased, Lesley couldn't wait till tomorrow to taste those tomatoes. She rinsed them off in water she'd heat for dishwashing and sliced them carefully, unable to resist eating a piece slowly, letting the juice fill her mouth and savoring it before she swallowed.

She heaped a platter for Micajah, spread a dish towel over the pan with the remaining biscuits, and started for the depot. There was a crunch of gravel. A tall figure loomed out of the night. "That smells tantalizing, Miss Morland. Would it be presumptuous of me to invite myself to supper one evening?"

She absolutely did not want him at the gala meal she was planning for tomorrow, but her father called from the platform, "You'd be welcome anytime, Mr. Benedict. In fact, if you fancy apple dumplings, there's likely some left. Sit down and have one and some coffee."

"That would be most enjoyable after an annoying session with that Oldsmobile. But first I need to send a telegraph message, Mr. Morland, if you would be so kind. Matthew confesses utter defeat with the engine."

"Certainly, sir. Do you have your message written out?"

"Here it is." Benedict extended a paper

and a bill. "Matthew believes the band of the planetary transmission was faulty. I'm ordering another one, and my friend Ransom Olds is getting an earful. May I help you, Miss Morland, with what you're carrying?"

"Thanks," she said, not very graciously, and acutely aware that her father had vanished inside the depot. "I can manage very well."

Thank goodness, here came Micajah and Jim, emerging into the light from the station. "Here's your supper, Micajah, and some of those lovely tomatoes." She put the platter and tomatoes down on a crate beside one of the chairs. "Would you like coffee now?"

"All the time, bless your heart, Miss Lesley. If you got plenty of sugar and Pet, I'd sure appreciate a good lacing of 'em." The grizzled teamster swept off his hat to her and tossed it under the chair before he eyed Benedict, who smiled and held out his well-kept hand.

"I'm Adam Benedict, sir."

Micajah squinted at him with pale blue eyes. "You the one, mister, as didn't pay the boss for that last load of ties he hauled out of Sunflower to your railroad?"

"He's settled up," put in Jim, though he looked rather grimly at the heavier man. "Benedict, this is Micajah Schatz, the other teamster in our outfit."

"Well, if we're square —" The teamster's weather-beaten face, where it showed between wild gray elflocks tangling with kinky eyebrows and the lower expanse of dense beard and mustache, was clean as a scrubbed schoolboy's, but it would have taken a currycomb and steel brush to impose discipline on his hair. He exuded an odor of tobacco smoke, leather, and sweat, human and animal. Grudgingly, Micajah extended a hand that resembled a clawed brown root.

Benedict didn't take it immediately. "I did *not* pay you for what you voluntarily did after you were discharged —"

"I quit before you fired me," Jim said.

"I paid you for hauling my automobile back to the tracks," said Benedict.

"No, you didn't. There's no way under the shining sun I'd ever charge for doing the neighborly thing — even to someone who doggone sure isn't neighborly!"

"Please!" Lesley frowned on them both. "Do shake hands, and I'll bring the apple dumplings and coffee."

Peace reigned as Micajah stowed away two platters of food and the rest of the biscuits while Benedict savored a golden glazed dumpling oozing syrupy juice.

"Is there a blacksmith anywhere around?" Micajah asked when his hunger was appeased and he was reveling in dessert. "We're going to need one."

"There's one at each construction camp, so you can get your work done at either place." Benedict smiled broadly. "However, a blacksmith's arriving any day to set up his anvil in Bountiful."

"We can't give him that much business!" Micajah protested.

"You won't have to. Work on the brick factory starts as soon as the builders get here, and the bank will go up as fast as the bricks are ready. After the bank's done, the next major construction is a larger brick depot with more comfortable living quarters."

"Oh, that's a big expense, Mr. Benedict," objected Ed. "Maybe you should wait and see if the town needs a new depot."

"It'll need one." Benedict's tone was positive. "The present depot will serve as storage and temporary living space for newcomers. A frame hotel and livery stable are going to be built to accommodate new citizens of Bountiful till their homes and businesses are ready. Farmers who've taken over abandoned places will be arriving by train and wagon. In six weeks Bountiful will be well on its way to becoming the center of commerce for the whole region."

Lesley thought with a sinking heart of the prairie dog town. If this drowsy little station mushroomed into a small city, all land near the tracks would be valuable. Too valuable for an entrepreneur to sell at a price she could afford, if he'd sell at all. As if reading her mind, his eyes rested on her, fathomless in the shadows.

"I've been contemplating your proposition concerning the prairie dog village, Miss Morland. A town planner must always look ahead. As the area resettles and attracts more people, these ground squirrels are going to lose most of their holdings. In time, maybe within a score of years, such villages will be scarce."

"You mean —"

"I mean that someday people will travel here to watch the little guys stand sentinel on their mounds and see the owls and other creatures that share the burrows. Why, rattlesnakes may be scarce before your hair turns gray."

"Not in western Kansas," asserted Micajah.

"Perhaps not, but even so, the village will be a good attraction. In time, a museum might be built close by to house arrowheads and other artifacts unearthed by the plow. We could fence a small pasture and bring up buffalo and longhorns from Charles Goodnight's ranch in the Texas Panhandle." Benedict warmed to the notion. "There could be penned coyotes and pronghorn antelope —"

"No!" Lesley's cry was involuntary. All the men stared at her, but she was too horrified to care. "That would be — it would be a *sin!*"

Benedict's already quizzical eyebrows arched higher. "What would be a sin, Miss Morland?"

"Shutting coyotes and pronghorns up in pens."

"Enclosures, if you will. Ample ones."

"Ample?" She gestured widely. "They're used to running for miles. Buffalo and longhorns are different. They'd be killed if they weren't protected by

173

fences and people. But the only more cruel way to treat wild things I can imagine is keeping far-flying birds like eagles and hawks in cages where they couldn't do more than flutter a little way."

"This would be educational," argued Benedict. "People would have more understanding of coyotes if they watched them close up."

"You might as well study human nature in a prison or insane asylum," Lesley retorted. "Imprisoned animals of that wide-ranging kind are bound to go crazy."

"You'd deny Bountiful an outstanding living museum?"

"I'd fight it every way I could!"

"Even if, as a part of it, I donated the prairie dog town to Bountiful?"

"Nothing you could do would make that a good thing."

He shrugged. "Let it be on your head, then, that our town won't boast a Museum of the High Plains."

"Let it."

He made a cathedral steeple of his fingers. "Nevertheless, in spite of your curtailing its promotion on a grander scale, the possibilities of the prairie dog village are great enough to make it wise business to preserve it as it is. I will wire my agents to remove that property from their prospectuses."

Instead of being relieved, Lesley was uneasy. The way his agile mind generated ideas, how long would he keep to this resolve? Besides, she had a suspicion that he was doing this to overshadow Jim Kelly.

"I'm glad you feel that way, Mr. Benedict," she said. "Still, I'd prefer to buy the village if your bank would accept a mortgage."

"You don't trust me?"

"It's not that, sir, but you could change your mind."

"I'll give the matter my deepest consideration. While my recalcitrant automobile is immobilized, I'm going to Denver. You'll have my answer when I return."

"But you will take the land off the market?"

He gazed at her. She tried not to visibly tense. "I will if you ask it, Miss Morland."

Jim cast them a smoldering look. Lesley hated asking a favor of this man to whom they already owed their living, but it would be disastrous if someone bought the property while Benedict was making up his mind. Cat-and-mousing, she thought resentfully, but she couldn't let pride endanger the bustling world of small beings who hadn't the faintest notion that their homes and lives could be wiped out in a few days of plowing.

"Of course I'll ask you to take the village off the market." She couldn't keep the edge out of her voice. "After all, I do want to buy it."

He beamed. "Ah, yes. But you see, my dear Miss Morland, that no more than you trust me to do right by your diminutive friends can I trust you not to imperil Bountiful's economic interests should there be a conflict." He bowed and bestowed a general smile on the gathering. "I wish you all a very good night and farewell for perhaps a week. Should messages come for me, Mr. Morland, kindly relay them to the Denver depot. Thank you, Miss Morland, for the most succulent dessert. You work such magic with dried fruit that I wonder what you might create from fresh."

He disappeared into the night. It wasn't till he emerged again in the light of his private car that anybody spoke. It was as if, till they knew where Benedict was, they thought he might be anywhere, listening.

"So you want to buy the dog town?" Jim asked in a neutral tone. "Why not just let Benedict make it an attraction? That'll keep the critters alive and won't cost you anything."

"It's fine for people to watch the village, but you heard the way he was thinking. He can't seem to keep from taking a simple idea and elaborating it into something complicated."

"Guess that's why he's rich," said Jim.

"I'm nervous about what he'll do if he owns the place. Not that a museum wouldn't be nice. I just don't think living creatures ought to be in it unless they can go on living the way they always have."

"I'm partial to the little fellas myself." Jim sounded less guarded. "Lots of times I've camped where I could watch them. They have savvy about getting along with each other. Young'uns can play around any mound till they're old enough to know better — then they get run off. But in danger, it's okay for any dog to dive into the closest burrow."

"Yeah, and a bunch are always on guard while others feed," supplied Micajah. "They got to live in towns. A dog by itself or even a little group of 'em are dead meat real sudden." He smothered a cavernous yawn. " 'Scuse me, Miss Lesley, but I'm plain tuckered out. Better stagger up on my hind legs while I still can. Know what we're doin' tomorrow, Jimmy?"

"I talked to the contractor this afternoon. We're hauling a windmill, couple of tanks, and other stuff down to where they're digging a well."

"Will you be back for supper?" Lesley asked. All those great vegetables! It would be a shame if Jim and Micajah didn't get to enjoy them.

"Should be. It's less than a mile beyond where the horseless carriage got plumb completely unhorsed. We'll leave before light in the morning, rest our teams through the noon heat, and ought to rattle in not much past sundown."

"If you run into Bella, tell her we sure hope she'll be here, too," said Father.

Both men praised the meal again before they moved off together toward the glow of Bella's tent. "On the other

178

hand," worried Ed, as he helped collect the dishes, "unless Mr. Benedict takes his private car, that dratted Frenchie'll have plenty of time to hang around Bella, bring her iced drinks and fancy eats."

"She'll be busy," Lesley comforted. "Anyhow, I'm sure she likes you best."

"I don't have ice or a pointy little beard, and I'm not from Paris."

"No, but the telegrapher's the most important person in town."

"If we get a town."

"Oh, we will. Maybe faster than we really want it."

"Mmph. Well, I just hope Mon-sewer Champagne goes to Denver with his boss!"

"I wish his boss would stay in Denver," Lesley said fervently. Avoiding her father's puzzled stare, she carried the dishes to the boxcar.

8

To Ed's delight, Henri did accompany his employer to Denver in the private car, and Bella appeared in time for supper the following evening, as did Micajah. "Jim'll camp out tonight," explained the older man. "When we went to load up this mornin', the contractor added a bunch of supplies for the next construction camp to Jim's freight, and then he's supposed to haul ties to that camp from a cedar-cuttin' outfit. Don't know when he'll be back."

An all-gone sensation in the pit of Lesley's stomach took away her appetite. Jim wasn't there to relish the squash made so tempting with tomatoes, chilies, and onions that squash-hating Micajah had three helpings, or to savor roasting ears tender enough that butter was scarcely missed, or finish the meal with cold, tangily ripe watermelon. It was hard to believe that Benedict would go to that much effort to make sure Jim was gone during his own absence, yet it certainly seemed that way.

"This garden stuff sure hits the spot," said Micajah, accepting another hunk of watermelon. "Onliest time I ever tried plantin' anything was 1874 —"

"Oh," cried Bella, "that was the first year — and the worst one — that the grasshoppers came!" She brushed an errant curl from her eyes. "The year I lost my hair, too."

"Can see why you remember the year," said Micajah. "Well, after the Civil War, I homesteaded. Got the four years I'd served in the army taken off the five-year provin'-up time, but I was too restless to stay put, so I sold out. Helped build the Union Pacific Railroad and worked buildin' other railroads till I joined up with some buffalo hunters in 'seventy-two. That winter when I finally got the stink off me —"

"Must have took most of the winter," Bella observed. "All the buffalo hunters I ever knew, you could smell farther away than you could see 'em if the wind was right."

"Can't recall as anybody smelled too good in them days 'ceptin' the — mm-um, 'scuse me, ladies. Anyhow, I got fumigated enough to court a purty gal who worked in her daddy's mercantile in Dodge. She convinced me we ought to farm — wouldn't marry me less'n I settled down. We bought land from the Atchison, Topeka and Santa Fe. Found out the first year you break sod, there's so many roots, 'bout all you can do is dig holes and plant corn, but by spring the roots had rotted. I plowed and harrowed and the soil looked rich as chocolate cake."

"None of my husbands was ever fool enough to farm," said Bella.

Micajah shrugged and looked back through the years, hoarse voice softening. "Our wheat and oats was cut and bound in the shock that July. Mary and me was expectin' our first baby in a few weeks. We was standin' out admirin' the corn — up to her waist, it was, she was the daintiest little thing — and all of a sudden this wind blew from the north and we saw a big cloud. Thought it was smoke or dust till the hoppers came down like sleet. They lit so thick on the big cottonwood by our soddy that a couple limbs broke off. I'd hauled in cedar shakes for our roof. Them hoppers hittin' it sounded like a hailstorm that wouldn't quit. Mary's chickens ate till their crops bulged out, but they couldn't make a dent on the pesky cusses."

"Hogs and turkeys got fat on 'em." Bella made a face. "Tasted like 'em, too."

"So'd our chickens. Anyhow, that proud purty corn bent down to the ground with hoppers. Sounded like a herd of cattle chompin' away. I ran down the rows knockin' em off with a branch, but more swarmed down. They smashed potato vines flat. Mary ran out with all the quilts we had — she and her mother had sewed many an hour to make 'em. Covered up the turnips and onions and green beans, Mary did, but the hoppers swarmed in from underneath. Ate the onions way down into the ground so there was little holes left."

"They made such a mess in the creeks that my mules wouldn't drink till they were nigh thirstin' to death." Bella shook her head at the memory. "Folks had to clean the hoppers out of their wells every day to keep them from ruinin' the water altogether."

"Mary tried so hard to fight off the hoppers that the baby came early and hard and we lost it," went on Micajah.

"I was lucky to get a job on a section gang, worked up to foreman. By then, trail drives was comin' up from Texas. Cowboys gave my wife puny little calves that'd lost their mamas or couldn't go no further. We pinched every penny till it hollered and bought a cow every time we could afford one. By the early eighties, what with gettin' a hundred sixty acres under the Timber Culture Act and buyin' out a coupla disgusted farmers, we had a pretty nice little ranch goin' and twin boys gettin' of a size to help. Looked like their mama. She had the goldenest hair and the smilin'est blue eyes . . ."

His words trailed off. Bella's tone was gruff. "I recollect when you asked Jim for work, you said the blizzard of 'eighty-six wiped you out."

"It did."

He bowed his head. Something in his tone kept anyone from asking questions, but after a moment, he looked up. "No sense makin' a mystery out of it. Not even Jimmy knows. Our boys were out rounding up cattle when the storm hit on New Year's Day. I was fixin' a windmill in the north pasture when I saw it comin'. Headed my horse across country toward home, cuttin' fences. Couldn't see a thing. Gave old Barney his head and somehow he found his way home. I prayed the boys'd be there. They wasn't. Mary, neither. I went huntin' for 'em. Stumbled into a draw and busted my leg. Onliest thing saved me — and it was a mighty long time before I stopped wishin' it hadn't — was crawlin' beneath a bunch of my cattle that were pilin' up against the bank. When the blizzard stopped, I crawled out. Same neighbor found me as saw one of the boys' red mittens stickin' out of the snow. Mary had her arms around the kids."

Bella rested her hand on his arm. "Leastways, they went out together."

Micajah nodded, got up abruptly, and strode across the tracks with a muttered thanks and good night. "Lord!" said Bella. "It's enough to make you wonder how come he stayed in this country!"

"You did," Lesley pointed out.

"Sure. But I never lost any kids." She added wistfully, "Never had any. Ain't it crazy? Seems like plenty who don't take care of the kids they got keep havin' more, and some who want 'em bad can't have even a teensy runt." She got to her feet. Ed's mesmerized gaze dwelt on the firming muscles revealed by her trousers. "Come on, Les. I'll help you with the dishes before I toddle off."

Ed put away while Bella wiped and regaled them with tales of the early rip-roaring days of Dodge City. Soon they were laughing. Lesley felt only a tiny sting when her father said he was walking Bella to her tent. Truly, she *was* glad they enjoyed each other's company. It filled a void in her heart to feel like — surely this wasn't disloyal to Mother — to feel almost like a family again, when her father gained new zest, Micajah shared his grief, and she, for the first time since that one brief childhood friendship, didn't feel isolated, cut off from others by a morose or drunken father.

Hoping with all her heart that Jim would want to be part of that family, she leaned on the dresser and studied her mother's face in the wedding portrait. "You don't mind, do you, about Father?" she whispered.

It must have been a trick of the light, but her mother's smile seemed to deepen.

By the end of that week, Bountiful could not be recognized as the once forlorn huddle of falling-down buildings. Trains from both directions unloaded lumber, tools, roofing, and supplies. A brick kiln was built well beyond the town lots and soon had twenty thousand bricks in the making. Benedict's expert masons laid stone foundations for a hotel, livery stable, wagon shop, and the bank while all the carpenters who could work without stumbling over each other raised the two-story frame hotel and more crews started on the other buildings. They lived in tents some distance northwest of the water tank and worked from dawn to dusk, taking meals under the shade of tarpaulins attached to poles with a sign that read The Three Sisters.

The sisters dispensing food that sent alluring aromas drifting toward the depot had arrived by train with tarps, poles, two kerosene stoves, dishes, pots, pans, and planks that quickly assembled to benches and tables. Lena, Lisa, and Lilibet Schiller had fair skin, rosy cheeks, taffy hair severely braided and pinned into coronets, and wore blue and white checked aprons to match the oilcloth on the tables. There similarities ended.

Dimpled Lena, probably Lesley's age, had pansy brown eyes, a well-curved but slender figure, and tinkling laughter. Plump Lisa, some years older, had merry blue eyes and laughter that began deep inside and overflowed. Lilibet wasn't old, but lines etched the corners of her mouth and cool green eyes, and they weren't put there by laughing. Cooking for perhaps forty hungry men kept them busy from before daylight till after dark, so Lesley hadn't talked with them since they left the station seated in Micajah's wagon amongst the furnishings of their open-air establishment. Bella was hauling supplies to the railroad camps, but Micajah had been given the task of delivering building materials to the various sites in between regular freighting.

Other freighters, mostly farmers earning some welcome cash, were also supplying the camps, so the blacksmith, brawny Hugh MacLeod, scarcely had his forge ready and the anvil unloaded from his wagon when he had two mules and a horse who needed new shoes, two broken wagon wheels, and assorted damaged or dulled tools to deal with. Hugh's lot was close to the water tank, and the ring of his hammer sounded over the more distant staccato of the carpenters. He took his meals at The Sisters and slept under the shelter made in the wagon by canvas stretched over hoops.

Every evening he lounged over to the depot to watch the eastbound pull in to disgorge the latest supplies or people. Powerfully built, with his curling red beard, mustache, and long hair, given a timeless aura by his stained leather apron, he looked to Lesley like the Norse god Thor of Longfellow's poem.

"Are you expecting someone, Mr. MacLeod?" Lesley asked the first time he came.

Broad white teeth flashed in the rusty beard. "Bless you, ma'am, no. Of course, you never know who or what may turn up. I've just always loved trains. I worked my way up to engineer after about ten years. Lost my job in the Pullman strike and got blackballed, so I decided to take up my pa's trade — be my own boss."

"After that, I'd think you wouldn't like

trains," Lesley ventured.

"Trains can't help who owns them." Hugh shrugged. He helped Ed wrestle off some large crates, watched with a faintly disappointed expression as half a dozen men in working clothes got off with their metal or cardboard suitcases, and then, as steam billowed and the train began to chug, he strolled back across the tracks.

"Don't let him kid you," said her father, chuckling. "Even if he doesn't know it, he's waiting for someone to get off that train."

Men hand-dug a well in the middle of what would be the main business section between the bank and hotel and livery stable, and soon clear, sweet water ran from the pump anyone could use and flowed into the huge trough for watering horses, mules, and the occasional ox team. Perhaps, as Benedict predicted, automobiles would eventually take the place of horses, but there were no signs of that in Bountiful. Besides the livery stable and wagon shop, two tents now proclaimed themselves to be feed stores, another was a harness shop, and another blacksmith had located on the far reaches of town without diminishing Hugh's trade in the slightest.

Almost every day another sign or two went up by tents where the proprietors tended to customers in between helping carpenters build their permanent places of business — a mercantile, grocer, butcher, lumberyard, hardware, and a drugstore.

"Outside of the barber with his bathtubs and that drugstore that's gettin' rich off 'medicinal spirits,' Lydia Pinkham's, Parker's Ginger Tonic, and such, they're sort of selling just to each other," surmised Ed. "By the way, did you see there *is* a laundry set up close to the builders' camp? Sam Welliver, who has the mercantile, reckoned it would be a good sideline. Before he came here himself, he wired Sears, Roebuck for two washing machines, real good wringers, tubs, sadirons, and something called a mangle to press sheets and such. The shipment came last evening along with the two widow ladies from Dodge who're going to run it. I want you to take our wash up there, Les, instead of scrubbing it out on a board."

"I'd rather buy a washing machine, Daddy." She had looked in the catalog, of course, had even begun to wonder if they couldn't afford a machine now that her father had been off drink for almost two months. "We don't have to get an expensive one, the kind that costs four or five dollars. The Chicago American is two dollars seventy-five cents. It wouldn't take long to pay for it out of what laundry would run us, and then we'd have it for good."

Ed Morland looked embarrassed. "I sure haven't paid much attention to making things easier for you, Les. I'm sorry — you make out that order to Sears just as quick as you can." He cleared his throat. "Things are going to be better, honey."

"They *are* better," she said, and brushed a kiss across his cheek. She hadn't known about the drugstore. That was disquieting, but surely he'd never start again, especially not when Bella had brought zest to his life.

One business she did know about was several rolled into one in the scrawny being of Rutherford Miles. He arrived on the westbound morning train with his Washington printing press and other furnishings. Well before sundown, an ornately lettered sign at the top of his tent pole declared it to house *The Bountiful Banner*. A more sedate sign beneath it announced: Rutherford Miles, Attorney at Law. Below that, block print proclaimed: CLOCKS AND WATCHES REPAIRED. Lowest of all on the tent pole was the modest announcement: SIGNS AND PORTRAITS PAINTED: PHOTOGRAPHS.

The editor-attorney-repairman-painter came to the station the night of his advent to claim a large heap of newspapers and magazines. "Any hot news, Mr. Morland?" Miles asked, with an engaging smile. He doffed his brown fedora to Lesley, revealing a head bald except for a halo of fine dark hair. His mustache reached almost to his ears, and his black eyes sparkled with exuberance.

"Sorry," said Father. "Nothing you probably wouldn't know coming from Wichita the way you did this morning. According to the papers, the Allies entered Peking and freed the folks in the foreign legations. The dowager empress hightailed it out of there with some of her loyal soldiers. The Boxers are still holding out in a few spots, but they're done for." He shook his head. "I'm glad we didn't send lots of soldiers to that one."

The men exchanged a glance of understanding. "I'm sorry a lot of missionaries got beheaded," Miles said. "But you can't blame the Boxers for wanting foreigners out of their country."

Father grunted. "What they got was troops — Russians, Austrians, Italians, French, Germans, Japanese, British, and two infantry regiments from us." He made a fist and waved it in mockery. "We told China she'd have an Open Door Policy, and she will if we have to hold it open with cannons and warships."

"Looks that way now we've decided to be a world power." Rutherford Miles gathered up his papers, and The Atlantic, *Harper's*, and *The Saturday Evening Post*. "Hope you won't mind if I stop by pretty often to see if anything exciting's happened."

"Glad to see you," Father said. "But except for special bulletins that come through bigger Western Union offices, our little station doesn't get news over the wire, just railroad orders and Western Union telegrams. Of course, I can use the wire for something special like elections or a big prize fight."

"Well, I can get news from folks getting off the train," said the editor. "And you're welcome to the papers and magazines after I'm finished."

"Would you mind if we had a shelf for them here in the depot?" Lesley asked. "One of the carpenters sprained his ankle yesterday, and a friend came hunting for something he could read. I gave him our old newspapers and *Life* magazines and lent him Mr. Winston Churchill's *Richard Carvel* and Charles Majors's *When Knighthood Was in Flower*. His friend thought a good many of the builders would enjoy something to read after supper."

"Much better than gambling or getting a pint from the drugstore," the editor said. "I'll be glad, certainly, to add to your lending library." Resuming his hat, he went his way.

"Maybe between all his professions, he'll scrape along," Ed said. "During homesteading years, lawyers used to make a dandy living out of helping settlers prove up on their claims or in arguing disputed ones, but Miles isn't old enough to have got in on the land office days."

"His newspaper's name's at the top of his pole," said Lesley. "That must be what he likes best. But what's he going to put in *The Banner* till we have more of a town?"

What he put in, she discovered next evening when he delivered a stack of papers, were the plans each business-person had for his or her undertaking, a little about their backgrounds and why they had come to Bountiful. Beneath a masthead that adjured *"As Bountiful prospers, so do we all,"* Miles praised the "mouth-watering viands and clean and pleasant atmosphere" of The Three Sisters. He said the water of the town well was pure and God's own elixir. No expense would be spared in making the bank the most imposing structure between Dodge City and Denver. The laundry, equipped with the best and latest machines, guaranteed impeccable white shirts and sheets while promising not to fade colored garments. Sewing on buttons and mending minor tears was included in the extremely reasonable charge.

Hugh MacLeod had never met the animal he couldn't shoe and was expert at repairing plows, wagons, and machinery. Wellivers' Mercantile stocked everything from the most popular brands of chewing gum and candy bars to phonographs and up-to-date clothing. New bargains were arriving daily.

"As for your humble scribe," ran the column titled "Miles's Musings," "he welcomes all news, some opinions — and advertisements. He would also appreciate your passing the word that he has successfully handled just about every legal difficulty a mortal can get into. Your $1 Brownie can't begin to give you quality photographs of your loved ones. I specialize in tasteful portraits of children gathered untimely by the grim reaper. Business signs large or small, discreet or dazzling."

A boxed notice at the bottom of the last page made Lesley's cheeks warm at seeing her name in print for the first time.

Many of you have made the acquaintance of our conscientious station agent, Edward Morland, and his charming daughter, Lesley, who may well be called the first residents of the reborn Bountiful. This public-spirited pair announce the establishment of a readers' shelf in the depot. Newspapers, magazines, and books may be borrowed at no cost. Contributions, cash or reading material, to this community library are extremely welcome.

"That sounds much too grand for our little collection," Lesley fretted. "I'm afraid people will be disappointed."

"Well then, let them contribute some cash to buy books," said her father. He glanced out the ticket window. "Holy smoke! Look at them come!"

Lesley gasped. It was like a mob changing from faceless dark shapes to individuals as they moved into the light from the depot. "Heavens, are they all coming for something to read? A few have books or magazines. I'll hurry and bring our other books — if you don't mind lending them?"

"Hang on to your mother's family Bible," her father said. "I'd be real sad if that book of Walt Whitman's poems you gave me one Christmas disappeared. Otherwise, sure, folks can read my books. Rather have neighbors who read than the kind who hang around pool halls and joints." At the look on her face, he added with a grin, "The way I used to!"

She wasn't letting go of her mother's recipe book, either, but she filled a box from their bookshelf and tucked in a tablet and pencil so that anyone taking a book could write down the name and date.

Hugh MacLeod met her halfway to the depot and swung the heavy box to his shoulder. "I brought Bobbie Burns's poems," he said. "And Jane Porter's *Scottish Chiefs*. That's champion, Miss Morland. Have you read it?"

"No, but I will when I get the chance. Father enjoyed this one a lot, H. G. Wells's *War of the Worlds*. And Joseph Conrad's *Lord Jim*."

"I won't hog 'em both," said Hugh. "Dibs on the war one."

The Wellivers put Lew Wallace's *Ben Hur* and Edward Westcott's *David Harum* on the shelf and examined the books Lesley had brought before she could take them out of the box. They selected five before moving enough to let other people choose reading material.

"Maybe we ought to have this at the

mercantile," Sam Welliver said. He was a clean-shaven, short, thick man of middle years with sandy brown eyes and hair. "It'd draw folks in."

"It'd clutter up the store and not bring in a cent. Handing out the mail works better," his wife said.

Since the population increase, some mail was dropped off nearly every day. The Wellivers had volunteered to take charge of it and outgoing letters. From all reports, anyone collecting a letter rarely made it out of the mercantile without being hectored into buying something. Agatha Welliver's scant red hair was combed over a brown hairpiece that showed through in numerous places. She had flinty, colorless eyes and a tight-set mouth that pulled tighter as she frowned at a book Rutherford Miles was adding to the trove. "*Sister Carrie*? Isn't that Theodore Dreiser's disgusting trash?"

"I found it excellent," said Miles.

Agatha gaped. "Isn't it about a — a hussy?"

"Why, no. It's about a young farm girl who comes to the city and becomes a rich man's mis—"

"Young man!" thundered Welliver as

Agatha's face crimsoned. "You will not use such language to my wife!"

"If I offended you, ma'am, I'm indeed sorry." Miles smiled at her pleasantly. "I had supposed that a lady of your years and experience would be aware of certain realities."

Her crimson turned purple. "Knowing something evil goes on isn't the same as wallowing in it!"

"I'm positive, ma'am, no one would dream of forcing you to read the book."

She skewered Lesley with pale eyes. "Are you going to allow such garbage in the library, Miss Morland?"

Lesley spread a hand toward the contributed assortment. The builders had brought mostly tattered dime novels, though she spied Rudyard Kipling's *Barrack Room Ballads*, a book of James Whitcomb Riley's poems, and Stephen Crane's *The Red Badge of Courage*, which her father considered the best book ever written about war.

"I don't think it's my place, Mrs. Welliver, to decide what people should read. Surely no one will bring anything too frightful to a public exchange."

"It *is* your responsibility since you started it." Mrs. Welliver switched her glare to Lesley's father, who had heard the ruckus and was advancing to his daughter's rescue. "Mr. Morland, you should not only examine all reading material displayed here, but you have an obligation to see it includes inspiring works like Theodore Roosevelt's *The Winning of the West* and that wonderful book by that Topeka minister, Charles Sheldon, *In His Steps*."

"Ah, yes." Ed's tone was mild, but there was a gleam in his eyes. "The last, I believe, is about what would happen if people behaved like Jesus. Strange. I can't recall that he ever took the slightest interest in what people read. However, ma'am, you are certainly free to donate books of which you highly approve." He squinted at one she held. "*Quo Vadis*! Now, that's an exciting story, ma'am. I ate it up. But it'll offend your sensibilities, I fear. Drunken orgies, lusting, Christians getting burned like torches —"

"It's due the martyrs that we remember their suffering!"

"To be sure, ma'am," Ed Morland soothed. "I kinda skipped over that part — turned my stomach. But I sure enjoyed the kissing between that good-looking centurion and Lygia, and the way his uncle had beautiful slave girls sashaying around in nothing much but a smile —"

Sam Welliver folded his arms. "Mr. Morland, I object to such indecent remarks!"

"Indecent? It's all in that book by Henryk Sienkiewicz your wife has there — that, and a lot more."

"Agatha," said the stocky merchant, "I will read the book first and decide whether it's suitable for you."

"Oh, it's a bang-up story, Mr. Welliver," Ed assured him. Lesley put the tablet and pencil on the desk near the shelf.

"If you'll just write down your name, the date, and the books you're taking, please?"

Mrs. Welliver bridled. "If you think we'd keep them —"

"Not at all, but books have a way of dropping under chairs or getting covered up by papers or something."

With ill grace, Mr. Welliver recorded that they were taking John Habberton's *Helen's Babies*, a book that had beguiled many lonely childhood hours for Lesley; R. D. Blackmore's *Lorna Doone*;

Jules Verne's *Around the World in Eighty Days*; and another often-read favorite of Lesley's, *Jane Eyre*.

Lesley met her father's wry look. They both burst out laughing. "Daddy! You were awful!" she said when she could speak. "I tried to get you to read *Quo Vadis*, but you said it was lurid rubbish tricked up with tortured Christians so people could claim they were reading about the early church."

Her father grinned. "I read the good parts, honey."

9

Ten days after he left for Denver, Adam Benedict's private car was back. He strode briskly into the depot while Ed was selling a ticket to a farmer's wife who was going to Wichita to help her ailing mother. Lesley finished transcribing a message from New York and handed it to Benedict.

"Your Panhard should be here in six weeks. What *is* a Panhard?"

"A French car with a Daimler engine that I trust will run better than the Oldsmobile." He gave a short laugh. "If I have two automobiles, perhaps Matthew can keep one of them running."

"You could get a horse or team from the livery stable."

"This is 1900. I don't intend to jog back to the eighties." He glanced out the window. "Well, Miss Morland, what do you think of my town?"

His possessive tone somehow startled and annoyed her. "A lot has happened since you left," she said noncommittally, refusing to meet his gaze.

"My agent has had a number of offers for that property you want."

She tensed but tried to keep her voice level. "Have you sold it?"

"No."

Breath filled her lungs again. She fought to keep pleading out of her tone, but there was a hint of it, and probably in her eyes, too, when at last she met his dark ones with their disconcerting flickers of emerald. "Will you sell it to us?"

He didn't answer immediately. He seemed to feast on whatever he read on her face. Till then, she hadn't noticed how full and fleshy and red his lips were. "Might I trust you'd be appreciative?"

"It's a business matter," she countered. "But of course, I'm glad you'll let us buy it."

He sighed mock ruefully. "I suppose I'll have to be content with that for now. Very well. As soon as my bank manager arrives — he'll operate out of the wagon shop till the bank's built — I'll have him draw up a mortgage."

"I'm sure you won't mind if we have

our lawyer look over the papers," Lesley said.

Benedict frowned. "You mean that fellow who stuck up a newspaper sign and I don't know what all? I mean to bring in an experienced editor, one who can help the town grow."

"Rutherford Miles seems capable," Father defended. "Surely, Mr. Benedict, you don't object to people starting enterprises on property they've bought?"

"A newspaper isn't just a business. It shapes opinion, reflects a community, and should spearhead progress." Benedict's lip curled. "I don't think that a clock-repairing photographer who doubtless became a lawyer after working in some hick attorney's office and passing the laughable bar exams is eminently qualified to produce the kind of paper I want to see in Bountiful."

"I should think," retorted Lesley, "that the important thing is for the townfolk to like it."

"*Like* it? They'll love it as long as it reports their marryings, buryings, babies, Ladies' Aid socials, and who shipped how many bushels of wheat!"

"Shouldn't it?"

He gave an irritated flip of his hand.

"Certainly, but a first-rate editor projects a vision for a town rather than just recording what's happening. Encourages here, admonishes there. He keeps the community focused on goals."

"Whose goals?"

"They're the same for any place that hopes to be prosperous and influential." He ticked them off on his manicured fingers. "Most essential is adequate rail service and communications. Next comes a sound financial base — substantial permanent merchants rather than fly-by-nights. Imposing buildings that indicate stability. A variety of industries and ventures that bring in revenue apart from surrounding farms. A first-rate hospital that will draw people from far away. A college is desirable, and of course, public schools must be the best possible." He paused and considered. "Something cultural helps. Perhaps an opera house."

"We already have a library," Lesley said, and indicated what had grown to two long shelves of books and several stacks of magazines. "From the books Mr. Miles contributes, he's not a hayseed. Have you read Henry Demarest

Lloyd's *Wealth Against Commonwealth*?"

"That scurrilous attack on trusts?" Benedict's eyes narrowed. "Of course I haven't."

"Then how do you know it's scurrilous?"

"Not wishing to have an apoplectic fit, I had Matthew read and summarize it. Lloyd is an incendiary blockhead who would undermine the complex business systems that have made the United States the model and envy of all advanced nations."

"You mean combinations like the Standard Oil Trust that control sugar, lead, beef, and all manner of needs?" Ed asked. "Another thing I give Kansas credit for is being the first state to pass an antitrust law over ten years ago."

"Kansas was settled by cranks!" snapped Benedict.

"If you mean the New Englanders who made it a free state instead of a slave-owning one —" Lesley's father began, face reddening.

Benedict tilted his head as if to listen better. "You sound like my father, Mr. Morland. Exactly." He gave the older man a magnanimous smile. "Let's not snarl at each other. If Mr. Miles fails to provide Bountiful with the paper it requires, another editor will. Let us return to cultural and educational attractions."

Lesley raised her eyebrows. His smile broadened. "The prairie dog town is such an attraction, Miss Morland." He raised his hand against her imminent protest. "No, we won't argue the Plains Museum again, though I hope in time you'll come to believe in its value. What we need to discuss is the means to allow the public to watch the animals."

"Can't they just be left in peace?"

"Absolutely!" He beamed. "That's why we have to consider some kind of fence or wall to keep humans from intruding."

Lesley made a sound of dismay. That would be necessary as the town grew. She could imagine the shambles a gang of boys could make of the mounds. But any kind of barrier around an area that large would be expensive. She glanced beseechingly at her father. He gave her a rather grim nod.

"Could your bank lend us enough for a fence, Mr. Benedict?"

"Actually, I'm willing to pay for a five-foot-high brick wall to surround the part of the village closest to town, and barbed-wire fencing around the rest."

"Why?" asked Lesley.

"What suspicion! Can't you credit me with a soft spot for the droll little creatures?"

"You'll have to pardon me," said Lesley, "but it's hard to imagine that you ever do anything without a dollars-and-cents reason."

"Miss Morland, you wound me!" He sounded tragic, but his eyes laughed. "However, in this case you're right. While my men put up the wall, they can make benches around the periphery so people may comfortably observe the dogs and —"

Lesley shook her head. The man was unbelievable, but his persistence was surely a large factor in his success. "Thank you, we'd prefer to borrow the wall money."

He wrinkled his brow. "Mistrustful as you good people are of me, doesn't it worry you to go so deep in debt to my bank?"

"Not," Ed said, grinning, "if it doesn't worry you! Gives you a reason to keep me hired." A whistle sounded. He took a parcel of letters and the train's orders, called, "Excuse me, Mr. Benedict," over his shoulder, and went out to meet the train.

Benedict watched Lesley in a way that made her nervous. She rose and looked out the window. "Oh, there's a lady getting off with a baby and little children. I'd better go help her —"

"The blacksmith seems to be doing that." Benedict positioned himself so that she was trapped between him and the desk and wall. "Do you know what I did in Denver, Miss Lesley Morland?"

"It's none of my affair, sir. If you'll let me by —"

"In a moment. I want you to know about my useless experiment."

It was clear he wasn't moving. After all, what could he do in broad daylight with her father in calling distance? "What experiment?" The words came out breathless, which added to her discomfort.

His eyes veiled and his lips looked redder and fuller than ever. "I found a woman with hair like yours, rich brown with glints of fire. Fox eyes, too, warm russet as autumn leaves. She was even of your height, and her complexion was almost as fresh and creamy."

"Please —"

"I had her for five days. I did with her everything I've dreamed of with you."

"Mr. Benedict, this is not decent!"

"It's true. And true that she bored me to distraction as I found she had no intelligence beyond contriving tricks to please a man, no ambition beyond owning her own carriage and mansion."

"She gave you what you paid for."

"But not what I desired. To be cured of you."

"You make me sound like scarlet fever." She hoped to make him laugh and dispel the charged tension.

"You're a fever in my blood." He took her hands. Something like fever ran from his touch through her entire body. When she drew her hands away, he let them go, but they tingled as if he still held them. "So, Lesley love, I'm doing what I never expected. Will you marry me?"

"*What?*"

"I'm sure you heard me."

"But — we don't love each other. We don't even know each other very well!"

"I'm not sure I can love in the usual way, my dear, but I want you more than

I've ever wanted anything."

"That's probably the trouble." She tried to speak lightly. "You're used to having what you want as soon as you decide you'd like it."

He ignored her. "I've proved to myself that it's not just your physical attractions that enchant me. I'm intrigued by the nature that will go in debt to protect creatures most people consider vermin. My heart, stony though it is, responds to the woman who stands by her drunken father —"

"I've told him that I won't anymore."

"You told him that to keep him sober."

"I did not! I told him that because I deserve better and I'm going to have it!"

"Wonderful! I couldn't stand a saintly martyr!" He reached for her hands again, but she locked them behind her. "Well, Lesley, do you belong to any particular church? I'll bring an excellent modiste from Denver to design your gown unless you'd enjoy going there for the fitting."

Too stunned to find words, she shook her head slowly, emphatically.

Covered by swelling pupils, Benedict's irises seemed totally black for a moment. Then the green of them flamed.

Was brimstone the sulfurous yellow she'd vaguely imagined or was it more the smoldering color of his eyes?

"Don't you understand, Lesley? I want to marry you."

"No. You just want me. If you could, you'd buy me the way you did the woman in Denver."

"If I could." He smiled, sure of himself again. "But I can't. So when and where shall the wedding be?"

"No time and nowhere! You're not a — a sultan, Mr. Benedict, who just nods at whatever woman he wants for the night."

He laughed in delight as blood heated her face. "Now, however did you learn about that convenient practice?" She blushed more hotly and he sobered. "I may not love you, Lesley. But I'm sure that I want you for all the nights of my life. And all the days."

"I can't marry you."

"Why not?" One eyebrow climbed to meet his silver hair. "Do you think I'm too old for you? Sixteen years difference isn't unusual."

His formidable charm and experience would trouble her more than the years. Feeling vulnerable and gauche as a newly emerged, damp-winged butterfly, she somehow managed to sound firm and unapologetic.

"I don't love you."

His gaze caressed her mouth, the throbbing pulse in her throat, the curving of her breasts. "I'll teach you. That will be sweet."

The force of his will was so strong, his hunger so imperative, that she clung to the memory of Jim as a drowning person in a flood might grasp at help. "I can't marry you, Mr. Benedict."

"Why on earth not? You'd have a life most women can only dream of instead of drudging in a boxcar by the railroad tracks." His voice took on a bantering tone as if he knew he had alarmed her. "You could have iced tea and chocolate wafers every meal, all the books you can read, and every prairie dog town situated on my properties."

Relieved at his change of manner, she laughed and said, "That would persuade me if anything could, sir."

He watched her intently though he still smiled. "Is there someone else?"

She hesitated for a split second too long. "Ah." He nodded. "You fancy someone but aren't sure he fancies you." She wanted to evade his gaze, but the jade sheen of his dark eyes compelled her to meet them. "Can it be you have a weakness for Jim Kelly?"

"You've no right to ask such questions!" Voices were approaching. Benedict moved to one side. She whisked by him.

"My dear," he murmured, making no attempt to halt her. "I always get what I want. Sometimes it just takes longer." Aloud, as her father entered, he said, "The mortgage papers will be ready soon. Good day, Miss Morland. Mr. Morland, when my Panhard comes, you get the first ride. Agreed?"

"That would suit me right down to the ground, sir." Ed's delighted smile faded as he turned to Lesley. "Can we do something for this lady and her kids, Les? Not to mention her menagerie? Mrs. Lee bought one of those old lots with a field on the edge of town, thinking the house on it was livable."

Lesley frowned at Benedict, who shrugged. "The prospectuses mentioned houses 'in need of repair,' I think."

"Those wrecks are worse than no house at all because they have to be torn down," Lesley accused.

Benedict surveyed the arklike assemblage on the platform — a yellow-haired woman in a blue gingham dress; a baby in the same gingham in her arms; a fair-haired toddler, also ginghamed, clinging to her skirt; a blond boy of about five in a matching shirt hanging on to the halter of a buckskin horse; two Holstein cows with calves at their sides, halters and ropes secured by Hugh MacLeod; a crate of hens squawking at a huge marmalade cat who was hissing at them; and, guarding them all as well as heaped belongings and tools, was a black and white dog with a piratical sable spot over one eye and a gently wafting feathery tail.

"They came in that emigrant car," Father explained. "We had to unload them quick because the car's needed farther on." There was a special rate for emigrant cars, which were usually left on a siding as near as possible to the moving family. They could have several days to load the boxcar before it was added to a train and brought to its destination. The conductor or some kindly folk must have watched out for the children in the passenger car, for only one person was allowed to ride with the family's belongings.

"Appealing and appalling," mused Benedict. "The animals will need a barn. Perhaps a couple of my carpenters can make one out of the old shack." Lesley still scowled at him. "All right," he surrendered. "Possibly the prospectus could mislead optimistic innocents. I've no wish to oppress a widow — she *is* a widow, Mr. Morland?"

"Very recent, sir. Her husband's shirt caught in the cylinder of a threshing machine. He was dead by the time they got it stopped. He was a hired man, and of course, the farmer could scarcely let Mrs. Lee and the children stay on."

"A pathetic story. How does she propose to maintain her brood?"

"The cows are grand milkers. She plans to sell milk and cream and butter, open a little bakery, do sewing."

Benedict gave a nod of grudging approval. "It seems she'll be a productive person, not a drag on the community. She qualifies for a business loan, and of course, her place of business can also be her home. I'll have the head carpenter work out with her what she needs. Now, if you'll excuse me, I'm going to check on how much of the roadbed's been built while I was gone."

Lesley and her father looked at each other. "Hugh MacLeod's offered Mrs. Lee his covered wagon, but it's not nearly big enough," said Ed. "She doesn't have a tent."

"Our boxcar's not big enough, either." Lesley's eye fell on the open baggage room door. "Daddy! The family can stay here till their house is built, make pallets in the freight room and cook at our place."

"Well — I guess so." She could almost see her father's station-agent set of mind click over to a neighborly view. "It's not as if we had so many passengers it would interfere, and most freight these days gets picked up on the platform. Come on, let's tell them."

"I'll make the hens a coop so they won't be so likely to make a picnic for hawks, Miz Lee," Hugh MacLeod was saying. "That couple of acres you bought behind your house lot joins Jim Kelly's and Bella Ballard's pasture. I bet that they won't mind your critters nippin' a little grass off their land till you get a fence up. In fact, here comes Micajah Schatz. We'll ask him."

Micajah said he was sure Jim and Bella wouldn't mind, and the Lee livestock could drink from the tank he'd put by the pump at the new well that had just been dug. "Can I haul your things somewhere, ma'am?" he asked Mrs. Lee.

"If you don't mind sleeping in the freight room, you're welcome to it, ma'am," said Ed. "My daughter, Lesley here, will help get you settled." He smiled, happy at being able to bring good news. "We can stow your belongings in the depot till your house gets built."

"Our house?" Deep blue eyes widened, seeming larger than they were in the thin face because of bruised-looking hollows. A tear edged from one of them to be fiercely scrubbed away as she jiggled the baby, who was flushed and whimpered fretfully. "We don't have one, Mr. Morland — just that falling-down ramshackle over there."

"You'll have a house, Mrs. Lee. Mr. Adam Benedict, the railroad builder and man who owns most of the town, agrees the prospectus was a mite misleading. If it suits you, his carpenters will turn the old shack into a barn and build you a home."

"A *new* one? I can't afford that."

"Mr. Benedict's bank will make business loans."

"A loan?" She looked frightened. "Big Tony always took care of things like that."

"Don't you worry, Mrs. Lee," said Hugh in a comforting tone. "I'll help you see about the loan and make sure you don't get cheated." He made a gesture that took in Micajah, the Morlands, and the town at large. "We'll help you."

Lesley swallowed the lump in her throat. "Of course we will. And now let's get you located and see about something to eat and drink."

"Don't you worry about the stock, ma'am," said Hugh. "I'll take the cows to their grazing if Dusty will lead the horse."

"Sally thirs'y, Mama," pleaded the little girl, peeking out from her mother's skirts where she had refuged from so many strangers.

Mrs. Lee considered for a moment. Her eyes were very bright, but her voice trembled only the slightest bit as she lifted a chin that was determined in spite of its dimple. "You're all so kind, I don't know how to thank you, but I hope I'll have a chance to give back your help." She rocked the fussing baby against her shoulder. "The calves can have all their mothers' milk this morning, but I'll have to milk tonight. After all, I'll have a house — a home — to pay for. We've never had a place of our own before."

She smiled for the first time, and at that sight, Hugh MacLeod glowed eager and joyous as a boy. He led the cattle off, Dusty at his side with the rawboned horse.

"Whether he knows it or not, Hugh's found what he came to meet the train for," Ed said in Lesley's ear. He and Micajah moved the Lees' possessions inside and spread two corn-shuck mattresses on top of each other in the baggage room. Lesley gave small Sally a cup of water from the big jug and dragged the most comfortable chair in by the bed, trunk, suitcase, and bundles.

The baby was wailing. Sweat plastered golden wisps to its face and scalp. "How can I help?" asked Lesley, feeling woefully ignorant of how to care for infants. "Would a bath make the baby cooler?"

"I think right now I'll try to feed him. He's been cranky for several days, but I think it's teething and maybe my milk isn't agreeing with him because moving's made me tired and upset." She hesitated. "But if you could help Sally go to the outhouse and give her a cracker or something, I'd be much obliged. Poor little thing's still a baby herself, but I don't have much time to see to her."

"Did you have breakfast, Mrs. Lee?" Lesley asked.

"Please — that makes me feel so old! Could you call me Susan? We had a little bread and cheese left from the nice basket Mrs. McCormick packed for us when we left yesterday morning — she's the wife of the farmer Big Tony worked for. We had to change trains and wait a long time in Wichita. I bought an apple from the train newsboy this morning and cut it in half for Dusty and Sally."

Lesley blessed the row of Van Camp's pork and beans and Campbell's soup in her food shelves. "I'll bring you bread and soup, and there's rice pudding," she said. "This evening I'll fix a proper meal."

"Oh, we can't put you to so much trouble and expense!"

"You can give us some milk," Lesley parried.

Sally was squirming, little legs pressed together. Lesley offered her hand. "Come along, honey, I'll show you where to go."

Twenty minutes later, Sally and Dusty perched on orange crates, eating noodle soup and crackers. Tabitha, the cat, and Cap, the dog, lapped up canned milk. Susan fed herself with one hand while the other supported small Tony, who drowsed against her buttoned waist.

"He acts colicky," Susan worried. "He'd nurse a little while and start to cry. Is there a doctor in Bountiful?"

She must be worried. People, especially those with money troubles, didn't call in doctors unless all home remedies had failed. "The nearest doctor's in Dodge City," Lesley said. "Would you like us to wire him? He could come on the morning train."

"Oh, bringing him all the way out here —" Susan Lee cuddled the drowsing baby. "Now we're here and everyone's being so kind, my milk ought to agree with him better."

"Why don't you all have a rest?" suggested Lesley, pulling the shade and collecting the dishes.

"I'm not sleepy!" scorned Dusty, whose freckles had much more color than his spiky sun-bleached hair. His thin chest puffed out. "Hugh said I could help him!"

"Mr. MacLeod," his mother corrected.

"He said 'Hugh'!"

"Uncle Hugh," she insisted.

"Is he my uncle?" Dusty's tone was hopeful.

"Of course not, but — well, young man, you call him that or Mr., take your pick. Don't get in his way, mind him, and be careful around that forge and anvil."

"I can go?"

"Yes, or the rest of us won't have a second's peace." He started to dash out, but his mother placed a restraining hand on his shoulder. "I'll want you to bring the cows for milking when the sun gets low. Now, where can I do that? Where will I keep the milk?"

"I'm sure the Schiller sisters will be

glad to let you leave the milk in their big tent. They're sure to want to buy a lot of it. I'll go talk to them about it while you have a rest."

"And H— *Uncle* Hugh said he'd clear out the shack and fix kind of a manger and posts where the cows can be tied till he can build proper stalls after the carpenters get through."

Susan Lee looked a little less exhausted. She glanced from the son wriggling with impatience to join his "uncle" to the small one in her arms to Sally, who had located a rag doll that had been loved into facelessness and nestled with it on the bed. "We can't have been here much over an hour," she said with a wondering smile. "But I feel like I've come home."

10

Lilibet Schiller's dour expression softened at the prospect of fresh milk. "A gallon we will take each night and morning if Mrs. Lee can spare it. Of course, she is welcome to leave it in our tent so long as it is out of the way. The baby is teething, you say, and cross? I will send some blackberry balsam. It will soothe him and settle his small stomach."

During her errands, Lesley had lifted her skirt enough to clear the uneven ground and avoid horse and mule droppings. What a quagmire this would be when it rained! If Bountiful was to be as important a town as Benedict planned, wouldn't there be sidewalks, or at least a boardwalk along the main street? Long skirts, it seemed to her, were a diabolical invention to hamper and aggravate women. Even if some man didn't accidentally squirt tobacco juice on you, it was impossible to get through the day without a badly draggled hem.

Tagged by Dusty, who was savoring a Hershey bar, Hugh MacLeod left off hammering on what must be the chicken coop situated not far from the Lee shack, where two carpenters were hard at work. The blacksmith hurried toward Lesley. "Is the wee one quieting down?"

"He's sort of napping, but he looks feverish."

Hugh tugged at a curl of his beard. "I'll pay a doctor if you have any idea of how we can get one out here."

"Susan says she'll see how Tony is in the morning."

"Kids take sick fast, get well fast — and die fast. I don't think we ought to wait."

Hugh had said *we*, not *she*, and his hazel eyes were so distressed that Lesley decided to tell him why Susan wanted to wait, though her cheeks burned as she confided the very private information to even this kind man.

He blushed, too, but nodded in relief. "That's likely the trouble. When she gets rested up, the laddie should be fine." He reached in his leather apron. "I sent Dusty up to the mercantile to get him a candy bar and to the drug-store for a bottle of Castroline. It's better than Castoria and it doesn't have morphine or opium in it."

At this rate, Susan could open a drugstore, a real one. "I'll milk the cows tonight," Hugh decreed. "In the morning, too. You tell that girl to look after herself and the little ones and leave the stock and chickens to Dusty and me and Cap. See how he's keeping an eye on them?"

The dog was indeed watching the cows, calves, and horse from a knoll. It was his job, his manner said, no matter where his humans chose to wander. Dusty chimed in importantly, "Yes, lady, you tell Mama me'n Uncle Hugh'll take care of everything!" He added quickly, "But I'll come home when it's dark. Sally's such a baby, she won't go to sleep without me pretty close."

Hugh tousled the cottony head, but his grin faded as he met Lesley's gaze. "If it looks like we need the doctor . . . If . . . well, you know, Miss Morland."

"I know. And I'd like you to call me Lesley."

"Honored, ma'am." He scuffed one laced work shoe against the other and studied the result. "You — you know how I feel about Susan Lee. Do you think I'm daft? Can it happen that fast?"

"Like lightning," Lesley said, and thought of Jim, suddenly, desperately wishing he were here, though what would he know about sick babies? She just felt that somehow he'd be able to help. Or that his presence would make her stronger.

"I'll tell Susan about the milking," she said. "When Dusty comes for supper, why don't you come along?"

The eager delight on Hugh's face changed to anxiety. "Let's wait and see how Tony is. If you have your hands full helping Susan, I'll get grub for all of us at The Sisters and bring it over. For dinner, this young feller" — another tousle of the hair — "can help me polish off the Mulligan stew I made last night."

The big man and the small boy went back to work, Dusty imitating Hugh's deliberate stride. It seemed too good to be true, that a young widow with three children could step out of a Noah's ark of a boxcar and practically fall into the arms of a man who seemed to accept the children as swiftly, as wholeheartedly, as he had their mother.

Wouldn't it be lovely if — Lesley's smile died as she crossed the tracks and heard the thin shrilling of an infant almost too sick or too weary to cry.

If strain had made Susan's milk indigestible before, it was horrid to imagine how it would taste to the baby now. Looking helpless and anguished, Lesley's father hovered outside the baggage room door. "I've wired the doctor. He'll come on the morning train. But —"

Lesley knew they were both thinking that might be too late. More than likely Tony did just have colic, something that could be alleviated by time or one of the hopefully contributed remedies she carried. "If he's not better by the time the eastbound comes through this evening," she said above the baby's wails, "I think I'd better go to Dodge with Susan and the baby."

Ed nodded. "That might be a sight better. Listen, honey, don't worry about fixing dinner. I'll open up some pork and beans and salmon."

Lesley thanked him, gave a light tap on the door, and entered. Tabitha shot past her with an indignant yowl, sprang into the window, and began to groom her striped honey and orange coat. Huddled with her doll, Sally slept in spite of the noise.

Walking back and forth, holding Tony against her shoulder, Susan tried to lull him to sleep, but the small body arced backward as if trying to escape its pain. "Maybe one of these will help." Lesley held up the medicines and read the less extravagant promises from the labels.

"How kind they all are!" Susan blinked back tears. "I've heard of Castroline. Let's try that."

He vomited it up immediately along with greenish bile. "He's so feverish," Susan lamented. "Maybe we could cool him with wet cloths. We did that with Dusty when he used to go into convulsions."

Lesley brought a pan of water and some towels. While Susan held the child, naked except for his flannel diaper, Lesley wrung out towels and held them on the small, hot body. He screamed his protest, but after a while he quieted to snuffles and accepted his teething ring. The next dose of Castroline stayed down and he slowly relaxed in Susan's arms, eyes closing. He looked so thin, so wasted. Lesley kept applying wet towels to his torso, arms, and legs, while she told Susan that Hugh would milk that evening and the milk could be kept with the Schiller sisters, who would buy several gallons.

"I can't believe people I don't even know are being so good to us," Susan marveled. "But I'll find some way to pay them all back. Dusty —"

"He's having a great time helping Hugh build the chicken coop and eat Mulligan stew."

Susan gave a tremulous smile. "I guess I don't have anything to worry about — except Tony." The fleeting smile gave way to stark fear. "He's lost so much weight, Lesley! Between not nursing or drinking to amount to anything and diarrhea and throwing up, he's just dried to his little bones."

And those, as Lesley kept wet towels on him, felt hollow as a bird's. His eyes were sunken deep in a skull that seemed much too large for the rest of him. "Susan," said Lesley, "if Tony won't nurse or drink when he wakes up, I think we'd better take him to the doctor. We can catch the evening train."

If only there were a doctor here, or a

faster way to reach one! No team could cover the forty miles in less time than it would take to wait for the train and ride it to Dodge.

The Oldsmobile! There was no road to Dodge, but there were only wagon tracks to the places Benedict traveled. If Tony wasn't markedly better when he roused, Lesley resolved to ask the builder of the town to do something for its newest family.

While Tony drowsed, Lesley rinsed out diapers. Tony was whimpering and chewing at his fists when she finished. It was more frightening than his shrieks, as if he were too weak to cry loudly. Lesley took the baby and assumed the chore of applying wet cloths to him, insisting that Susan eat, drink, and move around.

Susan was reaching for her baby in less than ten minutes. "I'm going to the camp to see if there's an automobile there that could take you to the doctor," Lesley said.

The measure of Susan's dread was that she didn't argue.

"I have to go to the second roadbed camp today." Benedict frowned from the Oldsmobile. "Bella Ballard thinks they're not doing a good job on the culverts. Have your father write a free pass for the woman on tonight's train."

"The baby's so sick! And he's so little. I — I'm afraid he may not live if he has to wait for the train."

"Oh? Have you then cared for so many infants?"

"No. But he's not getting any nourishment —"

"Miss Morland, I applaud your tender heart, but I cannot neglect vital business to drive children with upset stomachs to the doctor."

She stared at him, appalled, though he was probably only saying what ninety-nine out of a hundred successful businessmen would. "How will you feel if the baby dies?"

"That it would very likely have died even if I gave in to your preposterous wish. It sounds harsh, but I believe it's a good thing that nature weeds out the sickly."

"Anyone can get sick. Even you."

"You hope I will, don't you?"

"Sick enough so you'd have some sympathy for others."

"Sickness doesn't have that edifying

effect on me." He shrugged. "According to Matthew, I just get more demanding." He sprang down and came around to her. "I don't want you trudging back along the track. I'll drive you to the depot."

"If you won't help, there's no hurry." She avoided his hand. Bitterness left a metallic taste in her mouth. "We'll have to wait for the evening train."

"Miss Morland —" He blocked her way. She swerved around him.

"I'll never get in your automobile again," she flung at him. "Neither one of them! Never, ever!"

"I'll pay the doctor's bill and for any medicine," he called.

"And for a coffin?" she hurled over her shoulder.

Heartsick and angry, she had walked a mile when she heard the rumble, clank, and rattle of a wagon. Supposing it was one of the camp vehicles, she didn't glance back.

"Miss Lesley?"

Jim Kelly's voice flooded her with gladness and relief, though she realized even as she turned to him that, of course, he, like Micajah and Hugh and her father, was powerless to get little

Tony to the doctor faster than the evening train could.

All the same, as he leaned over to give her a hand up to the seat beside him, she felt as if half of a heavy load had shifted from her shoulders to his. She poured out the trouble as they traveled beside the tracks.

"Poor little guy," he said. "And that poor lady! But it's a good thing she landed where folks'll help her."

"It doesn't feel like we're helping much when all we can do is wait for the train!"

Jim pondered a moment. In spite of the fear that made a tight, hard ball of her stomach, Lesley wished she could trace the lean contours of his face, smooth the scar angling into his black hair. She wished she could touch the pulse of his throat, learn the rhythm of his blood and breath. She wished . . .

"Maybe we can do better than wait," Jim said.

"How? Benedict won't take her in his automobile."

"May be just as well since there's no road most of the way. What if he got stuck again? I'm thinking we'll borrow the handcar."

"The handcar?" she echoed. They

were designed to travel up and down the track, but she'd never heard of one being used to cover more than ten or fifteen miles.

"Hugh MacLeod's got a blacksmith's chest and shoulders. Rutherford will sure help, and so will Andy Hart from the livery. I'd reckon the four of us could propel that thing to Dodge in maybe three hours. Mrs. Lee and the baby can ride in the little trailer that usually carries water and tools. Could you go ask the men and tell Mrs. Lee to get ready while I leave my team with Micajah?"

"You have to eat first."

"Maybe you could make me a sandwich." He flashed her a smile that made her heart open warmly. "I'd sure like a cup of coffee, too, Miss Lesley."

She would have given him anything. Full of hope, she ran on her errands. First, Father must check with the dispatcher to make sure there were no incoming trains and that it was safe to use the handcar. In ten minutes, Susan with her sleeping or unconscious baby was seated on blankets heaped on the floor of the four-wheeled trailer car hooked to the handcar, shaded by a canvas awning rigged by the men, a bag of necessities at her feet. Hugh patted her shoulder as he and Andy Hart got in place across from Jim and Rutherford at the handles that worked back and forth to power the vehicle.

"Travel safe!" called Lilibet Schiller. She and her sisters waved starched aprons as the men started pumping the handles. "Have no worry, Mrs. Lee, I'll milk your cows."

Micajah, allowing Dusty to help water Jim's horses, shouted, "Good luck!" The Schillers flourished their handkerchiefs.

Sally, in Lesley's arm, began to cry and reach frantically toward the departing handcar. "Mama! Mama! Sally go, too!"

"You can't, honey," Lesley said. "Mama has to take Tony to the doctor, but they'll be home as soon as they can."

Sally's lips quivered. "Daddy didn't come home!"

"That was different, sweetheart. Your mama will come, she surely will."

Tears spilled from the blue eyes and Sally began to weep. "Dusty's here," Lesley tried to soothe. "Look, he's helping with the horses. Shall we go see them?"

"No!" wailed Sally. "Me scared of horsies. They gots big yellow teeth!"

Lilibet said offhandedly to Lesley, "I am in need of a girl who can sprinkle sugar and cinnamon on pieces of piecrust, one who can help mix raisins in cookie dough. If she helped me well, such a girl could have crusts and cookies and lemonade."

" 'Nough for her brother?" Sally inquired, gulping back a sob.

"Oh, I should think so, if she helps *very* nicely."

"Sally big 'nough?"

Lilibet's green eyes, no longer chill, showed flecks of gold. Strange how a smile covered the fine wrinkles and made her look years younger. "I think Sally Lee is just the correct size, *liebchen.*"

Sally pushed away from Lesley, who gratefully deposited her on the platform. "Thank you, Miss Schiller. I'll come fetch her in time for supper."

Taking Sally's hand, Lilibet said, "Ach, I think my good helper must eat in our restaurant, and her brother, too."

"Tabby and Cap can have some nice

scraps?" Sally asked.

"All they can eat," Lena said, and took the small girl's other hand.

Lesley stared after the handcar, which was getting smaller with each thrust of the handles. Hugh's prowess, gained from swinging his hammer, would never be put to better use. Her father touched her shoulder. "Guess we'd better wire Dodge so the agent can have a buggy at the station or maybe even get the doctor to meet them there." He shook his head between chagrin and admiration. "Jim Kelly's got his wits about him. I should have thought of the handcar."

"Oh, gracious!"

"What, Les?"

"Jim and Benedict are likely to fall out — again — over Jim's taking off for Dodge."

Father lifted a shoulder and dropped it. "Those two are going to have a big blowup sooner or later, child. At least this is worth it. I'll go send that wire."

Lesley and her father listened intently as, at five o'clock, the Dodge operator sent Jim's message that the doctor himself had met Susan and Tony Lee and taken them in his buggy to his office. "Will all be on morning train unless advise otherwise," the wire concluded, as Lilibet Schiller brought in neatly folded diapers and ironed garments.

"My, Mr. Kelly and Mr. MacLeod must be worn to nubs!" Lilibet exclaimed. "But they got the poor baby to the doctor three or four hours earlier than the train could, even if it's on time. I'll tell my sisters and Mr. Schatz."

"We'll let you know if we hear anything else," Lesley promised. She tidied the baggage room, giving Tabitha a scratch behind both ears, and went to the boxcar to fix supper.

Sally and Dusty ate at The Sisters and drank milk from their own cows, which Lilibet had milked. The three sisters and Micajah brought the children to the depot a little after sundown. Micajah carried Sally, who was all but asleep.

"Will you let me help take care of the horses and d'liver stuff tomorrow, Mr. Micajah?" Dusty asked.

"You bet! I hitch up early, so scoot on over soon as you've had enough breakfast to keep you trottin'." Micajah ruffled the towhead. "Don't know how I managed without a boy." Was he thinking of his twins, frozen to death when they were only a few years older than Dusty?

Lesley's eyes misted as she got Sally into her nightgown and settled her at the far side of the shuck mattress where Tabitha crouched in guardian stance. If only the feeling people had for lost loved ones could be directed to the living, who needed it, how much better that would be all the way around. She could never do things for her mother, but she could do them for others, in a fashion offering her efforts to her mother's spirit.

Dusty, without embarrassment, stripped to his drawers and curled up near the edge of the bed where Cap settled his muzzle. "Mama and the baby — they'll come back tonight?" Dusty whispered, blue eyes large and solemn.

"They'll probably come on the morning train." Lesley knelt beside him. After all, despite the exciting afternoon of "helping" Micajah, he was still a small boy among strangers. "You've got Tabitha and Cap for company, but I'll sleep there by the trunk."

"When?"

"Not too long, Dusty. Anyway, till

then, we'll be in the next room. I'll leave this door open a bit. The eastbound train'll roar through pretty soon, and you'll hear the telegraph clicking now and then. It's sort of a friendly sound."

The child's body was tense. He mumbled into his pillow, "Mama *will* come back?"

"Of course she will! Just as soon as she can." Lesley smoothed his hair, not daring to kiss him. "Goodness, she'll be proud of how you've worked with Micajah and looked after Sally!"

He held up one hand, splaying the fingers. "I'm that many! Sally's only three!"

"Yes. That's why you have to take care of her."

"Uh-huh," he said doubtfully. "But not while I help Micajah?"

"No. I'll see to her while you're busy, or maybe Aunt Lilibet and her sisters will."

"Aunt Lilibet gave us choclit cake after we ate our green beans and mashed potatoes. Aunt Lena gave Cap a nice bone. Aunt Lisa gave us each a nickel for our banks, but when I said we didn't have a bank, she said she'd get us each a piggy bank and feed them with the nickels." His brow puckered. "What's an aunt? We never had any before. No uncles, either, like Uncle Hugh."

"Sometimes aunts and uncles are your parents' brothers and sisters. Sometimes, like here, they're people who love you."

"Are you my aunt, Miss Lesley?"

Her throat tightened. "Yes, I am." That time, she kissed him.

Micajah was already in the depot. As darkness gathered, the Schiller sisters came in. So did some of the construction workers who'd heard about the sick baby.

They talked of ordinary things for the most part, but all eyes were on the sounder, and Lesley knew there was a lot of silent praying.

A little after nine, just as Lilibet and her sisters were saying good night, Lesley deciphered the message as father wrote it down.

"Tony —" Father's voice choked off. He tried to speak again, gave it up, and handed around what he'd written. BABY DEAD. UNKNOWN FEVER. RETURN MORNING TRAIN.

11

Hugh and Jim were on either side of Susan, steadying her as she got down from the train with her baby in her arms. His face was nestled to her breast. Perhaps he had died that way. Perhaps she had held him all the night long. Her eyes were red and swollen, but she seemed calm now, or dazed. Rutherford and Andy Hart followed with blankets and her little bag.

"Mama! Mama!" Sally ran to her, burrowing in her skirts. "Lesley say baby's dead!"

"Like Daddy," Dusty said. He had understood when Lesley tried to prepare them, but Sally had responded by weeping and asking, "Sally and Dusty die, too? Mama die?"

Susan let Lesley take the frail little body wrapped in a shawl. It was unnerving to feel its rigidity, as unyielding as a jointless wooden doll. Kneeling, Susan gathered both children close and held them till Dusty squirmed.

Two women, one in rather gaudy attire with a beplumed hat, the other in a perfectly tailored green traveling suit and straw hat with matching trim, had preceded Susan off the train. The plump blond younger one surveyed Bountiful with growing contempt and dismay on her pouting face, but the older watched Susan. Coming over to Lesley, the dark-eyed woman asked softly, "She's lost a baby?"

Lesley nodded and added under her breath, "Her husband was killed just a few weeks ago."

Rising, Susan held Sally, the stunned look replaced by pain, but pain that willed to live. "A minister offered to come, but I wanted just you people who've helped us so. Is — is the coffin ready?"

"I have a nice cedar chest," said Lilibet Schiller. "It's in the depot."

"The mercantile didn't have any velvet or silk to line it with," Lesley apologized. "I brought a pretty quilt, though."

The dark stranger woman said, "I have a blue velvet dress with a very full skirt. Please use it."

Rutherford Miles sucked in his breath and scribbled away. "Ellen!" shrieked

248

the blond woman. "Have you lost your mind? That dress came from Paris — and at your age, you won't be getting many more like it!"

"At my age, Tess, it doesn't matter." The woman called Ellen smiled wearily at her companion before she said to Susan, "Please. I want very much for you to use the dress. I lost a baby once. They buried him before I was conscious, so I never even saw him."

"I'm sorry." Susan took the older woman's hand and pressed it. "You're kind, truly kind. I'll be glad to wrap Tony in your dress."

"All aboarrrd!" the conductor shouted. "All aboard for Pueblo and Denver!"

Tess grabbed Ellen's arm. "Come on, Ellen! Let's get out of here! No place to stay — no trade except construction gangs and hayseeds! It sounded like a swell town, but look at it!"

Ellen gazed around at the neighbors gathered at the depot to meet and comfort a mother with a dead child. She looked at the train. She glanced at the tents and the start of buildings. "Go on to Denver, Tess," she said. "I'm staying here."

"Here?" Disbelief pitched darkened

249

eyebrows high. "Ellen, you're crazy!"

"As you say, my dear, at my age —" Ellen's smile was suddenly less tired. She gave her incredulous friend a swift kiss and a little shove. "Hurry!"

Tess cast her a horrified look, shrugged her elegant shoulders, and shouted at Ed Morland, who was trundling off the baggage cart. "Wait, mister! Put the two biggest trunks back on the train. And I'll need a ticket to Denver!"

There was a knoll on Jim and Bella's property where wild roses grew, and this was the spot Susan chose for Tony's grave. While Hugh and Jim and Micajah dug it, she asked Rutherford Miles to take a photograph of her holding the baby. To Lesley this seemed macabre until Susan, caressing the soft curls, said, "I'm afraid I'll forget how he looks if I don't have a picture. He lived such a little while. I want him to have that, at least — for me to remember."

Ellen Tremayne nodded. Although she had been a total stranger when she stepped off the train two hours ago, by sharing this grief, she already seemed to belong. "I wish I'd had a picture of my baby. For a long time I couldn't believe he was dead. In fact, I always wondered —" She bit her lip on the rest of that thought.

Even to Lesley it was apparent that Ellen belonged to that profession patronized by Benedict when he went to Denver. Had her baby really died or had outraged parents or some ruthless madam smothered it? Unlike Tess's, Ellen's voice, language, and deportment were ladylike. In spite of faint lines at her eyes and well-shaped mouth, she was still a handsome woman, and her deep brown eyes were magnificent.

Rutherford Miles clearly thought so, too. As soon as he had carefully taken several portraits of Susan and her baby, he watched Ellen Tremayne with fascinated admiration. Confidence was something he had never seemed to lack, but he approached her shyly, pad and pencil in hand.

"Mrs. Tremayne," he ventured, "I've worked on papers in a number of cities, but it's completely outside my experience for a lady to give a Parisian gown for such a purpose. Forgive me if I intrude, but why —"

She gave him a dazzling smile, a smile that made her far more alluring than the younger, fuller-bosomed Tess. "I won't need Parisian gowns in Bountiful, sir. But you could put an item in your paper saying that Ellen Tremayne, modiste and milliner, is familiar with the latest fashions and can sew anything from everyday wrappers to wedding dresses."

"You — you're opening a shop?" His dark eyes were luminous.

"As soon as it can be built on a lot I intend to purchase as soon as possible."

"Be assured, ma'am, that it will be my pleasure to feature your business as soon as you're established. Meanwhile, if I can be of service in any way . . ."

His voice trailed off as the men returned from digging the grave. Susan, very pale, went into the depot. The fragrant cedar chest lay open with deep blue velvet heaped loosely into it and draped over the sides and lid. Susan kissed the child. It seemed very hard for her to place him on the rich velvet. She did, finally, and stumbled away, sobbing, her other children clutching her skirts.

Lesley, Ellen Tremayne, and the Schiller sisters looked at each other through tears, and tears wet the sumptuous cloth as they folded it over the pallid face, tiny hands, and wasted body. They closed the lid and locked the ornate clasp as the men came in.

The gravediggers had washed and put on their coats. Now, joined by Father, Hugh, Jim, and Micajah, each lifted a corner of the chest, raised it to their shoulders, and proceeded toward the gentle slope. It was a half mile away, but no one had suggested hauling the casket in a wagon. "Let's carry the wee lad," Hugh said gruffly. "It's — friendlier."

The women followed. Oddly, it was Ellen Tremayne who walked with her arm around Susan. Lesley carried Sally, who was big-eyed and hushed. Dusty clung to Lilibet's hand, needing for a little while to be a small boy again.

When they reached the knoll, the men rested the casket on the buffalo grass. Hugh took a harmonica out of his pocket and played sweet and sad as the prairie wind with the song of the meadowlark winging in and out.

"This is the Lord's lamb," he said then. "If you know the Shepherd's Psalm, let's say it for the laddie and his mother and brother and sister."

The ancient words sounded in a blending of voices, men's deep, women's softer and higher. "He leadeth me beside the still waters, he maketh me to lie down in green pastures, he restoreth my soul . . ." They offered the Lord's Prayer, and then Lilibet drew her sisters forward.

"We know a German lullaby," Lilibet said to Susan. "It tells how the stars in heaven are the sheep, and the moon a shepherd boy. If you would like that —"

"Oh, we would! Thank you."

Lena's and Lisa's sopranos wreathed Lilibet's rich alto as they sang the words their mother must have sung to them back before the troubles came that grooved Lilibet's face. *"Schlaf, Kindchen, schlaf, am Himmel ziehen die Schaf . . ."* The listeners couldn't understand the song, but the tenderness was unmistakable.

"Sing it again," Hugh said, and played his harmonica with them as Micajah and Jim looped ropes around the casket and gently lowered it.

Sally, led by Dusty, had gathered purple coneflowers, brilliant orange butterfly weed, and big golden sunflowers.

They dropped these on the casket. Susan added a few wild roses Hugh cut for her with his pocketknife. Then, hoisting Sally to his shoulder, other hand under Susan's elbow, he guided the family away.

Only when they were out of earshot did Micajah, Jim, and Ed start filling in the grave.

It was a good thing the other children needed Susan's attention and she had the cows to care for. Hugh offered to go on milking them, but she said she had put her neighbors out too much as it was. "I'll never forget how you men pumped that handcar to get us to the doctor."

Hugh hung his head. "It didn't do any good."

"Yes, it did. I feel a lot better because if Tony had died here, I'd always wonder if the doctor could have saved him." Susan's gaze rested on Tony's slope. "I'll never leave here now."

"I'm mighty glad to hear that," Hugh said. He hesitated, decided it wasn't the time or place to speak his mind, and strode off to his forge with Dusty at his heels.

Jim, who had finished hauling bridge timbers for the second construction camp and was now freighting supplies to the grading crews as they moved south, had stopped by the depot several times, but the Lees were still there, and Ellen Tremayne, while her house was built, was sleeping on a bench curtained off from the waiting room.

That left no chance for private conversation, but when his gray eyes touched her, Lesley felt like a flower opening to the sun. Then she felt like one deprived of light when his face closed and he quickly looked away. After the way Benedict had refused to take Tony to the doctor, how could Jim possibly believe she welcomed Benedict's attentions?

If there were ever a chance for them to talk alone! Ironically, after the weeks of solitude that had sent Lesley to the prairie dogs for company, the Morlands were never by themselves these days.

"One good thing about folks being around the depot is that it sure ought to scare off train robbers," Ed said.

"Oh, Daddy! Train robbers!" Lesley thought of dime novels with bandits, lower faces covered by bandannas, galloping alongside a train. "Surely that can't happen in Bountiful."

"Why not? A payroll for the building gangs comes in every two weeks. The Dalton brothers held up plenty of trains before they got killed trying to rob two banks in Coffeyville eight years ago — good-lookin' men, they were, Bob and Grat, tall, yellow-haired, and blue-eyed. Bill Doolin robbed trains till Heck Thomas shotgunned him four years ago after he broke out of jail down in Oklahoma, and the Jennings Gang robbed trains down there till they got sent to the penitentiary three years ago."

Lesley knew about all these famous outlaws, of course, but it was hard to imagine the familiar depot as a place of violence and danger. She laughed and said teasingly, "Well, if having people around keeps robbers away, Daddy, we don't have anything to worry about. There were eleven people here for supper last night, counting Sally and Dusty."

"Is it a bother to you, Les?"

"Oh no, I like it! It's like a picnic and it's no more work for me since everyone brings their own dishes and something to share."

Her only regret was that she never got to see Jim alone. Like Bella, he spent most nights camped by the road, but when he was in Bountiful, he joined the supper group that spontaneously formed each evening on the platform and spread their food on the table made by sheet-covered planks laid across two packing crates. The variety made each meal like a party, and each household ate better than it could have on its own.

Susan's hens were laying again, comfortable in their new coop. Their eggs, milk, cream, butter, buttermilk, and cottage cheese were Susan's welcome additions to the common meals. Ellen Tremayne created marvelous soups from dried beans and peas, leftovers and canned tomatoes, corn and oysters, including vichyssoise from potatoes and onions, and French onion soup with croutons from onions and hard bread. She concocted fruit puddings that she said were in the Scandinavian manner from canned fruits and cornstarch, and she taught Lesley and Susan how to make Saratoga chips so that the potatoes came out crisp, not greasy.

Hugh told the women not to cook one

night and brought over a huge kettle of Mulligan stew and a Dutch oven of golden cornbread. Micajah visited his widow lady friend and returned with enough squash, melons, corn, green beans, peppers, and tomatoes to enliven their meals for days.

Susan baked the bread, long, crunchy sourdough loaves and whole wheat. "Miss Lilibet wants me to bake for the restaurant when I have my own kitchen," she said, and added in a tone of wonder, "It doesn't seem right, but with the milk and baking, I'll earn more than Big Tony could working hard on the farm with me helping." Her deceptively dimpled chin lifted. "Farming's a good life if you own your land. If you don't, you work your heart out for someone else and don't know where you'll be one year to the next. If Sally or Dusty farm, I hope I can give them a start on their own place."

One child had all the land he'd ever need, a small plot enclosed by a wrought-iron fence fashioned by Hugh MacLeod into roses and lilies and vines. He had also contrived a marker in the shape of a lamb with Tony's name and brief dates engraved on it. Lesley helped

Susan plant wildflower seeds on the raw mound, and there was already the clump of wild prairie roses visited by butterflies that looked like winged flowers.

"I learned that pretty lullaby from Miss Lilibet," Susan told Lesley as they walked back from planting the flowers. "I hope Tony can hear it." She shielded her eyes and watched a vehicle stop outside the depot. "Gracious, is that a horseless carriage?"

"It's Adam Benedict's Oldsmobile." Lesley's tone was grim. She had never told Susan that the town builder had refused to drive Tony to the doctor.

"Oh, I hope he'll let me keep the property," Susan worried. "It's been a big expense to build the new house."

"Maybe it'll teach him to be more careful about the wording of his prospectuses."

Benedict had tossed his gray silk duster over the seat. Now, as he approached, impeccable in a gracefully cut dark green Prince Albert coat and matching trousers, he swept off his steel gray crusher hat with a brim curled stylishly on the sides.

"Mrs. Lee? I'm Adam Benedict. Please

accept my sincere condolences in your grievous loss." His tone held just the right measure of sympathetic melancholy. "I'm sorry that your arrival in Bountiful was marred by such distress, but it's good news that you're already taking your place among our town's productive citizens." He smiled, not too fulsomely. "In Miss Morland, you have an invaluable friend, as I'm sure you know."

"Of course I do, Mr. Benedict. Thank you for your sympathy. Everyone's been very kind."

Except you, Adam Benedict, you smooth hypocrite! thought Lesley. He knew she would never tell on him and harrow up Susan's grief.

"I'd like to express my support in a concrete way." He reached inside his coat and produced a legal-looking document affixed with an impressive seal. "This is the deed to your property, the previously existing structure — which seems to have been turned into a creditable enough barn — and the house being raised to fulfill the wording of the prospectus."

"You can't give me the deed now, sir. It will take years to pay off the mortgage."

"Please, Mrs. Lee! You'll pay by being

a worthwhile resident of the caliber I want in my town, by rearing your children here, by building the future." He placed the deed in her hand and turned the full glow of his smile on her. "I consider this an excellent investment in Bountiful."

Her eyes searched him. Perhaps she was wondering if he might expect favors in return for his generosity. "Thank you, Mr. Benedict. I appreciate not being under pressure and I think it's fair enough for you to build my house since the prospectus advertised a livable dwelling. I will pay the mortgage as I can, though. I'd like to begin by supplying your cook with butter, cream, and eggs."

He inclined his silver head. "Henri will be ecstatic. Keep your own accounts, dear lady." He fell in step beside them. "Miss Morland, I have a document for you, too."

She hadn't seen him since the day almost two weeks ago when he refused to take the baby to Dodge. "Is it a mortgage for the prairie dog town?" she asked in a carefully neutral voice.

"That's what it is." He got another paper from inside his coat. "If you and your father will stop by the bank office and sign it, it'll make you, as soon as a nominal sum is paid, the sole proprietors of eighty acres of prairie dog mounds."

"Thank you."

"Don't mention it." The full lips quirked. "It's always a pleasure to do business with such a gracious lady."

To her annoyance, she blushed at that, but she had no intention of pretending a cordiality she didn't feel. They had reached the depot. Bowing to Susan, he said, "I'm sure you'll excuse us, Mrs. Lee, while we discuss the mortgage."

Before Lesley could bolt, he grasped her elbow and turned her toward the Oldsmobile. "Could we take a drive, Miss Morland?"

"We could not." It was impossible to free herself without an undignified struggle. "I told you I'd never drive with you again and I meant it."

"Then we'll stroll along the platform. Could I invite you into my abode for an iced lemonade?"

"No, thank you."

He sighed. "You can't actually blame me for that infant's death?"

"I blame you for not trying to help."

"If the automobile suffered no mishaps, we might have reached Dodge an hour and a half sooner than the handcar."

"You didn't know Jim Kelly was going to think of the handcar. You expected us to wait for the evening train."

"That kind of foolishness is exactly why Kelly works for me and not the other way around."

Lesley did wrest away from Benedict then. "And why you can afford to make grand gestures to Susan Lee! It makes me sick! You know none of us will tell her and she'll be grateful —"

"I'm not concerned with Susan Lee's opinion."

"There's not much you can do about mine."

"Truly?" One eyebrow lifted. "That stings, sweet Lesley, especially since to please you, I've abandoned the excellent idea of making a zoo of the prairie dog town."

"I'm glad you dropped the notion, but it doesn't change my opinion of you since you still don't see anything wrong with putting coyotes and pronghorns in cages."

"I thought," he said so lugubriously that she couldn't wholly maintain her ire, "that women loved to reform men. Look at the challenge you have with me!"

She shook her head, unable to restrain a grudging laugh. "You're too much of a challenge for me, Mr. Benedict."

His eyes narrowed. "I suppose Kelly's handcar exploit, useless as it was, makes him more than ever your hero."

"He thought of something that could have made a difference. *He tried.*"

Benedict shrugged. "Kelly's a born champion of lost causes, my dear. He'll try, yes. But he'll lose. So what's the point?"

"That he tried. That he cared."

The entrepreneur's broad face hardened. "If sentimental fumbling is what you admire, Miss Morland, I can't oblige you." With an abrupt nod, he swung around and took the few paces to his Oldsmobile. Matthew came rushing from the depot to crank the engine.

That should settle that! Lesley thought. There must be a limit even to Benedict's pursuit of something he couldn't have. If she'd fallen into his arms at his first advance, he'd already be tired of her.

"Daddy," she called, entering the depot. "Let's go to the bank and sign this paper before Benedict changes his mind!"

Bella and Jim both drove in that night. Their and Micajah's contribution to the common suppers had arrived from Sears, Roebuck the day before, a giant crate addressed to THE DEPOT DINING ROOM. It yielded a ten-pound cheese, a twenty-pound box of crackers, two gallon cans of honey, ten pounds of roasted mixed nuts, ten pounds of African Java coffee, and two cases each of Campbell's soup and Van Camp's pork and beans.

"You ordered far too much expensive food! You don't join us that often!" Lesley protested as the three freighters strolled across the tracks, Bella in the middle. She did a man's work well, but Micajah and Jim still treated her with as much deference as practicality allowed.

"We sure enjoy it when we do," said Bella. "The Schillers are overrun with hungry galoots and I'm glad to have a change from the kind of grub I scorch on the trail." She grinned at Jim and poked him in the ribs. "Hey, pardner, has Benedict talked to you?"

"Not lately."

"That's funny. He offered me three times what our outfit's worth. Said it'd be more efficient for him to own the teams and wagons and hire teamsters who'd stick to their jobs rather than take off on private business when the mood struck them. I asked him did he mean private business like taking a baby to the doctor and told him whether we sold was up to you."

Jim looked grimly amused. "Guess he knew what I'd say."

"Well, pardner, if we're not retirin', my Mollie mule has. She purely loves followin' Dusty and moochin' her way around town, visitin' here and there. She just don't want to be harnessed up anymore." The exasperation in Bella's tone mellowed into affection. "She's been a dandy, hauled her share of hundreds of thousands of pounds through sandhills and quagmires for the last sixteen years. I sure don't have the heart to beat her — not that it does any good to beat a mule. She's earned her rest. But I've got to get a new lead critter."

"Miz O'Brien, my widder lady friend, has a purty good mule she might sell," said Micajah, filling his plate and sitting down on the edge of the platform next to Dusty. The boy slipped an occasional morsel to Cap or the self-emancipated Mollie, who loitered across the track by the water tank, evidently believing that she was no longer limited to the company of her four-legged former associates. Tabitha reclined on the ticket window, her tail a languid and infrequent pendulum.

"I was thinkin' I'd look for a mule in Dodge," Bella said. Color brightened her cheeks. She looked a bit flustered as she glanced around the group of neighbors. She avoided Ed Morland's eyes in an embarrassed way that sent a ping of alarm through Lesley. "I — we've got a couple of announcements —"

It wasn't just twilight that made her face look young, shy and joyful as she flourished her cup toward the man descending from the private car. "Here comes Henri — I mean, Henry!"

"What do you mean, *Henry?*" demanded Ed. "That's Onray Champagne with his pointy little beard any decent man would be ashamed of and —"

"He's the man I'm going to marry!" Bella flashed. At the shock in Morland's face, she said contritely, "I'm sorry, Ed. I didn't mean to blurt it out that way, but — well, you see —"

"Yeah. He's been bringin' you ice and carrying on the way those Frenchies do and waxin' his beard and —"

"Hold on, Ed." The cook's accent was pure cowboy. Instead of his apron, Henri wore a dilapidated old leather vest stained with the smoke of many campfires and dust of many trails. "I'm no more French than you be, and Bella's known it since we started gettin' serious."

"A phony's worse than a Frenchie!"

"Now, you just take it easy, Ed," cautioned Henri. "I sure understand your bein' disappointed, but there's no use callin' names."

"Does Mr. Benedict know his fancy French cook's not French?"

"I just told him. He says he don't care as long as the grub's good — and I *can* cook French. That's not phony."

"Now, how did that happen, Onray?" Ed's tone was sarcastic. "Guess you studied in Pa-ree?"

"Sure did. And from now, just call me Henry. Henry Cantrell. You folks go on with your suppers and I'll tell you how it was." His gaze moved from Jim and Micajah back to Bella, where it rested fondly. "We've traveled the same trail into Dodge, but I did it cookin' for cattle drives till blizzards, barbed wire, quarantine laws, and railroads buildin' into the Texas plains put an end to that along in the mid-eighties. That was when I joined up with a Wild West show and toured France and England doin' trick ropin'. In Paris" — he grinned at Ed — "in Paris, sure enough, I got a little under the weather. The show manager left me enough money for the trip home, but I drank that up. So I sashayed into an eatin' place and offered to teach the chef how to cook cowboy style."

"Did you really?" laughed Ellen Tremayne. "What a brilliant idea, Mr. Cantrell!"

He nodded modestly. "First thing you knew, cowboy fixin's at Le Cowboy was the crème de crème. All the highfalutin young crowd hung out there, eatin' thick steaks and gravy and sourdough biscuits. I taught Charles cowboy cookin' and he taught me French."

"Sounds like you should have stayed there," Ed said.

"I sure made more money than I could spend. Saved some in spite of myself. After about a year, though, in spite of pretty women and good cheap wine, I got a cravin' for the plains. Told Charles I was goin' home and buyin' a little ranch."

"Yep," said Ed. "That's some ranch you got in that private car."

Loftily ignoring his chagrined rival, Henry smiled nostalgically at his enthralled listeners. "Kissed me on both cheeks, Charles did, and gave me a hefty check. 'Hen-ree,' he says to me like a father, 'here a cowboy cook is a sensation, but in your country they must be like — what you say — thick as fleas on a shaggy dog. So remember, if you need money in America, a French chef can earn beaucoup.' "

"Thought you had money," grumbled Ed.

Lesley was embarrassed for him. He was being a poor loser. Of course, it had been terribly sudden. For the courtship to have advanced to this stage, Henry must have been borrowing a horse and riding out to meet Bella along the trail while her mules grazed in the early afternoon or at the night stops.

Henry gave a philosophical shrug. "Before I got far enough west to buy that ranch, the money plumb evaporated."

"Into whiskey fumes," Ed muttered.

"One way and another," Henry conceded mildly. Winners can afford magnanimity. "Saw Mr. Benedict's ad in a St. Louis paper. When I heard what the pay was, I hired on and started savin' for that ranch again." Henry beamed at his intended. "Now that I got the best reason in the world to settle down, I just plunked all my savin's in on an old ranch a little north of here."

"You quitting me, Bella?" asked Jim, looking worried for the first time.

"Not for a good long while. We're both goin' to work and pay off the land. Then we got to stock it." She chuckled at her partner. "By the time I can quit, son, they may be makin' wagons that have engines like them dratted horseless carriages."

"When they do, I'll make my living

hauling them out of the mud or wherever they decide to break down," Jim scoffed. He raised his coffee cup. "But here's to your happiness! Henry, you're getting one of the best teamsters that ever drove a wagon to Texas and back."

"We'll give you a shivaree they'll hear all the way to Dodge," promised Micajah. His bushy eyebrows crinkled. "You're a lucky man, Henry Cantrell. Don't you forget it!"

"No chance of that." Henry eyed his wife-to-be adoringly and took her hand. "If I get out of line, Bella can flick off my whiskers one at a crack."

"Wish she'd start with that funny little beard," Ed snorted. He stalked inside the depot and didn't come back out.

Lesley thought of following but decided he needed time alone to get over the shock. People did seem to be pairing off, she thought, as she glanced around. Hugh sat protectively by Susan, little Sally falling asleep in his arms. On this still almost-frontier, few except the Wellivers would criticize a young widow's marrying less than a year after her bereavement when it would give two children such a good stepfather. Ellen Tremayne smiled at some remark of Rutherford Miles's as he brought her lemonade and some of the chocolate mousse she had made that day.

What her father ought to do was start dropping by The Sisters, Lesley decided, suppressing a pang. Bella was so merry and likable that Lesley had never felt jealous of his interest in her, but she discovered that she did feel differently at the prospect of his forming another attachment, desirable as she knew that was. Lilibet might be a bit too stern, Lisa too young, but Lena was the right age and laughed a lot.

Father had been so smitten with Bella that he hadn't paid any attention to the other women. That had to be remedied. There was, Lesley told herself, no use in brooding over someone you couldn't have.

Like Jim Kelly? Involuntarily she looked at him. Had his eyes rested on her, or had she only imagined it, in one brief second before he turned away?

12

By the time shimmering wedges of wild geese called high above on their southward flight, Bountiful was really a town, serving not only the railroad builders but its own people and the scores of farmers attracted by Benedict's cheap land and offer of Turkey Red seed wheat for that fall's planting. They must have been encouraged by the extra wheat cars passing through. The Santa Fe line about eighteen miles north was running several special wheat trains every day. Elevators were so full in western Kansas that grain was piled on the ground till it could be shipped.

This presaged well for Bountiful, for wheat would always be the make-it-or-break-it crop of that region. Often financed by generous loans, now there were more substantial frame businesses than tents. Several brick buildings were going up besides the Citizens Bank of Bountiful, which was temporarily housed in the most imposing wood structure with the longest hitching rack in town.

Presbyterians had Bible reading and hymns there Sunday mornings, and Methodists held forth in the afternoon. Neither denomination had enough members to build a church yet. The population of Bountiful was still mostly single, not very pious men. An attempt to pool Methodist and Presbyterian resources with those of the few stray Episcopalians, Lutherans, and Baptists in order to build a community church came to naught when Mrs. Welliver let slip her view that Methodists were too lenient with sinners and she couldn't imagine being edified by a minister of that faith. Thus, till the town acquired a larger class of devout citizens, the bank's hitching rack was as occupied Sunday as on any day of the week.

The overflow of buggies and wagons drew up to the hitching posts or racks outside every place of business: two blacksmiths; two wagon shops; the large livery stable located between two hotels; two harness shops; three feed stores; two barbers, one of whom did shoe repairs; a laundry; four drugstores, where filling self-written prescriptions for "medicinal" spirits seemed to be the main function; two lumberyards; two hardware stores; two meat markets; three grocers; two mercantiles; a lawyer on either side of the real estate office; a furniture store; another restaurant in addition to The Three Sisters; The Kurtchner Disc-Plow Manufacturing Company; the brick factory, and several home businesses like Ellen Tremayne's Millinery and Dressmaking — Also Gentlemen's Shirts, situated cozily between The Three Sisters and *The Bountiful Banner.* Rutherford Miles had artistically painted the sign displayed in scrolled wrought-iron brackets fashioned by Hugh MacLeod outside Susan's little white house with blue-gray shutters and trim: Lee's Family Bakery. Rutherford made the same fancy lettering on the small wagon Hugh had repaired.

Not long after the morning train chugged westward, Susan helped Sally into the wagon, Dusty scrambled up, and Buck trotted along Main Street, often whickering to other horses hitched along the way or drinking at the trough by the town well. They were usually escorted by Mollie, the retired white mule, who was so fond of Dusty. At The Three Sisters, Dusty carried in eggs and butter or cream while Susan brought a gallon of fresh milk. Sally descended to "help" her aunts Lilibet, Lisa, and Lena while her mother and brother delivered plump loaves of bread and cinnamon rolls to their customers.

"When I can afford it, I'm going to build a separate bakery," Susan confided to Lesley. "I hope someone moves here who can help me bake. People ask for pies and cakes, especially the builders, but I don't have time to make more than I do." She shook her head in wonderment. "It doesn't seem right that I'm earning more alone than Big Tony and I did together on the farm, but I think he'd be glad."

"Of course he would, and proud of you, too," Lesley said. "Those are really becoming outfits Ellen made for you."

"Mrs. Welliver sniffed about my not wearing mourning, but I don't have any black, and besides, it's not very practical when you're milking cows and baking." With pardonable satisfaction, Susan surveyed her striped blue skirt and matching shirtwaist over which she wore a ruffled white pinafore with blue trim. "Ellen made me a green stripe just like this and four pinafores. I put on a pinafore for deliveries. That way I look fresh and clean but can wear my suits longer. And it's wonderful to use your washing machine! No more bending over a scrub board or stirring sheets in the big copper boiler on top of the stove!"

"It is a lot easier. One of these days maybe we won't even have to turn the handle to swish the load around or run things through the wringer."

"I don't mind that so much," Susan said with a wry grin. "What I despise is filling up the machine and rinse tubs and emptying them. Washing and iron-ing are the worst jobs a woman has — or maybe it seems that way because everything just gets dirty again."

"Children go through heaps of clothes." Lesley spoke before she thought, and then could have bitten her tongue, remembering a little blue-eyed boy who would never be scolded for getting his things dirty.

Susan leaned over to give Dusty a hand up. "I'm lucky to have two young ones to wash for," she said, and Lesley could almost read the rest of her thought: *and work and live for.*

After losing her husband and baby within a month, it must seem to Susan that raising her children was her main purpose in life. However, Hugh, though he clearly respected her grief, was not the man to let her wither up with mourning. Lesley didn't think Bella's wedding gown was the last one Ellen would make before the geese winged south again next year.

Would Ellen ever sew Lesley a bride dress? For just a moment, she let herself dream, imagined Jim standing close beside her as they made their vows. That day would never come, though, if he remained so distant. If it was because of Benedict —

Her father stepped out of the depot. "Will you take over for a while, Les? I'm going to the mercantile for some shoe blacking and stop at the barber's for a haircut."

"Take your time," she said. "Why don't you stop at The Sisters for pie and coffee?"

"Hope I'll come back in a better mood?" he asked with a wry twitch of his lips. "I'm sorry I've been such a grouch, honey. Fact is, I could stand losing out to a Frenchie. Everybody knows they're the devil with women. But to have my time beat by a plain old cowboy cook —"

"Not so plain," Lesley comforted. "He was a roper with a Wild West show, and he *did* live and cook in Paris."

"It was the silly little beard that got her," Ed brooded. "That and plenty of ice in her lemonade."

"I'm not the only one who thinks you're handsomer than Henry," Lesley soothed. "Didn't Lilibet Schiller bring you cherry strudel because you sent a telegram for her after hours?"

"The eldest Miss Schiller scares me to death," her father admitted. "Those cat green eyes of hers go right through a man and out the other side. Anyhow, she must be nearly forty."

"What's wrong with that?"

One thing that outraged Lesley from the time she was old enough to notice was the way middle-aged and older men usually acquired younger wives, shunning widows and maiden ladies of their own years. Not so long ago, respectable single women of any age were scarce on the frontier, but Bountiful had attracted an unusual number of older ones, though only Susan, Lena Schiller, and Lesley herself were under twenty-five.

"Nothing's wrong with being forty-three." Ed sounded defensive. "It's the prime of life for a man. But — well, drat it, Les, I want a woman with spirit!"

"Miss Lilibet has plenty of that."

"Not the kind I want," he groused. "For Pete's sake, Les, don't start trying to marry me off!"

Bella picked that inopportune moment to appear in the open door of Ellen's house, pirouetting in a dress of pale blue-green chiffon with a matching veil.

"At least she's not crazy enough to get married in white," Ed said. He added bitterly, "I wonder if she's getting a new wig like she did for her other husbands."

"She says Henry likes this one," Lesley said. "Anyway, remember, her third bridegroom died on their wedding day. It's not as if she wore yellow curls much for him."

Her father snorted. Lesley wished there weren't any drugstores so temptingly close. "Do you have your notes ready to lead the book discussion tonight?" she asked.

"Rutherford's going to do it."

"But, Daddy! You were going to have such fun showing how *The Wonderful Wizard of Oz* is really about Populism!"

"Rutherford's the one who tipped me to that in the first place. I'd never have read a children's book otherwise."

"I loved reading it to Dusty and Sally without trying to figure out any parables. What wonderful creatures Mr. Baum dreamed up — the Scarecrow, Tin Woodman, and the Cowardly Lion!"

"Well, aren't they still wonderful if you take the Scarecrow for farmers who have more brains than they believe they do, the Tin Woodman for working men chopped to bits and used up by big business, and Dorothy for the average well-meaning person who'd like to help ordinary folks like the Munchkins?" Father laughed sourly. "William Jennings Bryan is the Cowardly Lion, all right. Roars big, but he doesn't have any more chance of defeating McKinley now than he did in 'ninety-six. There just aren't that many votes in the rural South and West."

"McKinley's the Wizard of Oz?"

"You bet he is. He's backed by all the

East's money and power. But just in case that's not enough, Teddy Roosevelt's campaigning so hard for him all over the country that McKinley can just stay in Washington."

Lesley hesitated. She wished her father would reassure her that he had no intention of buying anything but shoe blacking. He'd promised her at Sunflower, though, not to drink again. She didn't want to annoy him or make him think she didn't trust him. Still, she couldn't help considering it a bad omen that he'd surrendered leading Bountiful's first Literary, something he'd looked forward to ever since Rutherford handed him a copy of the book that had been published a little over a month ago.

The telegraph chattered. She hurried to take the message while her father crossed the tracks and walked down the street. When he returned in reasonable time in a better temper, she was much relieved and told herself she couldn't get nervous every time he had an errand near the drugstores, which were all in the far end of town close to the builders' camp.

Washing and household chores kept

her so busy the rest of the day that she saw her father only briefly at dinner. Because of the Literary, those gathering on the platform for supper didn't linger but took their dishes and leftovers home, planning to return after the eastbound rumbled through.

Bella was not among them, having left on a freighting trip after her dress fitting, but Lesley was glad to see Jim Kelly joking with her father, who, thank goodness, seemed in better spirits tonight than he had since Bella's announcement.

It was a shame that he wasn't going to launch Bountiful's Literary Society, but maybe he'd join in the discussion. Jim's face turned unreadable as Lesley came to take her father's plate. What was the matter with him, anyway? Sometimes he seemed to want to be around her, though he seemed careful not to get too close. Other times, like now, you'd think he suspected her of having some not very nice disease.

"You get ready for the program, Les," Father said benignly. "I'll take care of orders for the train." His breath carried an unusual spicy fragrance. He was fond of ginger creams and had probably treated himself to some when he went to the mercantile.

Lesley hurried through the dishes, nettled at Jim's cool behavior. It wasn't ladylike to ask a man what he felt about you, but that was a stupid rule! Why shouldn't she ask when her life and happiness were involved?

Out of her small wardrobe, she recklessly selected a ruffled white shirtwaist that had taken half an hour to iron. It gave a fresh look to her brown polka dot skirt. As she brushed her unruly hair and pinned it up to disguise the forehead she considered too high, she stared into mirrored eyes the color of autumn leaves and came to a decision.

The next time she could make an opportunity to speak to Jim alone, she was going to ask him point-blank what was the matter with him — or her, if that was the problem. If *he* didn't feel that sweet magic that pulsed between them when their eyes met in unguarded moments, if *he* didn't feel as if he'd been running hard when their hands brushed accidentally, the sooner she knew it, the better. It would be a long time, if ever, before she could care remotely as much for any other man as she did for Jim, but if he couldn't love her, she would command herself to battle this yearning, smother each longing impulse the moment it arose.

After her rootless childhood, she had dreamed of a home with a man she loved, of belonging to a real family and a certain place. Rather than marry without love, she'd stay single. Exciting and magnetic as Adam Benedict was, he might have, with persistence and imagination, overwhelmed her defenses, but she was safe from him now. She couldn't forget that he'd refused to help a dying baby.

Luckily, she could make her living as a telegrapher. Bountiful was her place, including the prairie dog town she was committed to protect. She'd watched the town grow from the depot and abandoned shacks; she had friends who were almost like family, especially Susan and Ellen, Micajah and Bella. Yes, Bella. Father was just going to have to make peace with that.

Without Jim, the years ahead looked bleak and interminable, but how dared she moan when Susan with her tragic double loss carried on so bravely; when the Schiller sisters fed hungry men every day, but never their own husbands; when Ellen Tremayne stepped off a train and, in an instant, chose to build a new life among strangers; when Micajah and Bella, after savage losses, still lived with gusto and courage — no, this wasn't a community in which to nurture self-pity.

She'd confront Jim Kelly as soon as she could and, with him or without him, get on with her life. She tossed a rust brown shawl around her shoulders and blew out the lamp.

The platform benches had been brought inside. People who owned chairs or stools that could be handily carried ranged them next to sturdy apple boxes. Over by the bookshelves, Rutherford Miles was urging Susan to read Mark Twain's *Personal Recollections of Joan of Arc* and saying it wouldn't be long till he'd read *The Adventures of Tom Sawyer* to Dusty.

Lena Schiller appropriated George du Maurier's *Trilby* as if she hoped Lilibet wouldn't notice, but Agatha Welliver's pinched mouth compressed even tighter. "I can't believe you're reading such trash, Miss Schiller. No decent girl would be an artists' model anywhere, let alone in Paris! And then for that nasty Hungarian Svengali to make her into an opera singer — the whole thing's silly, wicked garbage." She turned her pale, hard gaze on Lilibet. "I'm flabbergasted, Miss Schiller, that you don't keep an eye on what your young sister's reading."

"And I am flab— gas— gasterflabbed — no, astonished, Mrs. Welliver, that you stick your funny little nose in other people's affairs! My sister is a woman grown, she earns her living, she is modest and worthy." Green fire sparked in Lilibet's eyes. "Myself, I must read this most interesting book. May I ask how you so well know what is in it?"

Agatha's jaw dropped. Her face reddened before she swallowed and spoke haughtily. "My niece, who was working for us till the giddy, ungrateful girl married a carpenter, begged to read the novel. It was my duty to peruse it first."

"Of course," mocked Lilibet. "A Christian duty."

The older woman gave her head such a vigorous nod that it almost dislodged the form beneath the sparse strands of carroty hair. "You may be sure I told

Caroline she could never read such filth while she was under our roof."

"How fortunate for her that she no longer is." Lilibet turned her back on Mrs. Welliver and, like a hen with large chicks, ushered her sisters to the cane-bottomed chairs they had brought, for Rutherford Miles was getting ready to start the program.

"Fellow citizens and readers of Bountiful," he began. "Welcome to our very first cultural event. The only rule we're going to have as far as I'm concerned is that everybody gets to have their uninterrupted say — but no more than five minutes at a crack." He flourished his watch to general laughter. "I also submit to you that it's not fair to comment on a book if you haven't read it. As long as we can find someone willing to lead a discussion, we'll meet once a month —" At disappointed murmurs and faces, he cocked his head. "Every other week, then?"

That brought unanimous affirmation. "I'll publish the name of the book and the date in the paper," he said. "Just one more reason, folks, to subscribe to your weekly *Bountiful Banner*. Now then, our book for tonight is remarkable for several things. It begins on the Kansas prairie and is about a young girl, but it's already selling far beyond the publisher's wildest dreams. It's a children's book, but some critics hail or blast it as political satire. Wait! I'm adding another rule! No arguments over politics!"

"How about discussions?" asked Leroy Martin, a gangling redhead who ran one of the lumberyards and was a great admirer of Sockless Jerry Simpson, who had served three terms in the House of Representatives.

"The less said about politics, the better, till after the election." Rutherford's bald spot gleamed from encircling soft black hair as his dark eyes swept the gathering. "Can we agree on that right now?"

"*You* say plenty in your paper," jabbed Sam Welliver, scraped jowls wobbling. "That we're murdering innocents in the Philippines, that we're forcing the Cubans into vassalage —"

The editor held up a silencing hand. "Mr. Welliver, if you will write an article or letter setting forth your views and demolishing mine, I will be glad to print it. *The Banner* creates a forum for public opinion. But I wouldn't be an editor if I didn't have strong convictions that I intend to present as forcefully as I can."

Sam Welliver scowled. "That's no way to get advertising, young feller."

"I haven't got any from you," retorted the newspaperman cheerfully. "All right, folks. All in favor of banning politics from the Literaries till after the election, raise your right hands."

"Let's ban it permanent," Micajah boomed. "Them as craves to can wear out their jawbones at the barbershops or livery."

There was a chorus of amused agreement. "All opposed?" asked Rutherford.

The Wellivers glared, but neither spoke. Rutherford glanced at his notes. "First, a bit about the author. He's from South Dakota and published a newspaper there, though he's since moved to Chicago in hope of better things. He probably came to Kansas once with a traveling troupe of actors. One suspects he located his disastrous sunbaked farm here to keep from offending his South Dakota friends —"

"Hunh!" grunted Ed. "Kansas, South Dakota, Nebraska — what's the difference? Plenty of farmers in all of them have wished a cyclone would pick them up and set them down in some place a whole lot better!"

There was laughter at this, but Lesley stiffened in alarm and peered over her shoulder to where her father sat on a crate by the baggage room. His words had just that hint of slurring she had come to dread.

Rutherford laughed, too, though he looked a trifle annoyed at being interrupted. "Since the Gold Standard Act was passed by Congress in March, the issue of using gold alone as the standard unit of value for all other money has been settled —"

"Whether we like it or not!" supplied Ed to Lesley's mounting apprehension.

That spicy scent on Father's breath this morning . . . Had he been nipping all day at something he'd bought at the drugstore? Should she climb over the Schillers to go back and sit by him?

"So without venturing into forbidden ground," Rutherford continued with a slight frown, "I can point out that some think the Yellow Brick Road represents the Gold Standard, and its perils demonstrate the problems with that Standard. First, though, let's return to Kansas and the cyclone that scoops up Dorothy and her little dog and carries them over the Deadly Desert —"

"That'd be the Oklahoma Panhandle and all of West Texas," Ed called out.

There were giggles and chuckles, but Lilibet Schiller looked disgusted. "The station agent's drunk!" Agatha Welliver whispered to her husband, who nodded and whispered back, "Drunk as a skunk!"

"Ed," appealed the editor. "I thought we'd agreed there'd be no interruptions. Now then, as Dorothy follows the Yellow Brick Road to Oz, she has many adventures and meets some traveling companions. Miss Tremayne, would you describe these amazing creatures?"

Lesley scarcely heard. She could have gone through the floor with mortification, but outrage welled up in her, too, as she blindly muttered excuses and stumbled past the Schillers to make her way to her father. They had a fresh start here. Father was liked and respected and happier, till Bella's announcement, than he had ever been in Lesley's memory.

Why had he thrown that away? When he was buying his alcohol, had he given a thought to her, to his promises to keep sober? There was more anger in her than pity as she gripped his arm. "Come on, Father," she said under her breath.

"Aw, Les —" He grinned foolishly and tried to pat her hand. "This is a dis-dis-cussion. I'm just puttin' in my two cents worth."

"It's not worth two cents!" She tried to hoist him to his feet, but he was like heavy water, inertly resisting. "Come home!" she pleaded through tears of shame and disappointment.

As if things weren't bad enough, they were making a public scene. Hugh MacLeod, on the back row, started back, but before he could reach them, a long arm slid under Ed's.

Without roughness, Jim raised him to his feet and steered him through the baggage room and out the rear door. "Ed, you're just full of conversation to-night," Jim said as he eased the older man along, supporting him with one arm. "Let's go to your place, where I can listen to you proper."

"Les don' wanna listen to me."

"Well, Ed, she wanted to hear the discussion."

"She — she's mad at me."

"You just bet I am!" stormed Lesley. "But you're too — too *drunk* to talk to now!"

"Honey —"

"You're going to bed," she told him. "We'll talk after you've slept it off. But why in the world did you have to —"

"Miss Lesley," Jim interposed, "there's no use fussing. Why don't you go to the Literary? I'll get your father settled down."

"If you think I can go back in there as if nothing had happened, you must believe my skin's as thick as an elephant's!"

It upset her even more when he chuckled. "No, ma'am, I sure don't think that. Maybe you could start some coffee."

"He's too far gone for that to do him any good," she said with the bitterness of experience.

"I'd like some." Jim almost carried her father inside while she held the door. "I'll take care of Ed. You make that coffee."

It was an order. No please or will you.

296

Yet Jim Kelly had gotten her father to their home, which she couldn't have done alone. Stifling a retort, Lesley filled the coffeepot and lit the burner.

13

Sodden mumbles from behind the partition mixed with Jim's calming voice. Lesley heard the thump of shoes, the splash of water from pitcher to basin. By the time Jim emerged, she had better control of herself — was that why he had given her a task? — but she was still furious at her father and sorrowfully convinced that he had no real will to stay sober.

Deciding not to try to speak past the lump in her throat, she poured coffee for Jim. How often she had dreamed of doing this in their own home; how bitter it was to share the intimacy under these conditions.

" 'Drink your coffee fast and go home, Kelly.' "

He mimicked her voice with a kind of teasing tenderness, but she was in no mood to make light of what she considered betrayal by her father. He got down a cup, poured it half-full, and added milk to the brim — real milk, thanks to

Susan. "Let's go sit on that tie of yours down by the prairie dog town."

"They're in their burrows."

"Sure, but it's still a good place to talk."

"I don't feel like talking." All these months and weeks she had longed to be alone with him, and it was only now that he tried to make it happen, when she was desperately close to a raging outburst.

"We're going to talk," he said calmly. "Wherever you choose."

If she was going to cry, better it was in the dark. Besides, it was possible that Susan or Ellen might come to console her. That would complete her humiliation. She blew out the lamp so it would appear that she, too, was in bed, and moved out the door with her cup.

There was no moon, but as her eyes grew used to the darkness, the stars gave enough light for her to lead the short way down the familiar path. She sat at the edge of the tie and set the coffee cup between them.

He sat down, too, but not at the far end. In spite of her inner tumult, the closeness of him made her lungs swell, speeded her heart.

"It's grand coffee." His breath stirred the hair at her temples. "Drink up, Miss Lesley, and listen to me good. This isn't the end of the world. Your father didn't pick a fight or insult anyone."

When she couldn't speak, he added, "Most folks thought what he said was funny."

"Of course." Her tongue felt burned by acid. "I might have thought he was funny, too — if he weren't my father."

"Why are you set on making out that a lame horse is a plumb outlaw?"

The accusation snapped her restraint. "You know why! You saw him in Sunflower, Jim Kelly! You paid his fine!" She could feel Jim's shock and it roweled her on. "It's not so much what he did tonight, it's that he broke his promise!"

"His promise?" Jim echoed slowly.

"Yes. I told him before we came here that if he got drunk again, I was leaving."

"Now, hold on. He broke his promise. You can break yours."

"I won't. I *can't!* Life with him will always be this way. I can threaten him into staying sober for a while, but when anything goes wrong —" She bit hard into her lip, blinking back tears. The only place she had ever felt at home, and her father's weakness was forcing her to leave!

Jim Kelly took her hands. How could that send such a lightning shock through her yet still make her feel so comforted and protected? "I reckon I can guess how you feel," he said in a soft voice that reached and warmed her heart. "But you can stay in Bountiful, Miss Lesley. If you weren't living at your father's, you could still look after him some — and you're going to want to do that, no matter how mad you are at him right now — but you wouldn't be so torn up by what he does."

Cheered till she thought about it, she shook her head. "If I move out and stay in town, he'll feel deserted and drink worse."

"Not if you're married."

Were her ears playing tricks? Before she could say anything, Jim asked, "Can I ask something real personal?"

She gave a shaky laugh. "I think we are being pretty personal already."

"Adam Benedict wants to marry you." At her startled movement, Jim gave a wry chuckle. "He let it slip to Henri — I mean, Henry — who told Bella, who told me. Benedict's attractive to women. He could give you everything. But sometimes —" His long fingers slipped up to her wrists, where the pulses leaped and raced. "Sometimes it's seemed to me that you might like me a little."

"A little? Oh, Jim!"

He set the coffee on the ground and took her in his arms. His mouth was warm on hers, hard, yet tender. She gave herself utterly to his kiss, closed her hands behind his neck, caressing, delighting in the freedom to at last touch him, learn the feel of the muscle and bone and flesh that clothed this man she loved.

When at last Jim raised his head a little, she traced the angles of his face with her fingers, scarcely daring to believe her luck. "Jim —" How sweet it was to whisper his name. "You acted so strange most of the time. I thought you didn't even like me!"

"I liked you too much." His lips brushed her hair. "The reason we moved our business here instead of someplace else was because of you. But when I found you out driving with Benedict, it sure looked to me like he had the inside track." He laughed joyously. "Bella told me what Henry told her just a few days ago — that Benedict wants to marry you — so I've been waiting for the chance to find out how you felt."

"Silly! Why didn't you just ask?"

"I was scared you might not care. Till I asked, I could keep on hoping."

She heaved a sigh of loving exasperation. "It's a good thing you got pushed!"

"No one has to push me to do this." His kiss, his embrace, claimed her again. She could not believe there was such bliss in all the world. He began to tremble. Electric quivering spread through her. Mixed with the bliss came hunger, a craving for more of him, for all of him, the fierce need to be so close, body and spirit, that they would merge. Then she would be whole, complete, instead of the isolated, separated person she had been all her life till the friends and neighbors of Bountiful changed that.

"When?" he demanded. "When can we get married?"

The words she had longed to hear

took her breath away, threw her into panic. More than anything on earth, she wanted to live with him in love, but the prospect of doing so immediately overwhelmed her.

She didn't have any pretty night-gowns. No wedding dress. Would Jim think her extravagant to want a lacy, beautiful white one? Did he want children as much as she did? Above all, could she make him happy, could they stay in love their whole lives long?

"Was I too sudden?" He kissed her forehead, the tip of her nose. "I'm sorry, sweetheart. I'd like to carry you off right now and hunt a preacher, but you deserve a proper courting, a chance to get used to the idea."

That *was* it, she realized, with a surge of gratitude to him for understanding. She wanted to savor the pleasure of getting to know him, of being sweethearts, of looking forward to their marriage.

"Oh, Jim, I do love you! And we won't wait a long time —"

"We'll wait till you're ready." He brushed a teasing kiss across her cheek and down her throat. "How's that for getting acquainted?"

"Nice, but you don't have to be in such a hurry."

"Well, I do just now, honey."

"Why?"

"I'll tell you sometime."

He nuzzled her ear till she fidgeted and, laughing breathlessly, fended him off. She had never guessed lovers could have fun, that courting could be light-hearted as well as passionate.

"Don't get your feelings hurt, honey, if I set the coffee cup between us or say, like now, it's time we went for a walk."

"Oh!" Lesley's cheeks grew hot. Was she, Lord forbid, causing him distress?

From Jane Eyre's smoldering Mr. Rochester and heroes and villains of other novels, Lesley had deduced that men usually got more swiftly carried away by lovemaking than women did. When both lost their heads, a baby could result from this even if the man and woman weren't married.

That was a terrible disgrace. In several towns where the Morlands had lived, there had been scandals. One girl "ruined" by a married man had drunk Lysol. Several had put on weight, left town for some months, and returned thin. Had such a disaster sent Ellen

Tremayne into the life she'd led until she abandoned it at Bountiful?

These things passed swiftly through Lesley's mind. She smoothed Jim's cheekbones, the scar on his forehead, the angles of his jaw. How marvelous, how amazing, to be allowed to touch him! How lucky she was to know he would never betray or hurt her. She didn't want to hurt him, either, even if it was only a temporary male problem.

"I'll leave the — the courting up to you, Jim, till we're married." She added with delicious confidence in the effect she had on him, "After that, I'll court you, too."

"Will you, Les?" He chuckled and drew her to her feet. "That'll be pure heaven, but for now I reckon we'd better take a stroll."

They crossed the track beyond the spill of light and laughter from the depot, not the least tempted by it, and strolled hand in hand along what was called Main Street but was, in fact, Bountiful's only street except for tracks leading to Susan's place, Jim and Bella's freighting yard, and the brick factory.

They walked almost to the cluster of

drugstores at the end of town near the builders' camp. Men loafed inside and out, most quaffing from bottles.

"Might as well be saloons," said Jim. "These booze dealers better hope Carry Nation doesn't bust 'em up. Last year she closed every joint in Barber County."

"Do you know her?"

"We were never what you'd call introduced, but I was in Medicine Lodge — her husband's a preacher there — when she rolled a barrel of beer out in the street and smashed it with a sledgehammer."

"She must be strong!"

"In more ways than one. Big, too."

"Daddy says she's crazy."

"Her mama, they say, thought she was Queen Victoria. The husband bought her a fancy carriage and hired her a coachman. That's what the family traveled in when they moved from Kentucky to Missouri."

"Did her father drink?"

"Nothing remarkable far as I know, but her first husband, who'd been an army surgeon in the Civil War, was a real souse. He died early and left her with a baby to raise."

Sudden alarm shot through Lesley. She stopped in her tracks. "Do you drink, Jim?"

"I relish a cold beer when I come in from a trip, and I woke up a few times with bad headaches back when I was younger and dumber. Truth is, I don't like hard liquor much." He touched her cheek. "If it'd ease your mind, Les, I'll skip the beer."

"No," she said quickly. "I don't want to take away your pleasures. You might be sorry later that you promised."

"It's no pleasure if it worries you."

"It won't worry me as long as you don't — don't —"

"Get drunk?"

She nodded. He put his arms around her. "I'll promise you and myself this much. I won't get drunk. For the rest, let's just see if you get over feeling nervous when I've had a beer." He raised her face between his hands. "We'll get mad at each other sometimes. I've got some aggravatin' ways and you're human or I wouldn't love you. We'll fuss, I reckon, and hurt each other when we don't even mean to —"

She couldn't bear to think about that. "Jim —"

He placed one finger on her lips. "I love you every way I know of, honey, but I've never been deep enough in love before to want to get married. I'm guessin' there are ways I don't know about, that I'll have to learn. You've got the job of teachin' me."

"I can't believe I can teach you anything." She laughed fondly though her eyes blurred at his earnestness. "It'll be fun to try, though. See how long you can kiss me before we have to stop for breath."

"Now, that's the kind of lessons I like!"

They did some learning together, the advances and responses of loving, some subtle, some bold. How, standing, their bodies fitted excitingly, in spite of her corset waist, because she simply melted into him; how the back of her head fitted exactly in the spread of his palm; how a gentle, almost shy kiss could change to ardent fervor on his part and to a yielding intoxication on hers that made him gasp and straighten, drawing back.

"Lord, honey, we've got to walk!"

Shaken yet elated at her newfound power — and his power, too, for her knees wanted to go out from under her

— she slipped her arm through his. They walked slowly down the rough road to the brick factory, making the evening last as long as they could.

"How much longer will you be freighting for the railroad?" she asked. Benedict was going to be furious when he heard, as he inevitably would, that she and Jim were engaged.

Jim squeezed her hand. "Not much longer even if Benedict doesn't fire me when he hears our news. The roadbed's just about finished as well as most of the bridges. When the tracklayers begin, an engine and a construction train will haul ties and steel rails. The engine will push flatcars of rails as a crane helps place them." Jim hesitated.

"It's lookin' ahead a ways, but Micajah's got no family. When and if he gets to where he can't manage alone, could we build on a room for him or a separate little house? Likely he'll get hitched to his widow lady before too long, but if he doesn't —"

"He can be an extra grandfather for our children," Lesley said. "Won't they love his stories?"

"Sure," said Jim in a tone of obvious relief. He hesitated. "Lesley, you know there'll always be a place for your father."

Disgusted revulsion welled up in her. "Not if he's drinking. I'll pay someone to take care of him when he gets to that stage, but I won't do it!"

Jim put his arm around her. "You wouldn't have to do it alone, honey. While I'm alive and on my feet, you'll never have to do anything alone."

She felt a little ashamed, but not very. "You must think I'm cruel-hearted, but if he keeps on boozing, I don't want him around my children."

"You think it'd be better for *our* kids to know they have a grandpa we won't have at our table than for them to learn what drink does to good people that you love anyway and do what you can for?"

His voice was sympathetic, but she felt accused. She tried to withdraw from the comfort of his arm, but he wouldn't let her. "You don't know what it's like!" she cried. "You just don't know!"

"Les, it's nothing we have to settle tonight. Shucks, your daddy may never take another drink."

"Yes, and it may snow next Fourth of July, but I won't count on selling cold lemonade!"

"Well, anyhow, sweetheart, he's got a lot of years to change in. By the time he needs to live with somebody, you may be glad to have him. If you're not, we'll figure something out."

How could his reasonable manner annoy her at the same time it reassured, and moreover, made her feel guilty? Not very graciously, she said, "You're right. It's nothing we have to worry about right now." She hesitated but decided he'd already seen her unforgiving nature. He might as well know another drawback. "I want to go on working after we're married, Jim."

His arm stiffened a trifle. "At the depot?"

"Yes, if I can work it out with Father. More trains will run when the new railroad opens, and what with Bountiful growing, the station and telegraph get busier all the time. It won't be long, Daddy says, till he'll have to sleep at the depot to take night messages or a night operator will have to be hired."

"Whoa, Les! I've got other plans for you at night!"

He gave her a demonstration that left them both breathless. When she could speak, she hugged him. "I've got the same plans, dear." That sounded nice. She'd never called anyone but her father "dear" before. "The night operator's usually a boy who hangs around the station and just sort of starts helping out and learning how to use the telegraph. Sometimes he can get a job as night operator in a small place with just that much training and work his way up."

Jim seemed to be thinking hard. Goodness, as understanding as he'd been about everything else, was he going to balk at her wish to have a job? "I keep house now," she pointed out, "and still work at the depot."

He sighed. "You're used to bein' in the middle of folks' comings and goings. Guess I can see why you don't want to stay home all day, especially when I'll lots of times be off for two or three days at a crack. I just don't want people to think I can't support my wife."

"You wouldn't mind if I worked in our own business or on a farm if we had one," she argued. "Since you usually won't be home for dinner and will be gone often, there's no way, even with baking and laundry, that I can stay busy keeping house — and I like to be busy."

"How about when we have a baby?"

"The first one, I could take to the station. After that — well, we'll do what's best for the little ones, of course."

"Reckon I'm old-fashioned," he said ruefully. "Ever since I met you, I've been daydreamin' about coming in off the road dirty and tired and how you'd meet me at the door all pretty and sweet and —"

"You'd smell something good in the oven," she laughed, stroking his cheek, discovering and loving this small-boy part of him. "And there'd be a tub of water just the right temperature and soap and towels." Her thoughts ran on from there and she stood on tiptoe to brush her mouth along his jaw. "Why, you might not get to eat your supper till you'd seen how clean and sweet our bed was!"

"Say, honey, you've galloped plumb ahead of what I had the nerve to dream on! If you greet me like that even half the time, I'll be the luckiest man in the world."

"Oh, I think I can manage it most of the time," she assured him. "Because it's my dream, too."

A swift, sweet kiss before they walked on. "Benedict's not going to like this," Jim said.

"There's not much he can do about it except maybe say I can't work at the station." That was surely true, yet deep down she was apprehensive. "He can't hurt your freighting business, can he, once you're through hauling for the railroad?"

"Oh, he can put some dents in our outfit, especially if he opened up a competing company and undercut our prices, but as long as Bountiful is the trading center and shipping point for the region, I don't see how he can wreck us. If we hang on, he'll go build another railroad or town somewhere and leave us in peace."

A sudden thought struck her. "Is Henry going to keep working for Benedict when he moves on?"

"Nope. Henry's told him he'll stay here and open up a restaurant that'll serve both French and cowboy grub. Benedict took it pretty well. When he found out Henry wasn't Henri, he couldn't go on braggin' about his French cook. Next one he hires will probably have to show him a birth certificate."

"It'll be nice to have some weddings, especially since the first ceremony we had here was burying poor little Tony. I hope Susan feels ready to have Hugh before too long. Maybe sewing Bella's wedding dress will start Ellen thinking along those lines."

"My guess is that Ellen will just stay friends with Rutherford Miles."

"Why? If he knows about her and doesn't care —"

"I reckon she cares."

"But if they love each other —"

"Honey, she told Bella she can't have children."

"Maybe Rutherford doesn't want them more than he wants her."

Jim shrugged. "They'll have to work it out. I know I'd sure want you whether we had kids or not." He chuckled. "Fact is, the only reason I want 'em is because they'd be yours."

That led to another kiss, a long one, outside the boxcar. "I'll see you in the morning, Les. I'm picking up a shipment for the builders that's due in on the morning train." He held her against him so that she heard the strong, steady beat of his heart beneath her cheek. "Sleep sweet. And don't be too hard on your daddy. Between us, we can handle whatever we have to."

Between us. What strengthening words! She felt in that overflowing moment that the two of them could indeed do anything they had to — do it with grace, and even laughter.

"Thank you, Jim. I — I love you!"

"Praise be," he said. "Go on to bed, darlin'. So will I, and we'll each one dream our dream."

He gave her a fleeting kiss and strode away. As she moved past her father's partitioned bed, the sour odor and stertorous breathing she had hated and feared all her life made her lips tighten and diminished her joy a little, but she was too filled with hope and delight to brood.

She'd be cool in the morning, let her father stew awhile. He had that coming. It would serve him right to wonder if she was leaving. But then in a day or two, she'd tell him about Jim. Daddy liked Jim, and it would be a relief to him to know she'd be staying in town, that she'd like to go on working with him.

Maybe — maybe with Jim making them into a real family — Daddy would find it easier to keep off the bottle. She wouldn't count on it, but she could hope.

When she lay down, she pushed all troubles away and went back over every moment with Jim, relived their kisses, remembered his arms. In that happiness, the happiest night of all her life, she fell asleep.

14

Her father looked so shamefaced and forlorn at breakfast that Lesley felt sorry for him in spite of herself. Besides, she was so full of joy and bursting with her news that it took real effort to maintain a cool demeanor. Averting her eyes from his misery, she told herself that what he had done showed utter disregard for her and their place in the community. If it hadn't been for Jim, she would be going away, or at the least, moving out of their home. Her father deserved to suffer the result of his tippling. Maybe it would keep him from doing it again.

"Les," he began. He had nicked his chin as he shaved that morning, and his fingers shook as he thrust back the wispy hair falling across his forehead. "I'm sorry as I can be. If you'll just —"

Forgive you one more time? she thought savagely. She rose from the table, turning her back. "We'll talk about it later."

"Payroll should come in this morning," he mumbled. "I have to load the gun." He kept a Colt .45 in the drawer beneath the ticket counter, but while Susan and her children stayed at the depot, he'd taken out the bullets and must have forgotten to put them back in. The only time he wore the gun in its shiny holster was when the payroll or some other valuable shipment was due. He paused in the door, brown eyes pleading. "Honey —"

The whiskey smell was still on him, as it had been so many, many times. Lesley hardened her heart. She didn't respond. After a moment, he sighed and went out. She grew angry with him all over again for blighting her happiness and making her feel guilty when goodness only knew he was the one who'd broken his promise and disgraced them before the people she cared about.

It was wash day and Lesley was glad to vent her wrath in hard work. She carried buckets of water from the depot tank to heat in the half-bushel buckets set on the stove. She took off the sheets, wrinkling her nose at the gingery alcohol odor on her father's, and shaved a bar of laundry soap into the heating water. By the time the eastbound local whistled, she had filled the machine with hot, soapy water, the sheets and other white things, given the handle several turns, and left the laundry to soak while she filled the rinse tub. Now that she had the washing machine, she emptied the soapy, dirty water after the colored things were through the wringer, and then filled the machine with clean water for the final rinse.

Much easier to turn the handle and swish a whole load around than dip each item up and down before guiding it through the wringer. Washing was still a lot of work, especially since she had to carry the water from the tank, but the machine and wringer cut the labor in half. In olden days, and still in some countries, Lesley knew women took their soiled things to rivers or streams and pounded them clean on rocks or beat them with sticks before spreading them on bushes or limbs or grass to dry. That was how Nausicaa, the king's daughter, had met Odysseus, when she and her women brought the court's washing down to the seacoast and played games while it was drying.

Pounding stained mantles and bedding on rocks could be fun if you had company to laugh and talk with and could mix pleasure with toil. Machines could make work easier for women, but if they were shut up alone in a house all day, it could be drudgery, just from the loneliness.

She started turning the handle vigorously as the train clanged to a stop. The laundry churned with the motion of the agitator. This was a heavy load. Lesley's shoulder began to protest. After she hung out the washing, she'd go up to the station and tell her father about Jim and their plans. He'd been punished enough; in fact, she was already a bit sorry that she hadn't made peace with him that morning.

He was no longer the central figure in her life. Jim was. What her father did couldn't upset her so deeply, though of course, she hoped he'd leave alcohol alone. If he'd just take an interest in Lilibet or some nice woman . . .

The eastbound whistled and began to chug. Lesley heard a cry, a shout, and a barking explosion followed by several others. Gunfire! Her heart squeezed tight. She caught up her skirts and ran.

Two strangers, who looked like drummers, had dropped their suitcases and were helping Jim with her father, who lay by his desk, sprawled over a heavy canvas bag.

Another stranger with a bandanna tied over his lower face had crawled a little way, leaving a thick smear of blood. The back of his head was blown away. It oozed bone, blood, and other things. His fingers clawed feebly, his feet jerked, and he was still.

"Daddy!" The gun had fallen from his hand, the gun that had always seemed so alien to him though he had been a soldier.

Jim was stuffing his shirt over a wound below her father's shoulder blade while one of the strangers cut away the front of the shirt and vest to reveal a hole from which blood welled with each gasping breath. Lesley tore off her apron and pressed it over the opening as Adam Benedict ran in, Henry behind him. Each man held a revolver.

Her father reached for her hand. "Les, forgive me —"

"Oh, Daddy! You forgive me! I was so hateful this morning —"

"You had — every right to be —"

Weakly he patted her hand. His eyes wandered to Benedict. "Les can have my job, can't she?"

"Now, Ed." Benedict dropped to one knee. "You can't retire just as the town gets going!"

Ed Morland tried to smile, but it ended in a grimace. "I — I reckon I'm about to retire permanent like. If I knew Les —"

"She can work here as long as she wants to, Ed, but we're going to have you around for years."

Morland's eyelids fluttered and closed. Benedict cleared his throat. "You're a brave man, Ed. I'm proud to be your friend."

"I missed the robber," Ed panted. "Jim — got him —"

As if noticing Jim for the first time, Benedict frowned. He got to his feet, grasping Jim's arm. "Come on, Kelly. Leave Miss Lesley with her father."

"Reckon I'll stay," said Jim.

"Can't you see this is a place for family and women friends?" He nodded toward Susan and Ellen, who were just hurrying in.

"Guess I'm close to family, Benedict. Miss Lesley's going to marry me."

"What?" choked Benedict.

"Did I hear right?" Ed tried to lift himself. He sank back, but a smile followed the twist of the pain on his lips. "Jim, that — sure eases my mind —"

Jim put a hand on the dying man's shoulder. "I'll take care of her, Ed."

Lesley cradled her father's head. "Daddy, Daddy! I love you — I'm sorry —"

"Les —" He drew a convulsive breath, tightened his hand on hers, and then the life drained out of him in a sigh. His fingers loosened, he seemed to grow heavier as if the animating spirit left an inert mass.

Holding her father as if she could will him back to life, Lesley buried her face against his and wept. If only she could live that morning over again — if only she hadn't been so vindictive and self-righteous, meting out his punishment as if she were God! He had been weak when it came to drinking, he had caused her much unhappiness, but never had he been deliberately cruel.

She had.

As if from a great distance, she heard Benedict say, "I'll drive to Dodge City to order a coffin, get a minister, and send for a fill-in telegrapher station agent."

Still holding her father, she looked up. "I can wire for a coffin and preacher."

"But —"

"I'm the agent now."

"Miss Lesley," Benedict remonstrated. "You're distraught. For a few weeks, at least, let me get a relief telegrapher-agent."

"My father would want me to do my job. He died doing his."

Benedict looked in revulsion at the canvas bag. "I'd rather have lost the payroll."

The depot was full of people who had heard the shots. Jim called to Hugh, "Bring a door or wide plank."

"Aye," said Hugh. "And I'll have the lads knock together a box for that one." He jerked his head toward the robber and hurried off.

Rutherford Miles held back the crowd. For once, he wasn't asking questions for his newspaper. Jim dropped to his knees while Susan and Ellen knelt beside Lesley and each put an arm around her, Susan weeping. Ellen was pale, but her voice was steady. "We'll wash your father, Lesley, and dress him."

That was something she couldn't do. Clean away the blood, see the wound.

But she was the telegrapher now. There was a wire to send. All she could do for her father now was to see him decently buried and carry out the duties in which he had trained her. Hugh and Leroy Martin, the lanky redhead who ran one of the lumberyards, came in with an unpainted door.

Lesley held her father's remaining hand as Jim and the others lifted him onto the board. She kissed the fingers that would send no more messages, laid them at his side, and moved toward the telegraph key as her father was carried to the boxcar.

"If they don't have a mahogany casket in Dodge," said Benedict, "order the best one they have in Kansas City. Besides asking for a minister, Miss Lesley, you'd better have the Dodge agent notify the law and the coroner."

When that was done, when she had signed off with the initials that had also been her father's, there was nothing else to do but face his death and the way she had treated him that morning. Lesley sat staring at the telegraph key. Suddenly she remembered that the washing machine and tubs filled the front of the boxcar; the men would have trouble getting through to her father's bed — which had no clean sheets as yet . . .

Yes, he must lie on clean sheets. Susan had waited and was instantly at Lesley's side, slipping an arm around her, as she stumbled to her feet.

"Lesley dear." Susan's eyes were puffed and red. "Maybe you'd better come to my house for a while. Till — till things are ready —"

"I have to put clean sheets on Father's bed. I have to finish the laundry."

"We'll tend to all that," said Ellen, and Susan nodded. "Of course we will."

"We'll bring your meals — and see that you eat them." Lilibet Schiller's tone was stern, but tears softened her green eyes. "You have to keep your strength, *mein schatz.*"

"Thank you." Lesley's throat ached till it felt as if it were raw inside. Amazing that words came from it rather than blood. "Thanks very much, all of you. But I — I want to make my father's bed."

She would never do it again.

Ed Morland lay on his clean bed,

dressed in his good suit with the empty sleeve pinned up. Someone had brought a bottle of embalming fluid from the drugstore, and the women took turns wiping it on his face. Lilibet had arranged the pillows and some towels to keep his jaw from gaping.

Surrounded and helped by her women friends, Lesley hung out the wash, except for her father's things. How sad and useless clothes look when their owner is gone! Lesley couldn't bear to see them fluttering from the line. She left them in the willow basket and said to Susan, "Would you please hang these out at your place and give them to someone?"

Jim watered the rosebush and apple tree with the rinse water and hung the tubs on the back of the boxcar. The women tactfully went inside. He came and tried to take her hands, but she thrust them behind her.

His deep gray eyes went wide. "Les, sweetheart —"

"I was so awful to my father, Jim."

"He'd be the first to say you had reason."

"I wouldn't talk to him this morning. I didn't tell him about us — that I wasn't leaving town —"

"He knew at the end. That made him glad, Les."

"He said he was sorry. I told him we'd talk about it later. I wanted to hurt him."

"Honey, no one could blame you."

"I blame myself."

"Les —"

"It was pure meanness. He was never mean to me on purpose, never in his life."

Jim's jaw hardened. "Ed wasn't mean, but he sure didn't consider you much. You put up with a lot from him. I was there in Sunflower, remember. You were right to tell him you'd had enough of his drinking."

"But —"

"He's the one who went to the drug-store and bought that Ginger Elixir. He did it knowing what had happened before and would probably happen again. He didn't *want* to be cruel to you, darlin', but that's what it came down to. So you cut out this nonsense!"

He took her by the shoulders. She shrank so much that he let her go. "Lesley! You can't have got it into your head that we shouldn't get married!"

It hadn't worked into her mind that way. She could only stare at him, shaking her head. "I don't know, Jim."

"What do you mean?"

"I don't know — about us."

"But your father was glad to hear it! He went easier because he knew I'd look after you."

"Maybe I'll feel differently later on. I — I'm sorry, Jim, I hate to make you feel bad."

"How do you expect me to feel —" He broke off, swallowed hard. After a moment, he said quietly, "We shouldn't talk about this when you're so torn up, honey. For sure I'd like to marry you right away now and take care of you, but we'd figgered on courting for a while. We'll just do that."

"Please, Jim. I — I wouldn't feel right doing that, either."

"For the love of mud!" He reached out as if to shake her, then dropped his hands and clenched them. "All right! We won't kiss or hug or even hold hands. But you sure can't intend for us not to be together alone."

"Well —" Yearning for him overflowed her grief. "We can try."

He looked so hurt and bewildered that

she felt wicked. It came to her that he had killed a man. That couldn't be easy to bear. This time she took his hands and pressed them to her face before she released them. "Oh, Jim, I'm sorry you had to shoot that robber! I've been so selfish, not thinking about how that must be for you."

"I may have killed some poor devils in Cuba. I don't know, it was all so fast. I couldn't see if they fell." He drew a jagged breath. "Except for then, the only time I've ever killed anything was when a horse broke his shoulder and was suffering." He grinned crookedly. "Mother couldn't get me to kill chickens, though I put away my share of drumsticks." He sobered and passed an arm over his face. "If I'd just stepped into the depot a little faster —"

"Life's full of 'ifs.' "

"Yeah. I guess it is." He hesitated. "Shall we dig your daddy's grave close to little Tony's? Wouldn't be so lonesome for either one."

"Daddy enjoyed carrying Tony around before he got too sick for it. Yes, Jim, if it's all right with Susan, I'm sure Daddy would like being near Tony."

"I'll see to that then. Unless you want me here."

"I'm sure Ellen or Susan will stay."

"Maybe you should go home with one of them. We can work it out for somebody to sit with your father."

"No. I'd rather stay here."

He turned abruptly, as if he had to do that or take her in his arms. "I'll stop by later. If you need anything earlier, just send word."

"I will, Jim. Thank you."

Her dulled heart contracted as he moved away, bringing a stab of almost welcome pain. She knew, of course she knew, that her father wouldn't want her to feel this way. Maybe in time the guilt would fade to bearable regret. She certainly wouldn't nourish it. She'd had every justification for being angry with her father. What flayed her was her ruthless hard-heartedness that morning. She had refused to share her happy news with him, allow him that balm for his mortified spirit. Now her inner judge condemned her. As long as it did, she couldn't accept Jim's comfort and love, though she knew that hurt him.

That wasn't fair. Jim had pleaded her father's cause, had offered to give him a home. Jim himself needed solace for killing that man. She could give him sympathy, but that would only mock him when she couldn't show her love.

Her eyes blurred as she watched him disappear beyond the depot. Bella and Micajah were off freighting, but they should be home tomorrow. They'd help Jim. Lesley hoped they could understand what she couldn't understand herself but could only feel.

At noon Lilibet brought creamy dilled potato soup, fresh rolls, and lemon mousse. She set the table and summoned Ellen and Lesley from their vigil. "My sewing can wait," Ellen had told Susan as she shooed her out. "You need to take care of your business."

It had been agreed that Susan needed to be with her children that night, but Ellen and one or two of the Schiller sisters would take turns sharing Lesley's vigil.

"Eat," commanded Lilibet as Lesley put down her spoon after one bite. "Everything is better when you eat and sleep. You must rest tonight, *mein schatz*. I will bring chamomile tea and peppermint schnapps." At Lesley's startled look, Lilibet said, "I make it for my stomach's peace. Soothing it is, very."

Lesley stifled hysterical laughter. Father might have found Lilibet more to his liking than he could have dreamed. If he could have shared a companionable glass of schnapps with her of an evening, he might not have been lured by the drugstore.

Too late for that chance. The most awful thing about death was that there were no more chances. No chances, either, for those left alive to make amends. Lesley's heart felt like an aching hollow in her chest, but under Lilibet's commanding eye, she ate her meal, and such was the body's treachery that she did indeed feel stronger.

The black-coated minister, Marcus Sheridan, patted Lesley's hand and spoke to her kindly, but she was glad when he went off to view the burial site and prepare his service. A mahogany casket had arrived from Dodge, so the funeral would be in the morning, at sunrise, "a time of hope," the Reverend Sheridan said, but also allowing him and the coroner and marshal to catch the eastbound back to Dodge. They would take the dead robber with them.

He was, Marshal Robert Tower said, wanted for killing a teller while robbing a bank in Wichita.

"Don't blame you folks for not wanting him in your cemetery," the marshal said. "There is a reward on him."

"I don't want it." Jim gave his head a vehement shake. "Give it to an orphanage or something."

The gray-haired lawman gave him a keen glance of understanding. "Don't take it too hard, shootin' Thad Traylor, son. He killed two men and would probably have done for more if you hadn't got him." When Jim didn't speak, Marshal Tower's voice roughened. "Would you rather Traylor had got away?"

After a moment, Jim's head lifted. "No. No, I wouldn't."

"Remember that," the marshal advised. He bowed to Lesley. "I'm sure sorry about your father, ma'am, but he died in his duty."

"He died for a payroll."

"That wasn't the whole of it, Miss Morland. He was in charge of this station. It was his responsibility."

"Perhaps that's how men see it. But I'm the agent now, sir. If someone holds a gun on me and wants a payroll, they can have it."

"You're the agent?" He looked startled. "Bless you, ma'am, even most robbers aren't low enough to draw a gun on a lady!"

"Then it's too bad I wasn't in the depot this morning instead of my father."

Marshal Tower gave her the same weighing yet sympathetic glance he had given Jim. "For the good Lord's sake, girl, don't blame yourself over that. There's a time for each of us, I reckon. It was your daddy's time. Be proud' of him and let him rest."

He'll rest, rest forever, but I don't know if I can. Still, she understood that it wasn't the payroll, really, that her father had defended. It was his responsibility, his honor. She said, and felt a stirring of gratitude that it was so, "I am proud of my father, marshal."

Something she had not been for a long, long time.

15

The service was held in the depot, which was completely filled. Almost everyone in Bountiful had arrived by train, sent or received telegraph messages, or picked up freight at the station. Coming down to watch the trains come in highlighted the day, gave people a chance to visit, as well as creating a sense of being connected to the outer world. Ed Morland had been cheerful and obliging, storing freight till it could be collected, tracing strayed shipments, walking down to the construction camp to find someone who'd received a wire.

It wasn't curiosity that brought most of the town to the funeral, but respect for their station agent and sympathy for his daughter. All the same, Lesley was glad to be surrounded by her women friends, especially when the Wellivers, with their prying stares, pushed as close as they could to her.

Jim, Bella, and Micajah stepped in front of them, completely shielding her, and Bella, who must have just come in from a freighting trip, gave her a swift hug and murmur as Reverend Sheridan took his place by the handsome casket.

Someone had placed a rug over where the porous wood floor must be stained by blood. Lesley was grateful for that, but she would always know it was there. Could she go on working in this building where her father had died along with his murderer? Would that awful memory ever fade so she could enter the depot without a surge of horror?

The minister's words about Ed Morland's doing his duty and keeping trust could not comfort her. There was no way to take back the cold hatefulness with which she had treated her father the last morning of his life.

It was not far to the knoll where little Tony slept. After a few hymns, pallbearers Jim, Micajah, Hugh, Rutherford, Leroy Martin, and Adam Benedict took their places and lifted the coffin. Till Benedict moved forward, Lesley hadn't known he was at the service. Father would have appreciated the honor, and so, perforce, must she.

The grave was ready, yellow clods

piled to the side. Reverend Sheridan spoke again. "The Lord gave, and the Lord hath taken away; blessed be the name of the Lord. Let us pray."

Dusty pressed a straggly bunch of gayfeather and goldenrod into her hands. She could not bring herself to toss in the first handful of earth, but when the men had filled the grave and mounded it as neatly as the hard soil allowed, she knelt and arranged the flowers so they wouldn't blow away.

"I've ordered a tombstone from Denver." Benedict's bare head gleamed silver. He wore a black slubbed silk suit, the first time she had seen him in that color.

"That was kind of you."

He made an irritated gesture. "I thought a lot of your father, Miss Lesley. As you know, he reminded me of my own."

"Yes."

"My builders will start the new depot today. Why don't you let me send for a relief agent till it's ready? It'll be hard for you to work where" — Benedict was seldom at a loss for words; now he stumbled — "where it happened."

"You're kind," she said again. "But I'd

rather keep busy."

"If you change your mind, you have only to say so."

"Thank you."

"We'll need to discuss the design of your living quarters, Miss Lesley. Perhaps in a week or two, we could go over some plans."

Even in her numb state, she thrilled at the prospect of clean, brand-new quarters that would surely be more spacious and light than the boxcar. It seemed so unfair, though, that her father would never enjoy them that her excitement guttered and failed like a candle in a storm. "It's your depot, Mr. Benedict. I'm sure whatever you decide will be perfectly adequate." The jade depths of his eyes caught the sun as he gazed at her in such disappointed bewilderment that she said, "Believe me, I will appreciate getting out of the boxcar."

"It was a poor time to bring it up. Forgive me." For a brief moment he held her hands between both of his. "Please remember, dear Miss Lesley, I am always at your service."

He moved away, shadowed by Henry, who had kept very much in the background as if to avoid any hint of triumphing over his rival for Bella. Jim was talking to the marshal, but he had watched Lesley and Benedict with a grim expression.

"I have to get back to the station," she told the women surrounding her. "There may be orders for the eastbound fast freight."

"I'll come with you," Ellen offered.

"Thank you, but —" Lesley glanced around the circle of friends, the Schillers, Ellen, Bella, and Susan. "I'm so lucky to have you near. I don't know what I'd have done without you. But now — please, I think I'll manage better if things are as normal as they can be."

"We understand." Susan, so recently bereaved, spoke for them all. "But we will run in to see you."

"And at night, someone will stay with you." Lilibet's tone allowed no argument. "Days pass, but nights crawl."

"I would like that," Lesley admitted. Tears filled her eyes, but these were tears of gratefulness and burned less than those of self-blame. "You've all been wonderfully good."

"You were to me," Susan said, and Ellen nodded.

"Neighbors are to share sorrow as well as joy, dear," said Ellen. "Apart from defending themselves, it must be the main reason people started living in groups, so we can take turns carrying each other's burdens when they get too heavy for a while."

Lesley's friends walked her to the depot, and each gave her a hug and comforting word before going off to her own work as Lesley turned to hers. She wrote the shipping label for Thad Traylor's rough coffin with a steady hand. She made out tickets to Dodge for two construction workers, and transcribed the orders that came over the wire to give to the engineer and conductor.

She did this when the train groaned to a stop like a dying monster, as she was trying to ignore the long box that Jim and Hugh helped the brakeman load into a boxcar. "Sure sorry about your daddy, Miss Morland," said the conductor, graying Jared Crane. "He was a fine agent. Is it true you're taking over?"

"That's right."

"Well —" He shrugged. "Don't see why you shouldn't manage all right. Guess you've sort of grown up in depots, and the dispatchers brag on how you handle a key." He shook her hand. "Good luck, young lady."

The burly construction workers got on, slicked up for their trip to Dodge. The train hooted, belched clouds of steam, and slowly clanked into motion. Lesley retreated from the flying cinders, shielding her eyes as she gazed after it.

Father would never wave a train on its way again. He was buried. His killer was departing. Now there was living to do, getting through days and nights till pain and guilt dulled to more bearable aching.

Jim said at her shoulder, "I need to haul a load of machinery to a farm way out northwest of here. Won't get back till tomorrow night. Will you be all right, Lesley?"

She nodded. "Lilibet put her foot down. Some friend will stay with me every night."

Their eyes met. Something flared in his, then burned with a steady flame. "Till I can stay with you, till you get over whatever craziness you're putting yourself through, honey, I guess that's the next best thing."

He touched her cheek. On an irresistible impulse, she brought his fingers to her lips. He caught in his breath and swept her against him. His mouth found hers. For a moment she clung to him, rapt in his strength, the force of his loving. Then her father's face, sad and pleading as it had been that last morning — only yesterday, though it seemed an age — rose before her. She'd had no mercy on him. That torment wouldn't let her have any on herself.

"I'm sorry," she whispered, drawing away. "It's not fair to you, Jim, but I just can't —"

His mouth, warm and urgent on hers the moment before, hardened to a grim line, and the scar on his temple was livid. "Take care of yourself, Les. I'll see you tomorrow night. I reckon I can *see* you, can't I?"

"Oh Jim, I'm sorry!"

His mouth bent down. "God help us, don't get all guilty about me, too. I wish you could help feelin' the way you do over your daddy, but I guess you can't." He released her with a resigned sigh. "So long for now."

He strode across the tracks without looking back. Lesley's eyes followed him till, without conscious volition, they swept toward the slope, the longer, broader mound beside the tiny one.

The clatter of the telegraph roused her. She blinked away the tears and hurried to take the message.

Susan was Lesley's closest friend, but she couldn't leave Dusty and Sally alone at night, so it was the youngest Schiller sister, brown-eyed Lena, who occupied Ed Morland's bed. If this bothered her, she gave no sign of it, but chatted from the time she came after The Sisters closed until Lesley suggested that they retire.

"I'm really all right, Lena," Lesley said on the second night. Jim hadn't returned, so she supposed he must have been delayed. "I don't like keeping you away from home."

"I like it," Lena bubbled, dimpling. "For me it is this way possible to read the books I want to without Lilibet scolding." Lena imitated her older sister's piercing look and dry tone. "She says I should read to elevate my mind and that things do not happen between men and women the way they do in *Trilby* and Mr. Majors's *When Knighthood Was in Flower* — that I am stuffing my head with nonsense."

"It does seem unlikely that Svengali or knights in armor will arrive in Bountiful by train," Lesley said.

Lena whooped at this mild witticism, clapped her hand over her mouth, and said contritely, "Forgive me, *schatz.* I should not laugh when —"

"Of course you should," Lesley assured her, and smiled consciously for the first time since her father's death. "Daddy would want to be remembered, but he'd hate for people to go around for weeks with long faces."

Lena widened her long-lashed pansy eyes. "That is what Lilibet says about you." Whatever expression was on Lesley's face made the other young woman falter. "I mean —"

"What do you mean?"

"I heard my sisters talking with Miss Tremayne and Susan." Lena gulped unhappily. "They know you must grieve, dear Lesley, but they are troubled."

"Are they?" Lesley was not sure whether she appreciated her friends' concern more than she hated being talked about. "Why? Susan didn't laugh for weeks after little Tony died, and she still has swollen eyes some mornings.

No one thinks that's peculiar."

"No, but —" Lena threw up her plump little hands. "A bungler, I am, as Lilibet says, making things worse! It is that — that —"

"It is what?"

"Early on the morning it — it all happened, Mr. Kelly told Hugh MacLeod that you would marry him. Full of joy, he was. Now he has nothing to say to anyone, hardly even 'Gee' and 'Haw' to his horses, Mr. Micajah told us."

Lesley's cheeks burned. "It seems that everyone is minding our business!"

"Sorry, I am." Lena stared fixedly at a loose button on her shoe, then glanced up pleadingly. "But, Lesley, it is because we all love you and like Mr. Kelly. So fine you look together and so brave he was, getting between the robber and your father —"

"I know." The energy roused by indignation drained from Lesley. "I don't want or try to feel this way, Lena. I just do. You read or go to bed, dear. I'm going down by the prairie dog town for a while."

"There may be snakes."

"I'll try not to bite them."

Again, Lena shrieked at the feeble joke. Lesley tossed a shawl around her shoulders and followed the path she had worn to the old railroad tie. The chubby little creatures would be curled up in their sleeping chambers, but unlike their white-tailed cousins of Utah and Colorado, they'd pop out of their burrows with the morning light and greet their friends, for all the world like human neighbors.

Any burrowing owls that hadn't yet gone south for the winter would be hunting in the night. As autumn deepened into winter, the snakes would hibernate, but it was still mild enough for them to be active. Lesley hadn't worried much about snakes since Bella told her that they could sense how big an interloper was, and if it was not of a size that could be enjoyably digested, they didn't strike unless molested.

"It's a lot of hogwash that rattlers will die to defend baby prairie dogs and that burrowing owls stand sentry for the whole caboodle," sniffed Bella. "Snakes and owls will both have a nice feed off prairie dog pups if they have a chance. What they like is the dandy holes the dogs dig for them."

"It seems they ought to show a little gratitude." Lesley had grinned.

Bella shrugged. "They're just tryin' to make a livin'. I got nothin' against that. It's the silly yarns about them that aggravate me."

Bella was putting off her wedding till Christmas. "She wants to show respect to your father," Ellen had explained. "She says she and Henry aren't so young and hot-blooded they can't wait, and that by then maybe Susan and Hugh —" The usually self-assured Ellen broke off, floundering.

"That's all right, Ellen," Lesley said. "Jim and I had agreed to wait even before — before this happened."

"I'd love to make your wedding dress."

"I hope you will. Someday."

As if her thoughts had summoned him, Jim called softly from a distance. "Sayin' good night to the critters, Les?"

"Just thinking."

"Room for me on the tie?"

She'd said they shouldn't be alone, but it seemed rude to enforce that rigidly, especially when he'd been away. "Plenty of room," she said, moving to the far end. She started to protest as he came right up to her, but a plaintive mew and a protesting one startled her.

"I brought you something — two of 'em." She heard his smile in the dark as he placed two warm, furry creatures in her lap. "Meet Atchison and Fe. And don't let 'em run off! They're black as coal except for Fe, who has a white cross on her chest."

"They're tiny!" Needle-toothed little mouths nuzzled at her fingers and tried to suck. "Have they had some milk lately?"

"I begged a bottle off Susan on my way here, but I figgered you could do better with feedin' than I could."

"I've never had a kitten." Or a dog. Father hadn't thought it professional to keep animals in a depot.

"High time, then."

"Where'd you find them?"

"The farmer I freighted for, Dan Nelson, had heard from a neighbor that the station agent at Buckeye — the Atchison, Topeka and Santa Fe runs through there — had a mama cat who'd done what mama cats do. She had six kitties, and he was tryin' to give four away rather than drown them."

"What happened to the other two?"

"He'd given the biggest ones to a

farmer. These were the runts, and I reckon if I hadn't got there about when I did, they'd be floatin' down Buffalo Creek."

Lesley shivered at the idea. "We'd better go feed them before they nibble my fingers off."

"Oh, the cunning *katzies!*" Lena cried, putting her novel aside and kneeling by the saucers as Jim poured milk into them and Lesley set them down.

They seemed bewildered. Fe looked at Lesley with sapphire eyes and gave a piteous meow. The white cross on the downy black of her breast looked like a miniature crusader's blazon. Atchison arched his back high, erected his tail and hair, laid back ears, hissed, and glowered mistrustfully at the humans from golden eyes.

"What a tiger!" Lesley dipped a finger of each hand in the saucers and offered them to the kittens. Avid little pink tongues followed her fingers down and into the milk.

Fe made a sound of content. Atchison relaxed. Their small sides visibly expanded and they purred like diminutive trains. "I'll fill a box with gravel for them," Jim said. "Two boxes, if you'd like to have one in the depot."

"Now, wait a minute, Jim Kelly! You didn't ask me if I wanted any cats!"

"No." He grinned, head atilt, and a flicker of warmth sparked in her chill heart. "But you do, don't you?"

How could she not? Trusting little Fe and dauntless Atchison? "Of course I do, but you still have a nerve to decide I need some pets."

Looking straight at her, he said, "You need something to keep you warm at night."

A deep, slow blush spread from her toes to the roots of her hair. Lena giggled, then, abashed, covered her mouth and started to flee behind the partition. Lesley caught her arm. "Stay here, Lena!"

"The little dickenses slept with me last night." There was a glint in Jim's eye. "I had to be careful not to mash 'em, but outside of that, it was real nice to snuggle."

"Take them home with you, then!"

"I couldn't deprive you" — Jim heaved a wistful sigh — "and them."

In spite of herself, she had to smile and shake her head. "What can a person do with you, Jim Kelly?"

"Want me to show you?"

"I think as full as these kitties are, you'd better bring in their gravel."

"Yes, ma'am. And I'll leave a box in the depot."

"Thanks, though it's the least you can do after foisting these small beasts off on me. If you think they're going to soften me up —"

"They'll give you something to take care of and play with, they'll warm you at night and make you laugh. I happen to be simple-minded enough to think that's what you need." Again that irrepressible, lopsided grin. "I could do all those things real well, Les, but if you won't let me —"

"Get that gravel!" she commanded.

Fe curled up beside Lesley at once, nestling in the hollow of her body where the tight, cold knot of her stomach began to loosen. Atchison stalked all over the bed and then up and down her prostrate form, trying to stamp his wee feet. Finally he settled in the curve behind her knees.

Ridiculous to be so comforted by two little waif cats, but she was, and since she was saving their lives, she didn't feel she was trying to escape the penalties of her lack of charity.

Clever Jim. Stroking Fe, Lesley had to smile in the darkness as she remembered his brazen insinuations. Clearly he had no intention of treating her with formal politeness. She had to admit she was glad of that since it didn't inflict the extra guilt of seeing him sunk in gloom. But it would be a very long time before she could accept from him all those kitten-derived benefits he'd enumerated.

She said a prayer for her father's peace and, solaced by the warmth of two small living creatures, drifted into sleep unbroken by nightmares and stricken awakenings.

16

Ed Morland's tombstone arrived on the eastbound two weeks after his death. Hugh MacLeod, who hadn't met the train since Susan stepped off it, started turning up to see if there was anything heavy to unload and trundle to the baggage room. The huge crate was addressed to Adam Benedict. When Lesley read MONUMENTS OF DISTINCTION on the label, she began to tremble.

"Why don't you go over to Susan or Ellen, lass?" Hugh asked gruffly. "I'll tell Mr. Benedict — I see his private car was switched off on its siding last night, so he's probably around — and we'll find a team and wagon. You can come see the stone after it's in place and all."

"I'll stay with it."

For some reason, that seemed important, something she could do for her father. Hugh shrugged and hurried off. Lesley stared at the crate. Her knees dissolved. Blackness swirled around her. She sank dizzily to the threshold of the depot, holding her lowered head in her hands.

The gravestone made it irrevocable. Her father would lie beneath it forever. She would never see him again, and the last time she had before he lay wounded to his death in her arms, she had scarcely looked at him, scorned his apologies. There was nothing she could . . .

"Mee-yuuu?" entreated Fe, trying to scramble into Lesley's lap. Once there, the minute creature rubbed her head against Lesley till it was impossible not to scratch gently behind her ears and accept the ministrations of a rough rose-petal tongue.

Atchison pounced on her shoe and began chewing a button. She picked his squirming body up and tried to hold him, but he yowled and writhed till she let him go.

"Ungrateful little demon!" she accused.

"Yowrrr!" he retorted, swishing his bottle brush of a tail.

"You'll come to a bad end, *katzchen.* It starts with gnawing shoe buttons and winds up with stealing baby chicks and staying out all night!"

Benedict's approach had been soft, for she hadn't detected it till he said from the far end of the platform, "Good heavens, Miss Lesley, you sound like a mother with an erring son! Where did you get those pathetic strays? Had I known you wanted a cat, I'd have brought you a handsome Siamese."

She set Fe down with a caress and rose, ignoring Benedict's proffered hand. The temporary faintness was past. She looked him in the eye and decided that he himself considerably resembled a regal, massive, slightly diabolical Siamese.

"I like Fe and Atchison."

"You mean you're sorry for them."

Atchison arched and hissed as if he resented Benedict's unflattering remarks. Lesley couldn't keep from laughing and bent to smooth the taut backbone. "I mean I don't know what I did without them! I strongly recommend a pair of cats, Mr. Benedict, if you would be instructed, infuriated, and beguiled all at once."

He looked at her with real horror. "Take care! You don't want to be one of those cat-crazed women who never marry and are found dead at an advanced age in a chaos of felines, litter, sardines, and dead mice!"

"I hope not," she said demurely.

Henry and Matthew had followed their employer. They waited by the crate as Hugh said, "Jim and Bella are gone, but there's Micajah just hitching up. I'm sure he'll haul the stone."

"Get him," said Benedict. "There's no need for you to come along, Miss Lesley."

"I want to."

"Then perhaps you'd like Mrs. Lee or Miss Tremayne to accompany you."

"It's not necessary, but thanks for your concern. I'll just walk on over."

"I'll go with you."

Short of insulting rudeness, there was no way to evade him. Besides, it was broad daylight and the others would be along shortly. She put the kittens inside the depot and shut the door. Till they got bigger, they mustn't tempt hawks or the coyotes that often *yi-yi-yi*ed from the cemetery slope. Her father had always liked to hear them, and Lesley was glad they sang to him and Tony Lee, but she didn't want her kittens to be a coyote snack.

As she started to step across the

track, Benedict slipped his hand beneath her elbow. She tensed, then decided to accept his assistance. The quarter mile to the graves was rough and uneven, and in addition to the fact that her eyes kept blurring, she still felt rather light-headed and off balance.

"The builders are ready to start the new depot," he said. "I do wish, Miss Lesley, that you'd look at the plans so they can be altered to suit you."

"It's your depot, Mr. Benedict."

"But it'll be your home. Not for long, I trust. Still, it's my wish that you be comfortable."

That was beyond the capabilities of any building, but it would be discourteous and unappreciative to say so. "Won't you let Henry prepare us a good meal and look the plans over at leisure this evening?"

"Why don't you bring the plans to the depot, sir? Miss Tremayne and I are invited to supper tonight at Mrs. Lee's."

"So, no doubt, are Hugh MacLeod and Rutherford Miles."

"Indeed, why shouldn't they be?"

If he paid any attention to comings and goings, and it seemed that he did, he'd have noticed that the group suppers on the platform had stopped, not only because of her father's death, but because it was chilly now after sunset. He would also know that Ellen and Susan took turns making supper and inviting Lesley and their men friends as well as Micajah, Jim, and Bella, when they weren't on the road. Bella had made supper for them all a few times, with Hugh contributing his Mulligan stew. When Lesley said it was far past her turn to cook, Susan gave her a hug. "If I cooked for you the rest of our lives, I couldn't repay the way you helped when I needed it so much!"

"No more could I," said Ellen. "Just wait till the day you really *yearn* to fix a meal."

Lesley couldn't imagine yearning to do much of anything except be with Jim, which her guilt wouldn't let her enjoy. People survived devastating losses. Susan had lost both her husband and baby within a few months, but she had carried on her business, and from the way she and Hugh smiled at each other, he might not have to wait too much longer. Susan had Dusty and Sally, though, and nothing to reproach herself for.

As they neared the small and large graves, Benedict said, "It's not MacLeod and Miles I worry about. They have sweethearts. It's Jim Kelly who makes me greener-eyed than I am by nature, but at least I don't see you alone with him of late. Are you still engaged?"

"I don't know."

The points of his silver eyebrows climbed. Almost imperceptibly, his hold on her arm tightened. "How can that be?"

Too late, she gave the answer deserved by his first query. "It's a private matter."

"Let's not pretend that it's not of very private interest to me."

Fair enough, and like it or not, she was beholden to him. "I told Mr. Kelly that I didn't know when I could marry him."

"What did the redoubtable Kelly say?"

"That really is none of your affair."

"It doesn't matter." Benedict's voice was exultant. "You aren't rushing to become his wife. That gives me hope."

"Why?"

"Because, my sweet, since you've postponed the wedding when no one could blame you, alone as you are, for a hasty one —"

"I'm not alone!" She realized how lucky she was that that was true. "My friends have been wonderful, better than most families!"

"Susan Lee and Bella, I can understand, but the Tremayne woman? And that battle-ax of an elder Schiller sister —"

"Lilibet Schiller's truly kind. And for you, of all people, you with your 'cousins,' to hold Miss Tremayne's past against her —"

"Words fail you," he supplied amiably. "Still, it would be entertaining to see how quickly your reformed paragon would revert to her old ways if I offered her a tour in my private car and a fashionable apartment in San Francisco."

"You wouldn't!"

"Of course not." He stifled a yawn. "In theory I have nothing against scarlet women bleaching their robes. Why should I lure an aging trollop away from her forgiving yokel editor in order to prove a point of small concern?"

Shocked and resentful, Lesley didn't answer. He went on imperturbably,

"What intrigues me is your turning to your wondrously varied associates for comfort instead of your fiancé."

"It's nothing to do with Mr. Kelly."

"He, I daresay, would think it's everything to do with him."

Again she had no retort. The nearing wagon rumbled behind them. "It doesn't matter, Lesley." Benedict spoke into her ear, dropping any title. "Until you're soundly, thoroughly married in front of God, man, and the devil, I won't give up. Maybe not then."

She did try now to withdraw her arm. "Considering the fondness you alleged for my father, Mr. Benedict, I'm amazed that you'd take advantage of this occasion."

"When else have I had an opportunity?"

"There's no point in your having opportunities. You're an attractive and charming man, but I don't love you."

"You might if you tried."

"Why should I try?"

"Any number of reasons." He swept his arm in a dismissive gesture. "For a start, are you really, at the ripe age of twenty or whatever it is, content for this to be your world?"

"Yes. I've wanted a home — a place to belong — all my life."

"If you're so attached to Bountiful, I'll build a mansion. We could spend part of our time here."

"A mansion in Bountiful?" She gave an incredulous laugh. "That would cut me off from everything I care about!"

"Instead of a couple of shelves of books in the depot, there could be a real library. You could build a hospital, a church, a school, an auditorium for cultural affairs — design a park with a bandstand and playground."

She shook her head. "Bountiful can have all those things someday, but we'll do it ourselves. Of course, Bountiful's your town, too. If you want to build a hospital, we'd name it for you."

The wagon pulled around them. No weeds were allowed to grow on the small length of Baby Tony's grave, but Hugh had mounded it several times as it sank lower than the earth around it. A morning glory vine with heaven blue trumpets twined around the wrought-iron marker, and late-blooming verbena brightened sere buffalo grass that softened the broken earth. Lesley tried to remember the little boy's face, but it was eclipsed by Dusty's and Sally's. Was that why Susan found comfort in the photo Rutherford had made, so that time and the living faces of her other children would never erase the memory of the child who left her arms so soon?

Compelled to look at her father's grave, Lesley knelt and rested her hand on the sod. The men strained to guide the gray marble stone down a ramp to the head of the mound. Among engraved lilies and vines were her father's name, the years of his birth and death, and two lines:

A MAN OF HONOR
FAITHFUL TO HIS TRUST

Through her tears, Lesley looked up at Benedict and said, "Father would have liked that."

Benedict's Panhard arrived on the westbound local that evening. Someone rushed to the private car with the news. By the time Matthew and Benedict arrived, every man in town had dropped whatever he was doing and headed for the depot. As the gleaming black chassis with its brass trim was disrobed of padding and tarps, whistles, sighs, and exclamations filled the air.

"That baby cost almost nine thousand dollars without the body," Leroy Martin breathed. "Look, it's got a steering wheel instead of a tiller, and the engine's up front."

"This has twenty-four horsepower," Matthew informed the admiring throng. "Rear-wheel drive, pneumatic tires, four speeds and reverse. Nifty, huh?"

There was no lack of help to maneuver the vehicle across the ramp from flatcar to platform. Then, while Matthew set to work readying the Panhard for Benedict, the better part of Bountiful's male population prowled around it, peered under it, and obviously struggled with the urge to touch it but were deterred by its owner's proprietary vigilance.

It was the way, Lesley thought with an inner chuckle, that they would have inspected another man's dazzling wife or mistress had discretion permitted. Then she thought of how thrilled her father would have been and remembered with a pang that he had never gotten his ride in the Oldsmobile.

Benedict slanted an inquiring glance

at her, nodding toward the luxuriously upholstered front seat. She moved her head in a quiet negative and went to attend to less glamorous freight.

During the next days, as the builders started framing up the new depot across the tracks from the hotel, bank, livery, town well, windmill, and watering trough, the insouciant little curved-dash Oldsmobile perched like an abandoned toy outside the private railroad car while Benedict and Matthew wooed the Panhard and tried its paces. Lesley suspected that Jim was as impressed as the other men by the glittering machine, but he made no comment — fair or foul — on it or the new depot.

Toward the end of that week, Benedict departed in his private home on wheels. According to Bella, grumpy over Henry's enforced absence, Benedict wanted to entertain some San Francisco tycoons before he lost his French cook.

"They ought to finish layin' track south by Christmas." Bella didn't have to raise her usual tone much to be heard above the hammering and sawing of the builders. "Benedict'll be toodlin' off to build a railroad in California. Henry and me thought — well, if you won't feel like it's disrespectin' your pa — we'd like to slip into double harness at Thanksgiving, 'cause we sure are thankful for each other."

"Why, that's a lovely idea, Bella!" Lesley ignored the twist of her heart at remembering her father's hopes. "Romantic, too. Wouldn't it be nice if Micajah and his widow lady made it a double wedding?"

"We've asked them," Bella said. "The more the merrier. If you and Jim —"

The look on Lesley's face stopped Bella cold. Ellen, who had crossed the tracks to chat when she saw them on the platform, nodded toward the rising wooden frame and called above the din, "Susan and I thought the wedding could be in the new depot and we'd have a dance afterward, if you don't mind."

"It's a grand notion!" Lesley yelled back. "A happy christening for the depot! I can't hear the telegraph over all this commotion, so I'd better get back inside."

Life swept on like a river, though she felt the current of her own was blocked, choked off by her self-blame. Susan would marry Hugh before long, surely; Micajah believed his widow friend was weakening; and Ellen had blushed like a girl when Susan asked when she was going to make her own bride gown.

Instead of radiating joy through her as it had that one rapturous night of their mutual confession, Lesley's love for Jim ached like a wound, the only powerful sensation she had apart from the protective tenderness and delight caused by Fe and Atchison. Was she indeed fated to become one of Benedict's addled cat-mad spinsters?

The sounder began to click. It was a wire for Sam Welliver. As Lesley wrote down what her ears decoded, she could scarcely believe it and asked the sending operator to repeat the message.

What she had transcribed was correct. Filling in letters commonly left out by telegraphers to speed a wire, this one read: TEN ORPHANS LEFT. HOPE WILL FILL YOUR NEEDS. ARRIVE BOUNTIFUL WESTBOUND TRAIN TONIGHT. OLIVE ELLIS, CHRISTIAN MISSION.

Ten orphans? Sam Welliver's needs? Stunned and worried, Lesley frowned at the words. She'd heard of orphan trains, though one had never stopped at any station where she'd lived. As orphaned or homeless children became an increasing problem in the streets of New York and other large eastern cities, the idea of sending them westward had been seized on by a number of orphanages and religious organizations. The theory was that children could be rescued from a sordid life of thievery and despair by being "placed out" with families who would give them room and board in return for work.

Lesley had gone to school for a time with a pretty blond girl who'd been adopted by a well-to-do couple who'd lost their only child to pneumonia. Sybilla had lovely clothes for which she was envied, and had to take piano and elocution lessons, for which she was not. However, in another town, there had been a twelve-year-old boy off an orphan train who came to school black and blue, often with marks on his thin face, and once with a broken arm. Everyone knew he was worked hard and beaten by the farmer who'd taken him. That spring he was kept out of school to work in the fields. Sometime that summer, he disappeared. Some thought he'd run away, but there were dark hints that the farmer had accidentally killed him and buried the body.

Some "placing" groups tried to enlist a local person, perhaps a minister, to watch out for an orphan's welfare, but Lesley had heard that especially in earlier times, placed-out youngsters had to depend on the grace of God and those accepting them, for there was neither will nor way for eastern charities to concern themselves with their erstwhile charges.

In spite of the Wellivers' righteous posturings, or perhaps because of them, Lesley hated to think of any child coming under their control, but she had to deliver the wire. Occasional messages came or were sent between train times, but most depot business — receiving orders for the trains, selling tickets, sending or collecting freight — was concentrated around the arrival of the local trains each morning and evening. Lesley was in the station most of the day, but she could have left long enough to walk to Wellivers' mercantile.

She was saved from that necessity by the jingling approach of Susan and Dusty starting their morning delivery rounds. Sally would be dropped off with her Schiller "aunts." The brightly painted cart was followed by Mollie, the retired white mule who usually accompanied them and then hung around the town water trough to visit or jeer mule-fashion at working animals.

Susan said it would be no trouble to start her deliveries at the Wellivers and work back this direction. She'd be glad to give them the wire and wouldn't even peek at it.

Lesley went back to her father's desk, trying not to think of the dark stain soaked into the wood beneath the rug. It was bound to be less harrowing in the new depot. Here, everything she saw, everything she touched, was permeated with his memory, tainted with the way he had died.

She was making out shipping papers for an unsatisfactory corn planter a farmer was returning to Sears when Sam Welliver scurried in. "Isn't it your job to deliver wires, Miss Morland?"

"Yours got there faster with Mrs. Lee."

"Mmph. That's as may be. However, I'm in charge of local arrangements for these orphans."

"What kind of arrangements?"

"Informing people who might take

them in, preparing a place where the waifs can be on display —"

"*Display?*"

He stared at her from pale brown eyes. "You can scarcely expect people to accept orphans into their homes without looking at them pretty thoroughly first."

"Like prying open their jaws to look at their teeth the way one does a horse?"

"There's nothing wrong with asking a child to open its mouth. Rotted teeth can be a great expense and cause sickliness." He turned his back on her to study the platform. "It'll be dark when the train stops. How many lanterns do you have?"

"Two, but —"

"I'll bring two more. That should light the platform adequately. If the builders will lend some flooring planks, they can be set up on crates to put the orphans at a level where they can be clearly examined without stooping or kneeling."

Lesley's jaw dropped. When she could speak, she said with cold fury, "It sounds like a slave market. I won't allow it, Mr. Welliver, not for a second."

"You don't own the depot!" Welliver

blasted when he recovered. "The young'uns are coming in on a train, so I reckon they're like freight. You're responsible for 'em till they're collected!" He beamed at his reasoning.

Lesley choked down a withering retort and compelled herself to think. The children were coming. They would be chosen or sent on to another station with whoever was in charge of them. So what was the best way for the children to meet their potential guardians?

They would be tired and probably hungry. Good hot food and something nice to drink would help a lot. So would a little time to rest or move around.

Why not a sort of welcoming party? Something to make the unwanted young feel wanted?

"All right, Mr. Welliver." She gave him a smile of steel. "I'm responsible for the children. I'll arrange supper for them here, and you may inform your prospects that they're welcome to bring a covered dish and join in the meal or drop by later in a casual and friendly manner. There'll be no display. None."

"Who do you think you are?" Welliver began. His brow puckered. "But the brats do have to be fed, I suppose, at least the ones that are headed out to farms." He thrust his jowls forward, blue from close shaving. "I'll be here when the train pulls up. I'm the one who wrote The Christian Mission in New York and asked for orphans. So I get first choice."

"Fine, if your choice chooses to go with you."

"It'll be none of your say, Miss Nosy!"

"I assure you that it will."

"What can you do?"

"I hope we don't both have to find out." The smile hurt her mouth, but she broadened it. "Just save us both trouble, and pick a child who's willing to go with you."

His face turned ugly red. "I guess you think you can get away with anything because of all your friends!"

"I guess I do." His eyes dropped first. "Good-bye, Mr. Welliver," she said briskly, returning to her task. "If you do come early, please be sure to bring a dish."

17

Ladling hot cocoa from the big enameled kettle Ellen had brought, Lesley smiled at the elfin child whose light brown hair wisped over a high, pale forehead. "You're Bridget O'Hara and you're six years old." Lesley got her information from a heart-shaped piece of paper pinned to the girl's patched, faded, and too large gingham dress. The fancy-shaped name tags were Susan's idea. She had stationed herself at the ticket window and made out a tag for everyone so the children, too, would know people's names and not feel like curiosities.

"I'm Bridgie," said the girl, big hazel eyes regarding Lesley. "I can't read. What's your name?"

"Call me Lesley."

A girl with curling tawny hair, almost a young woman to judge by her voluptuous figure, hurried over and took the child's hand. "Come on, Bridgie! Let's get something to eat before it's all gone."

"We won't run out," Lesley assured her. "Hugh has another pot of Mulligan stew ready; Mrs. Lee has four more pies in the oven; and the ladies who run the restaurant are frying more doughnuts and bringing more macaroni and cheese and custard."

The older girl looked suspiciously at Lesley. "How come people are being so nice to us, putting out this grand feed? The other places we stopped, people who wanted an orphan just came to the station to look at us and ask questions."

Taken aback, Lesley said, "We thought you'd be hungry —"

"We are that! All we've had since we left New York was bread and jelly."

"That's more than you often had in the street!" Mrs. Ellis, the skinny, sharp-featured chaperon, looked strained and exhausted. "You're a thankless chit, Elizabeth O'Hara, almost grown and not helping me at all even after my poor husband got sick and had to get off in Wichita —"

"Drunk, wasn't he?" the girl sneered. "I've looked after my brother and sister, but it's the pair of you that's getting paid to parcel us out."

The woman glared at her. "I'll tell you

one thing straight, my girl! You've put folks off of you at every stop because you say they have to take the three of you. Well, you either get places here, or you're coming back to the home! I wired the matron from Dodge City and told her I can't take this bunch any farther without my husband to help."

"Scared he'll be gone if you don't get back to Wichita pretty quick?" asked Elizabeth O'Hara. "I'd say you have reason, *Mrs.* Ellis. I had the devil of a time keeping him out of my drawers even on a train and you watching him like a bilious chicken hawk."

"You little slut!" Mrs. Ellis raised her hand.

The girl dodged, laughing. Her head turned so that for the first time Lesley saw that the right side of her face and throat were horribly scarred. "You'll get shut of us here one way or another, you old trout! We're not going back to that home. Come, Bridgie. Let's fill our plates and sit over there with Jamie."

Mrs. Ellis glared after them. "Is there a whorehouse in this town?"

Lesley blinked. She'd never heard the word spoken aloud. It took her a minute to understand. "Mrs. Ellis!"

"That's where the hussy belongs! The people who run the home believed her when she begged to be taken in — vowed she'd work hard enough to pay the keep for all three. I guess she was a good enough worker, but the minute there was a chance to go west, she jumped at it."

"That seems reasonable. They *are* orphans?"

The chaperon gave a shrug. "Matron told me the father disappeared years ago. The mother burned to death three years ago shielding the girl when the shirt factory where they both worked caught fire."

"How terrible! Why was a child that young working in a factory?"

"She must've been twelve because she's almost fifteen. Thousands younger than that work twelve hours a day or longer. Anyhow, with a face like that, it's no wonder she couldn't find work. Look at the way she swings her hips! I bet I know how she supported her crew." Mrs. Ellis shook her head till the cherries on her hat bounced alarmingly. "Along the way, several families would have taken the boy or the little girl, but no one would take both, much less all three. Excuse me, I'm really quite hungry myself."

The woman took one of the plates supplied by the Schillers, filled it from the contributed food, and retired to a corner, where she seemed more interested in her meal than the children.

These didn't suffer from lack of attention, though. Except for the O'Haras, who sat close together on a crate, all the orphans were eating and talking with local people. None of the boys was out of knee pants. The girls' skirts were of all lengths depending on where obvious hand-me-downs struck them. Most garments were more suited to summer than autumn on the High Plains, but all of them had a sweater or jacket, however shabby and ill-fitting. Whoever took the children would have to immediately supply them with better clothing.

Dan Nelson, a lanky, sunburned young farmer, had introduced himself to Lesley as the one who'd told Jim Kelly about Atchison and Fe. He'd come alone since someone, in this case his wife, had to see to the milking and other chores. They had no children and needed help on the farm.

"You mean I can have a horse to ride?" the redheaded, big-eared boy of fourteen or so asked Dan as they tucked away Lesley's biscuits slathered with Susan's butter. "Jumpin' gee-whillikers, mister, I've always wanted to have a horse!"

"Well, Tom, he's a dandy little quarter horse who can plow all week and race on Sunday," Dan chuckled. "Ridin' for fun comes after the work's done. There'll be plenty of days when I bet neither you nor Buck's goin' to move a hair more'n you have to after you come in from the field. But it won't be all work, I promise you that. You're a mite old to be our son, but we'll treat you like a kid brother and see you get an education. There's a school with a good teacher two miles away. It runs from November to April. I won't keep you out a day more'n I have to."

Tom pulled a face. "I'd ruther work than go to school."

"Wait'll you've helped with harvest or threshing, lad, sunup till after sundown the longest days of the year."

"When I grow up, I want to be a cowboy."

"Well, I reckon you can, but trail-drivin' days are over and it's mostly hard, dusty work. I grew up on a two-bit ranch in the Texas Panhandle, son. I wasn't much older'n you when I'd had a bellyful of cleanin' screwworms out of cows while they sprayed me with somethin' that sure wasn't honey."

"Don't you have cows?"

"We have five, but they're milk cows, not the kind you chase and rope — and don't think for a second about tryin' it. My wife'd scalp anyone who made one of her Jersey cows dry up."

"Shucks!"

"What I'm going to do next summer, God willin', is buy a steam engine and thresh grain for my neighbors and around the countryside. If you take to it, you can run the engine while I take charge of the threshing machine."

Tom's freckled face lit up as a new dream blotted out those of cowboy glamour. "A steam engine, Mr. Nelson? Oh, gee-whillikers! You bet I'll learn everything about it!"

"We both will." The young farmer grinned. "And say, if you're comin' home with me, you'd better call me Dan."

Ann and Avery Roberts were talking

with dark-haired twins, Helen and Mark Altman, who were perhaps thirteen. The middle-aged Robertses' children had grown up during the hard years and moved away from the farm in search of better opportunities. The graying, pleasant-faced Robertses needed help — and company, too, Lesley suspected.

She was surprised and touched to see Ellen befriending a shy little boy of about five with big brown eyes, taking him over to sit with her and Rutherford. Andy Hart from the livery stable was offering to take an eager boy up to see the horses and vehicles.

Lilibet Schiller had left her sisters to serve out food while she cajoled a scared-looking pigtailed child of six or seven into filling a plate and talking to her.

The Wellivers had secured the strongest-looking boy, and he watched his prospective guardians with shrewd eyes. Lesley suspected that he could hold his own with them, but she didn't like the way Sam Welliver kept stealing glances at Elizabeth O'Hara, who, with her brother and sister, occupied the crate as if it were a citadel.

By now, everyone was eating. Lesley leaned the ladle against the side of the cocoa kettle and got a plate. Since Mrs. Ellis was sitting morosely alone, Lesley took a place on a nearby keg and said, "It looks as if most of the children have found places."

"Yes, and a good thing, too. These are the culls." She scowled at the O'Haras. "Look at that brassy piece! Daring anyone to come near them unless they're willing to have the lot!"

Lesley hadn't liked Elizabeth's strident manner, but it was impossible not to admire the way she guarded her family and presented them as indivisible. "What if no one takes them?"

"They go back with me unless that hussy runs off — and it's good riddance if she does."

Sam Welliver said something to his wife, who glared but went with him unwillingly to speak to Elizabeth O'Hara. Lesley couldn't hear what they were saying, but there was no mistaking the way the older sister put an arm around each of the younger children.

A three-way argument went on: Agatha Welliver fuming at Sam while he obviously tried to bargain with the adamant Elizabeth, whose clear voice rose over the hum of other conversations. "Jamie's quick and smart. He'll earn his keep. I'll feed Bridgie out of what you allow me and I'll look after her. She'll be no bother to you, missus."

At last, Sam nodded reluctantly and gave his irate wife a quelling look. Her shoulders sagged, her mouth was tight, and her colorless eyes were bleak as she trailed him to Mrs. Ellis.

"Guess the wife and I can take four off your hands, ma'am," the merchant said expansively. "We'll have Oliver Black, the husky young sprout, and the O'Hara bunch."

"Talked you into it, did she?" The chaperon's smile was at once malicious and relieved. Her gaze stretched to Agatha. "You'll have your hands full with Beth O'Hara, lady."

"*She'll* have her hands full," snapped Agatha. "I'll work her so hard, she'll have no time or energy for foolishness."

Lesley recoiled at the venom in the woman's voice. There no doubt she'd make a drudge of the girl. For Elizabeth to prefer that and what Welliver would expect to the life her family had led on the streets or in the orphanage showed how desperate she was. Probably she was deliberately sacrificing herself to give Jamie and Bridget a better chance.

Without considering all the problems — the ones that immediately leaped to mind were daunting enough — Lesley said, "Wait a minute!"

She hurried over to the O'Haras. "Elizabeth, would you like to live with me?"

The scarred side of the girl's face whitened. "All of us?"

"Of course."

Elizabeth frowned. "You got a man?"

Did she? Lesley hadn't seen much of Jim lately, and when they met, he seemed remote. By the time she felt able to marry, he might not want to. Pushing away that horrid possibility, Lesley said only, "I'm not married."

The wariness in those golden eyes deepened. "Then how do you make a living?"

Between shock and amusement, Lesley wondered if she was suspected of being a genteel go-between for a brothel. "I'm the station agent and telegrapher. The boxcar I live in will be a little crowded, but new quarters are going up. They should be large enough."

"Why do you want us?"

I don't want you — especially not you yourself with your grudges, distrust, and that ripe figure that any man, including Jim, can't help but notice. Sure that Beth would at once detect insincerity, Lesley spoke too softly to be overheard. "I think you'll be better off with me than with the Wellivers."

"You got work I can do to pay our keep?"

"I'd expect help with the cooking, housework, and laundry."

Beth's eyes dropped. She bit her full lower lip. "About laundry," she muttered. "Jamie wets the bed. I'll wash his sheets, but you better know about it now." She gave Lesley a defiant stare. "I won't have you slappin' or beatin' or shamin' him like they did at the orphanage."

Inwardly shrinking at the thought of the odor and piles of sheets, Lesley said more cheerfully than she felt, "Maybe he'll get over it when he finds out he's safe here. Anyway, Beth, I certainly won't fuss at him for something he must already feel terrible about."

"We'll need clothes and things. Will

you let me work out somewhere to earn a bit?"

"Of course, but if we get a school started now that there are more children, wouldn't you like to go?"

Beth flushed. "I never been to school. I'd feel silly with the little 'uns in primer."

"I'd help you study at home. You'd be out of the primer in no time."

A sudden light in the girl's eyes faded. "Book learnin's no use to me. No one'll hire me to work in a shop or anywhere customers'd get put off by my face."

"Now, Beth —"

"I know! After Ma died in the fire and I was burned, I was scared to work in a factory. They lock the doors, you know, to make sure everyone stays hard at work. Then, if there's a fire, and there's lots of them, you can't get out." Beth's shoulders slumped. "I was scared of factories. No one else would hire me. So I — well, I looked older than I was and I found out lots of men didn't care about my face, specially when it was dark."

Lesley considered her own childhood dreary, but it was paradisiacal compared to the O'Hara's. "You don't have any relatives?"

"Ma's sister used to live with us, but she died of consumption." Beth grinned cheekily and for the first time looked close to her true age. "If we'd had a rich uncle, I'd have sure got us to him, lady, even if he lived in Timbuktu."

Smiling back, Lesley said, "Well, since there's no rich uncle, would you like to share my boxcar?"

Wariness again. "We don't have to call you 'Mother'?"

"Gracious, no! I can't be your mother and won't try, but I hope to be your friend. I think you should call me Lesley." At a slight curl of Beth's lip, Lesley added, "I'll try not to be unreasonably bossy, but since I'll be responsible for you, I expect you to cooperate."

The curled lip twisted even more. "Do what you say, you mean."

Lesley started to demur. Then she realized that with this girl only four years younger than herself and infinitely more experienced in many ways, she would have to establish control or let herself in for an intolerable situation. She spoke as pleasantly and matter-of-factly as she could. "When it comes right down to it, yes, Beth. That is what I mean."

"I thought so!" Beth sounded triumphant but also cornered.

"If you live with me, it's your free choice, so it should be your free choice to help all of us to get along."

Beth pondered. "How's this, lady? If you think the kids need beatin', you tell me and I'll do it."

Lesley gasped. "Neither one of us is going to beat them!"

"Honest?" Beth's tawny eyebrows rose in disbelief. "People always beat kids."

"Not here, they don't!" Lesley nodded toward Susan, who held a drowsing Sally on her lap while Dusty snoozed against Hugh. "Mrs. Lee over there might spank her children or punish them some other way, but she'd never really hurt them."

"Will you want to spank the kids?"

It was Lesley's turn to reflect. "I may want to, but I won't. If we can't live together without a lot of trouble, we'll have to think of something else for you." She spread her hands. "I'm not old enough to be even Bridgie's mother. I'm certainly not wise and patient enough.

But if we all do our best, maybe it'll work."

Beth encountered Sam Welliver's avid stare and seemed to shrivel. "I guess there's not much choice." Then, as if conscious of how rude that sounded, she added, "I'm obliged, lady — I mean, Lesley. We all are. Look, Bridgie's going to sleep on those sacks. You suppose you could show us where your boxcar is?"

"I'll take you. But first let's tell Mrs. Ellis."

Sam Welliver glowered at the news, but Agatha looked relieved. "Better you than me," she told Lesley. "You've got a handful and then some. Come along, Sam. Let's take Oliver home. We can show him around the store tonight so he won't start out plumb ignorant in the morning."

"You need to sign a paper for the orphanage." Mrs. Ellis sounded close to amiable in her gratification of having disposed of her problem charges. "You agree to supply the children with a home and adequate food and clothing till they're eighteen. You also undertake to keep them in school till they complete eighth grade or are fourteen."

"There's no school here," objected Agatha.

"We'll have to start one," Lesley said.

"That'll be a big expense," growled Sam. "Folks like us who don't have kids shouldn't have to pay."

"You've got a boy now," Lesley pointed out.

"Fine lot of help he'll be if he has to go to school half the year!" Sam glared at the chunky lad. "How old are you, Oliver?"

"I'll be fourteen in February, sir, and I've finished sixth grade."

Sam brightened. "Don't see how you can get a school going before then, Miss Busybody," he said to Lesley. "And even if you do, Oliver won't have to go very long."

"Maybe he'll want to finish eighth grade."

Sam looked into the wide blue eyes of the boy who was as tall as he was. "You want to keep your nose stuck in books for the next two years?"

"No, sir. I reckon I'll learn what I need to know by just working hard in your store."

Young as Oliver was, Lesley thought he saw himself as the Wellivers' prospective heir. Indeed, why shouldn't he be? They certainly seemed to think alike. It seemed a little sad for a boy to lack an adventurous spirit and settle in to storekeeping at such a young age, but Oliver's past may well have held risks and uncertainties enough to last him all his life.

The Wellivers signed the paper and went off smugly with their prize, though Sam did steal a regretful look at Beth. She gave him a stare of such scornful hostility that he reddened and hurried after his wife.

Mrs. Ellis coughed. "Now, Miss Morland, am I to understand that you're taking all three O'Haras?"

"Yes."

"You look very young for such responsibility."

"I'm the station agent, so I'm used to being responsible."

Mrs. Ellis gave her a condescending smile. "You'll find that handling young ones, especially the O'Haras, is a far cry from selling tickets and keeping an eye on shipping crates."

"We'll manage. Beth's agreed to help."

The chaperon snorted and glanced bitterly to where Beth and Jamie were putting several carpetbags beside the sleeping Bridget. "If you believe anything that one tells you! Not to mention what she doesn't! I'll wager she never told you that James wets the bed."

"Yes, she did," Lesley flashed. "Now, if you wish to investigate my character, Mrs. Ellis, just ask around. I'll sign the papers after I've put the children to bed."

"It would be much more suitable if you were married."

"Well, I'm not, and —"

"She's engaged to me, though," said a deep, laughing voice. Lesley whirled. She hadn't heard Jim approach, hadn't even known he was in town. Gladness welled up in her and overflowed at seeing him so unexpectedly at a time she was besieged. Jim grinned and looked from Lesley to the chaperon. "Now, what is this, ladies, that would be more suitable if Miss Morland were married? I'm ready to do my part to make her that way."

"Are you ready to act as parent to three children?" inquired Mrs. Ellis in an acid tone.

Jim's jaw dropped. He blinked, looked

at Lesley, sensed her anxiety, and responded magnificently. "I sure hoped to be a parent one of these days, ma'am. If Lesley wants us to start early, I reckon we can."

"You'd better look at the children first, sir." The cherries bobbed as Mrs. Ellis jerked her head toward the O'Haras. Jamie had sat down on the sacks by his slumbering little sister while Beth stood guard over them and the carpetbags. Mrs. Ellis gave a malicious laugh. "One of them, you must observe, is scarcely of tender years."

Jim didn't answer the woman. His deep gray eyes searched Lesley. "Honey, it'll sure be a job. Maybe —"

"The boy wets the bed," warned Mrs. Ellis.

"Shame on you!" blazed Lesley. "Beth and I have that worked out. It's no concern at all of Mr. Kelly's. Shall I sign or come back after you've satisfied yourself about me?"

"If your young man will sign as your fiancé, it'll look better to the orphanage officials."

Though somewhat sobered by the prospect, Jim was clearly enjoying the situation. Lesley scowled at him. "I don't know when we'll be married, or even if!"

"We'll fight that out later, dear." Jim's tone was infuriatingly indulgent. "Sign the paper and let's get our kids to bed before they all go to sleep."

"They're my kids," Lesley informed him.

"That's not what it says here." He smiled sunnily as he scrawled his name by Lesley's. "How the heck do you spell fiancé?" Mrs. Ellis told him. With a flourish, he wrote it after his name. "Thank you, ma'am, for givin' us such a good start on our family."

"I hope you'll thank me six months from now," the woman said, but his smile was so infectious that she unwillingly returned it. "Good luck to you, I'm sure. You'll need it."

"What a dragon," Jim said under his breath as he followed Lesley. Beth watched him with wondering golden eyes but didn't offer her hand. He took it anyway. "My name's Jim Kelly, Beth." He had seen her name and age on the papers. "Welcome to Bountiful." He smiled down at Jamie, who had roused at their coming and was rubbing his eyes. "Hello, Jamie. You look like you're ready to hit the hay, but maybe tomorrow you'd like to help me hitch up my team and deliver some stuff around town."

"A team?" Jamie's brown eyes got bigger. "Horses?"

"You bet."

Beth was trying to lift Bridget, but in spite of her curves, the older girl was small and fine-boned. "Let me have her," Jim said.

He scooped up the child effortlessly, studied her heart-shaped face, and said, "She's a darling — like a little fairy."

Beth gazed at him with such open worship that Lesley's heart contracted. She tried to soothe a startling blaze of jealousy by reasoning that, of course, it must overwhelm Beth, after the kind of men she'd known, to meet one like Jim, who was kind and wholeheartedly accepted her brother and sister.

Still, jealousy smoldered in Lesley like fiery poison. She caught up the larger carpetbag and said breathlessly to her oldest ward, whose eyes were still fixed on the man Lesley loved, "Beth, will you bring the other bag, please?"

Holding Bridget against his shoulder

with one arm, Jim held out his other hand to Jamie. "Come on, son."

At the door of the boxcar, Lesley looked over her shoulder and saw the four of them silhouetted against the spill of yellow light from the depot window. A tall man close to a girl with a woman's body, and two children. *They looked like a family.*

Lesley felt as if a knife had pierced her heart and twisted. Could the family be hers or was she sheltering a child-woman who would bring disaster?

18

It was no surprise that Jamie wet his pallet, train-weary and overexcited as he was. The rubber sheet from one of the carpetbags protected the quilts beneath it, but his sheets were soaked, as was his nightshirt. When Lesley got up to fix breakfast, Bridget was still nestled in Ed Morland's bed, which she'd shared with her sister, Fe snuggled against her, but Lesley found Beth outside running sheets through the wringer of one of the washtubs that sat on the bench. Jamie was sloshing buckets of water over the rubber sheet hung on the clothesline.

"I didn't use the washing machine, la— Lesley," explained Beth. "Just heated water enough to melt the soap shavings and sloshed the sheets around in one tub before I rinsed them in the other." She gave a resigned sigh. "On days when you've got other white things, I can wash them first. Might as well get good use out of the water when it has to be packed so far."

"I — I'll carry the water!" Jamie vowed in a breaking voice. He turned to watch Lesley with swollen, shamed, and frightened eyes. "I guess you won't want us now, lady. But please keep Beth and Bridgie! I — I'll go back to the orphanage with ole Miss Ellis."

Lesley grasped him by both shoulders. "No, you won't! This is your *home* now, Jamie — where you belong. Boys don't get sent away from their homes, you know. Not ever."

Cautious hope dawned in his brown eyes. "You ain't mad?"

"No. Anyway, dear, I believe you'll get over it once you're all settled down and used to living here."

"Beth says you're not going to try to be our mother," he puzzled, "so what are you, lady?"

"By law, I'm your guardian, someone who's supposed to look after you, but when we get used to each other, I'll probably seem more like a big sister." She smiled, wishing she could hug him but afraid of going too fast. "Do you think you can call me Lesley?"

He nodded.

"Try."

"Lesley," he ventured as if tasting the sounds. "That's a pretty name."

"I'm glad you like it." She helped Beth hang up the sheets while Jamie pegged up his much-mended nightshirt. "I'll make the oatmeal," said Lesley. "Will you pour the rinse water on the tree and rosebush, please?"

"How about the soapy?" asked Beth.

"Just carry it fifty feet away or so and dump it — but not in the prairie dog town."

"Prairie dogs?" the New York children chorused.

"They're not dogs. More like fat squirrels with stub tails. They'll be out of their burrows by now. You can watch them till I call you for breakfast."

"Watch what?" Bridget appeared in the door in a shabby gown, hugging Fe while Atchison stalked them. The children all needed new clothes. "Can I watch, too, Beth? Where are we? How come we're in a train car that's not on the track?"

"Get dressed, you little question box!" ordered Beth. "Then you can come with us to see the prairie dogs."

The child stared up at Lesley. "You're the one who gave us cocoa!"

"Yes, and you can have some for breakfast if you'd like it."

Bridget jumped with pleasure. "I like it!"

"So do I," said Jamie hopefully.

"Coffee or cocoa, Beth?" asked Lesley.

"Water's fine."

"It is, but I'm making coffee for myself and cocoa for the children, so you can have either one."

Beth hesitated. "Well, if you're sure, I love good coffee — but no offense, Lesley, if it's brewed out of grounds used more than twice, I'd rather have water."

"So would I!" Lesley grinned, warming to this human side of the girl who seemed so unnaturally grown-up. "Don't worry, Beth. I pinch my pennies, but not where my coffee is concerned. Maybe you could grind it before you go visit the prairie dogs."

When they sat down to breakfast, Jamie looked up in wonder from his cereal. "There's raisins in here!"

"It's not slimy like what we got in the orphanage," Beth allowed, and savored a sip of aromatic coffee richly laced with Pet.

"Is there lots and lots of cocoa?"

Bridget ran a pink tongue over her brown mustache as she drained her cup.

"Lots and lots," assured Lesley. "But finish your oatmeal first."

Jamie darted her an anxious glance. "I — I guess I can't go help Jim harness the horses?"

"Why not? He'll be expecting you."

Warmth flickered in the dark chill of Lesley's heart. She had a family to make supper for. The empty house was alive again, more than it had ever been. And if Jim was taking Jamie on the day's deliveries, it made sense to invite him to supper. She could have his company, uncomplicated by courtship, without feeling guilty. Beth kept her eyes lowered as she ate, but the way she held her body visibly softened at mention of Jim. Lesley remembered how they had looked last night when Jim carried Bridget home and fought down a surge of misgiving. Beth, for all her experience, was a child. Jim Kelly was not a man to take advantage of a girl. No, but could he be seduced by her?

"I have to get to the station," Lesley said, pouring a little hot water into the dishpan. "Jamie, you'd better hustle across the tracks and help Jim." She paused for emphasis. "Now, listen, all of you. It's good to form a habit of looking both ways every time you cross the tracks."

"You always hear the train a long way off, don't you?" asked Beth.

"It seems that way, but it's shocking how many people, especially children, get run down by trains. It happened to a boy I went to school with. There wasn't much left of him. The friend he was playing with lost both legs."

Beth paled and shook a finger at her brother and sister. "Do you understand that? Stop before you're close to the tracks and look good in both directions."

"Don't play on the tracks, either," said Lesley, recalling some of her juvenile trespasses. "It looks like fun to jump from tie to tie, but it's too dangerous. The best rule is just to cross the tracks when you have to and keep away from them the rest of the time." She remembered one of her father's fascinating tidbits of railroad lore and knew it would please him to have it passed on. "Do you know why the space between standard-gauge tracks is four feet eight and one-half inches?"

"We didn't know it was," said Beth.

"Why?" chorused the younger ones.

"That was the space between the old Roman chariot wheels that traveled the roads in what's now England."

"What's a charyet?" demanded Bridget.

"Sort of a fancy cart. Anyway, stage-coaches and roads were made to fit the old, old tracks, and when they began making trains and laying tracks, they just used the same measures."

"Did we have Roman charyets here?" asked Jamie.

"No, dear. But we got our first train engines from England. Now, Jamie, run along and help Jim. Tell him he's invited to supper tonight. Beth and Bridget, you can come with me or stay here or sort of explore Bountiful."

Beth glanced up and down the box-car. "I want to earn our keep, and there's not much to do here." Her hand went to her scarred cheek. "Do you think someone would hire me?"

Lesley thought. "Susan could probably give you work in her bakery, or the Schiller sisters might need help in their restaurant, but unless you're sick of sewing after working in the factory, you might enjoy working with Ellen Tremayne. I know she's got more sewing than she can get to quickly." *And she will understand the life you've led and show you it's possible to leave it.*

"I don't want to wait tables and have men staring at my face and bottom," Beth said. "I could learn to bake, I guess, but if this lady needs a seamstress — Is she snooty?"

"No. Maybe you noticed her last night. She was the dark, pretty woman in the maroon suit and matching hat who was eating with a little brown-eyed boy who looked to be about five."

"Oh, that was Robbie. He doesn't have any last name." Beth, drying dishes after Lesley rinsed them, spoke with the condescending pity of one who at least had known a parent and had a name. "Someone just left him on the orphanage steps before his navel cord had even healed. I tried to watch out for him on the train. Do you think your friend took him? He wouldn't be much help."

"I think she'd like to have a child."

"She married to that baldheaded guy with the wide mustache?"

"Not yet, but it could happen."

Beth pondered. "Your Miss Tremayne looks nice, but I bet she knows what's what. Would you show me where she lives?"

"I'll take you over after the eastbound passenger train passes through."

"If she takes me on, I'll do real good for her," Beth promised. "Maybe she'll have some scraps and let me sew Bridgie a dress."

All three children needed clothes. Lesley had intended to order from Sears what couldn't be found locally, but Beth clearly wanted to make her family's way as much as possible. Resolving to have a private word with Ellen about replenishing the O'Haras' garments, Lesley said, "I'm sure Miss Tremayne has lots of material and probably some nice things that can be altered or made over. I'd like to get new shoes for all of you, though, as a kind of welcome-to-Bountiful present."

"New shoes?" Bridget looked up with rounded eyes from her second cup of cocoa. "I never had any new shoes, never ever!"

"Do we get to pick them out?" breathed Jamie.

The glee of her brother and sister

smothered Beth's beginning protest. "I'll pay you back," she told Lesley. "I don't need shoes myself." She blushed as Lesley's gaze involuntarily fixed on the hole in the toe of one of the girl's scuffed, run-over shoes. Turning to Bridget, Beth said crossly, "Finish that cocoa and wash your face, Bridgie."

Jamie ran ahead across the railroad tracks to where Jim was starting to harness his horses. Stocky, fair-haired Andy Hart from the livery, accompanied by the skinny black-haired boy he'd chosen, was waiting to send a wire for a new buggy shaft. "Did you meet Alan last night, Miss Morland? He's going to make a great hand with the horses." Andy grinned and glanced from the O'Hara girls across the way to Jamie. "Looks like you have quite a family yourself. We're going to have to start a school."

Lesley was glad he didn't see Alan as simply cheap help to be worked as hard as possible. "Those of us with children will have to get together and talk about how to do it," she said. "Do you know of anyone who's taught school?"

"Mrs. Roberts did back when there were enough farmers with kids to have a one-room school about five miles north of here. Just about everybody went broke and moved away when things got so bad. Some rancher bought the little school and hauled it off to use for a bunkhouse."

"The Robertses took a brother and sister, so maybe she'd consider getting a new teaching certificate," Lesley said.

She sent the message as the girls watched with interest. Then orders for the eastbound clicked through; a wire came for a drummer staying at the hotel; and two construction workers bought tickets, one to Kansas City, one to Chicago.

Near train time, Mrs. Ellis appeared with her carpetbag. She sniffed at the sight of Beth O'Hara. "I hope you appreciate the chance you're getting, young lady!" To Lesley the chaperon said with an edge of spite, "Once you've signed the papers, you can't change your mind, you know."

"Why would I do that?" asked Lesley.

Beth's smile was oversweet and sympathetic. "I do hope you find Mr. Ellis, ma'am. Drunk as he was, he may still be sleeping it off."

The woman's thin nostrils swelled.

She whirled from the window and pinned her hat on tighter against the ebullient morning wind. When the train ground to a halt, she was on it before Jared Crane could put out the steps or assist her.

Jim and Hugh came to help unload the freight. Jamie was close at Jim's heels. As soon as the train chugged on, Jim brought his team over to load the crates he was supposed to deliver. With Jamie proudly beside him, he drove across the tracks. Bridget's lip quivered. "I wish I could go, too!"

"We're going to Miss Tremayne's," said Lesley. "Maybe you can play with Robbie."

"Robbie's a baby!" complained Bridget.

"Don't you be one!" Beth warned.

Just then Susan brought her cart down the lane to Main Street. When she saw Lesley and the girls crossing the tracks, she smiled at them all, but especially at Bridget. "Would you like to help Dusty and me?" she invited.

Ellen came out, Robbie peering from behind her skirts. He wore the same summer cotton knee pants and sailor top that he had on last night. Lesley was sure it wouldn't take long for Ellen to outfit him, something she herself must do for the O'Haras. Susan smiled straight at Robbie and repeated her invitation.

His brown eyes went over Buck and the cart, Dusty and Sally and Cap. He took a step forward as if drawn by a magnet, then retreated behind Ellen and shook his head. Ellen placed a reassuring hand on his shoulder. "Maybe he'll go tomorrow. Thanks for asking him, Susan. Could Dusty eat dinner with us and stay to play awhile?"

"Can I, Mama?" Dusty begged.

"You may, as soon as you help me rub Buck down and give him his oats. Are you coming, Bridget?"

Lesley nodded at Bridget's questioning look. "I'm not scared of horses," Bridget announced as she marched forward. Still she kept a wary eye on the patient Buck till she had scrambled up with a hand from Susan.

As the cart rattled off, Bridget waving jauntily, a tear rolled down Robbie's snub nose. "You can go tomorrow," Ellen comforted. "And Dusty's coming to play —"

Another tear soaked into her skirt.

Then Robbie scrubbed his eyes and pointed. "Look! White horsie!"

It was Mollie on her leisurely amble in the wake of the employed Buck. "Actually Mollie's a mule, dear," said Ellen. The mule approached, extending a sociable and hopeful nose. "Would you like to give her a pancake?"

"With syrup?"

"By all means with syrup."

"Oh, yes!"

Beth watched bemused as Ellen and the boy hurried inside, and turned a suspicious gaze on Mollie. "Is this mule just allowed to roam around?"

"She's retired."

"Mules don't retire!"

"This one did." Lesley smiled at the memory. "As soon as the Lee children came to town, she decided she'd rather hang around with them and just enjoy herself than haul freight anymore."

"Why didn't her owner sell her to a tallow factory?"

"Bella wouldn't do that. She said Mollie had worked hard for years and deserved her rest."

Beth's straight, heavy eyebrows almost met above her shapely nose. "I can't figure you people out. First you have a good supper for us, kind of a party. This morning Mr. Kelly takes Jamie with him, that pretty blond lady took Bridget, and now Miss Tremayne's going to give a pancake *with syrup* to a mule that doesn't work!"

"The Wellivers wouldn't do that," Lesley pointed out. "But people here do know each other, and most help when they can. Mrs. Lee had just lost her husband when she came here, and didn't know a soul. Her baby died a few days later. She'll never get over that, but she's made a home for her children, and someday —" Lesley broke off and glanced up the street toward Hugh, who had intercepted Susan.

"Yes, she's pretty, and she'll marry that big nice man!" Beth's tone was bitter and her hand went up to hide the scar as Ellen came out with Robbie.

Eyes shining, he advanced on Mollie with awed delight and held the rolled pancake out as far as he could. The mule expertly lipped a drop of syrup in the air and fairly inhaled the pancake, wafting her tail in gratification. She then put her head down almost to the ground so that her neck slanted like a ramp.

"She wants to give you a ride," Lesley explained. "Get on her neck and she'll lift you up slow and easy and let you slide onto her back. That's how she helps Dusty and Sally on."

Robbie hesitated, torn between fear and longing. "Don't hurt her feelings, Rob," Beth admonished. "Here, just put your leg over her neck."

"But I'll be upside down!"

"Not for long. Anyway, I'll hold the back of your pants. Just hug her neck. Great! See, you're sliding down and there you are!"

Robbie leaned forward, resting against Mollie's mane, short legs jutting out from either side of her neck. As if understanding that her rider was nervous, Mollie paraded sedately up the lane a hundred yards or so and then returned. She put down her neck and Robbie slid off, calling ecstatically, "I rode her, Mama! She letted me ride her!"

"She'll take you farther when you want her to," Lesley told him.

Robbie didn't hide behind Ellen now. Sighting Rutherford Miles coming out of his office, the boy raced to him. "Uncle Ruff! Did you see me?"

The editor hoisted Robbie to his shoulder. "Indeed I did! I'm going to take a photograph of you for your mama next time you ride, or paint your portrait if she'd prefer. Would you like to help me set type for the newspaper?"

Robbie nodded eagerly and then blinked. "What's set-type, Uncle Ruff?"

"Do you know your alphabet?"

The boy shook his head. "I don't think so. What is it?"

"Well, there's no better way to learn than hunting letters," Rutherford said. "I'm just now setting type for the story of all Bountiful's new citizens."

"Cit-zens?"

"He means us." Beth's lip curled as it so often did, spoiling its tender curve. "Yes, I suppose you'll praise everyone who took orphans, make them sound like Jesus Christ come back to earth, and not mention most of them were just after cheap labor."

"I'll give the names of the people who took in children, certainly." Rutherford's sparkling black eyes were somber as they studied the hostile girl. "Has Lesley got you slaving away, then? I thought your brother looked thrilled when he helped Jim harness up, and your little sister couldn't climb into Susan's wagon fast enough."

Beth flushed, the livid scar standing out like the print of a slap. "I wasn't talking about us!" she snapped. She looked at Ellen, more embattled than appealing. "I want to ask this lady for work so we won't be so beholden to Lesley. But you know, mister, the kids who went with those hayseed farmers'll work like slaves!"

"They'll work the way farmers' children would," said Rutherford mildly. "I stopped at the livery this morning. Young Alan was currying a chestnut mare and talking to her like she was his sweetheart. And I dropped in the mercantile and found Oliver rearranging merchandise so it shows to best advantage." Rutherford grinned. "I didn't dare talk to him long. In the ten minutes I was interviewing him for my story, he sold me one of those newfangled safety razors, a pocket knife, mustache pomade, and a telescope."

"A telescope?" Beth laughed derisively. "Is that so you can spy on everyone and write it up in your paper?"

"It'll come in handy." He grinned at Beth, not in the least ruffled. "You seem to have the instincts of a good reporter — indignation at wrongs, suspicion, and inspirations on collecting information. Should Ellen not keep you fully occupied, I'd welcome your help with *The Banner.*"

Beth colored again, even more painfully. Her amber eyes dropped to the hole in her shoe. "I can write my name, mister, and spell out a few words. That's all."

The three adults shared a startled glance, then tried to pretend they hadn't. "We've got to have a school," Lesley said. "Just as soon as we can start one."

Ellen and Rutherford nodded, but Beth said violently, "I'm not hunching down with a bunch of primer kids like him!" She jerked her head toward Robbie. "Anyway, I have to work."

"We'll have classes at night," Lesley said. "That way Oliver and Alan could go on studying. And there might be quite a few grown-ups who'd like more education."

"Who's going to pay for a night teacher on top of a day one?" Beth's tone was scoffing, but there was a shine of eagerness in her eyes.

"If our regular teacher — we're hoping to get Mrs. Roberts, who taught north of here till so many families moved away — if she can't do night classes, maybe some of us could at least tutor reading, writing, and arithmetic."

Rutherford and Ellen looked at each other and he sighed. It was no secret that they spent most evenings together. "I guess we can," he said.

"Cheer up, editor!" Beth adjured. "The more folks who can read, the more papers you'll sell!"

He laughed and gave her a look of true respect. "And the sooner you can read and write, Beth, the sooner I'll have a very capable reporter."

"Are you trying to steal my assistant out from under my nose?" demanded Ellen in mock indignation. If she was at all jealous of the appreciative way her man friend watched the girl, it didn't show in the smile she gave Beth. "My dear, I'm in dire need of a helper. You can start right now if you wish. I have only one sewing machine, but there's plenty of basting, hemming, and buttonholes to do by hand. I can pay a set wage if you like, but it would be fairer to give you a percentage of what we earn above expenses."

"No offense, Miss Tremayne, but I'd better have the wage, at least to begin with."

"Till she has a chance to figure what a percentage would pay," added Rutherford with a glint of admiring mischief.

Beth was getting used to him. She only turned pink instead of scarlet and followed Ellen into her house. "I think," said Rutherford, addressing Robbie as much as Lesley, "that I shall take it upon myself to call around on those with children and, if the results are encouraging, take this young man with me to visit Mrs. Roberts and ascertain her willingness to instruct. But where shall we have the school?"

They both looked toward the depot and the new structure rising a distance from it. Lesley did mental calculations. "I think we'll have about seven day pupils to start with, though by the time word gets around, more may come in from the farms. Between trains, the depot's usually not busy. We could use the waiting room part from nine to four."

"Would Benedict mind?"

"I'll ask him when he turns up, but I'll take responsibility, Rutherford, if Mrs. Roberts can start right away."

"Excellent!" Rutherford twinkled. "I can't imagine our lordly entrepreneur denying you anything."

"I hope he won't." Lesley refused to act coy. "Because I'm going to ask that he give us the old depot for a school, library, and meeting room."

"Your father would like that," said Rutherford gently.

Lesley nodded and hurried off to hide the tears that sprang to her eyes. *Maybe we can call the building after you,* she told her father as she entered the depot. *Maybe, if we use it enough for good and happy things, it won't hurt so much to remember that you died there, that your blood stained the floor.* The murmur of children learning might exorcise the shots and screams. But would she ever feel she had a right to happiness when she had been so cruel to him that last sad morning of his life?

Harry Brinkman, the telegrapher at Chadwick, the next depot to the west, was full of questions about the orphan train. By the time she had satisfied his curiosity, Hugh MacLeod came in to wire for horseshoes, nails for them, and toe calks.

"All of a sudden, seems like every horse in town needs shod," he grumbled. "Feast or famine."

"At least the shoes won't spoil," Lesley teased.

19

Bridget skipped into the depot that afternoon with Mattie, the young girl Lilibet had befriended, who proudly declared that her name was Schiller now and she had *three* mamas. She looked it. Her yellow hair, tied back with a blue ribbon, flowed in waves crimped by the former scalp-tugging pigtails, and she wore shiny patent leather sandals with fancy buckles.

"There weren't any dresses at either of the mercantiles," she said, fingering a patch in her skirt. "But there was some pretty material. I picked what I liked best and each of my mamas is going to make me a dress! I'll have three!" She held up her fingers to demonstrate while Bridget looked so wistful that Lesley vowed silently that the child was going to have at least one new dress as soon as possible.

"We setted the tables!" Bridget said, claiming a share of glory. Laboriously she untied a knot in a pretty handkerchief the Schillers must have given her. "Look, Lesley! Some of the men left nickels under their plates!"

Mattie flourished a similarly knotted hankie. "Mutti Bet said Bridgie and me could have the nickels under the plates we carried back to the kitchen, but we have to save them for *important* things like shoes and clothes."

"But she gave us each five pennies for a nickel," said Bridgie. "We got to spend a penny each, and she said I could have two more to get something for Beth and Jamie." From the pocket that had held the hankie, she produced three peanut sticks. "I got four for a penny, so there's one for you, too, Lesley!"

"How sweet of you!" Touched deep by this generosity from a child who had probably never before had pennies to spend, Lesley ignored the bits of lint that clung to the sticky bar and munched away. "Delicious!"

"I got this many nickels." Bridget held up eight fingers. "There were some beeyootiful red shoes at the mercantile, Lesley. They costed ninety cents. Aunt Lena says I need ten more nickels and three pennies to buy them. Can I help

Mattie tomorrow? Can I get the pretty red shoes?"

"I think you'd better run back right now, give Mr. or Mrs. Welliver your money, and ask them to put the shoes up for you till you have the rest. Red shoes don't turn up every day. But first let's clean off your face a little."

Lesley was using her own handkerchief for this task when a smartly dressed young woman in a green twill suit swept into the depot. Her leghorn hat, draped with maize chiffon, was trimmed with green velvet and bronze and golden wildflowers. She wore fashionable Colonial Dame shoes with fancy pointed tongues and large pewter buckles that Lesley had admired in magazines, and carried a shopping bag.

"Beth!" cried Bridget. "Beth, where'd you get so swell?"

Lesley stifled a gasp and tried to cover her shock with what was indeed unfeigned delight. "What a lovely outfit, Beth! You look like a grown-up gorgeous lady!"

Beth's joy radiated from her like sunlight, and her golden eyes were luminous. "See what Miss Ellen did for my face? It's — it's magic!"

"Did she take off your burn?" asked Bridget in wonder.

Some of the shine faded from Beth's face, but she located the mirror placed in the waiting room for the passengers' convenience and went to examine herself closely.

"Of course, the hat's such a stunner that people won't look too sharp at my face," she said. "But the scar really doesn't show much, does it?"

"What did you do to it?" Bridget persisted.

"Miss Ellen has a birthmark she used to cover up when she wore low-cut gowns. She has this flesh-colored cream she spread over the burn. Then she dusted me with face powder and — Would you guess I have on rouge?"

"It looks perfectly natural and very nice," Lesley said. "Is the clothing an advance on wages?"

"Lord, no, ma'am — I mean Lesley! She says the suit makes her skin look sallow and she never wears it. The top fitted, but we cut off the skirt several inches. She let me make the hat for practice out of odds and ends."

"These are brand-new shoes," said Bridget, bending to touch the buckles.

"She ordered them from Sears. They pinch her toes. She's letting me work them out at half price rather than go to the fuss of sending them back." Beth reached into the shopping bag and shook out a full-skirted red plaid dress with a wide, ruffled collar. "Look what we made out of leftover cloth — and there's enough scrap gingham for another dress. Go in the baggage room and try this on!"

"Oh, Bethie! You didn't forget about me!"

"Of course I didn't, goose! And tomorrow we'll make Jamie a shirt and pants."

"It sounds like Miss Ellen's working for you," observed Bridget as she ran off to the baggage room, followed by Fe.

"I'll make it up to Ellen," Beth vowed. "She says I have a flair for hat design and she's tickled that I do buttonholes fast and nice because she hates 'em! And —"

She stopped and stared as Adam Benedict filled the door. Atchison arched his back, fluffed out his hair to make himself large, and hissed like a steam kettle. The evening sun slanted through the back window to strike emerald flame from Benedict's dark eyes and illumine his silver hair as he swept off his hat.

"Well, Miss Lesley, I see we have another charming lady in Bountiful!"

"Elizabeth," said Lesley, struggling not to smile. If a not quite fifteen-year-old could dazzle this experienced man, Beth's future might bloom in ways none of them could yet imagine. "This is Mr. Adam Benedict, who owns this railroad and is building one south. Mr. Benedict, this is Miss Elizabeth O'Hara, lately of New York."

Bowing, the man said in velvet tones, "I'm honored to make your acquaintance, Miss O'Hara. I hope you'll be staying in our town."

Before the flustered girl could think of an answer, Mattie danced in front of Benedict. "I'm Mattie Schiller!" she boasted. "I'm not an orphan now. I've got three mamas!"

Benedict passed his hand across his forehead. "So it's true! I pelted over here as fast as I could when I learned an orphan train had arrived during my absence and you, Miss Lesley, took on not one but *three* of the waifs!"

Bridget pirouetted from the baggage

room, twirling her full skirt and ruffles. "It's the prettiest dress in the world, Beth! Wait till I get my red shoes!"

She noticed Benedict, whose massive presence intimidated most adults, let alone a child who had reason to fear strangers. Beth reached her in a gliding step and rested her hands protectively and proudly on her sister's thin shoulders.

"I'm one of those waifs, Mr. Benedict. This is my sister, Bridget, and my brother, Jamie, is the third of those pesky waifs Lesley's taken."

His broad jaw dropped. The admiration in his eyes for a pretty woman changed to something deeper. "I beg your pardon, Miss O'Hara, most humbly. But allow me to correct you on one point. A waif, you are not. And though you must be much younger than you seem, you're not a child. You are a very regal, lovely woman."

In spite of her love for Jim, Benedict held a fascination for Lesley. It had been flattering to be courted by him. She felt a twinge at his obvious and immediate interest in the girl.

This did not deter him from weighing Lesley with a penetrating gaze as he turned to her. "My dear Miss Lesley, with all respect, you are simply too young for such responsibility. The person charged with placing the children should have saved you from your hasty impulse."

"It's none of your concern, sir."

"You're my employee."

"Yes, but you don't control my private life."

"Would that I did," he said with a wicked grin. "However, even in this brief time of foster parenthood, you must have glimmerings that you're in beyond your depth."

She'd had more than glimmerings, especially with Beth, but she said in a cool tone, "Actually, sir, what I'm learning is that my friends are taking more care of the children than I am. Bridget spent the day with Mattie at the Schillers' and earned a pocketful of nickels for setting and clearing tables. Jamie's helped Jim Kelly with his deliveries. And Beth, who's an accomplished seamstress, is working with Miss Tremayne. Beth made the hat she's wearing, so you can see that she's talented and artistic."

"Yes, I see that." He smiled at the

eldest O'Hara. "However, Miss Lesley, I do most earnestly suggest that I locate a sensible, middle-aged woman to live with you and look after the two young ones. The new depot with living quarters will soon be finished. An undemanding widow could be fitted in somewhere."

"I'm sure we'll manage very well. What we do need is a school."

"A school?"

"It must have occurred to you that Bountiful would need one in time. Well, the time is now."

"And you think I should build it?"

"No. I just hope you'll let us use this building. We're going to see if Mrs. Roberts will teach. Those of us with children will pay her salary till Bountiful enacts some kind of school tax. We'll have night tutoring for the older youngsters who work days."

His brow wrinkled. "You've certainly been planning. I suppose a school is a reasonable use for the depot."

She laughed audaciously. "Perhaps you'd teach a class in business or basic engineering."

He shuddered. "No, thank you." He glanced around the sparsely furnished room. "You'll need desks, smaller chairs or benches —"

"We'll make those." Jim Kelly came in with Jamie trotting worshipfully at his heels. "Leroy Martin's giving us the lumber at cost and sawing it for us. Rutherford and Andy Hart and Hugh and I can hammer the whole works together in a couple of hours and make some shelves to boot."

Benedict regarded him coldly. "Did *you* adopt an orphan, Kelly?"

"No." Jim dropped a hand to Jamie's shoulder, and the two grinned at each other. "But I sure hope I've got me a boy here."

Benedict's tone was almost jeering. "Ah, yes. You're currying favor with Miss Lesley."

Jim's smile vanished and his eyes were darkly gray. "I reckon we're all God's orphans, Benedict, so it's fittin' that we help one another. Besides, you'd better understand that Miss Lesley promised to marry me the night before her father died." He hesitated. Lesley felt a stab of grief as she met his gaze along with an almost uncontrollable need to go into his arms. Jim added slowly, speaking to her more than Benedict, "I do believe knowing that made him pass easier."

Benedict's arched brows climbed level with his silvery widow's peak. "I'm sure Miss Lesley respects her father's memory too much to marry in less than a year, Kelly. Many things can happen in a year."

"Yes, I expect by then you'll be finishin' up another railroad, maybe in California."

Benedict chuckled. "The farther away the better?" His amusement faded. He regarded Jim with deliberate challenge. "Who knows, Kelly? It might be you who shifts your base of operations."

"You tried to buy me out before. I'm still not interested."

"That could change."

The men confronted each other, the same heights but Jim so much thinner that, though muscularly built, he looked slight against the older man's hard bulk. The nape of Lesley's neck chilled. Surely they wouldn't fight, not with fists, but a deeper elemental struggle went on beneath their stillness.

The wail of a train jolted her into remembering the special due to hurtle through in a few minutes. It wouldn't stop. She had the orders ready on the hoops. It was only when she reached the door that she realized the smaller children weren't in the depot. Bored by the adults' talk, the three had gone outside.

She couldn't see them on the platform or across the tracks. Suddenly terrified, remembering all the dreadful accidents that had befallen children playing on tracks, she ran out, calling their names, looking frantically in all directions.

What she saw froze her for an instant before she screamed and ran as fast as skirts and heels allowed down the track toward the siding where the handcar was kept. The siding was on the slightest of inclines. The lock on the switch was very hard to unlock. Lesley could only suppose that someone had carelessly left it open.

Somehow, the three children, doubtless using all their weight to drag the four-man handle down, had got the vehicle onto the main track and headed facing away from the oncoming train. It could never stop in time.

In a nightmare that seemed to last forever, hoarse with screaming, Lesley watched the three children look back.

They had been so thrilled with their adventure that they hadn't heard or heeded the train. They clung petrified to the handle.

Jim sprinted past Lesley with a steel pry bar he had grabbed from somewhere. He swooped all three youngsters off the car, tumbling them well away from the tracks. In almost a continuous motion, with the train nearly on top of him, he set the pry bar under the car and heaved it off the track on its back.

The train thundered by, but it was beginning to slow. How horrified the engineer must be! Lesley, sobbing for breath, sank down to sweep the children against her. Beth dropped to the gravel at the same moment.

They huddled together, terror giving way to thanksgiving. The train groaned to a stop several hundred yards down the track. The conductor emerged, followed by the engineer, fireman, and brakeman. Benedict panted up at the same time that Hugh MacLeod, Ellen, and Rutherford cleared the tracks. The Schillers weren't far behind.

The young engineer, face still blanched, shook Jim's hand. "Thank God you got them off the track! And the handcar, too. That would have wrecked us."

The three Schiller sisters had claimed Mattie and were dusting her off, fretting over a skinned knee and elbow. Lilibet, tears in her usually cool green eyes, threw her arms around Jim and gave him a kiss on the cheek. "*Gott sei Dank!* And you, Jim Kelly! Never again will you pay for a meal at our restaurant!" She whirled sternly to Mattie. "You, Matt-chen! Another trick like that and instead of toys and good things, you'll get sticks and stones for Christmas!"

"I'm sorry, Mutti Bet!" Mattie, sobbing, buried her face in her eldest mama's blue and white checked apron. "Please don't send me back to the orphanage! I — I'll go to bed without supper a whole week and you can have all my nickels!"

"Now, would we let our daughter go?" scolded Lilibet. "Never! You will come home, wash, and have arnica on your scratches. Then you will have a good supper and go to bed." The child was too big for her to lift, but she did. "First you will kiss Mr. Kelly and thank him. Always, always you will remember you owe him your life."

"Aw, Miss Schiller —" pleaded Jim.

Mattie hushed him with a resounding kiss on the mouth and was spirited off by her mothers, who mixed chidings with endearments. Bridget tugged at Jim's elbow. "Uncle Jim, I want to kiss you, too!"

He turned red but leaned down. "All right, honey, but make it quick, will you? I can't stand all this fussin'!" As he straightened from an even louder smack than Mattie's, Jamie pumped his hand and said, "Much obliged, Uncle Jim."

Bridget nudged him. "You ought to kiss him."

"Boys don't kiss people," her brother retorted.

"Right now I could kiss and hug everybody!" declared the engineer.

"I'll get your orders," Lesley cried, remembering. She hurried back to where she had dropped the hoops on the platform when she first spotted the children. She handed their orders to the engineer and conductor, who had recovered enough to smile as they thanked her and hurried to the train, followed by the crew, who called back thanks and goodbyes.

Watching Jim with shining adoration, Beth rose on tiptoe and kissed him, not a brush of lips across his jaw but a firm, full kiss on his astonished mouth. "I'll never, ever forget, Mr. Kelly! There's no way to pay you back, but —"

"I consider him well paid, indeed," growled Benedict, still flushed from his unaccustomed dash along the track. "The town hero, and what's more to the point, the ladies'!" He added grudgingly, "I suppose I have to thank you, too, Kelly, though if your fiancée hadn't —"

He broke off at Beth's fierce assault. "I'll bet you're more glad that your train didn't wreck than that it didn't hit the kids!"

Benedict, eyes intent on the angry girl, didn't speak for a moment. When he did, he was in full control again and gave Beth his most winning smile. "I trust you'll allow me to be equally grateful that neither calamity befell?"

Mollified but distrustful, she gave a brief nod and started to the boxcar with her brother and sister. Hugh and Rutherford helped Jim wrestle the handcar back on the siding and then hurried across the tracks to reassure Ellen and Susan, who had heard or seen the commotion and were heading that way. Apparently the men convinced the women that it was best to keep away while Benedict talked with Jim.

"I'm indebted to you, Kelly," the big man said abruptly. "So I'm going to offer you a lucrative business deal. There'll be at least five depots along the new railroad, and hauling out of each, which will increase as towns spring up. Because ranches, farms, and settlements are so far apart, it's a region that'll rely on teamsters for years, until motor vehicles and roads take over. I'd like to put an experienced freighter in charge of a company located at a midway point that would organize freight service out of all these depots. With my money and your know-how, we can roll wagons through the Panhandles for a good long while. It'll almost be like the old days."

"Except teams'll freight in town or ten, twenty, thirty miles instead of two hundred."

"Those days died with the first railroad through Dodge."

Clever of Benedict to link his bold scheme with an appeal to Jim's feeling for the old wagon road days that bonded far-flung settlers as neighbors. But *mid-way?* That would situate Jim at least sixty miles away, with responsibilities running south for that same distance. Lesley waited in apprehension for Jim's answer.

"I reckon your company headquarters being midway is the main point of this," he said.

"It's the logical place."

"Sure. It's logical."

"Well?"

"I like the idea just like you figured I would." Jim glanced at Lesley as she caught in her breath. "I'll do it, Benedict — if I can do it out of Bountiful."

"You know that's ridiculous."

"I know I could do it."

Benedict's eyes narrowed. "I'll start the company without you, Kelly. And the branch at the depot closest to Bountiful can offer cheap rates long enough to close you down."

"Cheap, all right," Jim agreed.

Lesley burst out, "This is a fine way to thank Jim for keeping your train on the tracks!"

Benedict looked at her. "Miss Lesley, let us be candid. I want Kelly out of Bountiful, and not simply because it's possible that in time you might look on my suit with more favor." He waved his hand toward the handsome brick bank building and hotel that were nearing completion, at the other substantial frame buildings for which he had advanced loans, at the impressive new depot. "You know how I've poured money into Bountiful. I've built towns before, but this one is different." His usual mocking air had vanished and his voice deepened. "I've intended it to be *my* town — where I would build my real home, where I would rear my children."

"No one's stopping you," she said coldly. In spite of herself, though, she was touched by his earnestness and almost felt guilty because she was certain that she had figured in his dream.

"What's the old saying?" Benedict's smile was sardonic, but it was clear he measured out and meant every word he said. " 'This town's not big enough for both of us.' I have money and power, Kelly, but you're the one who shot the robber who killed Mr. Morland, and now you're the one who rescued three children and kept a train from crashing."

"Benedict —" Jim began almost sheepishly.

The entrepreneur raised his hand. "Townfolk will let me build schools and an opera house and city hall and fire station. They'll be glad to have the benefits of my creating the kind of town I want. But it's you they'll elect mayor, Kelly. You they'd trust to be sheriff. You'll be their leader. If, on top of that, you marry Lesley Morland, who must be the best-beloved person in town, Bountiful cannot be my town."

Jim sighed. "That's plain enough, I reckon. But why does it have to be any one person's town? Why can't it be everybody's?"

Benedict's lip curled. "If it's everybody's, it can't be mine."

"I'm sorry you feel that way."

"Save your sorrow for yourself." Benedict looked tigerish. "If Bountiful can't be my town, I'll wipe it off the map — and you with it, Kelly!"

"Now, just how are you going to do that?" asked Jim.

"Make the first depot on the new road the main hub that Bountiful was going to be. Abandon service through Bountiful from both directions by spring." He laughed at Jim's stunned expression. "And yes, I can get permission to do that. The railroad commissioner is a great friend of mine. It's amazing what officials will do for the use of a private car several times a year."

"Then how'll you use your new road?" Jim asked slowly. Like Lesley, he clearly couldn't believe his ears.

"It'll get the traffic from Pueblo. I'll build a connection from a point west of Bountiful to my new town. For west-bound service from Dodge, I'll build a spur from Clover, the next station east of here, to connect with my road at the new main depot."

"So there won't be a depot here." Lesley spelled out the devastating facts. "The tracks from Clover to here just won't be used and traffic from Pueblo will go through your town."

"You are warmly urged, my dear, to be the agent-telegrapher at the new depot town."

Lesley gestured along the street at the thriving little center where less than four months ago there had been only deserted falling-down shacks. "That's cruel, Adam Benedict! What about the people who've started businesses here

— borrowed from you because they believed you'd back the town?"

"I'll finance their move to — Shall we call my new town Zenith? Yes, I like the sound of that. I'll give them building lots there in exchange for these and credit what they're out on structures here towards what they'll need at Zenith."

"And your fancy bank?"

"It can stand as a reminder of what Kelly's stubbornness cost the town. Its life, no less." He smiled savagely, showing his teeth. "When anyone foolish enough to stay on here gives up and crawls away, be that two years or twenty, I may open up the town again."

To Lesley's astonishment, Jim laughed. "I've heard of rail rogues, Benedict. Now you're showing me one. Just don't be too sure this town will curl up and die without you."

"You think you can keep it going with your freight service?" Benedict's tone was almost pitying. "Those days are gone, Kelly, and you've passed up your only chance to hang on to them for a while. Unless you'd like to change your mind?"

"Thanks, but no, thanks." Jim turned

to Lesley. "Say, is it true I'm asked to supper?"

"True as true." She smiled, responding to his lead. "Let's see if Beth's put the soup on to heat." She tucked her hand through his arm and wasn't sure whether she did it more for Benedict's observation or for Beth's, who had come to stand in the boxcar door.

Somehow, irrationally, though Benedict had in effect erased her job and planned to do the same with her town, she felt a twinge of sympathy for him because he stood alone while she and Jim walked together — toward two children who wouldn't have their lives if he hadn't risked his.

"Do you have any ideas on how Bountiful can survive?" she asked.

"Nary a one yet," Jim said cheerfully. "But we'll have to call a meeting right away to talk about our school. That's when we can decide what to do about Benedict pulling out."

She couldn't bear to tell him that she was afraid most of their neighbors would pull out, too. What other choice, really, did they have?

Beth's eyes glowed golden as the sunset behind her as they approached. Jim smiled appreciatively back, and Lesley, with a wrench of shamed jealousy, wondered if she had waited too late to reach out for her lover's arm.

20

Jim took a chastened Bridget and Jamie to watch the prairie dogs whisk into their burrows for the night. Beth, an apron over her good suit, intently watched Lesley make biscuits. "I don't know how to cook except for making stew over a campfire in some alley out of whatever we could get," the girl confessed. "After Mama died, we never had a cookstove even when I could afford to pay for a room. What we did was live outside summers so we could rent a room when it went real cold."

"It must have been awful."

Beth shrugged. "There were plenty more like us. Mostly we helped each other as much as we could, though there was some mean enough to scrag your last potato off you."

"Wouldn't the orphanage have been better?"

Even under the expert makeup, Beth's grimace showed the thicker patch of her burns. "I was scared the little 'uns would be adopted by different folks and we'd lose track of each other — that I wouldn't know whether the kids were all right or not. I kept hoping something would happen — something good." She brooded for a moment. Lesley ached to think how it must have been for her, a child herself, to feel responsible for younger ones. "It never did, and the kids were getting old enough to start wondering why I went off with men they didn't know."

"Oh, Beth!"

The girl squared her shoulders. "When the chance came for us to head west, I thought maybe we could all work on a farm or something." She looked around the boxcar, which Lesley considered so inadequate. "I never dreamed we'd hit it lucky. I love making hats. It's not like work at all. Miss Tremayne thinks we can do real well by advertising a suit or dress with a matching hat designed to look nice on a particular woman."

"That's a terrific idea," Lesley said. "In fact, let me be your first customer for an ensemble. I really would like something new for Bella's wedding. Is her gown finished?"

"Yes, and she looks wonderful in it! It's sort of a misty green that brings out the color of her eyes, and I get to make her hat — mostly." Beth lowered her voice. "Do you know she was *scalped?*"

Lesley nodded and Beth shuddered. Her hand strayed absently to her concealed scar. "Mrs. Ballard jokes about it! Says she tried on all her wigs for her bridegroom and she'll go to her grave a blonde 'cause he's partial to the yellow curls."

"It'd take more than scalping to stop Bella. It certainly didn't keep her from finding four husbands." Beth would hear it sometime if she hadn't already. Putting the biscuits in the oven, Lesley forced herself to say as offhandedly as she could, "My father hadn't looked at a woman since my mother died, but he looked at Bella."

Beth said awkwardly, "Miss Tremayne told me about — about your father. It's grand of you to take us in so soon after it happened and all —"

"It's good to have something else to think about." Lesley spoke almost automatically, but realized it was true. From the time she'd learned of the orphan train yesterday morning, she hadn't had a moment to relapse into grief and guilt. Also, she was sure Ed Morland would have applauded her new family. That slightly eased the dull, constant ache of loss and regret.

"You're engaged to Mr. Kelly." Beth's forehead puckered as she helped set the table. "Seems like that'd give you lots of nice things to think about." She sighed worshipfully. "Wasn't he brave — and smart — to derail the handcar like that?"

"Yes, but who could have guessed Adam Benedict would decide to kill the town?"

"Can he?"

"I'm afraid so. A town with no train service will just shrivel up."

Beth looked scared. "If there's no train —"

"I won't have a job," Lesley finished.

Beth's eyes flickered like the lamplight. "I thought Mr. Benedict was a swell gentleman at first, but now I think he's mean!"

"We've got a few months. Maybe we'll think of something."

"What?"

"We haven't thought of it yet." Lesley tried to joke and stirred the simmering potato soup that smelled deliciously of dill. "Would you go call the others in for supper?"

Even in her worry over Benedict's threat, her heart warmed to see the table set for five instead of one, for a shared meal, not a lonely one — and one of the five was Jim.

He came in with laughter, Bridget clinging tight to one hand, Jamie close to his other side, and Beth behind them, face aglow. More even than last night, when the O'Haras had been so weary, they looked like a family.

Lesley was glad the youngsters and Jim had taken to each other, but Beth's open adoration made Lesley feel that *she* was unnecessary, that she'd never be missed by the family gathering at her table. Beth was already the children's mother — and from the way she watched Jim, however young she was in years, she was ripe and ready to be his woman.

Still, in spite of jealous qualms, Lesley felt hungry for the first time since her father's death. She tasted and enjoyed the rich potato soup and flaky biscuits instead of chewing a few mouthfuls as if they were sawdust.

"I never saw it myself," Jim was telling the wide-eyed children. "I was just a baby when the hunters wiped out the last buffalo on the South Plains. But my dad helped string the transcontinental telegraph wires, and he told me how the buffalo rubbed against the poles till they knocked them down."

"Why'd they do that?" asked Jamie.

"Well, son, there weren't hardly any trees on the prairies, and the critters were wild to scratch their hides, specially when they were shedding." Jim chuckled. "Somebody decided to drive spikes in the poles to keep the buffalo off, but you know what?"

"What?" echoed Bridget.

"They purely loved the spikes! Scratched those buffalo so good, my dad says you could almost hear 'em sighin' with contentment."

"I wisht there was still lots of buffalo." Jamie's tone was wistful. "Were you just a baby when there were Indians?"

"Bless your heart, there's still all kinds of Indians! Fact is, we're pretty close to the border of Indian Territory and the Osage country. There's quite a few Indian nations inside that Territory — the Cherokee Nation, the Chickasaw, the Creek and Seminole, the Choctaw. And there are more tribes in Oklahoma Territory. Each has its own government."

"They won't much longer." Lesley quoted her father. "When the United States forced those tribes out of the East back in the eighteen thirties from the Carolinas down through Florida, the Indians were given lands in Indian Territory which were promised to them forever. It didn't take forever long to come and go."

"If they still have the land —" started Beth.

"They have some of it. But as white people spread west, the government kept finding excuses to take land away from the Indians and give it to settlers."

"Indians from all over wound up in the Twin Territories," Jim added. "The Comanches and Kiowas who used to range through here have reservations south of the Osages. There's Sac and Fox and Delaware and Shawnee — more tribes than I can name."

"Many tribes don't live in the Territories," Lesley explained to the surprised New York children. "There are Sioux and Cheyenne in Montana, and Nez

Percé in Oregon and —"

"Where are the 'Paches?" whispered Bridget.

"Apaches? Some live on reservations in Arizona and New Mexico, but some called the Chiricahua were sent to forts in Florida and Alabama after Geronimo surrendered fourteen years ago. They were used to mountains and deserts, and many sickened and died. General George Crook, who had fought them, worked and pleaded till his death to get them sent back west."

"The Comanches let them have land around Fort Sill," Jim explained. "I knew one of the teamsters who brought them the last part of the way by wagon in 'ninety-four. He says when they heard coyotes again after so many years, they wept with gladness. They still aren't home, but at least they're where they can see a long way, and that's what their leaders said they wanted."

Bridget and Jamie exchanged solemn glances. "I'm sorry they can't go home," said Jamie.

"But I'm glad we won't get scalped like Mrs. Ballard," said Bridget with a fervent bounce of her head.

Jamie looked sad. "I guess the buffaloes wouldn't have liked the telegraph poles so much if they'd known the white people would kill them all."

"It's hard to believe that Mrs. Ballard and lots of folks can remember when the Indians and buffalo roamed free here," marveled Beth.

"Dad helped string the first telegraph wire west of the Missouri River in 1860," Jim said. "California and Oregon were already states with cities and industries, but a couple thousand miles of prairies and mountains stretched between the Missouri River outposts and the West Coast. During the Civil War, Congress appropriated money to help two big railroad companies, the Union Pacific and the Central Pacific, start building from both sides. Their tracks didn't join till May of 1869."

"The telegraph flashed the news to both coasts," Lesley said. "My father was a telegrapher when President Lincoln died in April of 1865. The transcontinental telegraph got the news to San Francisco within an hour, but London didn't hear of the assassination till a ship docked eleven days later."

"Sure." Beth shrugged. "But London's

across the ocean."

"It's not much farther from New York than San Francisco," Lesley said. "A cable was laid across the bottom of the Atlantic Ocean in 1858, but the wires weren't properly insulated, so any messages that got through at all were badly garbled."

"Aw, Lesley, you're teasing!" protested Jamie. "How could they spread wires across the bottom of the ocean?"

"They did, my boy, and finally made it work in 1866." Jim paused to savor a bite of golden biscuit. "That put an end to one of the most fantastical ideas a human being ever came up with — stringing telegraph wires two thirds of the way around the world, sixteen thousand miles!"

"Why?" asked Bridget.

Jim chuckled. "Well, honey, you saw the prairie dogs chatter away at each other before they dived down their holes for the night. Folks are the same way. The ones in Paris and London and New York and everywhere else like to know what's happening somewhere else."

"It's what Mr. Rudyard Kipling calls 'insatiable curiosity.'" Lesley smiled. "I'll read you that story, Bridget, about the elephant's child."

"Me, too?" begged Jamie.

"Of course, you, too!"

"Did they build the tele-telegraph?" asked Bridget.

"They made a good start," said Jim, "from California up through Canada and Alaska, which still belonged to Russia. Another work party landed in Siberia with twenty thousand telegraph poles and all the supplies for stringing almost two thousand miles of wire to meet with the line the Russians were building from Saint Petersburg."

"Daddy used to laugh about the way the work party got rid of all that stuff when a boat brought them the message to sell their supplies to the natives and come home," put in Lesley. "They sold glass insulators as teacups, crossarm brackets as kindling, and gave candles and soap and frozen cucumber pickles to anyone who'd buy their dried apples, lime juice, salt pork, and shovels. They couldn't sell the telegraph poles, but the natives probably chopped them up for fuel."

"Speaking of dried apples," said Jim, with an appreciative sniff, "is that a pie I smell?"

"It's a cobbler."

When the last crumb was polished off, Beth collected plates and put them in the dishpan of heated water and shaved soap. "You dry, Jamie. Bridgie, you put things away."

"I can't reach the top of the cupboard."

"Then climb up on a chair, goosie!"

Jim grinned at Lesley in a way that flustered her. "Looks like we're not needed here."

More primly than she felt, she said, "I've got to get up to the depot for the westbound local."

"I'll walk you there. But first I need to ask if Jamie can freight a load north with me tomorrow, and if he could spend the night at my place so we can get an early start."

The quick, joyful excitement in the boy's face turned to dread. "I — I don't think I better, Uncle Jim. Stay all night, I mean. But I can get up real early, can't I, Lesley?"

She smiled at the boy, trying to ease his humiliation. "Of course you can, Jamie."

"I wish you'd think it over." Jim dropped a big, brown hand on the thin shoulder. "You see, I've got this buffalo robe you could cuddle up in."

"A *buffalo* robe?"

"You bet. It's kind of magic."

"Honest Injun?"

"Sure. I was having lots of bad dreams a few years ago. Micajah got tired of my groaning and moaning and asked an old Comanche friend of his, a medicine man, how to help me. The Comanche gave him this robe. Roll up in it and you sleep better'n any baby I ever heard of."

"Wow!" gasped Jamie. "A real Comanche medicine man!"

"Did it stop your bad dreams?" asked Beth, with concern.

Jim nodded. "It'll take care of most problems. Now, Jamie, how can you pass up a chance like that?"

The boy glanced beseechingly at Lesley. She pitied his quandary. Would the magic robe work — or would he commit the horrible accident of soaking it? You couldn't toss a hide in hot water and wash it out. As the responsible adult, she was in a quandary, too. This might be a cure, but if it wasn't, how excruciating it would be for Jamie!

Above the boy's dark head, Jim's eyes

459

caught hers. He gave an almost imperceptible nod.

"I think you should sleep in the robe, Jamie," Lesley assured him. "Not everyone gets a chance at a magic one."

The child threw back his head and gazed at Jim with such hope and trust that Lesley's throat tightened. "All right, Uncle Jim! I'll wash my feet good before I curl up in that robe."

"Great. I'll come back for you after I walk Lesley to the depot."

"I'll dry these ole dishes fast as Beth can wash 'em." Jamie tackled his job with gusto. Lesley tossed her shawl around her shoulders and stepped out into the darkness. Jim slipped his hand under her elbow. She was glad to feel it there, glad of his closeness, but please, please, let him understand that she couldn't kiss him yet, couldn't embrace him.

"I hope your robe won't be ruined."

"Oh, I reckon we'd salvage it. Anyhow, I don't need it anymore."

"You really did have bad dreams?"

"I really did."

"The war?"

"Yes."

He'd never talked about the war except to agree with Father that instead of helping Cubans win their freedom, the United States had made them vassals. He clearly didn't want to talk about it now, so Lesley asked, "Did the robe truly help you?"

"Something did. Maybe it was knowing that Micajah cared that much. Maybe it was talking to him. After all, he fought in the Civil War. He's had his nightmares."

One of the worst must have been finding his children frozen. Yet he could laugh now and court his widow lady. Just as Bella could be jolly and preparing for her wedding after her scalping and loss of three husbands. Just as Susan Lee, doubly bereaved, would surely marry Hugh someday. Life did go on, Lesley knew. In time, surely, zest would flow back into hers.

But when? When would she feel she had the right to laugh, to love, to be happy? That brought her back to Benedict's ominous plans. "Jim, have you thought of any way to keep Benedict from ruining Bountiful?"

"I have a kind of notion, but I don't want to talk about it till I see if there's a chance of it working."

"Jim!"

"Now, if you want to coax me —"

"There's the telegraph!" She jerked her arm away and rushed inside.

Jim lounged by the desk while she took down a message for the westbound local. "Lesley, will you make sure that everybody hears about the meeting tomorrow night?"

"There doesn't seem much use in starting a school when we may not have a town by March."

"Starting a school could be one way we'll keep the town. Anyhow, four months of school for the kids beats nothing."

He was right. Ashamed of her defeatism, Lesley said, "I'll get the word around."

"That's my girl." Before she could step back, he brushed a kiss across the tip of her nose. "Pretend that was a butterfly." He grinned and went out.

The sound of his boots on the platform echoed in her heart. For a moment she closed her eyes, thought of how it would be to rest in his arms in his robe, and knew, with a surge of longing, that any covering they shared, however tattered and worn, would be magic indeed.

Next morning as Lesley and the O'Hara sisters hurried across the tracks to meet Susan, Beth anxiously scanned the area around Jim and Bella's board-sided tents and wagon-yard. All three freighters were gone.

"The magic must have worked for Jamie," Lesley assured the girl. "The robe's not hanging over the corral. That's what Jim, Bella, and Micajah use for a clothesline."

"I hope so. Maybe I should have warned Jim, but that would have mortified Jamie."

No *Uncle* Jim? Of course, Beth was a little old for honorary uncles, especially young, handsome ones. "Jim knew," Lesley said. "Mrs. Ellis told him."

Beth's tawny eyes softened. "So he took a chance on ruining the robe in hopes it would cure Jamie!" She drew a deep breath that lifted her full, youthful breasts provocatively. "I think Jim Kelly is the most wonderful man in the whole world!"

"Mm-hm." It was good to hear Jim praised, but Lesley felt uneasy at Beth's enthusiasm.

"Don't you think so?" Beth demanded.

"Think what?"

"That Jim's wonderful!"

"Well, I — uh —"

Beth stopped as Bridget ran on down the lane to meet Susan. Planting her hands on her hips, Beth stared accusingly at Lesley. "If — if you don't *know* he's wonderful, you don't deserve him!" She called to her sister, "Behave yourself, Bridgie!" and stalked toward Ellen Tremayne's.

A little dazed and more than a little resentful, Lesley helped Bridget scramble into Susan's cart for the short ride to the Schillers'. The way everyone was helping with the children, it was more as if Bountiful, rather than Lesley, had taken them in. She was telling a horrified Susan about Benedict's threat and that night's meeting when Rutherford Miles came out of his office, Robbie tagging him, and strolled up to the women.

With a tousling of Robbie's brown curls, the editor chuckled. "As soon as Ann Roberts knew this young man would be one of her pupils, she said she'd love to start a school here. She'd have to teach the twins anyway —

seems they can't read past primer, though they're eleven — and of course, even a small salary will come in handy." He frowned as he glanced from Susan to Lesley. "What's the matter, ladies? Aren't you glad we'll have a school?"

They told him. He whistled long and loud. "Holy smoke! Benedict's acting like a jealous lover, just like the town jilted him! He'll lose a bundle if he pulls out of Bountiful and finances business-people who'll move with him."

"He doesn't care." Lesley swallowed the lump in her throat. "He can't stand for Jim to be important and looked up to in the town he'd intended to be his showcase."

"After the way Jim saved his train last night and kept it from hitting those children, you'd think Benedict would be grateful!" Susan cried.

"Not as grateful as he is jealous." Lesley shook her head. "He offered to make Jim head of a big freighting outfit operating out of one of the depots on the new railroad. That was his grati-tude. When Jim turned him down, Benedict evidently felt justified in wrecking Jim's business."

"What about you?" Susan asked.

465

"You'd think after the way your father was killed protecting that payroll —"

Lesley couldn't keep an edge of derisive bitterness out of her voice. "Oh, he offered me the job of agent-telegrapher at his new queen city. Zenith, he plans to call it."

"You didn't accept?" asked Rutherford with a lift of eyebrows.

"Of course not — and he knew I wouldn't. It was just to salve his conscience."

"Doesn't sound to me as if he has one!" Susan burst out. "Luring people here with promises that Bountiful was going to be a principal center, lending them money for farms and businesses, and then, just as Bountiful's becoming a town, he yanks the rug out from under us!"

"Actually," murmured Rutherford, "he's yanking the railroad."

"Whatever you call it, it's wicked and mean! I don't want to move, but even if I did, I couldn't. Every cent I have is sunk in my home and business." A tear glinted in Susan's eye. "I didn't borrow from Benedict's dratted old bank, so he won't finance me."

"Oh, I'm sure he would," said Lesley.

"He'll delight in coaxing everyone he can away from Bountiful."

The hope in Susan's face turned to embarrassment. "If it were just me, I'd never leave while you and Jim stay, Lesley. But I have the children to think of."

"We can't blame you for doing what's best for Dusty and Sally." Lesley smiled at them now as they hugged Cap to give Bridget room. "That's why we're having the meeting, to talk over what people can do."

Her gaze swept from the knoll where her father rested near Susan's baby, touched the homes and businesses she had watched come into being, and traveled past the well and watering trough at the bustling heart of the community to the fringe where the drugstores clustered near the construction camp.

Echoing her thought, Susan said, "It all looks so prosperous! After all, there were towns before there were railroads!"

"Yes," said Lesley, "but none of those towns had railroads. They all depended on wagon freighting or water shipping. A town these days that doesn't have rail service has to compete with those that do."

"That's why so many withered away," Rutherford said glumly. "It costs more and takes a lot longer to haul supplies and manufactures and farm products in and out by wagon. People aren't likely to move by wagon or buggy when they can take a train and transport all their belongings cheap and fast."

Lesley had a sudden appalling thought. "Without a railroad, the newspapers won't come in, Rutherford. You won't know what's going on in time to print it." Rutherford prided himself on not using the "ready print" sheets many small papers did. These had state, national, and international news printed on one side of a sheet, leaving the other side blank for local news.

The editor blinked. Then he recovered and flourished a hand toward his other occupations. "Ah, dear lady, I can still take photographs, paint portraits and signs, repair clocks and watches, and practice law!"

"Yes," protested Susan, "but a town without a paper is —"

She floundered. "Like a person without a voice," Rutherford supplied. "Well, I could still print local news. That's what people like best."

"They aren't going to like this," predicted Lesley.

"It's a big story. Lots of drama." Rutherford's large nose twitched as if tracking sensational news. He suddenly laughed and furled his mustache a jaunty bit higher on both sides. "By jiminy, I'm going to interview Mr. Benedict! Then I'll talk to the businesspeople he's leaving high and dry unless they move to his new town. I'll print a special edition and send it to every newspaper in the state. Adam Benedict's going to look like a heartless, power-crazy robber baron."

"You won't have to invent much," Lesley said. "But that'll cut your throat, Rutherford. He won't make good your losses or help you set up in Zenith."

"Call me Ruff, please, like the children do. I think it's rather dashing."

Lesley had to grin, though she shook her head. "You'd better think it over, Ruff." The affectionate name came easily. He probably missed her father more than anyone except her, and Father had loved their wide-ranging arguments. "Of course, it would be thrilling and glorious to expose the villain just like Henry Demarest Lloyd denounced

Standard Oil and other monopolies in *Wealth Against Commonwealth.* But this is real life. If almost everybody leaves Bountiful, there'll be no one to read *The Banner* — and not enough call for signs and portraits, watch repairs, and lawyering to keep you going."

"Are *you* leaving?"

"Not if I can think of any way to make a living." She smiled across the tracks toward the mounds of the prairie dog town. "I want to make sure no one plows up that village, and I watched this one change from a ghost town to what it is now. For the first time in my life, I belong, and not just because my father's buried here."

Susan nodded and glanced toward the little grave on the slope beside the larger one. "That's how I feel. You were all so good to me when I came here not knowing a soul. It was finding a family I didn't know I had. This is home."

The three friends looked at each other solemnly. Lesley's eyes blurred. "Let's go ahead and start our school. Try to get everyone to come to the meeting tonight, Susan. Maybe we can think of some way to keep the town alive."

"Rob and I will drive out and ask the

Robertses to come," said Rutherford. He snapped his brown fedora down smartly on his gleaming crown, and the sparkle in his eyes changed from mischief to battle lust. "Then we're calling on Mr. Benedict. Rob, go tell your mama where we're going while I fetch the buggy."

The boy ran into Ellen's, the man rushed up the street, and Susan turned her cart after him. " 'Bye, Lesley!" called Bridget, waving. "Mattie and me won't get in trouble today! Cross my heart and hope to die!"

"Don't say such an awful thing!" Lesley shuddered. "Just behave yourself and keep a long, long way from the railroad tracks!"

She crossed them herself as Elden Griffith drove up with six ten-gallon steel milk cans. The wiry, graying dairy farmer had recently taken up land a few miles from town. When Lesley told him about the meeting and why it was being held, he smothered the first words that sprang to his lips, gulped heavily, and said, "We'll be there, Miss Morland, me'n the missus. Who does Benedict think he is, playin' these games? I moved here because it was close enough to haul my milk and cream to the railroad!"

"To be fair, Mr. Benedict would probably help you start over somewhere along his new line."

"Start over!" Faded blue eyes glared from a face lined and weathered by many seasons of wind and sun. "That's what we done here! Just got a new floor laid in the old farmhouse, put on a new roof, dug a new well! We're settled. We want to stay that way."

"Come to the meeting," Lesley said.

21

The meeting was set for eight o'clock so the westbound local should have roared on its way and farm people could do their chores before driving in. Late that afternoon, Lesley had built a fire in the potbellied stove so the waiting room was comfortable. Jim, who'd got back in time to collect extra chairs and benches in his wagon and bring them to the depot, had a glint in his eye as he and Rutherford arranged the seats, but not even the editor could get him to say much about what, if any, inspirations he'd come up with. There was an air of contained excitement about him, though, that made Lesley think that against all probability — possibility, almost — he'd hit on some thread of hope for Bountiful.

The Schiller sisters had brought vats of hot cocoa. Beth, in her green suit, delectable hat, and perfect makeup, unrecognizable as the embattled waif who'd arrived in this depot only two nights before, helped dispense cups of cocoa to people coming in from the chill night. Jamie, with Mark and Helen, the dark-haired twins taken in by Ann and Avery Roberts, proudly offered trays of chocolate-iced lady fingers, almond macaroons, sugar cookies, and date bars baked by Ann, Ellen, Susan, and Lesley.

"Does it not warm the heart to see how the young ones already are at home?" Lilibet's green eyes shone as they dotingly rested on Mattie, who was taking turns with Bridget in crooning to Fe and cuddling the little cat. Atchison had curved his back at them, hissed, and fled to his accustomed perch on top of the highest bookshelf.

Indeed, the decently clothed, well-scrubbed children no longer looked like the nervous orphans who had met their guardians such a short time ago. Robbie snuggled up to Ellen, munching a cookie. Alan Meadows, seated by Andy Hart, the livery owner, already looked less starved. His black hair, no longer scruffy, was neatly trimmed, and his plaid flannel shirt was new, as were cowboy boots displayed by rolled-up new Levi's. The Wellivers' Oliver followed their example, filling one hand with gingerbread and the other with cookies.

The doors were open between office and waiting room. These rooms were packed. There were even people in the baggage room. Even the Literary hadn't filled the depot this full. Memory of her father's last night engulfed Lesley with raw pain. It seemed a lifetime since she had seen him, yet it was really only six weeks. He would have enjoyed seeing people gather like this to plan a school, but he would have been devastated by the prospect of Bountiful without a railroad.

"Why don't you run this show, Ruff?" asked Jim. "You use words a whole lot better than I do."

"You called the meeting," the editor parried.

"Yeah, I guess I'm to blame for the fix we're in. All the more reason I shouldn't ramrod this prayer meeting."

As if they'd rehearsed it, both men swung toward Lesley. "Will you do it, Lesley?" asked Jim.

"After all," pointed out Rutherford, "the depot is your territory."

"I'll handle the school business if one

of you takes over the discussion of what we're going to do without rail service."

"Fair enough." What did Jim have up his sleeve? His eyes sparkled as he cupped his hands and called, "All right, folks! Find your seats. If there aren't enough of them, some of you younger fellas can lean against the wall. Miss Lesley Morland has the floor."

She had never spoken at a public meeting, much less presided at one. Warm, unexpected applause began as she walked to the center of the waiting room and didn't diminish till she raised a protesting hand. The nervousness that had made people look strange for a moment dissolved as she looked from Susan to Ellen and the Schillers.

"Friends and neighbors," she began. "Most of you know that rail service to Bountiful will probably end next spring. Before we talk about that, we need to decide if we'll have a school."

"Seems to me that we need to know if we'll have a town first," said Elden Griffith, who had brought his rosy, blond, considerably younger wife and three yellow-haired stair-step children who all looked to be under ten or eleven.

"It could be that starting the school

will help us keep the town," countered Lesley.

"How?" The graying dairy farmer wasn't being rude. He just didn't see any value in beginning something that might only last four or five months.

"Having a school shows we care about our children. It'll prove we can work together for something good and important." Lesley searched for words and they came. "A school is for the children we hope will grow up and live here. A school is faith that we have a future."

Susan, face aglow, led the clapping.

"That all sounds very fine." Sam Welliver puffed to his feet, and his sand brown eyes flitted around the room as if seeking allies. "But schools cost money. Oliver here's through sixth grade; he don't need no more book-learning. Why should people without kids in school pay to support it?"

"For all the reasons Miss Morland just voiced so eloquently," flashed Rutherford.

"It may be we can have night classes for children needed at work and any adults who'd like to come," Lesley said. "It's our school; we can arrange things to fit our needs as long as we satisfy state requirements."

"Pure-dee foolishness," Sam grunted. "We're not giving a dime. We —"

"Those of us who do will not bar your Oliver from night school if he wants to come," cut in Lilibet Schiller. She turned to Ann Roberts, who was sitting right behind her. "Is it true, Mrs. Roberts, that you will teach?"

"I'd love to." Ann Roberts's steel gray hair was pulled back in a plain bun beneath her sedate black bonnet, but her dark eyes sparkled with zest. "I've missed teaching, and I'd be tutoring Helen and Mark anyway." She glanced fondly at the dark-haired girl and boy who sat between her and her husband as if they'd fitted there from birth. "I used to be paid forty dollars a month, but I'd like to make half of that our contribution to the school."

"The first thing a businessperson learns is to beware of cut-rate products," Agatha Welliver sniffed.

Ellen frowned at her before turning to Mrs. Roberts. "It would be far more than your share if you reduced your salary five dollars a month."

"If the rest of us can't raise thirty-five dollars amongst us, we don't deserve a school," Susan said.

"Where's it going to be?" demanded Welliver. "You giving up your old barn to it, Mrs. Lee?"

Before Susan could answer, Lesley said, "Unless he's changed his mind, Mr. Benedict will let us use the depot. It has to be heated anyway, so except for night classes, we won't need extra coal."

"I'm giving lumber at cost for desks and benches," said redheaded Leroy Martin.

"Ruff, Jim, Andy Hart, and me can make everything and even put up more shelves," said Hugh.

"I've got my old teacher's trunk," Ann Roberts said happily. "Thank goodness, mice haven't got to the globe and maps and lots of things I saved."

"What about textbooks?" nattered Agatha. "What about subjects? No use to a lot of this newfangled stuff like science and civics!"

"If you won't support the school, madam," said Rutherford icily, "I submit that the curriculum is none of your concern."

They glared at each other. Before anyone else leaped into the fray, Lesley raised her hands and swept the crowd with a look that hushed them.

"We can work out the details later, folks! What we need to decide right now is: Are we going to have a school?"

"You bet we are!" roared Hugh MacLeod. The husky blacksmith rose with Dusty half-asleep on his broad shoulder, fair head partly hidden by Hugh's curly red beard. "I move we vote by acclamation to hire Mrs. Roberts at thirty-five dollars a month and elect a school board here and now with Rutherford Miles as president."

Amid the chorus of "Aye!" the Wellivers' "Nay" was scarcely audible. "I don't have children," Rutherford demurred.

"You got me!" cried Robbie.

"You're the best-educated, Ruff," argued Hugh.

"Lesley should be on the board," suggested Susan. "She's got three children and has charge of the depot."

Another affirmative chorus. "The Griffiths have three children, too," said Jim. "Would either of you make our third member?"

"Let the missus." Elden ducked his graying head, then lifted it and grinned.

"I'd admire to be in one of them night classes. I can cipher a little and write my name, but that's doggone near all of it."

Alice Griffith was quickly approved. The furniture builders conferred with Leroy Martin and said they could have the depot fitted up for classes by Monday.

"Splendid!" For an instant, Lesley saw her father at the telegraph, smiling. When she stared, he was gone, but her heart weighed less like a frosty stone in her breast. She believed he did know what was happening to his depot, and that he was pleased. Blinking away the moisture in her eyes, she said, "Let's give a hand to our teacher and our new school!"

"And the school board and Madam Chairman here!" proposed Jim, stepping toward the front to swell the subsiding ovation into a fresh one.

The door opened and closed. Adam Benedict towered there. He clapped heartily and bowed to Lesley with an extravagant sweep of his gray hat, but his appearance changed the atmosphere in the room from one of warmth and trust to guardedness.

In spite of this intrusion, Lesley was flushed with the sense of having rather creditably run the first part of Bountiful's first town meeting. She sat down in the space Jamie and Bridget made for her between them on the bench. Beth was at the end. Her gaze was fixed on Jim in a way that made Lesley's insides contract.

He did look handsome, got up for the occasion in black coat and tie and a white shirt starched and ironed to perfection. The scar that disappeared into unruly black hair on his right temple showed he had been through danger. Lesley ached to touch the lean, hard angle of his jaw and wondered how a mouth that had such a firm set could soften on hers so tenderly. Feeling Benedict's jade-depthed dark eyes on her, Lesley reached down to scoop up Fe, who was purring beneath her skirt, and settled the kitten in Bridget's possessive arms.

"Folks," said Jim, "now that we've got our school, we have to figure out how to keep our town." He looked at the expensively dressed man in the door. "Since you've come to our meeting, Benedict, I reckon that means you'll answer questions."

Benedict inclined his shining head. "Indeed. Though I must say that the sudden shift in mood when I entered makes me feel like the bad fairy who wasn't invited to the christening but came anyway." His amused scrutiny noted everyone there, Lesley was sure. "Or," went on the railroad builder in a bantering tone, "is this a burial?"

"Bountiful's going to be the liveliest corpse you ever saw," Jim promised. He set his back toward Benedict and faced the assembly. "You've all heard that we won't have rail service as of this coming spring. You've probably also heard that Benedict will help merchants and farmers who've borrowed from his bank relocate if they want to."

Sam Welliver heaved to his feet and crossed his arms across his bulging front. "We intend to avail ourselves of Mr. Benedict's generous offer," he said pompously. "I'd advise those of you who can to do the same."

"We never borrowed," Elden said bitterly. "We just sunk all our savings in land and buildings here, countin' on the railroad to haul our dairy stuff to market."

"I regret the inconvenience," said the entrepreneur blandly.

"Inconvenience!" sputtered Elden.

"So I will exchange your land for an equal amount along the route, pay for your improvements at fair valuation, and transport your livestock and belongings free."

The farmer blinked and his jaw dropped. He glanced at his wife. She shook her head, put her arms protectively around her two youngest, and looked straight at Benedict. "And what happens, sir, when you decide to abandon that railroad, too? We will not go. We will not help you kill Bountiful."

He shrugged. "You may change your mind, ma'am. I understand your exasperation and won't hold it against you."

His magnanimous tone infuriated Lesley, but she couldn't have blamed any of these people for accepting his offer. For those totally dependent on the railroad, it was the only apparent alternative to bankruptcy.

One of these, Leroy Martin, who got his lumber and supplies by rail, spoke gingerly. "Maybe we could haul stuff from the depot I reckon you'll build a couple miles west where the new road joins this one. We could manage that, I guess."

"Ah, but there won't be a depot there." Benedict sighed as if regretting it. "My new plans call for a depot about twenty miles to the north on the line I'll build to connect with the Santa Fe, and another fifteen miles south. Neither very helpful to Bountiful, I fear."

"That's the idea, isn't it?" asked Jim. "Fifteen miles either way means a day and a half or two by freight wagon, which adds a lot to the cost of everything we buy or sell. You're deliberately cutting us off from a railroad."

"Of course I am. Otherwise what would be the point in all this?" Benedict's eyes traveled over the faces, widening slightly as they rested on Beth, whose own eyes were a blaze of golden fury. He smiled at her and Lesley. "Are there any other questions?"

"You've made your aim to destroy the town you started abundantly clear," said Rutherford. "I assure you, sir, this story will reach every newspaper in the state."

"I've never lost money for my stockholders," said Benedict with cool nonchalance. "They won't question me."

"Businesspeople may be wary of investing in your new town of Zenith," the editor pointed out.

"Not if the incentives are great enough — and they will be." The magnate beamed at the Wellivers. "Including these good folks, several other businesspeople have decided to move." His voice hardened. "Why delude yourselves? You know and I know you may hang on for a while, but the skin of your teeth does wear out. Without a railroad, Bountiful is dead. All you can delay is the funeral."

He bowed and went out with that grace so surprising in such a massive man. As he shut that door, the back one opened. A slight swarthy man in stained work clothes stood there, clutching a battered hat in his hands.

"*Señores y señoras,*" he began. "*Yo* — I — I wish —" He pointed to himself. "*Mis niños* — children —" Baffled, he sighted the shelves of books and took one. Opening it, he pretended to read. "Children — read *Inglés?*" he ventured hopefully. "*Escuela?*"

While Lesley and the others looked helplessly at each other, Jim spoke to the stranger. After several courteous questions, he explained, "Señor Carbajal is one of the section gang that'll keep the nearest stretch of new railroad in repair. Their camp is at the first construction site, the junction of this road with the southern one. He heard we might start a school and he wonders if his children might attend."

The small, wiry man spoke quickly, spreading his hands. Jim listened, nodded his understanding, and explained, "He and his wife very much wish for their two children to learn English, and so does a neighbor who has an eight-year-old. They want to pay."

Everyone looked at Ann Roberts. "I'd be glad to have the children," she said with an apologetic smile at the dark-skinned man. "I don't know any Spanish, though."

Jim translated back and forth. "Señor Carbajal says that is good. The children will learn faster that way because they'll have to." Jim looked around. "Is it okay if I tell him to send the kids Monday? It's fair enough for the families to chip in on the teacher's salary — and important to their pride, too, I'd reckon."

Rutherford, as head of the school board, had been doing some figuring.

"It looks like we have eleven full-time pupils, not counting the Robertses' two, as well as several night students. Dividing thirty-five dollars by eleven comes out a tad over three dollars per child. Or would you rather divide it per family?"

"I think by family is fairer," said Leroy Martin. "Folks with more kids to shoe and feed need their cash."

There was general agreement. Jim said, "Most of us without children would like to help. Count me in — and I bet Micajah and Bella will want to help."

"Me, too," called Hugh.

"And I want to help sponsor young Rob here." Rutherford counted again. "All right. Assuming Micajah and Bella come through, that gives thirteen supporters. Comes to two seventy each."

Jim told Señor Carbajal what had been decided. The man nodded and bowed in courtly fashion.

"*Mil gracias,*" he said, smiling. "Thank you, much much thank you!"

He went out into the night, closing the squeaking door as carefully as he could. The Wellivers rose as one, Oliver between them. "That beats all!" Sam was so angry that he sounded out of breath. "Letting Meskins into school! We'll have no art nor part of it! The sooner we can get out of this crazy place, the better!"

They slammed out. The glances exchanged all over the room said that the Wellivers had better move since no one here would trade with them again except in dire necessity. The other mercantile owner, Mr. Beasley, a reclusive old bachelor, didn't mingle, but neither did he jangle.

"I'm glad no one else feels that way," said Rutherford, "or the town might not be worth saving. Now, Jim, how're we going to do that?"

"Yeah," said Elden Griffith gloomily. "How are we going to get along without a railroad?"

Jim stepped to the front, and again that suppressed eagerness gave his eyes the brilliance of sunlight behind a thunderhead. "We aren't going to get along without a railroad. We're going to build one — if you'll all help."

There was a collective gasp. Lesley wondered if outrage at Benedict had addled Jim's thinking. "Build a railroad?" Hugh shook his fiery head. "Lad, do you know what you're saying?"

489

"It's possible. Tough, but possible."

"How?"

"The farmers are pretty much through with fall planting. Mr. Roberts, I know you hired on with your team to help build the first part of the southern railroad."

Avery Roberts nodded. "So did several others who couldn't come tonight."

"I've got a team and wagon," said Elden, "but I got too many cows to milk morning and evening to take on other jobs."

"Someone could use your outfit, though?"

"Sure, if they'll take good care of my horses." Elden frowned. "I think you're saying we could build a roadbed, Jim. But where? Benedict won't let us connect with his lines."

"We'll build to the Santa Fe twenty miles north to Buckeye. During the boom, the Santa Fe surveyed a spur south of there but only built across the Arkansas River when they abandoned the idea. They've maintained that few miles because of a gravel pit they haul from. I wired the officials from the Buckeye depot today. They have no objection — after all, it'll increase their revenue. They held on to the land they got for proposing the spur and will sell that to us cheap, on credit."

"Don't see how a bunch of people can just up and build a railroad," said Leroy doubtfully. "Course, that's what I worked at till I saved enough to open my lumberyard."

"A little town in the Panhandle just built their own road in order not to wither away," said Jim. "Haven't a lot of you worked on the railroad one way or another?"

Every man there made affirmative nods or sounds. "I did everything from lay tracks to run the engine," said Hugh.

"I've laid track, too, and was a fireman," said Andy Hart. "Got to run the engine once in a while, but it would have been a long time till I could've been a full-time engineer. I got tired of shovelin' coal and decided it was more fun to work with horses."

"I hammered spikes one summer," Rutherford said. "Wanted to see what it was like — and I needed the money."

"Dan Nelson will round up neighbors to help when we get halfway," Jim went on. "It would be a big convenience for them to have rails by their farms. Dan's sure all of them will gladly give a right-of-way."

Hugh's hopeful look faded. "I can't hammer out twenty miles of track. And there's the ties and spikes."

"The Railroad Commission will have to approve it." Avery Roberts's voice was rueful. "I hear Benedict's a great pal of the commissioner."

"The Commission would have a hard time justifying a denial to a town cut off from service." Jim grinned at Rutherford. "Especially with our editor here able and ready to expose them."

"Would I ever!"

"Of course, we'll have to hire a surveyor and do it right," Jim planned. "If we agree this is what we want, several of us need to go to Topeka and talk to the commissioners. And we need to see the big boys at the Santa Fe and wheedle them into leasing us an engine with a few cars to run out of Bountiful and back a couple of times a week."

"A 'try-weekly'?" quipped Rutherford. His dark eyes glinted with the joy of battle. "We'll sure raise hel—iotropes if the Commission tries to give us the run-around. The editor of the Topeka paper is a good friend of mine. He'll roast them brown up there in the capital, where the governor and legislature will have to take notice."

"I still want to know where the rails and ties are coming from," persisted Leroy. "I can probably get a good deal on cedar ties out of Missouri and I'd let the builders have 'em at cost — but I got to have the cost, or a fair share of it. It's worth plenty to me not to have to move to Benedict's town, but I can't afford to go bankrupt, either."

Ellen Tremayne spoke for the first time, with quiet authority. "Everyone the road will help has to be asked if they'll contribute money or work or both. Mr. Martin can get quotes on what the materials will cost." She showed an unexpected dimple. "We can't borrow from Mr. Benedict's bank, but I have banker friends in Saint Louis and Kansas City. I'm sure they'd lend me generous sums."

If anyone caught a genteel whiff of blackmail, they didn't say so. "I went to school with a banker in Dodge," said Elden. "I hate to borrow on my farm and cows, but we'd rather do that than move." He turned to his wife. "Wouldn't we, Alice?"

She nodded. Lilibet, cradling Mattie's blond head in her lap, cleared her throat and said gruffly, "We have savings, and our father" — her face went stony — "he died in August without a will, so all came to us, a good farm and livestock, which we sold to a neighbor. There was also money — silver dollars and gold pieces. We will invest most of this in the railroad."

"We'll have to work out shares and all of that," Jim said. "I've talked it over with Micajah and Bella. We've agreed to mortgage our business to help with this, and we have some cash to boot."

"And I've a bit put by," rumbled Hugh. "Maybe we can do it, lad!"

Lesley had never felt so poor as now, when she didn't have anything to contribute. Feeding and clothing the three youngsters she'd taken in would at least triple her expenses, and she had to save what she could to make payments on the prairie dog town.

This must have shown on her face. Jim said, "Don't anybody fret if they can't kick in money. The will to keep our town is just as important. Benedict offered Miss Lesley the job of agent in the big, fancy depot he'll build at Zenith, but she's staying here."

"So am I," said Susan. "You gave me a new life when I thought I'd never smile again, and my baby's buried on the slope."

"I'll stay as long as I can earn a living," said Andy Hart.

Rutherford nodded. "No one can say fairer than that. I nominate Jim Kelly as president of the Bountiful Railroad with power to negotiate, contract, and make needful decisions on our behalf."

"Whoa!" called Jim, as the "Ayes" resounded. "I nominate — if they're willing — Rutherford Miles, Hugh MacLeod, and Leroy Martin to serve with me as a committee — and I entreat Miss Ellen Tremayne to keep us straight and be secretary-treasurer, with a full vote on all proceedings."

The slate met with united acclaim. "Here we go then, folks," said Jim. "We'll call another meeting when Ruff and I get back from Topeka. But first we're going to make the desks and such so school can start up Monday."

"Monday's election day!" Rutherford looked pleadingly at Lesley. "Could we pay you to stay up late while the returns come in, Miss Lesley? I'm praying Bryan will win, but I'm afraid Rough Rider Roosevelt's campaign has put him in the shade."

"You won't have to pay me," Lesley said. With a pang, she remembered how her father had always chalked up the returns on the blackboard and had never gone to bed till the results were certain. "Anyone who wants to can come listen. It'll probably be pretty well settled by midnight."

The gathering broke up, expressions varying from Rutherford's jubilant grin to Elden Griffith's dogged resolve. "I'll haul these chairs back where they belong in the morning," Jim said as Lesley prepared to close the depot for the night. Bridget had gone to sleep on Beth's shoulder, and Jamie could hardly keep his eyes open. "Let me carry your little sister home, son. Then we'll go let you snuggle up in that magic robe."

Lesley went ahead to open the door to the boxcar and light a lamp. Jim's plan was daring, but with everyone behind it, it just might work.

22

All the town, except for the Wellivers and some customers and proprietors of the drugstore joints, came to hear the election returns wired in. Benedict was off somewhere in his private car, and Micajah and Bella were on the road.

Bountiful wasn't yet organized as a voting district, so the men eligible to vote had traveled to the polls at Providence School, where the boy taken in by Dan Nelson was a student.

Lesley looked around the depot, which that day had become a classroom. "Maybe next election, people can vote right here."

"People!" snapped Lilibet, banging down a huge bowl of doughnuts. "Men are the only ones who vote, Leschen, so don't say *people!*"

"Well, men are people, I guess," said Lesley in peaceable fashion. She had grown up so worried about her father's drinking that she hadn't developed much interest in women's voting. She spread some old newspapers on her desk to insulate the wood from the five-gallon enameled coffeepot Lisa and Lena carried along with a basket of blue enameled cups. Next to the yeastily fragrant golden brown doughnuts was the dishpan of popcorn Beth had popped and whisked with Susan's melted butter and a little salt.

"Is it not *wunderschön*," said Lena, "to have a school so quickly? Mattie learned already to write her new name and all of ours."

Mattie, in yet another pretty frock, turned the globe that occupied a corner of the sturdy table serving Ann Roberts as a temporary desk. The little blond girl pointed to Germany. "Here's where my mothers' parents came from," she said. "Look how big the ocean is they had to cross!"

Maps of the world, the United States, and Kansas brightened the formerly dull walls. The seven simple desks and benches were of varying heights to fit children of different sizes, two to a desk with one place left over. The sand-papering wasn't finished, so as people drifted in, the men tackled that task while the women sewed or mended or knitted.

The raggedness of Jamie's clothes had compelled Lesley to buy him two complete new outfits, but darning the toes and heels of his wool stockings should get a little more wear out of them. He was playing marbles with Mark Altman at the back of the room, proudly attired in the green cheviot Norfolk jacket with the Kitchener yoke that Jim had bought for him. Lesley had darned her own and her father's socks as a matter of course. That hadn't given her the warm, responsible feeling of doing something for the boy who was too old to be her son, but might well have been her younger brother.

As results tapped out on the sounder, Lesley recorded them on the blackboard amidst disgust or elation. As the night wore on, it was clear that Kansas would go completely Republican except for a few congressional seats.

Rutherford shook his head over the latest heavy returns for McKinley and Roosevelt. "The Democrats did themselves in more thoroughly than usual this time. First, they enraged the Populists and Free Silver backers by nominating Adlai Stevenson as Bryan's running mate. Then they hammered another nail in their coffin by adopting an anti-imperialist plank."

"That's the main reason I voted for 'em," said Jim, brushing sawdust off the edge of a bench now rounded so it wouldn't cut little legs. "I know doggone well, Ruff, that you don't think we have any business taking over the Philippines or forcing Cuba to do what we say."

"Now, hold on, Jim." Andy Hart blew sawdust off his upper lip. "Them Filipinos ought to be glad we helped 'em run off the Spaniards."

"Did you read in my paper," asked Rutherford, "that Major Littleton Waller, accused of killing eleven helpless Filipinos, replied that his commander, General Smith, had ordered him to kill every male above the age of ten?"

"That's a lie!" growled Andy.

"I wish it were." The editor's eyes blazed. "To Kansas's shame, Andy, the Twentieth Kansas swept through Caloocan. Of seventeen thousand inhabitants, not one living native remains. One soldier from Washington wrote home to say that shooting human beings beats rabbit hunting all to pieces."

Troubled by the usually genial Rutherford's impassioned outburst, everyone worked in silence for a while. When Dusty, Sally, and Rob got sleepy, Susan took them to her house, saying Rob could spend the night. "And since I don't get to vote," she said to Hugh, in what was for her an unusually severe tone, "don't bother to wake me up to say who won!"

"Aw, Susie!" protested Hugh. "Kansas does better by women than most states."

Ann Roberts said in a peacemaking tone, "Women got equal control of children and property and the right to vote in school board elections not long after the Civil War. I think it was 1887 when the legislature passed a law allowing them to vote in city and bond elections."

"All well and good," sniffed Ellen Tremayne. "But we still can't elect the president or congressmen or state officials."

"One reason men are scared to give women the vote is that so many campaigners for suffrage like Susan B. Anthony and Elizabeth Cady Stanton are also leaders in the temperance movement," said Rutherford. "Men fond of the bottle are afraid women'll take it away from them as soon as they can vote."

"That is a poor reason to keep half the population from voting," pronounced Lilibet Schiller. She scowled at Rutherford. "Do not tell me, please, that it will cheapen and degrade women to have some voice in who governs and makes laws. It is more degrading to be dependent on a drunken man, be he husband or father."

"I couldn't agree more, Miss Lilibet." The editor crossed his heart with a flourish. "I always have supported women's suffrage, though I think prohibition can't stop drinking and nurtures lawbreaking like that evidenced by our drugstores on the edge of town."

"Sometimes I think Carry Nation has the correct methods," retorted Lilibet. "Mattchen, you are asleep almost!" She thrust her knitting in a bag and took her new daughter's hand. "Come, we shall go home, you and I." She gave her younger sisters an admonishing look. "Stay if you wish, but I expect help with breakfast in the morning."

Lisa and Lena stayed, probably savoring the rare opportunity to elude Lilibet's watchful eye. Beth took a drowsy Bridget home, and the Roberts departed since they had an hour's drive ahead.

"When you're finished fixing up the school," said Ellen, "there's another community improvement I wish you men would undertake."

"What's that, my dear?" asked Rutherford.

"Make sidewalks or boardwalks! And do it before we get snow that'll turn the streets to slushy mud!"

Lesley shuddered at the thought. Dust was bad enough, but mud — Susan gave a heartfelt sigh. "A walkway would be wonderful! You gentlemen have no notion of how dirty our skirts get."

"Indeed," said Ellen, with a freezing stare at Andy Hart. "Or how annoying it is to lift one's skirts to avoid a mudhole or memento of a horse and discover a bunch of oglers loafing in front of the livery stable!"

"Now, hold on, Miss Tremayne!" Andy protested, coloring to the roots of his fair hair. "It's just natural for menfolk to — to —" He gulped at Rutherford's stern look and ended in a mutter, "To appreciate nice — well, shucks, what they appreciate!"

"I guess I appreciate what men appreciate as much as anyone," said Jim with a chuckle. "But we do owe it to our women to give them a clean place to walk. Is it okay with everybody if we take it out of the railroad fund?"

There was no dissent. Andy Hart lifted a philosophical shoulder. "I can't leave my business to work on the railroad, so I'll take charge of the boardwalk and pay for the stretch in front of the livery."

"I'll supply the lumber at cost," said Leroy Martin. "I can't leave my business, either, but I can hammer down planks and go tend to customers when they turn up."

Ellen's asperity toward him softened, but she still spoke as one with accumulated grievances. "Another thing, Mr. Hart: When you rent buggies to young men, would you kindly tell them that racing down Main Street is dangerous to themselves and anyone in their vicinity? Not to mention the dust they raise!"

"I'll tell 'em, ma'am," said Andy

meekly. The supporter of Sockless Jerry Simpson's anti-big-business policies rose in disgust as Lesley chalked up the latest returns. "Looks like McKinley has it sewed up with his dratted 'four more years of the full dinner pail.' " He gave the dozing Alan a gentle shake. "Come along, son. Guess we won't hang around for the final sad story."

When the footfalls of the livery owner and his apprentice faded from the platform, Lisa Schiller said, "Mr. Hart is a nice man. I wish him no ill. And I do love horses! But they make such a mess of the streets! Automobiles, I suppose, will never replace them, but they'd be so much cleaner!"

"They'd churn up dust, too," Jim argued. "And you can just bet automobiles would run races around the town pump same as buggies do."

By midnight, there was no doubt of the outcome. "Do you have enough for your story, Ruff?" asked Lesley.

He nodded somberly. "This finishes the Populists, though the Democrats will keep some of their ideas. Big business and imperialists will have everything their own way."

"Give Roosevelt credit for one thing," said Jim. "He does praise the way Indians and Negroes fight as soldiers in the army — not that Negroes have officers of their own race."

"I can acknowledge that," said Rutherford, "and still have plenty to tax him with."

Jim walked Lesley home. "Win some, lose some," he said. "We lost the election, but good things happened here tonight for Bountiful."

"You really believe we can build that railroad?"

"We will."

Jim took her in his arms. Though she yearned to melt against him, she stiffened. "Oh, Lesley, sweetheart!" He brushed her forehead with his lips. "I know we can't get married for a while, but it drives me wild not to get to hold and kiss you —"

"I — I just can't, Jim."

He let her go so abruptly that she almost stumbled. "How long," he said roughly, "do you have to bang your head against a rock to show you're sorry?"

"Jim!"

"Your daddy wouldn't want this. He'd

want you to be happy."

"I know."

He kept his distance but touched her hair. "Does it bother you — working in the depot? I've worried about that."

"It won't, now that we have the school. Daddy would have liked that. And he'd be proud and excited at the way we're planning to build the railroad." She smiled through her tears and gave a little laugh. "He'd have loved being there tonight, even though he'd hate the way the election went."

"You did it!" he whooped. Catching her hands, he pressed them to his heart.

"Did what?"

"Laughed when you spoke of your father!" he said. "That's a start, darlin'! Ruff and I are off to Topeka in the morning, so I'll see you bright and early."

His warm fingers caressed her cheek, just for a heart-stopped moment. Then he was gone. Lesley didn't wash that side of her face before she went to bed but pressed it against the pillow to treasure that touch, so fleeting, that reached into her heart.

Jim and Rutherford returned that Saturday from Topeka with permission to build the spur line and a surveying team they'd picked up in Dodge. Meanwhile, Ellen's wires to her old friends had placed substantial loans at the disposal of the Bountiful Railroad Company. These and other monies were deposited with a Dodge City bank.

The boardwalk was finished before the first snow flurry made a sticky morass of the street. "The Wellivers wouldn't chip in," said Andy, "but we laid it past them anyway, and out to the one drugstore that's decent enough for ladies."

From nine to four, the waiting room of the depot buzzed with children. When they sang, they drowned out the hammering and racket at the new depot, which was nearing completion. Even though it would only be used briefly as a station, Benedict had apparently felt honor-bound to carry out his promise. Lesley thought with a wry smile that it wouldn't do her much good to have new quarters if she didn't have a job, but of course, to that, he'd retort that he'd offered her the depot of his proposed queen city.

When Lesley wasn't busy at her job,

she often tutored dark, sparkling-eyed Luis and Juanita Carbajal and red-haired, green-eyed Pablo Terrazas. It was a pleasure because they were so eager and treasured every new word learned as if it were a prize. The boys were eight, Juanita seven and shy. Since she was glad to follow Mattie's lead, she was accepted by Mattie, Bridget, and Caroline Griffith.

Pablo and Luis were younger than Jamie, eleven-year-old Mark, and tow-headed Danny and George Griffith, who were ten and nine, respectively. Ann Roberts's manner said clearer than words that she would tolerate no teasing of the children from the section gang camp.

Textbooks and supplies stored in Ann's amazing trunk were augmented by any old texts families had and those she asked Jim and Ruff to buy in Topeka. To give Ann a rest from teaching everything from primer to sixth grade, Susan, Ellen, Beth, and the younger Schiller sisters took turns coming in teams of two at lunch play time and morning and afternoon recesses. Bountiful resounded with their shouts and laughter as they played red rover, drop the handkerchief, hide-and-go-seek, tag, or pop the whip.

Sometimes they chalked squares on the platform to play hopscotch or jumped rope, with special glee in giving the harried jumper "red pepper" till his or her feet tangled in the swinging rope. On rare days of snow or drizzle, the girls might play jacks at one end of the room while the boys shot marbles or spun tops at the other.

When Mattie kicked up a fuss about coming home for lunch, the Schillers offered to serve all the children hot soup, bread, butter, and cookies for five cents each a day. "That doesn't cover your costs," protested Lesley.

"It gives the *kinder* something warm in their bellies." Lilibet shrugged. "And it keeps Mattchen happy."

Mattie, darling of three mothers after seven years of neglect, was becoming a bit spoiled, but she wore her unofficial crown with generosity. "We can at least take turns making cookies," Lesley said. "We won't bother the Carbajals or Terrazas with it."

But somehow, Luis, Juanita, and Pablo must have learned where the lunch cookies came from. In the second week of school, they came trudging up with two lard buckets apiece and carried them to the restaurant at noon, after they bestowed cinnamon-and-sugar-fragrant rolls of glaze-crusted sweet bread upon Lesley and Ann.

Night school convened three nights a week after the evening train went through. Alan Meadows came more willingly when Andy Hart, his idol, decided a little more book-learning wouldn't hurt him. Beth, aided by Ellen, was soon sounding out three-syllable words. Oliver, the Wellivers' boy, came in hesitantly the first night.

"Could I pay by sweeping out and starting the fire in the mornings?" he asked Lesley, blue eyes pleading. "Mr. and Missus Welliver, they say I don't need more schooling, but I want all I can get."

"You don't have to pay," said Lesley. "But it would help me a lot if you swept after class." She indicated the shelf of such textbooks as weren't stored in the single shelves beneath the desks. "I think you said you'd finished sixth grade. Do you want to try that seventh grade reader?"

Micajah was the third adult, along

with Elden Griffith and Andy, to study under Ruff's tutelage. "Looks like my widder lady may break down and marry me when Bella and Henry slide into double harness." He had worried at his snarled gray hair, but it persisted in tangling with his crinkly eyebrows. Andy Hart was redolent of tobacco smoke and horses, but Micajah's odor overwhelmed that of the liveryman. "I don't want Lilyun to know how igernut I am, so lead me to a speller, Ruff, I'm set to rassle it!"

There were indirect night students as well. Pablo and Luis told Lesley that each evening they taught their mothers and fathers what they'd learned that day.

"They could come here," Lesley said, with gestures more than words.

Pablo shook his carroty head and imitated a wearily sagging body and tired back. "Too *cansado, señorita.* Too far, but *mil gracias.*"

As soon as the surveyors finished, Jim and the others with teams started building the roadbed. When they got far enough along to camp out instead of coming home at night, Jim brought Jamie's magic robe to Lesley so the boy could stay with her.

Though he was tired and work-stained, Jim looked so confident and happy that the coldness in Lesley's heart melted a little more. "What with Dan Nelson and his crew starting from the gravel pit south of the Arkansas River bridge and other farmers along the way helping," he said over the supper she insisted that he share, "we hope we can get the roadbed done before the ground freezes, say by mid-December. We only have to build one bridge, over Buffalo Creek. Funny, it's running pretty high, being spring-fed, but the Arkansas River is bone-dry for miles."

"When do you think the rails will be laid?"

"With luck, we might finish by New Year's."

"That would be a great thing to celebrate." Lesley's smile turned to a frown. "Is there anything Benedict can do to stop you?"

"Can't think of what it would be short of blowing up the tracks. We're cleared with the Railroad Commission and have an agreement with the Santa Fe."

"Yes, but —"

Jim caught Lesley's hands and held

them. "I reckon Benedict's through with Bountiful, for good or ill, honey. Since he can't have it all his way here — includin' you — my guess is that he's wiped us off his slate. He'll put his energy into building up Zenith and making it his showplace."

"I hope you're right."

Beth's tawny eyes shone with adoration. "You'll do it, Jim! You'll build the road and keep Bountiful alive!"

That's what I should have said! thought Lesley, stricken. Maybe, in spite of the difference in age, the girl might in a few years make a better wife than she could, she with her remorse and distrust of men engendered by her father's weakness and self-absorption.

No, that wasn't it. Lesley couldn't refuge behind her strange upbringing. Compared to Beth's, it had been protected near-luxury. And as for men — Maybe knowing so many who'd take advantage of a child made Beth truly appreciate a good one.

Blushing with shy pleasure, Jim released Lesley's hands. "Beth, if we don't get that road built, it won't be for lack of tryin'." He tousled Jamie's head. "So long, son. You take care of your sisters and Lesley while I'm away."

Solemnly Jamie nodded. "I'll take care of 'em all, Uncle Jim." He thrust out his hand, man-fashion. "Shake on it?"

"You bet!"

That ritual performed, Jim bent over for Bridget's hearty kiss. "Good-bye, ladies." He was teasing only slightly when he grinned and included Beth.

He went whistling out into the frosty morning. Lesley looked at Beth, as tall as she and curvier, still with that sheen on her face. Oh Lord! It was going to be bad either way, whether Beth broke her heart over Jim or Lesley did.

One thing was sure. Even if Jim didn't fall in love with the girl who offered him such worship, he and Lesley couldn't marry so long as Beth was in her care. It would be cruel to the girl, even if Jim managed somehow to refrain from tasting the sweet fruit so temptingly offered.

Swallowing a taste of metal, Lesley turned to dish out the oatmeal. Pouring coffee and milk, Beth said dreamily, "Isn't he wonderful?"

"Yes," said Lesley, and hated herself for the blaze of jealousy that twisted through her like a red-hot crooked sword.

23

As Thanksgiving neared, some of Bountiful's attention turned from the progress of the railroad to the festive wedding wherein not only Bella and Henry would join destinies, but Micajah and Lillian O'Brien as well as Ellen and Rutherford.

"Might as well do it while the parson's here," said Micajah. His pale blue eyes twinkled from beneath his untamed eyebrows. "Kinda helps to take the plunge if you got company."

"With Robbie back and forth between us all the time, it just seems a good idea to be a family." The bright natural color in Ellen's cheeks made her more lovely than artful rouge, and her dark brown eyes were brilliant as she smiled at the editor, who took her hand possessively.

"Lucky for me Rob came along, my dear. You sure never let me get a proposal out of my mouth before."

She looked at him, eyes darkening.

"I'll try to make sure you're never sorry, Ruff."

He smiled and bowed to kiss her hand. "How could I be?"

Strange, thought Lesley, how Ellen's orphan had brought them together while hers — at least the eldest one — would serve as a barrier against her marrying Jim for years to come, even if he didn't succumb before that to Beth's allure.

All the volunteer road builders from the Bountiful area would come to the wedding, as would many of Bella's and Micajah's longtime friends and customers from along the old wagon road that ran south of Dodge through the Oklahoma and Texas Panhandles.

Fortunately, the new depot was finished the week before Thanksgiving. Lesley and the O'Hara youngsters moved into spanking clean new quarters, which seemed luxurious after the cramped, dark boxcar.

"A sink with a pump!" cried Beth. "Oh, that'll be wonderful, especially on washdays!"

"Isn't the wallpaper nice?" Even though she was sharply aware that this was Benedict's property with embellishments of his choosing, Lesley couldn't help being delighted with the fresh-looking tile-effect wallpaper with a border and matching ceiling that repeated the linoleum colors. What she liked best of all was the light given by four windows.

"The floor's bee-yoo-tiful!" Bridget squealed. She knelt to touch the green, gold, and brown linoleum that covered the floor of the large room that was kitchen, living, and dining space. Jumping up, Bridget looked hopefully at Lesley. "Is the bedroom floor this pretty?"

"Let's see." The linoleum, of course, had come in by train from Sears, but this was the first time Lesley had seen it unrolled, and she was forced to admire Benedict's choice.

The back entrance led into a room that could hold the washing machine, tubs, and such, and had a pantry adjoining the kitchen area. Next to the pantry was a small room that Jamie claimed for his. This and the utility-storage space were floored with the same warm-colored linoleum as the main room and had the same wallpaper.

Bridget opened the door of one of the two larger bedrooms. "Carpet! A *big* one! On top of linoleum!"

After the bare wood floor of the box-car, that did seem extravagant. Bridget opened the other door. "Another carpet! Which room do you want, Lesley? The blue-green squiggles or the yellow roses?"

"You and Beth choose. After all, there's two of you."

Bending to stroke the flowered wool carpet, Beth said, "The roses are so pretty and happy! Could — could we have this room?"

"I'm glad you picked it," Lesley admitted. "I love the turquoise, especially the wallpaper."

Andy Hart and young Alan, with help from Rutherford, moved Lesley's furnishings from the boxcar that day. Atchison yowled imprecations at the upheaval and Fe mewed plaintively, but when they discovered what fine sunning places the wide window ledges were, and found their familiar dishes beside the familiar stove, they were reconciled.

"These shades are grand," Beth said that night, as she pulled down the olive green window shades with lace inserts at the bottom. "But drapes would look lovely and make it warmer. I could sew them, Lesley, and pay for the material out of my wages."

Lesley's pennies were stretched and Christmas was approaching — Christmas with three children! — but they were so excited about their first decent home — and in truth, so was she — that she said, "You can pay for the drapes in your room, Beth, but if you're kind enough to sew the rest, I'll buy the material." She glanced around at the sparse furnishings that had crowded the boxcar and sighed. "After New Year's, we'll save up for a sofa and maybe a rocking chair."

"It's just as well not to have a lot of stuff in the way when we have the wedding party here," Beth comforted. "Can we order the drapery material tonight, Lesley? Can we?"

They did, and the material arrived in time for striped gold and green damask drapes to hang in the main room on Thanksgiving Day, where borrowed tables stretched with Lesley's down the middle of the room. The Schillers had supplied starched white sheets to serve as tablecloths, and for a decoration, Beth, Bridget, and Mattie filled Lesley's emptied mending basket with many-hued grasses, dried thistles, and milkweed pods.

The Reverend Marcus Sheridan came in on the train the night before the wedding. "Evenin', Miss Morland." The kind-faced, heavyset minister doffed his hat as he stepped off the westbound local with his satchel. "It's mighty good to be a part of such a happy occasion. Three couples tyin' the knot at once! I've done doubles before, but never a triple."

It did seem to Lesley that almost everyone else was getting married. If Susan hadn't told Hugh that she needed a bit more time, Lesley would be the only unmarried young woman in Bountiful except for Lena Schiller, who was going on frequent buggy rides with her construction worker beau.

Forcing a smile, Lesley shook the minister's hand. "It is a happy time, Reverend Sheridan, and we're glad to have you with us."

In the same moment, they both glanced involuntarily toward the slope where he had prayed over Lesley's father. "Your daddy was a brave man, my dear. You can be proud when you remember him."

Not of how I treated him that last morning. But Lesley realized that she was proud of the way Ed Morland had defended his honor — not the payroll, but the trust it represented. That was balm on the wound of her grief and remorse. She told the minister good night and went across the tracks to Ellen's.

"Good gracious!" She gazed in admiration at the three wedding gowns, each beautiful but different. Bella's was pale green, molded to show off her figure. No one had seen Lillian O'Brien yet, but from the look of the beige lace dress designed from measurements Micajah had given Ellen, she was a big lady. Ellen's gown was cream satin trimmed with ecru lace. "There'll never be such a wedding again in Bountiful!"

"Oh, yours will be special, Lesley, and Susan's, too." Ellen held up a rich mahogany suit jacket of Venetian wool with velvet trim along the deeply cut lapels and at the back and cuffs. "I'm sure the skirt fits right, but let's just be sure the cuffs aren't too long."

"They're perfect." Lesley looked at herself in the mirror. It was the most becoming outfit she'd ever had, and the first tailored to fit exactly. "You took a lot of trouble with this, Ellen."

"The color's good with your hair and eyes and makes your skin positively translucent." Ellen smiled. "Beth fussed and fussed to get your hat just so."

"Did she?" Lesley couldn't guess her ward's feelings toward her any better than she understood hers toward the girl. She respected Beth and abhorred the misery she'd endured, yet she often felt that Beth regarded her with something near contempt. And she herself — no amount of reasoning calmed the jealousy that blazed when Beth openly flattered Jim or he watched the girl with admiration.

As if reading Lesley's thoughts, Ellen said, "Don't worry too much about Beth's moods, Lesley. Even girls with normal upbringings can be trying at that age."

"Does she talk about me?"

Ellen hesitated. "Sometimes she talks as if she wants to be exactly like you. Other times — sometimes she sounds as if you were Bridget."

That hurt. "In some ways, compared to Beth, I suppose I am."

"That's not her fault, dear."

"I know! That's why I feel so beastly when I'm jeal—" Lesley broke off the word. Ellen pressed her hand.

"How could you not be when she worships Jim with those golden eyes?"

"But she's not fifteen yet!"

"She's a hundred in some ways, Lesley, but in her heart she hungers for a mother. You're too young to be that — and you have the man she adores." Ellen's brown eyes softened as they held Lesley's. "Don't wait too long to marry him."

"I can't while — while I feel the way I do about Daddy. And even if I didn't, how can I marry a man she's crazy about?"

"A good deal of that must come from not having a father. Beth needs that kind of tenderness much more than passion, though I doubt that she knows that." Ellen thought back to something that still pained. "If only one of those men who used her had been decent and kind enough to act as a father — Some of them probably had children her age. Why couldn't they be merciful?"

The cry twisted from Ellen. At Lesley's startled look, Ellen gave herself a shake. "Beth's here. She's smart and beautiful, except for that scar. She has a chance now. And I'm so lucky, I can't believe it, Lesley! I'm getting married tomorrow to a man I don't have to lie to, and we already have a wonderful little boy! I don't deserve it, but I'll spend the rest of my life trying to."

"Ruff thinks he's the lucky one," Lesley said. "And Robbie is for sure." Ellen's reserve usually discouraged hugs, but Lesley gave her one, got one back, and departed with her new ensemble, complete with the draped brown satin and velvet shepherdess hat adorned with bronze chrysanthemums.

The old depot was jammed with people. There was no room to sit even had there been enough chairs, but the taller men stood in back, and shorter people and children were in front. The brides all looked beautiful despite Bella's weathered features and Lillian O'Brien's gray hair. Robbie stood in front of his new parents, so it was as if the three were being united.

Jim acted as best man to all three

grooms, handing them the rings, but the brides craved more pomp. Beth, ravishing in her green suit, attended Bella; Lesley stood up with Ellen; and a pretty young niece of Lillian's served as her bridesmaid.

When the vows were made, the brides kissed, and the couples turned to their friends. Micajah snorted and brushed his sleeve across his eyes.

"Durned if you ladies don't all look like flowers," he blurted.

"My petals are a mite faded." Lillian chuckled in a way that endeared her to everyone who'd wondered if their beloved Micajah was getting someone nice enough for him. Those doubts were dispelled by the way the two looked at each other. "But who knows? I feel all set to bloom again!"

Lesley couldn't repress a pang at watching Henry tuck Bella's arm through his. If only Bella could have loved her father — but he would still have defied the robber. He would still be dead, killed right over there where the minister was standing. He wouldn't have started drinking, though, and she, Lesley, wouldn't have been so cold and unforgiving.

Feeling as if her smile would crack her face, Lesley embraced Bella and shook Henry's hand. Spiked goatee shaved, formerly waxed mustache allowed to fluff, he looked like what he was, an old-time trail hand and cowboy cook.

"I sure appreciate your good wishes, Miss Lesley," he said.

"You have them, Mr. —"

"Henry," he corrected. "I'm part of this now, I reckon." He waved his free hand to encompass the circle of friends. "Mr. Benedict's found him a new cook. Now I can put both feet in Bountiful, where they belong." He grinned at Jim. "I may not be stout enough to lay rails or hammer 'em down, but I can drive a wagon."

"We can use you," Jim said. "But you're entitled to some kind of honeymoon."

"Shucks, I'll drive a wagon, too," said Bella. "We'll honeymoon at night." She blushed like a girl when everyone laughed, and covered her confusion by hauling her bridegroom toward the door. "Isn't there some grub around? I didn't eat breakfast so's I could squeeze into my dress and I'm plumb famished!"

Outside, Lesley was surprised to see the Carbajal children and Pablo Terrazas waiting by her door. Each child held a towel-covered bucket. Their nervous little faces lit up when they saw Bella. They offered her the buckets.

"For you, señora," said Pablo.

"Happy wedding!" the three chorused. "Happy life!"

Bella unfolded some towels. A delicious fragrance floated out. "Tamales!" she cried. "Bless you, what a treat!" She bent to kiss Juanita and shook hands with the boys.

Jim eased forward to translate. "They say, Bella, that their mamas want to thank you for bringing them home when it started snowing last week when you met them along the way. Not being used to snow, they got scared and confused and might have got lost."

"Aw, it was nuthin'." Bella beamed at the children. "You come on in and eat, kids."

She swept them inside and the children's eyes shone with delight as Lesley emptied the dozens of corn-shuck-wrapped tamales into her biggest blue-enameled kettle and covered them with towels.

Reverend Sheridan blessed the food, those sharing it, and the lives of the newly married couples. These were thrust to the front of the food line and led the way in filling plates from the feast that more than lived up to the town's name. The tamales, cornmeal mush steamed around a filling of white cheese and green chilies, were the most relished food, but the guests quickly went through mounds of fluffy mashed potatoes; baskets of rolls, cornbread, and biscuits; bowls of green beans, lima beans, navy beans, buttered beets, corn, hominy, sweet-sour cabbage, and creamed peas; hot cabbage salad; cole-slaw; cranberries; all kinds of pickles, relishes, and preserves; and heaps of ham and fried chicken as well as what was probably rabbit.

Susan and Alice Griffith had brought platters of deviled eggs. These disappeared like candy. There were a dozen pumpkin pies, but there were also pies of apple, rhubarb, and wild plum, as well as vinegar and chess pie. Beth, with much "help" from Bridget and Jamie, had made and frosted a devil's food cake. The Schillers' towering coconut cake rose between bowls of rice and bread pudding, but the dessert most oohed and ahhed over was Ellen's ambrosia, as appealing to the eye as to taste. In a sparkling glass bowl, she had arranged layers of canned pineapple, shredded coconut, and carefully peeled sliced oranges, ending with swirls of whipped cream studded with toasted coconut and almond slivers.

There was coffee for those who needed it to top off the meal. The crowd had spilled into the new depot, which wasn't yet in use — and might not be used very long, if Benedict had his wish.

Ann Roberts rose and rang her teacher's bell. "Our school hasn't had time to prepare a real Thanksgiving program," she said as those in other rooms pressed near the doors to listen. "But we'd like to sing a few songs and recite some poems before Mr. Faraday starts his fiddling."

"You and your pupils have the floor, ma'am," said Rutherford gallantly.

"We need to let our dinners settle afore we start cavortin'," added Micajah, winking at his bride and squeezing her hand.

The children sang "America the Beautiful," shrill, sweet voices breaking at the high notes, cracking on the low. On the last verse, Ann Roberts spread her arms, and everybody joined in.

> *"America! America! God shed His*
>   *grace on thee*
> *And crown thy good with brother-*
>   *hood*
> *From sea to shining sea!"*

Jamie recited James Whitcomb Riley's "When the Frost is on the Punkin." Danny Griffith raced through Edward Rowland Sills's "The Fool's Prayer." Mark Altman Roberts gave a stirring ring to the same poet's "Opportunity," and his dark-haired twin, Helen, began shyly with "Little Boy Blue," by Eugene Field, but got so carried away with the faithful little toy dog and soldier that the tears in her eyes were reflected in those of the audience. George Griffith gave Field's "Seein' Things at Night" an eerie tone. His sister, Caroline, blondest of all three fair-haired children, Mattie, and Bridget brought down the house with Riley's "Little Orphant Annie." As they curtsied with flushed faces to resounding applause, Bridget caught Mattie's hand

and said, "We chose this poem 'cause it's about an orphan."

"An' 'cause we're real glad we aren't anymore," added Mattie.

That brought cheers that didn't stop till Ann Roberts rose.

"Thank you," she said. "We're planning an exciting program for Christmas and hope you'll all come."

"If it's as much fun as this, we sure will." The fiddler, Jack Faraday, who lived out near Buffalo Creek and was helping build roadbed, got to his feet at a nod from Micajah. Faraday was a wiry gnome with leathery skin and kinky hair as white as thistledown. "All right, folks! Let's redd up the tables and shove 'em against the wall in the office."

As everyone hurried to help, Lesley opened the big door that led into the freight room. "We can spread in here to dance," she called without looking in front of her.

Her collision with a broad chest covered by a fine gray cheviot Prince Albert coat was softened by hands on her shoulders that restrained her advance. "May I have the first dance, Miss Lesley?" asked Adam Benedict.

She slipped back from his hands. "I'm not dancing, sir."

"What a pity." Sweeping the crowd, which had gone silent at his appearance, his gaze touched Beth with surprised approval and came to rest on Henry and Bella. "I hope it's all right if I've come to dance at your wedding, old friend," he said to his former cook, and bowed his gleaming head to Bella. "Henry gets to lead out with you, I know, ma'am, but then I hope you'll honor me?"

"Not on your life!" Bella set her hands on her shapely hips. Leaf green eyes glared into some of darkest jade. "You've got brass, sonny! Tryin' to kill our town and then sashayin' in here and thinkin' us women'll be thrilled to have a whirl with the great Adam Benedict!"

"Now, Bella honey —" began Henry.

"*You* dance with him if you want!" Bella snapped at her bridegroom. "I'd sooner be scalped all over again, even if there wasn't a wig left in the whole country!"

Henry reddened unhappily. Benedict sighed. "I don't suppose it would cool your ire, ma'am, if I said my wedding present to you should arrive any day now." He grinned at Henry, a benevolent man overlooking female tantrums. "As thanks for all the good meals you've served me over the years, Henry, I'm equipping your kitchen with the best. Coal-burning steel range, kerosene cookstove for summer, stoneware sink, a porcelain-enameled steel-lined icebox that'll hold six hundred fifty pounds of ice, and a golden oak cupboard, chairs, and round table that I hope's big enough for me to slide my legs under someday for more of your cooking."

Bella snorted. "The table ain't made that'll hold you and me, boy. You just send all that fancy stuff back or use it your own self. We don't want it! Do we, sugar?"

Henry gulped. "I guess we don't. But thanks all the same, boss. I sure appreciate it —"

"I don't!" Bella stormed. "He's not your boss, Henry, so don't call him that. You're one sorry varmint, Benedict, and if I wasn't a lady and it wasn't my weddin' day, I'd blister your ears worse'n ever I did a team of mean mules!"

"How fortunate that you are a lady,

Mrs. Cantrell." The imposing silver-haired man beamed at her. "I wish you and Henry happy." He turned to his cook with a twinkle. "Henry, dare you shake my hand?"

"Sure, bo— I mean, Mr. Benedict!" Henry gripped his erstwhile employer's hand.

"My new cook really is from Paris," Benedict went on, "but André doesn't have your knack with soufflés. What'll you do now, Henry? Open up a restaurant?"

Henry drew himself up and looked at once stronger and bolder. "Reckon I'll decide on that after we finish our railroad."

Benedict shook his head. "I'm saddened to hear you're wasting your time on that ridiculous scheme, old friend."

"Don't see what's ridiculous about it."

"You may be able to run a few trains a week, but how's that going to compete with daily service both ways through Zenith? Nobody in their right mind will start a business here when they can locate in my town."

Reaching for a large envelope he must have set down inside the door, he held up a bright-colored brochure. ZENITH —

QUEEN CITY OF THE PLAINS, it boasted, and opened to a panorama of a thriving city surrounded by grainfields and grazing cattle. Below was print that presumably listed all the prospective town's benefits. Beneath the smaller type, large letters proclaimed: EXCELLENT DAILY RAIL SERVICE, UNBEATABLE SHIPPING RATES.

"In case anyone's interested." Benedict flashed a smile and splayed out the brochures on a table. Then, before anyone could guess his intention, he reached Beth in an easy stride and laughed down at her. "You'll dance with me, won't you, Miss Beth?"

She neither blushed nor fidgeted. Meeting his gaze with the appraising eyes of a woman, not a girl, she smiled, and the glow of those tawny eyes was dazzling. "I don't know how to dance, mister, but if you'll show me —"

"It'll be my pleasure."

Jack Faraday bent to his fiddle. "Choose your partners!" he yelled. "All set for the Grand March!"

The newlyweds led off. Benedict swept Beth along, light and beautiful in his arms. Susan and Hugh, of course; Lena Schiller dimpling up at her big, blond carpenter; Leroy Martin and Lisa

Schiller, and all the rest. Even Lilibet Schiller was whirled willy-nilly into the dance by a crony of Micajah's.

Only Lesley and the children looked on — but where was Jim? He came in from outside and dodged around the dancers to reach her. She had scarcely seen him since the roadbed builders got too far from town to return nights.

He looked browner and thinner and his eyes were hollowed as if he weren't sleeping too well. No wonder. Following his lead, his friends and neighbors had put all they had in the new road, Bountiful's lifeline. If it proved not to be enough — if, as Benedict predicted, Zenith's superior rail service slowly but surely stifled this little town — then Jim would feel to blame, all the more since it was Benedict's jealousy of him that had brought on the establishment of a rival center.

Whatever his worries, Jim's eyes lighted as he grinned at her. "You sure are lookin' pretty, Lesley. Guess it's not proper to ask you to dance?"

"No. But you should dance, Jim."

"Don't seem to be any ladies left. Anyhow, I'd rather be with you." He sat down. He was several inches away, but

537

she felt the warmth of him radiating toward her. "How are you, darlin'?" he asked softly.

Had she ever known that straight, slightly down-curved mouth on hers? Had she ever been held close in those lean, hard arms, hearing and feeling the strong, steady beat of his heart? She knew she had. It was like a sweet, unrecapturable dream.

"I'm all right, Jim."

"No." His dark gray eyes wouldn't let hers escape. "I'm sure you do your work and look after the kids and tutor at the school. But how are you really, inside?"

She shook her head in a helpless motion. "Inside, I — I'm like a field that's burned to the roots. I feel all charred and dead."

He caught in his breath. "Oh, Lesley — poor sweetheart! Listen, your daddy wouldn't want this!"

"I know." She swallowed hard. "Believe me, I'm not trying to wallow in guilt."

"It takes time." He pressed her hand, like a friend, not a lover. "But it tears me up, honey, not bein' able to help."

"You do help me, Jim." She paused, tormented, had to force out the words.

"I don't know if I'll ever be fit to marry you, though. It — it's not fair to keep you waiting."

"Now, Lesley Edwina Morland, you hush that kind of nonsense!" He wiggled a finger in front of her nose. "Lots of people are engaged for a year before they get married. We haven't even known each other a year. There's loads of time."

"Yes, but —"

"When I think I've waited long enough, I'll let you know," he teased with an undertone of seriousness. The clasp of his hand was no longer simply that of a friend. It sent shocks through her numbness that were almost painful. "Come spring, Les, if some blossoming doesn't start for you, I may just swing you into the buckboard and go hunt a place by the creek where the meadow-larks are singin' and wingin' and the sun's bright on the water and the sky spreads forever. We'll sit on the new grass and smell the spring and hear it, and you know what?"

"What?"

"I bet you won't make me wait anymore." He closed his eyes for a moment and smiled. "I bet we come back to town and name a day and have a wedding bigger'n this one. Maybe with Susan and Hugh. Wouldn't that be great?"

The fact that he didn't intend to let her grieve indefinitely was more comfort than threat. Also, she was touched that he was careful of her feelings at a time when *he* needed support and cheering. Repressed tears scalded her throat, but she found a smile for him.

"It would be great," she said. "Bless you, Jim. I think building the railroad is a wonderful thing to do, and I'm really proud of you for thinking of a way to keep Bountiful alive."

"Let's hope it does. I sure felt like a fool when Benedict plunked down his grand and glorious brochures." His voice dropped. "No one can blame new businesses or people for settling where there's daily rail service rather than twice or three times a week."

"Maybe not. But we've got people who care about each other and care about our town. We've got a school and a good newspaper and we can work together. I think that'll mean more to the kind of folks we want than having a train through every day."

"I sure hope you're right."

"I am. People who can build their own railroad can do just about anything." Encouraging him made her feel confident and strong. She squeezed his hand. "Jim, Zenith may have more and bigger buildings, but we've got better people. We'll have the best town."

"Thanks," he said. "Thanks, Lesley. If —"

"Grab your partners for a quadrille!" Jack Faraday called.

Beth, high young bosom rising and falling fast from pleasant exertion, came to stand almost between them. "Jim, please, will you dance with me?"

"Why, sure, Beth, but you'll find me a pretty clumsy partner compared to Benedict."

"Please, Jim."

It would have taken a strange masculine heart to resist that plea, but he glanced at Lesley. "Go ahead," she told him. "Good gracious, you're supposed to dance at weddings!"

"I hope the next one's ours," he said, but he laughed down at Beth as he brought her into the dance. What male wouldn't? With her terrible scar concealed, she was the prettiest, freshest girl or woman on the floor, though El-

541

len's regal carriage and striking features put her in a class by herself.

"Swing the one that looks so sweet —
Now the one that's dressed so neat —
Now the one with the little bitty feet —
Now the belle of the ballroom!"

The music made Lesley's foot tap in spite of herself. "We could go outside and whirl," said Benedict in her ear. He had moved stealthily or the music and flying feet had muffled his approach.

"You know I can't do that!" She added with asperity, "Even if I could dance with you, I wouldn't!"

"Splendid. We can converse better this way."

"I don't see what we have to talk about."

"I do." He settled beside her with the air of a mountain taking root and glanced around the spacious room. "How do you like your new quarters?"

"They're very nice. But it's beyond me why you should go to the expense when the new depot will only be in use till spring."

"Call it clearing my debt to your father."

She had several bitter responses to that but stifled them. She wouldn't play mouse to his cat. Far from acknowledging her silence as a rebuke, he crossed his arms over his chest and leaned back expansively to watch the dance.

The newlyweds all happened to be at their end of the room. He said in a tone of mocking condolence, "Looks like everybody's getting married except you."

She ignored him. He clapped as the quadrille ended but didn't get to his feet. "Since the new Mrs. Cantrell scorns my gifts," he said, "I'd like to equip your kitchen with them."

"I don't want them."

"Sorry, love. This is my property. If I choose to partially furnish it, I can."

He could, so Lesley shrugged. "I suppose your new tenant will appreciate it."

"New tenant?"

"I'll move out, of course, as soon as your railroad suspends service."

He smothered whatever he'd started to say. His jaw clamped hard. "Into Jim Kelly's tent?"

"That's none of your business."

"You don't need to leave, Lesley. As long as you want it, the place is yours."

"You just told me plainly that it's *yours*, sir."

"You're the most provoking woman I've ever known!" He scowled at her. "I suppose you'll move back in the old boxcar and run the old depot for your Try-Weekly Railroad."

"You gave the old depot to the town, Mr. Benedict. Of course we'll use it." In spite of her determination to show him no weakness, a lump rose in her throat and caused an annoying tremor in her voice. "I don't know how you can pretend to care what happens to me when you're taking away my job!"

His eyes plunged into hers. She felt as if twin spears pierced her. "Say the word, Lesley. You'll never have to worry about jobs or money again."

"You know I won't marry you."

He raised a pointed eyebrow and nodded toward where Jim was whirling Beth in the "Blue Danube." "That lithe young body of hers responds to every touch. No man, dancing with her, could help but wonder how making love to her would be. I know that I did, and I have, I believe, considerably more experience of women than your virtuous Jim."

"No doubt." A pang shot through Lesley at watching the dark head bent close to the brown-gold one, but she strove for a careless smile. "Maybe that's why you had lecherous thoughts about a fourteen-year-old."

That dented his composure not a whit. "You know and I know she's no ordinary growing girl."

"Oh?"

"I have a pretty shrewd notion of how she supported those kids in the New York slums."

Lesley stifled a gasp. It was like seeing Beth stripped, or her scar revealed, and not being able to protect her. "You — you wouldn't —"

"Good heavens, Lesley! Of course I won't prey on her. I'm not a complete degenerate, whatever you may think."

"Your 'cousins' —"

"All over eighteen and well set on their course when I took up with them."

This highly improper conversation relieved Lesley's mind, she grinned inwardly at Benedict's moral outburst. "If you won't take advantage of Beth, sir, I'm sure Jim wouldn't."

"Seduce her, no, though it might work the other way around, considering the way she adores him with those burnished golden eyes." Benedict rose at last. "He might marry her, though, Lesley. Had you thought of that?"

Before she could collect her shattered thoughts, he bowed and walked away.

24

The bridegrooms returned with Jim and the rest of the crew to work on the roadbed. Bountiful seemed a bit lonely without them, but as Ellen said, "They ought to finish soon, and we'll have the biggest New Year celebration ever!"

"Maybe we can all ride the first train to the Santa Fe junction and have a picnic," said Susan.

"A January picnic could be a mite frosty," cautioned Rutherford. "We could banquet at the depot there, though, and invite all the local folks."

So Bountiful looked forward to that while, apart from the children preparing a gala Christmas program, life fell back into its accustomed routine. On the evening of November 29, the men left around town offered to pay Lesley to stay late by the telegraph to report on the annual football game between Kansas University and Missouri in Kansas City. She declined payment but obliged them anyway. The six-six tie gave partisans of either persuasion nothing to brag or groan about.

Alice of Old Vincennes, by Maurice Thompson, was the topic of the next Literary, worked in on a night free of classes. Remembering the last one, the night before her father was killed, it was hard for Lesley to attend, but she took gingerbread and hot cocoa to serve, and somehow, as she recalled her father's ad libs on Rutherford's serious comments, they did seem funny rather than the lugubrious mouthings of a drunkard.

Jim had told her that at the time, but she couldn't believe him. No, she had self-righteously, cruelly — *When* would it stop hurting? One thing that did help, that made her feel close to her father, was, on nights when she wasn't tutoring, to tell the children railroading stories he had told her, of trains marooned in blizzards, pursued by prairie fires started by a spark from an engine, or slipping on rails greasy with drifts of mangled grasshoppers. Jamie's favorite story was about how during a bitter 1889 county seat war between Cimarron and Ingalls west of Dodge City, lawmen had broken into the Cimarron courthouse to pick up the records. Under heavy fire, some managed to get in a wagon and make it to Ingalls, but Jim Masterson, brother of the famed Bat, and a friend were trapped in the courthouse, besieged by two hundred men.

"And then," Jamie would interrupt delightedly, once he'd heard the story, "the mob let the lawmen leave town on the train. They didn't dare not to! 'Cause Bat Masterson heard about the fight up in Denver! And he wired Cimarron and told 'em if they didn't let his brother and the other off'cer go, he'd hire a train and come in with enough men to blow Cimarron right off the map!"

How her father would have loved telling the children stories! Lesley thought. That had been the happiest part of her childhood, listening to him. Starting to lapse into useless regret, she gave herself a mental shake.

Ed Morland could never tell his grandchildren wonderful yarns, but she could, and the brightest, bravest one was how he had died in the line of duty. His grandchildren — if there were any — could touch his old telegraph key, perch in his chair, know where he fell, and visit his grave. He wouldn't be forgotten. She caught herself smiling to think that apart from his heroic death, the most repeated bit of his legend would be his acerbic if inebriated comments on *The Wizard of Oz*'s political meaning.

She wished he could have enjoyed the comfort of the new quarters. Even though Lesley wouldn't indulge in the extravagance of ordering ice except for some grand occasion — it would have been enjoyable to have ice cream at the wedding, for instance — the huge, handsome wood icebox was a convenient, mouse-proof place to store food. The cupboard kept dishes, pans, and other food tucked out of dust and smoke. It was wonderfully helpful to have two sinks, and the large coal-burning range cooked, heated water in the reservoir, and warmed the main room all at the same time. The old kerosene stove had been put in the baggage room, awaiting the time that Lesley would move out when the depot closed.

Where would she move her family? The boxcar seemed the only answer within her means, but how the children would regret losing their rooms, the first time in their lives they'd had comfort and privacy!

The rooms were sparse of furnishings — Father's bed and chest of drawers in the girls' room, a cot in Jamie's along with a scuffed, cherished leather chest Jim had given him — but the wallpaper, carpets, and curtains Beth had made gave them a homelike feeling. By soliciting coffee package labels from friends and putting these with Lesley's, Bridget had a bright chromo of three calico kittens playing on a rug, and Jamie's wall boasted a pair of collie pups.

Jim would build a house if she married him, but how could she marry him till she was freed of the burden on her heart? After she sped the westbound local on its way and the children were busy at homework around the big oak table, on nights when she wasn't tutoring, she often bundled up warmly and went to sit by the prairie dog town. The little creatures were snug in their burrows, but she liked to picture them nestled together, safe from cold and enemies.

If Bountiful survived and grew, a stout fence or wall must be raised around the part of the village close enough to town to be invaded by dogs or mischievous youngsters. Within a human generation or two, such an expanse of burrows might indeed be like a living museum, a remnant of wild prairie. On the other hand, if Bountiful shriveled and died, its buildings might again be a dust-buried ghost town while the small animals thrived as they had for hundreds of years.

The north wind, only murmurous when Lesley had come out, knifed through her coat and the shawl draped around her head and shoulders. Was a storm rising? Thinking of Jim and the men racing to finish the roadbed before the ground froze, Lesley prayed for just a few more weeks of moderate weather. A blizzard or days of icy rain could delay completion of the road till the farmers would have to leave off to start spring plowing. Should that happen, Bountiful's railroad might well not be in operation when Benedict closed down service.

Shivering as she wished the prairie dog village a safe good night, Lesley thought that for all their inventions, people were as helpless against nature as the little ground squirrels were against the plows and poisons that destroyed them. One would think that would teach humans compassion and humility . . .

She stifled a cry. Someone had forgotten to pull the drapes of the main room in the dwelling part of the new depot. In the warm lamplight, Beth's hair shone as she moved in front of the window and threw her arms around the neck of a tall, black-haired man. His back was to Lesley, but there was no mistaking the easy, confident set of his shoulders, the way he held his head.

If Jim drew back . . . But he didn't! At least, not right away. He bent his head. It looked as if he kissed the girl, but briefly. It might have been on the cheek rather than lips, Lesley couldn't be sure. Then he did step away.

The two were laughing. Like great friends? Or lovers? Jim picked up his jacket and hat. Lesley steeled herself for him to come out in search of her, call her name.

What should she do? How could she act as if nothing had happened? Excuses for him welled up. Beth adored him. She had taken the lead. Was he supposed to shove her away, a girl he might regard almost as a foster daughter?

Foster daughter? Don't be a fool, Lesley. Jamie came racing to Jim, Bridget behind him. They both got hugs and some kind of treat fished out of Jim's pockets. Glad of the delay that gave her a little time to try to tame the scalding hurt and anger, Lesley threw the shawl from her head and deliberately turned in to the wind. It would sting and whip her face till her expression shouldn't give her away.

The back door opened. "Lesley?"

Even in her turbulent shock, his deep voice resonated through her, reaching every fiber. She might *wish* he had put Beth firmly aside, but when she herself kept him at arm's length, could he be blamed for responding to a ripe-bodied girl who hurled herself at him?

And who could blame Beth, Beth who had endured such cruelties and bad treatment, for worshiping a man who could be all to her that she had missed — lover, father, older brother? If I could fight for him! Lesley thought despairingly. Fight with a kiss, with holding him close! But something inside her would not allow that, some law of her own nature forbade her. She was not yet freed of the debt she owed her father. If she lost Jim, she lost him, though life without him stretched like a charred wasteland.

"Jim!" she called, moving toward him. "What brings you to town?"

"Couple of errands. I've got to get back. We're pushing hard to finish the roadbed next week."

"Will you come in for Christmas?"

"Not if we're still laying rails. We'll get through and then we'll celebrate."

"We'll have Christmas and New Year's all at once," Lesley said.

"Sure." Jim took her hands. "Maybe we can run our first train on New Year's Day. Now come in out of this wind, honey."

Outside the door, he brushed her forehead with his mouth, nothing so long and intimate a kiss as Beth had given him and he had perhaps given her. Opening the door, he thrust her inside almost roughly.

"Good night," he said, and was gone, quick strides crunching the ground as he moved to where his horse must be tethered at the post beside the depot.

Lesley couldn't bear to look at or speak to Beth, but she could feel the joyous glow emanating from her. Consumed with a jealousy she must not show, Lesley made cocoa for everyone and succumbed to Bridget's pleas to read another chapter from Twain's *The Prince and the Pauper*. By the time the younger children were off to bed, Lesley was able to wish Beth a civil good night, but she still couldn't bear to meet what she was sure would be the triumphant glory of those golden eyes.

The worst thing was that she couldn't blame either Beth or Jim for whatever might happen between them. She could only blame herself.

Waking or sleeping, what she had glimpsed through the window haunted Lesley, Beth throwing her arms around Jim, molding her body to him, the bending of the dark head to the tawny one. Jim would never take advantage of Beth; that, Lesley was sure of. But what if she took advantage of him till the only honorable thing he could do would be to marry her? She was young, true enough, but girls her age did marry, just as they got into trouble.

Lesley tried not to think of that embrace, but the image constantly rose before her. As Beth's guardian, was it her duty to warn her? The thought was so ridiculous that Lesley gave a grim laugh. Beth, unfortunately, doubtless knew all too well what she was doing. Lesley couldn't help a certain reserve with Beth, but if the girl noticed, she gave no sign.

That Saturday Jamie and Bridget rushed breathlessly into the station. Bridget caught Lesley's free hand. "Can we ride in Mr. Benedict's big Panhard, Lesley? Can we?"

"*May* you?" Lesley corrected automatically.

"I dunno," said Bridget. "That's why we're asking you!"

"Please, Lesley!" coaxed Jamie.

"Yes," said Benedict, lounging in and surveying her with laughing eyes, head atilt. "Please, Miss Lesley? Of course, they'll need an adult in back with them."

"You put them up to this!"

"Certainly."

"I'm busy."

"We'll wait."

Two pairs of eyes beseeched her,

Bridget's hazel, Jamie's soft brown, very like her father's — who had longed for an automobile ride he never got. Lesley gave the boy a gentle push. "Run across to Aunt Ellen's, Jamie. Ask Beth to ride with you."

"Oh, boy! Wait till the other kids see us!" Jamie tore out the door.

Benedict gave Bridget a pat on the shoulder. "Go with him, little one. Then your sister will see it's very important."

Bridget pelted after her brother. Lesley would have escaped out the door, but the big man lazed in front of it. "Clever of you, my dear. I'm not too cheated. Beth's spritely company. It would be interesting to see what she might become with the right training."

"Don't talk as if she were a horse or hound!" Lesley snapped. "She is taking night classes, and she enjoys working with Ellen."

The full lips curled. "Designing and sewing dresses for other women when, with that figure, she should be wearing gowns from France and London?"

Very conscious of the stays in her corset waist beneath her green twill jacket, Lesley said in chill tones, "That's an indecent way to speak of a girl not yet fifteen, Mr. Benedict. As her guardian, I insist that you promise to treat her with propriety should she agree to drive with you."

"You could come along to be sure that I do."

"I want your promise."

His smile vanished. "Good Lord, do you think I'm an ogre?"

"You're a man. By your own admission, you've noticed her — her —"

"Endowments?"

"They're coming." Through the window, Lesley saw Beth laughing as she walked between the younger children, holding their hands. Remembering how scared and neglected they had looked only six weeks ago, Lesley couldn't keep her eyes from misting. "Look at them," she told Benedict. "This is the first time Beth's been able to be a child. Don't rob her."

There were no mocking green glints in the darkness of his eyes. "I won't. I swear to you that I won't rob that girl of anything. But you must pay me a forfeit, Lesley, for losing your company."

Before she could guess or evade his purpose, he closed his hands on her shoulders and dropped a swift yet thorough kiss on her startled mouth.

"We'll be good." He bowed low and went out to the O'Haras.

Lesley opened the door. "Try not to get stuck somewhere!" she yelled. "There might not be a team handy to pull you out!"

Matthew Reid turned his face to hide a grin as he helped the smaller children into the backseat and climbed in with them. Benedict settled Beth in the front passenger seat and laughed gaily back at Lesley. "This Panhard has a twenty-four-horsepower engine compared to my little Oldsmobile's four. We won't get stuck, my very dear Miss Lesley, and if we do, my new chef, André — who *is* French — has packed us a picnic we'll enjoy while Matthew extricates us from the difficulty." He showed most of his broad white teeth. "Sure you won't come along? You're acquiring an indoor pallor that's not at all becoming."

Bellowing at him from this distance was not at all becoming, either. Lesley ignored him and waved at Bridget and Jamie, who were bouncing up and down on the luxurious tufted cushions. An irrational sense of abandonment swept over Lesley, the way she'd felt when everyone in her class was invited to a party except for her.

Benedict had guessed how Beth had supported her orphaned family. But would he be revolted by the scar she kept so artfully covered? Lesley gave herself a mental shake.

There was no reason why Benedict would ever see the naked scar. As he'd said, he wasn't a monster. He might flirt lightly with the girl who challenged his jaded palate, but he wouldn't go beyond that.

Still, as Lesley hurried to take a message that was clicking in, she wished that Benedict would move his private car down to Zenith and leave in peace the town he had fathered and now wished to destroy. And with the jealous-woman part of her, Lesley couldn't help but wish he'd take Beth with him.

Four days before Christmas, crews began laying rails from either end of the new Bountiful railroad. "We're not as fast as the lads who can stretch out two lengths of track in a minute," said Hugh, "and we don't have an army of spikers and bolters to follow along and fasten the rails tight to the tracks. But with the kindness of God, we'll finish in time to run our first train New Year's — and won't I bust my buttons at bein' an engineer again!"

"You're going to run the engine?"

"That's the plan. As long as the train only goes back and forth twice a week, I can do it and still keep on top of my blacksmithing. Andy Hart'll be my fireman. He can leave young Alan in charge of the livery."

By common consent it was agreed that the school would hold its Christmas program in the old depot on New Year's Eve, when the railroad builders should be triumphantly home. Then, early on the first day of January 1901, the citizens of Bountiful would decorate *their* train with bunting and flags, climb aboard, and, stopping en route for farmers like the Nelsons who had helped, would steam into the solitary Santa Fe depot that would soon be Bountiful's only link with the outer world. There they would have a gala dinner, welcoming anyone who cared to come, and then chug home, beginning the new year and new century with jubilation and hope.

Most families, including Lesley's, decided to keep their presents under whatever served for a tree until the men returned. Buying clothes for the children had used up most of Lesley's savings, but for a dollar, she contrived a pearl-handled pocket knife for Jamie, the cardinal red tam-o'-shanter with brass-button trim that Bridget had longed for ever since Mattie got a navy one, and a pompadour comb set with turquoise that would look beautiful in Beth's hair. She was young to do her hair up, but Ellen helped her with it for special occasions.

The whole new depot building was permeated with the rich, spicy smell of applesauce–black walnut cakes Lesley baked for friends and her own family — how wonderful that was, *her* family, especially with her father gone. For a chilling moment, she understood how wretched, how lonely, this holiday would be without the children to plan and care for, despite the kindness of her friends. The children called her out of herself, compelled her to think of them and their joys and woes. That was the most solacing balm for a wound only time could heal.

Jim's gift? What did a woman give the man she loved and was half-engaged to when it looked as if he had more than a fatherly interest in her young ward? The Wellivers had already moved lock, stock, and barrel to Zenith, but Mr. Beasley's mercantile carried a better selection than they had, at more reasonable prices. As Lesley roamed the aisles and counters in search of something more imaginative than handkerchiefs or a muffler, yet not too personal, her gaze caught on a compass.

Perfect. Jim had lost his and she remembered his saying he must get another because one could be lifesaving in a storm or useful when freighting to a remote ranch where floods or dust had covered the ruts or tracks that passed for a road.

And it might be a subtle reminder in case his masculinity was magnetized off course by Beth's appeal. The three dollars it cost took all her remaining savings, but Mr. Beasley assured her the woodman's compass with its double-thick oxidized case and jeweled English bar needle would stand up to the roughest use. He put it in a green velvet box, and Lesley was as content as she could be with a present till she had the right to buy wifely things for him.

Presents might wait for New Year's Eve, but caroling could not. On Christmas Eve, everyone but the railroad builders gathered in the old depot to sing the beloved songs and drink hot spiced cider. The evening ended with a public prayer led by Lilibet Schiller for the absent men and the success of their endeavor.

Susan gave Lesley a hug as they parted. "Soon! The men'll be home, God willing, in a few days now." She shifted a drowsy Sally to her hip and ruffled Dusty's yellow hair. "We'll be glad to see Hugh, won't we?"

"Why can't he be our daddy?" Dusty asked, seizing the advantage. "He says he really wants a little girl and boy and a dog like Cap!"

Susan would have no problem in getting her children to welcome Hugh into their home. Lesley smiled at her blushing friend, glad for her, and marveling at her strength in surviving with a bright, unembittered spirit the loss of her husband and dear little baby within a matter of weeks.

"Hugh met the trains every day till you

stepped off," Lesley remembered. "He didn't know he was waiting for you, but he was."

Susan's blue eyes glistened. "Do you think it'd be awful if we didn't wait a year?"

"I think you should wait till *you* feel ready," Lesley assured her. "Whether it's next week or next year."

"I'm ready," Susan said softly. "I didn't know how much I and the children would miss him till he left to work on the railroad."

Ellen must have been listening intently. She laughed and hugged Susan, children and all. "Come in, then, and we'll fit you for your wedding gown!"

"Oh, we won't go to all that fuss and expense," Susan protested. "It's a second marriage and —"

"It's your first to each other," Ellen said firmly. "You buy the material, and Beth and I will make it for your wedding gift. Won't we, Beth?"

"Of course we will!" Beth's eyes glowed with the prideful joy of giving, a luxury she'd never had. Her smile, perhaps a bit challenging, broadened to include Lesley. "I love to make wedding dresses!"

Especially your own? Lesley thought. Well, my child-woman, foster-daughter rival, if you can throw Jim off course, you're welcome to him. I only want him if he's true to his direction, true to me. Yet how long can he be steadfast if my heart stays bleak and cold?

25

In the days after Christmas, all eyes eagerly watched for the coming of the men. On the twenty-seventh, when the newspapers brought an account of Carry Nation's assault on the Carey Hotel saloon in Wichita, only Ruff got excited.

"So she smashed up the plate glass and bar with rocks and an iron rod, by jingo!" he chuckled, then looked rueful. "I've seen John Noble's painting of *Cleopatra at the Bath.* Wonderful art. A shame Mrs. Nation wrecked it."

"I'm sure most men would agree with you," said Ellen, who had come in to check the news. She arched a well-shaped eyebrow at her husband. "But most women would agree with Mrs. Nation."

"I'd love to interview her," said Ruff. "But now that the builders have moved to Zenith, and the joints with them, she'll have nothing to bust up in Bountiful."

The two almost newlyweds went out, Ellen's arm linked through her husband's. From the way he smiled at her, it was clear that Cleopatra, even bathing, couldn't have diverted his attention more than momentarily.

Through Ellen's front window across the tracks, Lesley could see Beth at the sewing machine. Lesley had scarcely seen her since that night she had seen all too much. Beth left for work as soon as the breakfast dishes were done and didn't get home till supper. Shortly after the kitchen was tidy, she went to bed, sometimes before Bridget.

"I'm afraid you're working too hard," Lesley admonished. "Ellen does make you eat dinner, I hope?"

"Of course!" Beth's eyes sparkled. "I'm just making something special that has to be done by New Year's."

A new dress to dazzle Jim? Lesley wondered. Looking into the girl's radiant face with the hidden scar, Lesley marveled at Beth and came close to loving and hating her at the same time. To endure so much and still shine bright and fresh as spring — by comparison, it made Lesley feel worn and poor-spirited. Why should Jim wait for her uncertain thawing when a vibrant young beauty was all too eager to throw herself into his arms?

What would happen when Jim came home? The days crawled as Lesley's painful suspense grew, yet sped with Bountiful's hopeful preparations. The leased engine with its tender, baggage car, passenger car, and two boxcars arrived via the old track and was turned on a wye connecting to the just-laid rails to await its exultant journey north.

Alan Meadows, the livery apprentice, polished the brass works till they glittered. Ruff painted the cab crimson and in golden curlicued letters proclaimed it THE BOUNTIFUL CITIZENS' NO. 1. Ellen supervised the artistic draping of red, white, and blue bunting punctuated by rosettes, on the engine and cars.

"It'll be the grandest train I ever took up a track," said Hugh MacLeod, when the crews returned dirty, exhausted, but jubilant late December 30. He grinned at Dusty, who was hanging on to his leg. "Think your mama'd let you sit on my knee and help run the engine?"

Dusty squealed. Susan told him yes, smiling at the big, redheaded blacksmith-engineer in a way that told everyone how glad she was to have him back.

Jamie still clung to Jim, but he pulled up short beside Hugh. "Can I help, too, Uncle Mac?" he begged.

"Sure, if it's okay with Lesley."

Lesley nodded. Hugh would be careful of the boys. In fact, he was sure to give any boy who wanted it a turn on this memorable trip, a thrill they'd always remember. Sitting with the engineer on any locomotive was the fondest dream of most boys, but to go over a track their own men had made — well, that was glory indeed.

Bridget had hold of one of Jim's hands, Jamie held the other, but it was Beth who faced him with proud confidence, as if they had a secret. Stabbed, Lesley kept a wooden smile on her face as she greeted Hugh, Andy Hart, Leroy Martin, Elden Griffith, and Henry Cantrell, and hugged Micajah and Bella.

"Some honeymoon, hauling rails." Bella grinned.

"At least you got to be with your sweetie!" Micajah caught his Lillian in his arms and whirled her around the platform. "We done it, folks! We got our railroad! Let's have three cheers for Jim, who figured out a way to keep our town alive!"

"Three cheers for everyone!" called Jim. "We're all in it together!"

Amidst uproarious applause, the weary men were hustled off to their homes and good hot suppers and baths. Jim made as if to turn toward his wood-walled tent, but Jamie and Bridget tugged at him. "Come home, Uncle Jim!" Jamie urged. "We got loads to eat, don't we, Lesley?"

"There's beans and coleslaw, and the cornbread should be just about ready," she said, and knew she sounded stiff. He deserved better than that for what he had done even if he was captivated by Beth's vivacious charm. "You're very welcome."

He studied her, dark eyebrows knitting. "Am I, Les?"

"I said you were."

How dare he take that tone of hurt puzzlement? Lesley hurried along to the new depot and managed to be so busy getting supper on the table when Jim was towed in that she didn't have to look at him.

Through the meal, while Jim regaled

the children with stories and Beth laughed and flirted, Lesley felt like an old-maid chaperon. This couldn't go on. After the gala journey and celebration tomorrow, she would take the first opportunity to have things out with Jim. The galling thought that he hadn't told her about the change in his feelings because he was sorry for her brought a taste of blood to her mouth, but she couldn't hate either one of them. She just felt stricken and betrayed. At least it would be several years before Jim would marry Beth. By then, Lesley hoped, the wound would be an old one that wouldn't hurt so much.

Pleading weariness, Jim left right after supper with Jamie's magic robe slung over his shoulder and Jamie hanging on to his arm. Smiling after them, Beth picked up the dish towel to wipe while Lesley washed. "Isn't it wonderful how Jim acts just like a father to Jamie?"

"You seem to think everything Jim does is wonderful." Lesley couldn't keep the sharpness from her voice.

Beth lifted the eyebrows Ellen had taught her how to shape. "Don't you?"

"What I think of Jim Kelly is none of

your business!" Lesley went hot and cold with shame at the infantile retort, but there was no way to call it back.

With real or feigned surprise, Beth said in a tone that was very much a woman's, "You're right. It's none of my business. But it's your business, Lesley."

"And I'll take care of it."

They finished the dishes in silence.

Right after sunup next morning, Hugh and Andy Hart fired up the engine. Bunting riffling in the breeze, the train puffed on the siding like a segmented dragon eager to snort along the tracks that gleamed out of sight northwards in the slanting rays of the early sun.

Bridget and Jamie were so eager to get aboard that Lesley let them go under Beth's supervision, carrying the laundry basket that held baked beans, potato salad, and two apple pies with sugared juice oozing through the slits.

The whole community assembled, some, like the Griffiths and Robertses, driving in and leaving their teams at the livery. Since Andy was busy with the engine, they took care of their own horses with some help from young Alan. Men and boys climbed into the engineer's cab, and mothers called to their children not to get into the coal heaped in the open tender and not to crawl beneath the cars.

Rutherford Miles took photographs, and then displayed another talent by producing a trombone and joining in the cacophony of Andy Hart's clarinet and Leroy Martin's trumpet. By the Fourth of July, Lesley dreamed, maybe Bountiful would have a real band, even a baseball team, to travel with the whole town for an escort to play another community's team as part of the year's most festive celebration. Would she still be here? How could she bear to go anywhere else?

Giving herself a mental and emotional shake, she closed the depot. Within the next few days, she'd talk with Jim. Time enough then to worry about the future.

Today she was going to rejoice with the town, *her* town, that she had watched grow from a few deserted shacks to a small but thriving center with a school and hopes and aims that brought people together. Today she was going to celebrate with her friends and neighbors.

She hurried to her room to get her hat and cloak, and paused as she remembered that Bridget had worn only a sweater. All very well for while she was racing about, but she might get cold during the ride. Lesley went into the girls' room, touched by its proud neatness and the chromo of playful kittens.

They'd had so little in their lives, the children. It had seemed a staggering responsibility to take them, yet with so much help, especially from the Schillers, Ellen, and Jim, the O'Haras had enriched her days, kept her from despair. However things turned out with Beth, Lesley owed the children more than they owed her.

With fabric matching the drapes, Beth had curtained off a corner for their clothes. Lifting the curtain aside, Lesley froze. Her heart stopped, then pounded in her ears.

There on a wooden hanger shimmered the ivory satin of what could only be a wedding dress. Beth and Jim didn't intend to wait! When were they going to tell her? Sick with betrayal and shock, Lesley had to steady herself against the chest of drawers.

Outrage heated her for a moment, then ebbed. What could she expect, constantly rebuffing Jim, when he had only to turn his head to meet an adoring welcome? More than likely, just as she was putting off a confrontation, so were they until after today's celebration.

With an effort that made her feel like a badly wounded person who was trying to get up and walk, she pulled herself together and reached for Bridget's coat. When Beth saw it, she might think it had been somewhere except behind the curtain. Unless she asked point-blank, explanations would better wait.

Let me get through the day, Lesley thought. *And then let me get through the rest of it without turning into a storming, crying, pathetic mess.* Securing her hat firmly, she slipped into her cloak and went out to the train.

Bridget was glad to have her coat as soon as everyone had settled into the hard wooden seats, except for the boys, who had crammed into the cab to wait their turn to, for just a moment, share the controls with Hugh. There was no stove in the passenger car. It had been decided that for such a short distance, it was better for people to bundle up rather than have the risk and mess of a coal fire.

The eighteen miles of roadbed and rails that had taken weeks to build were rumbled over in an hour, including several stops for farm families who had helped. On the other side of the Buffalo Creek bridge, the train picked up Dan Nelson and his wife with redheaded Tom, who seemed to have grown several inches on good food and fresh air. It was a happy reunion for all the youngsters who'd stepped off the orphan train, except for the Wellivers' boy, Oliver, who had, of course, moved to Zenith to help run the new mercantile.

At each stop, the three-man band struck up a welcome. They saluted the Buffalo Creek bridge, which had been the trickiest part of the whole enterprise, and as Hugh signaled the approach to the Santa Fe junction at Buckeye with a long, thrilling whistle and slowing of the train, the musicians played for all they were worth, and kept it up till the last passenger stepped out on the platform by the siding.

With the help of the Buckeye station

agent, Hugh and Andy got the train switched to the wye and turned so the engine faced toward home. The boiler wouldn't have time to cool before they'd start off again.

The potbellied stove in the depot exuded pleasant warmth. The bachelor agent, Mr. Alexander Thomason, a gaunt, white-haired man with a kindly smile, had laid planks over sawhorses. He got out a clarinet and added his efforts to the Bountiful band's as children played outside and women spread the planks with starched sheets and brought in the food. Rising from the center of the table was Henry's donation, a richly frosted and decorated four-tiered chocolate cake with a miniature train on top.

Mr. Thomason said it warmed the cockles of his heart to see neighbors work together and succeed in such a grand venture. Ruff took a photograph of the agent shaking hands with Hugh while Dusty proudly hung on to the smith-engineer's other hand.

"This was your idea, Jim," called the editor. "Give us a speech, man!"

Jim blushed to the roots of his black hair. "I'll just say thanks to all of you.

You've built a railroad for Bountiful that'll keep our town going. Before we light into all this scrumptious food, why don't we ask Micajah — he's the oldest person here — to give thanks and ask a blessing?"

Micajah stared, gulped, and would have fled, but Lillian stopped him, as much with her smile as her hand on his wrist. Micajah squeezed his eyes shut. His voice quavered for a second, then grew strong.

"Lord, we sure do thank you for helping us finish what we started. We thank you for friends and neighbors, and for what we are about to receive."

Into the echoing "Amen," a voice slashed like a wire whip. "You won't be thankful, I'm afraid, for what you're about to receive."

Adam Benedict bulked in the door a moment before he closed it. He beamed around him and held out a paper. "This wire reached me from Santa Fe's Topeka headquarters before I left Zenith this morning on the new connection to the west of here. The company has wisely decided to void its agreement to supply Bountiful with a train."

Into the stunned silence, Thomason

said, "I never heard that message on the wire, sir."

Benedict flashed white teeth. "You couldn't. I asked that it be relayed south and then west to Zenith. No disparagement of you, Agent Thomason, but you'll understand that I preferred to bring the news myself."

"We've got a signed agreement," Ruff said hotly. "The Santa Fe can't break it, no matter what you promised the bigwigs. I'm a lawyer —"

"And a photographer and editor, not to mention sign and portrait painter." Benedict smiled pityingly. "What chance would you have against the Santa Fe's high-paid, full-time attorneys who do nothing but keep the company clear of trouble? All they have to do is cast doubts on the safety of letting a blackballed engineer run one of their engines over a farmer-built railroad."

He flicked a bit of lint from his elegant dark green sleeve. For just an instant, his eyes met Lesley's. "Do proceed with your feast." He handed the message to Mr. Thomason. "This authorizes you to impound the Bountiful train. For the sake of the women and children, we won't do that." His eyes swept over the hushed crowd. "Enjoy your ride back to Bountiful, my friends. It'll be the last run on this expensive folly of a rail-road."

Jim's voice was barely audible. "You'd do this to these folks just to get at me, Benedict? You're that set on ruining our town because you can't be mayor, sheriff, fire department, and brass band rolled into one?"

"I'm a poor loser. You took my woman and my town, Kelly."

"I never was your woman," Lesley said. "And you never made Bountiful your town, not in the ways that counted."

"My bank didn't count? Easy loans and free lots?" Benedict's gaze, sardonic yet bewildered, wandered from Lesley's face to others', lingered on Susan, who held Sally on her lap. He let out an exasperated sigh as he turned back to Lesley. "I had business to attend to. I'd only have damaged my automobile if I'd tried to drive that baby to Dodge."

"You'd have shown you were one of us."

"If that takes being a fool, then I'm not and never can be." He bowed. "I'll leave you to your dinner. Don't trouble to invite me," he added mockingly. "André has mine waiting in my private car."

A whistle blared. Matthew Reid burst into the depot, followed by a pall of smoke and a stranger in a white apron and tall cap. "Dining car's on fire, Mr. Benedict! Can't put it out, it's spread to the grass! We've got to get out of here —"

26

Somebody screamed. Jim took one look outside and shouted above the rising confusion, "Get on the Bountiful train, everybody! Don't trample! Buffalo Creek's running high and wide enough to stop most any fire. If we can get across the bridge, we'll be fine!"

Lilibet Schiller started to collect the giant cake. "Leave it!" Jim ordered. "Leave everything but the kids! Hurry!" He gave Lesley a push and swung toward Benedict, who stood with his arms crossed. "Get on the train, you and your men!"

The ghost of a smile tugged at Benedict's lips. "We'll get on last. I'll call the crew, who are doubtless trying to quench the blaze. Mr. Thomason, be so good as to wire news of the fire and advise that no trains run this way till further notice." He strolled out into the thickening smoke.

Thomason swiftly tapped out his message as Lesley hustled Bridget and

Jamie outside. Smoke billowed around the figures of what must be the engineer, fireman, and brakeman. One played the hose from the water tank on the flaming train. The others used buckets, but the water only seemed to enrage the flames furling from the kitchen car through the palace car and engine. On both sides, the prairie was ablaze and spreading.

"Leave it, boys!" called Benedict. "Come on, we're catching a ride!"

Blackened and gasping, they abandoned the hopeless fight and made for the train that was already gusting out clouds of vapor. Thank goodness, the engine hadn't stopped long enough for the fire to die or the boiler to cool! It wasn't taking Hugh and Andy long to get up steam.

But the erupting grass! It licked at Mr. Thomason's feet as he leaped into the baggage car, where Lesley and Beth had boosted the children to avoid the crowd scrambling into the passenger car. The baggage car was just behind the tender, which held both coal and water for the engine, the coal in reach of the fireman, who had to keep the firebox stoked.

Lesley and Beth struggled frantically

with their skirts. The fire howled through the grass like a starving beast. If their garments caught — Benedict cupped a big hand under an arm of each of them and practically tossed them aboard.

His crew and men followed, lifting in a limping man whose sootier clothes proclaimed him the fireman. Benedict leaped up behind them as the engine jerked forward. Matthew and André helped him beat out smoldering char at the hem of his wool trousers.

Through the open door, Lesley saw Jim whip his hat at the embers torching his clothes as he vaulted into the cab. The prairie on either side exploded.

Screams came from the passenger car. A groan went up from those staring at each other in the dark baggage hold. Except for the wheels and metal parts of the engine, the train was wood.

"Fires'll be breaking out all over," said the begrimed young man in the engineer's visored black leather cap. "Mr. Benedict, can you and Mr. Reid get back to the passenger car and organize to put out fires? When the drinking water's used, you'll need to fill buckets or such from the tender unless there's a hose for siphoning. You'll have to climb the ladder up the front of the tender and down the one on the other end. Take care working your way across the coal. It'll shift under you. If you fall —"

He didn't need to finish, but Benedict and Matthew Reid were on their way out the other end of the baggage car as Jim balanced precariously on the rim of the tender and lifted the lid to the water compartment. He filled a bucket, leaped back into the cab, sloshed the water on Hugh, and returned to that narrow footing for another bucket. Lesley cringed at his danger. Flames shriveled the paint on the cab, though Andy played the steam hose from the boiler on the ceiling and walls.

If any of them were to live, Hugh and the controls had to be kept wetted down. Every time Jim moved back and forth, his chances of slipping increased. It would save time to have someone in the cab to toss the water and hand the bucket back. Even as she thought, Lesley shed her cumbersome skirt, stepped across, and clambered on top of the coal in the tender.

She had meant to crawl into the cab,

but now she was close to the water tank. Why not fill buckets and hand them to Jim? Turning from dumping his last load, Jim stared at her, jaw dropping.

"Get off of there!"

"No." She made her way amidst the shifting coal till she could brace her feet against the cab end of the tender and reach into the tank. "See, I'm perfectly safe! I'll fill the bucket."

No time for argument. He handed her the bucket, took it from her with a stretch of his long arm and body between cab and tender, and handed her another pail. "While you're at it —"

He actually grinned!

The fireman with the disabled leg crawled toward the door opening to the tender. He gripped a long hose. "Can you stick the end of this in the tank, ma'am?" he shouted. "They need more water back in the passenger car."

"I can't hang on to the tender and fill buckets," the engineer said. "Burned my hands too bad. But I can stand here and take filled buckets to the passenger car."

"I can get on the tender, too!" What it must have cost Beth, badly burned once, to sit in the open with flames shooting up!

"The children need you!" Lesley cried, but Beth kilted her skirts and was soon beside Lesley. The engineer handed her a bucket. She filled and handed it back to him. He carried it to the next car.

Dear God! Steaming smoke spewed from the cab windows. The bright paint was eaten through, and bits of charred wood fell away as the engine surged along the narrow road, the slender avenue of escape. How could buckets passed with agonizing slowness from tender to cab and passenger car possibly hold the fire at bay?

If only there were more buckets, more people! And then, amazingly, there were! Through the baggage car door, she saw Benedict's massive form sway with the rhythm of the wheels as he took the bucket from the engineer and handed it to Micajah, who passed it on. Ruff hurried through the baggage car with a short length of hose and pair of five-gallon milk cans. He set one beside the hurt fireman to siphon into, crawled over the coal and into the cab, where he set down the can and handed Lesley the hose. She started water siphoning into it and in the same breath handed Jim a bucket.

"The passenger car?" she yelled at Ruff.

"Ellen, Susan, Lilibet, and Ann Roberts are each in charge of a section, with Bella running the whole show. They're soaking rugs and blankets to put out fires as soon as they start. If we can just keep moving —"

"Ruff! Your coat!" Lesley sloshed the bucket she'd just received over his back and down the igniting rear of the cab.

"Your underskirt!" yelled Ruff.

The edges had caught. Ruff yanked off his wet coat, but before he could swing it over her, Beth dashed a bucket right on the fire. It died in smoke. In the baggage car, the lamed fireman doused any flicker with the siphoning hose.

Lesley's hat tore loose and went up in a fiery puff. She shuddered, reached for the bucket, passed it, reached again. How much water was in the tender? How much farther was Buffalo Creek? It seemed an eternity since they'd left the junction, though it could only be minutes.

Buffalo Creek — eight miles, nine? A

mile, even a fraction of one, could mean horrible death or injury to everyone on the train. Lesley prayed for Hugh at the controls, for Jim, reaching far out for the buckets with death almost certain if he slipped. She prayed for them all as the wind ripped her hair loose from its pins. If it flamed —

"Here!" Ruff gave her his brown fedora. "Stuff your hair up into it."

She did, caught a bucket, passed it, caught the next. Her arms ached. Tears streamed from cinders in her eyes; her throat and nostrils felt scorched.

Pure fresh sweet air! If they only lived to breathe it again! Nothing else mattered compared to that. If Jim and Beth loved each other, they'd have her blessing. How gladly she'd help Beth into that lovely gown rather than a coffin! If they could all just live, draw in the sparkling air . . .

A few cottonwoods had been left along the opposite side of the creek. Lesley saw them with a rush of thanks and hope. She swung the water along. The trees grew larger, naked branches uplifted to the smoke-hazed sky.

There was a blast from the whistle; the engine churned through darting, seeking flames that seemed to reach and grasp like avid hands. Then they were across the bridge, the wide, high-flowing creek between them and the fire.

Now that the train could safely stop, it didn't take long to quench the fires on board, though the damage was heavy. Jim and Benedict led the party that stood on the bridge and hauled up buckets on ropes to battle the fire as it tried to devour the wood supports.

There was no heavy brush and no trees on that side to sustain the grass fire long or power it to lunge across the water. Sullenly, grudgingly, it ebbed into scorched roots, whipped now and then into brief flaring.

"I'm sure glad I plowed that fireguard all around my fields," said Dan Nelson, watching the flames hurtle and subside along the broad strip protecting his farm, which was reached by a lane going back a quarter mile from the railroad. He squinted at the smoking, blackened land. "Reckon we can walk up the tracks to our road."

Other farmers from north of the creek decided to do the same. They had livestock and chores that wouldn't keep while they rode to Bountiful and waited for the engine to be serviced — even if it could be put in safe running condition that day.

Dan Nelson looked over the charred train and blistered engine. "I sure am thankful no one's hurt bad, but otherwise it don't look like we got a lot to celebrate."

Adam Benedict cleared his throat. His elegant suit was filthy, the brightness of his hair sullied, yet he smiled as he looked around at these farmers and townfolk who had defied him and whose dream he had destroyed.

"There is much to celebrate, sir. I pay my debts. I owe my life to this — um — peculiar railroad company. I'll make good all the damage, even to the dishes you ladies lost at the Santa Fe depot." He met Lesley's startled gaze and laughed softly. "We'll need to work out how my line can best cooperate with yours, of course."

"You aren't closing the Bountiful depot down?" asked Bella.

"No, ma'am. The difference is you'll now have a choice of whether to ship by Santa Fe or me." He turned to Hugh, whose burned hands and arms had been bandaged tenderly by Susan. "My engineer can bring the train in if you like, MacLeod."

"No, thanks, sir," said the Citizens' Railroad engineer. "Reckon I will."

Everyone was too exhausted for merriment that night, but it was agreed to meet at noon in the old depot for the children's program and a dinner of whatever could be put together. Then they could go home to enjoy their delayed Christmas gifts. Jamie had gone off with Jim after a hasty meal of soup and biscuits, but it took hours for Bridget, Beth, and Lesley to heat water to wash their hair and take turns bathing in the big metal washtub.

Lesley was last and, towel draped around her clean hair, soaked a long time after the sisters had gone to bed. Beth had given her a few searching glances, but apparently she no more felt up to a talk about Jim than did Lesley.

They might all have died so terribly! Compared to that, Lesley knew she could live through whatever happened, and she was minded to stay right here in Bountiful with her friends. If anyone moved, it could be Jim and Beth, but if they stayed, somehow in time she'd manage to accept it.

Benedict?

He had asked her, as he helped her down from the train, "Have you changed your mind about — anything?"

She looked him straight in those green-depthed dark eyes. "No. I never will."

"You know, my dear, I am compelled to believe you."

"I — I do wish you well."

"Thank you." He gave her a sudden dazzling smile and held out his hand to assist Beth to the platform. Nor did he release her. He'd walked her home.

Sighing as she relaxed in the soothing water, Lesley refused to speculate on his obvious interest in the girl. He knew, surely, that he couldn't make Lesley jealous, but he'd said he was no degenerate. Lesley believed him. He was no more than six or seven years older than Jim, but that made a considerable difference in paying court to a not-quite-fifteen-year-old.

As she slipped on her gown, robe, and slippers and dumped the cooled bath-water on the rosebush and apple tree Jim had given her, she tried not to think of the breathtaking gown behind Beth's curtain, but it haunted her dreams that night, along with the fire.

The children were a little nervous next day, either because of the harrowing race with the fire or because Adam Benedict joined the audience. He clapped as appreciatively as any proud parent, though, and when it was time to eat and he started to go, Bridget and Mattie caught his hands.

"Everybody's got to have New Year's dinner together even if it is a day late!" Bridget urged.

"Do they?" He arched a tufted eyebrow at Lesley.

"Certainly. It's not as fancy as what we had yesterday, but it's good and there's plenty."

"Ah," he said, looking around at what seemed more like a gathering of family than diverse folk whose bond was a shared town. "I can believe that if you ran out of food, there'd be another miracle of many loaves and fishes." He smiled at Beth in a way that made even that self-possessed young woman drop her eyes, and helped himself to corn fritters.

Hugh's hands and wrists were still swathed in bandages, but since this caused Susan to heap his plate and feed him, he concealed any pain he might be feeling. "We're getting married," he announced blissfully as Lesley sat down by Susan. "Just as soon as we can get Reverend Sheridan to come down from Dodge."

Susan nodded. "When you think of what could have happened —" She pushed a tumble of dark red curls off Hugh's forehead. "I don't want to wait."

"Why, that's wonderful!" Lesley meant it, in spite of the pain that wrenched her to see Jim and Beth approaching.

They looked joyous, as if they shared a secret. Throughout the meal they exchanged happy glances. Lesley could scarcely swallow. Tears of mortification stung her eyes. They could at least refrain from making her the object of pity and speculation.

She started to rise, excusing herself, but Beth caught her arm. "Wait, Lesley! Please, just a minute!"

The girl hurried away. Lesley frowned at Jim, but he wouldn't meet her gaze. He actually fidgeted! What was coming next? If she could have escaped without arousing wonder in Hugh and Susan, Lesley would have, but she grimly determined not to make an exhibition of herself, whatever happened.

Till she saw the dress. Could Beth be so crass? She held the ivory satin and lace cradled in her arms. A sleeve seemed to reflect the glow of her hair.

Lesley sat paralyzed, blood pounding in her ears. Was this how it was going to be? Flaunting the gown in front of everyone, announcing the wedding?

Beth tried to put the softly glowing dress in Lesley's lap, but Lesley thrust it away. "It — it's very pretty." Her voice trembled despite her resolve. "I'm sure you'll look lovely in it."

Beth gasped. "Me? It's your dress, Lesley!"

"Mine?"

Jim closed his hand over hers. "It's your Christmas present, honey! And for New Year's and all the life in front of us."

"But — but I haven't said I'll marry you."

"I figure if you have the dress hangin' where you'll see it every day, the idea will sort of grow on you." Jim didn't fidget now, and it was she who had trouble answering his look. "You will marry me someday. Won't you, dar-lin'?"

She thought of him clinging to the lip of the tender, handing down the water that had saved their lives. She thought of what might have happened, and of what she had feared about Beth. Beth, who watched them with a curious intensity.

Jim didn't love Beth except as a kind of elder brother-uncle. But Lesley, watching the girl, knew she loved Jim. Yet she had sewn this wedding dress. Young though she was, she could accept reality without a whimper.

"Yes, Jim," Lesley said, and took the gown from Beth. "I'll marry you, and I'll wear this beautiful dress. Thank you, Beth."

Beth dipped her head. She blinked at what might have been a sheen of tears in her golden eyes. Benedict had been watching. He rose from between Mattie and Bridget, advanced on Lesley, and bowed.

"It seems I must wish you happy, Miss Lesley, Kelly. I do, with a respectable portion of my heart." He turned to Beth. "I believe you've said, Elizabeth, that

Miss Morland and Mr. Kelly are your guardians."

"Yes, sir."

"Then, with your consent, my dear, I'll ask them to approve of what we've spoken of from time to time."

Beth went crimson. "I — I thought you were joking, sir! And I never spoke — it was you!"

"True enough. And of course I joked. I always do when something matters."

Jim said, "Since we are Beth's family, Benedict, sounds like you better tell us what's on your mind."

"Marriage." Everyone in earshot gasped. Before Jim or Lesley could protest, Benedict smiled across their heads at Beth and went on, "Not till Beth's at least several years older, of course, but that's in my mind."

"You can't expect her to make such a decision now!" Lesley chided. "She's little more than a girl —"

Benedict made an impatient gesture. "We all know better than that."

"But —"

"What I propose," he said with forced patience, "is to provide Beth with an all-expense scholarship at whatever design institute she and Mrs. Miles decide on. She will, at the same time, pursue her education with a tutor. I undertake most solemnly not to see her except when a suitable chaperon is present."

"But she'll be obligated to you," Jim argued.

"No. There are no strings on the scholarship, and if she wishes, I'll finance further study abroad."

"Oh, I don't want to get that far from Bridget and Jamie!" Beth cried. She bit her lip. "I would so love to study design! But I don't want to leave Bridget and Jamie. Besides, it's not fair, Lesley. You and Jim aren't really our parents."

"Don't worry about that," comforted Lesley, herself still dazzled at this prospect for her ward. "We'll all miss you, but you'll come home on visits."

"So it's agreed?" asked Benedict.

Jim pondered. He glanced at Lesley. She said carefully, "It sounds like what Beth really wants —"

"Wait!" Beth's mouth trembled, but she drew herself up as if facing an enemy. "There's something I have to show Mr. Benedict."

She ran from the depot. They all stared after her. What could be the matter? Lesley hurried after her. She

601

found Beth at the sink in their home, scrubbing her face.

"Oh, Beth! You don't have to show him that!"

"Yes, I do." The scar was livid. It was so long since Lesley had seen it that she was shocked at how it changed Beth's face.

This must have showed in Lesley's expression. Beth gave her a sad, bitter smile. "I intend to marry Mr. Benedict. But not unless he still wants me when he sees my scar."

"But, Beth, you don't love him!"

"Don't I?" Beth grinned. "I can learn. And you'll admit he's — interesting."

"Yes." Lesley felt very much the younger. "He's that."

"Let's see if he has guts."

"Beth!"

The answer was a laugh, but Lesley heard the taut-strung bravado in it. Beth almost ran to the old depot. Lesley heard the abrupt stillness as she hung back, unwilling to see the revulsion that would surely spring to Benedict's eyes, Benedict with his beautiful "cousins."

She stepped inside as Benedict strode toward Beth and kissed her full on the scar, then kissed her hands, bowing his head in homage.

"By God, you are beautiful, Beth O'Hara! You were pretty before, but now you have what few women do — the beauty of courage."

"Adam!"

"You'll be my woman one day. My beautiful, brave woman." His voice warmed with delight. "But you'll have some of your childhood back, for I'll have mine, too. We're going to share all ages and many things, Elizabeth."

He swept a bow to the assemblage. "With your consent, I'll build my principal home here. I can't think of a better place for my children to grow up."

Jim glanced around, reading faces. "Looks like you're welcome, Benedict. But let's have one thing real clear. Bountiful isn't my town or your town. It's *our* town."

"That's right!" Hugh flourished his bandaged hands above his head while others clapped and cheered.

Benedict inclined his head and departed. In his wake, Lesley met Beth's eyes. What a world had opened in those minutes for a girl from the New York slums! One day, with Benedict, she'd walk in that world as if born to it. He was too fascinating and magnetic a man not to win her. But it was Jim who'd had her heart's first love.

Women crowded around Lesley now, marveling at the dress, complimenting Beth and Ellen on the details, the sweetheart neckline, pointed cuffs, and medallions of lace on each puffed sleeve and around the swirl of a skirt that fitted snugly over the hips before it flared.

"It's a shame to keep that dress hid away!" bellowed Hugh. "Why don't you get married when Susie and I do, lass?"

"Why don't we?" Jim asked.

Like spring breaking the last ice blocking a river, a torrent of warmth surged through Lesley. She felt as if she glowed inside, sparkled and rejoiced. Rising, she handed the dress to Beth with a look that said more than her words.

"Thanks more than I can say for making this, Beth. It's the most wonderful present anyone ever had."

Beth shook her head. "Oh, no! Coming to Bountiful and you was the best." She swallowed hard. "I want to be your bridesmaid."

"Thank you," Lesley said again, to a woman, not a child. She tucked her arm through Jim's and smiled up at him. "Let's go sit on the tie by the prairie dog town and talk about all this."

"Be ready for more than talk," he said in her ear.

They went out with the applause and teasing of their friends in their ears, but the sounds faded as they neared the rim of the prairie. There was not even a prairie dog or owl to watch when they turned in to each other's arms.

The employees of Thorndike Press hope you have enjoyed this Large Print book. All our Large Print titles are designed for easy reading, and all our books are made to last. Other Thorndike Large Print books are available at your library, through selected bookstores, or directly from us.

For information about titles, please call:

(800) 223-2336

To share your comments, please write:

Publisher
Thorndike Press
P.O. Box 159
Thorndike, Maine 04986